BONE AND BREAD

BONE AND BREAD

SALEEMA NAWAZ

ANANSI

This edition published in Canada in 2013 by House of Anansi Press Inc.
www.houseofanansi.com

House of Anansi Press is committed to protecting our natural environment.
As part of our efforts, the interior of this book is printed on paper that contains
100% post-consumer recycled fibres, is acid-free, and is processed chlorine-free.

20 19 18 17 16   5 6 7 8 9

Library and Archives Canada Cataloguing in Publication

Nawaz, Saleema, 1979–
Bone and bread / Saleema Nawaz.

Issued also in an electronic format.

ISBN 978-1-77089-009-1

I. Title.

PS8627.A94B66 2013   C813'.6   C2012-905959-5

Cover design: Alysia Shewchuk
Text design and typesetting: Alysia Shewchuk

 Canada Council   Conseil des Arts   ONTARIO ARTS COUNCIL
for the Arts   du Canada   CONSEIL DES ARTS DE L'ONTARIO

*We acknowledge for their financial support of our publishing program
the Canada Council for the Arts, the Ontario Arts Council, and the Government of
Canada through the Canada Book Fund.*

Printed and bound in Canada

MIX
Paper from
responsible sources
FSC® C004071

If you listen, you can almost hear the sound of my son's heart breaking. In the backyard, under the drone of the lawnmower, there's a dull clanking, a sick rasp of metal like iron on bone, the chafing of something serrated. It could be a fallen branch from the lilac bush or a stray rock caught against the blade, but from where I sit looking out the kitchen window, the muted noise of the mowing comes through like a throbbing ache.

Since my sister, Sadhana, died, we move through the house like tenants awaiting eviction, silent and worn with guilt, nerves frayed. I buy the groceries alone and unpack them in stealth, going slowly to keep the plastic from rustling, the cupboards from slamming closed. Our grief is distended, sluggish as Sadhana's illness, so that talking or eating — eating above all things — still seems like an affront to its fragile sanctity.

The sun on Quinn's face is giving him a squint that looks like closed eyes; with the mower he is like a blind man feeling his way through the world, an electric cutter before him for a cane. The yard is small, but the mowing seems to take forever. When Quinn leaves for university at the end of the summer, I will think about planting a garden, though it might be more work, not less. Maybe concrete. Maybe I'll be the one paving paradise. But the lilacs that line the inside of the fence are my heaven, so I remind myself to look into what else can be put in that will bring itself up and earn me no disgrace or ire from the neighbours.

If we were speaking more, it might be a project for Quinn, but in the past six months we've been like bad reproductions of ourselves, our conversations only shadow plays of the dialogues we used to have. Even before the unthinkable happened, we used to keep it light. No family-drama-sharing circles, only the diversions, the drippings, the scuff and froth of everyday life: pop culture, homework, occasionally the news. Now there is not even that. At nearly eighteen, he is tall and independent, and his inner world is mostly a secret from me, a fact that at alternating times makes me resentful and relieved.

He's a good kid. We are never taken for mother and son, rarely but more often for cousins, or brother and sister. He is thinner than me, and darker, with Sadhana's deep liveliness of expression and grace of movement. When he turns to push the lawnmower back into the peeling shed, his red T-shirt reveals patches of sweat across his broadening back. For his birthday last year, Sadhana bought him a gym membership. Coming back to the house, he returns my smile when I catch his eye, but he slips in through the screen door and up to the second floor without a word.

And that quiet inhalation, audible as he pushes past? That's the sound of him blaming me.

When I am sure that Quinn is upstairs, can imagine I hear his fingers skimming in a light patter over his keyboard, I bring out the notebook where I've taken down the message. Three days alone with it, held secret like a key around my neck. The woman with the lilting voice and the strange request. She says she wants us to meet.

Hello, this is Libby Carr calling. I'm hoping to get ahold of Beena Singh. I found this number online. Ms. Singh, if this is you, I'm not sure if Sadhana ever mentioned me, and maybe you wouldn't remember, anyway. But your sister—well, she was a very dear friend of mine, and I was hoping you wouldn't mind getting in touch. I'm sorry to be calling out of the blue like this. It's selfish, but I've been wishing I had someone to talk to. About Sadhana. I miss her all the time, really. And there's something else I think you ought to know.

She left a Montreal number. I wonder how long she had been waiting to call. It has been almost six months since the funeral. The name Carr doesn't ring a bell, though Sadhana had legions of friends and even more acquaintances, or so it seemed from my vantage point in Ottawa, where I'd hear about them only as a string of names over the phone line, first names, drizzled over a tale of a night out.

It seems as though the woman has found my name on the internet, on the modest web page for freelance editing services that Andrew, an old boyfriend, set up for me, with clean graphics and a couple of testimonials. I listened to the message three times before deleting it, taking it down along with the name and number, and I have stopped myself from mentioning it to Quinn. In his hands, everything is a puzzle to be teased out to its solution. Even Sadhana.

I hold the cordless phone in my palm, its smooth black case feeling heavier than usual, weighted with possibility. With its small antenna, sticking out like a pinky finger at tea, it reminds me of a walkie-talkie, of the ones Sadhana and I had as girls. Of trying to whisper from either end of the apartment, still so close together that we could hear the other speaking without needing to listen through the receiver. And of the newer, long-range ones that Sadhana bought when Quinn was thirteen, driving him out to the Gatineau Hills, where they used borrowed GPS units to play at geocaching, hiding and finding buried capsules at specific coordinates, radioing to each other as they hurried along the trails.

I remember Quinn coming home from that excursion filthy and exhausted. I could tell by the way he scratched and wrinkled up his nose that, even through the shelter of the trees, he'd gotten a bit of a sunburn, invisible on his brown skin.

Sadhana herself was giddy, exultant. This was during one of her good periods. She was thin but energetic, even more so around Quinn. She sat before me at the kitchen table and ate a plate of pasta and pesto I put before her. "That kid of ours is something else," she said between mouthfuls. "Wading through muck. Climbing trees. You should have come with us."

But we both knew that I hadn't been invited.

As I stare at the page where I've written the number, the name blurs in and out of focus. I blink, noticing the doodles I've scribbled around it, loops and triangles. Capital letters shaded in thick double strokes. I haven't really spoken to anyone about Sadhana, or about the hollow in our lives she left behind. Even Sadhana's things are still untouched, exactly as she left them in her Montreal apartment. I've been putting off the task of sorting through all her worldly belongings. Packing up, throwing out, *contending* with those things — my dread assignment.

After a moment, I return the phone to the cradle. There is nothing for me to say to this woman. At least not yet.

Tilting forward and back on the legs of the kitchen stool, I sigh aloud, a bad habit I've given way to in recent months. I've traced it to Uncle, whose chest often heaved with theatrical exhalations, usually to express irritation with me and Sadhana. If we were chattering across the table to each other at dinner, he would say, "Give a man some peace," the thick fingers of his right hand curled against his brow. Uncle preferred to eat in silence. When we were teenagers, we viewed this as a mark of his misanthropy, but more and more I've found myself cultivating moments of perfect solitude, falling into them gratefully, becoming protective of my small preferences and routines. And the sighs just happen. So far, Quinn hasn't noticed. He hasn't been around enough. Then again, it could be that my new enjoyment of isolation is just a reaction to my circumstances, taking the path of least resistance towards self-preservation.

As usual, thoughts like this send me reaching for the phone. Thirty-four is too young to embrace seclusion, so I call Evan, the man I've been seeing. He is, of all improbable things, a cop.

"Hi," I say. "You busy?"

"Sweet cheeks," he says. This is a joke. "Beena. I'm glad you called."

"How's it going? What are you doing?"

"I'm just pulling up to the gas station, then I'm heading into work."

"Too bad. I'm feeling lonely."

"That *is* too bad. Are you okay?"

"I'm fine. Just looking for some diversion from my melancholy."

"I might fall into melancholy myself if I hear any more

about this. You make it hard for a man to go to work."

"Sorry," I say.

"No, you're not," says Evan. "You just want to make sure I'm thinking about you all shift."

"Well."

"Can I call you when I'm off? I should finish around midnight."

"I'll be up," I say. "Call my cell so it doesn't wake Quinn." As if Quinn would be asleep.

"Sure thing," he says, and hangs up.

Evan is twenty-six, halfway between my age and Quinn's. He seems older, though—something about the uniform. I find myself getting defensive when I think about him, preparing arguments to counter whatever teasing assault Sadhana might choose to set in motion, but of course there is no need. Even Quinn hasn't met him yet. We have decided for the time being to keep things quiet.

As if on cue, Quinn turns up behind me, close over my shoulder. I can smell the fresh scent of cut grass, along with something soapier and the peculiar odour of his loft bedroom, like sweaty sheets and dust piled and scorching on a hard drive.

"Calling your secret boyfriend?" he asks, seeing my hand on the phone, and I wonder for a moment whether he knows, until I remember that he has always used this term for my boyfriends, a jibe at all my failed attempts at discretion in the past.

"You bet."

He's over my head, grabbing a glass from the cupboard, then he's in the fridge, pouring the orange juice with the door resting against his hip. "Hot up there," he says, meaning his

BONE AND BREAD   7

room. He closes the fridge and follows up the juice with cold water from the tap.

"If you say so. Hungry?"

"Nah. Later."

I try to evaluate whether there's a new looseness here, something like our old easiness coming back. I wonder how he would react if I told him about the message, said Sadhana's name out loud, let it float at last through the air between us, its syllables finally turned into something that could be measured. Sound wavelengths in peaks and valleys like a chart of our memories, all the highs and lows.

"Want to go for a walk?" I ask. "Grab a coffee?"

"No thanks." Quinn puts down his glass by the sink and in a moment he is back at the stairs, some barely contained energy propelling him up two at a time.

I pour my own glass of cold water. "I'm going out," I call. "To work." I grab my purse, a voluminous orange shoulder bag, tucking into its largest compartment the black padded pouch with my laptop.

"Bye," I call again, and this time I hear a faint echo of it coming down to me from Quinn's bedroom.

The computer is heavy enough that I never go far. There's no need. It's enough to be out in the air. There's a diner I go to a couple of blocks up, with an inclined cobblestone patio and sloping green plastic chairs and tables, where after the lunch rush they don't mind if you linger for hours over two cups of coffee.

I head in that direction, closing my eyes for a moment to feel the sun warming my cheeks. The woman's voice from the message is still with me, her throaty civility, the exigent trace I think I can detect: an insistence in the chosen words that tells me how much she wants me to return her call. I can sense she shares some of our deep sorrow, that she is sensitive to the consuming occupation of grief. How she might have checked off the weeks as they passed, tracing an imagined progression of healing, how six months by her reckoning should have brought us all to an equilibrium, a weary peace. Instead of our fractured channels, the swooping pain. Insulating silence.

There's a tranquility in the city in the early afternoon. The streets are busier than at mid-morning but less frenetic, as though the people venturing out after lunch are doing so at their leisure, in pursuit of personal, rather than occupational, ends. Pleasure, in other words, instead of business. The luxury of being partly self-employed has never left me, and on the days I'm not doing my impression of a paralegal, I try to remain conscious of its simple enjoyments, like this—unfiltered light on my face in the afternoon, wrists free of any timepiece. I sometimes scan the faces of the people I see out at this hour, try to pinpoint the source of their workaday freedom. Students, some parents with children, usually mothers. The odd high school student cutting class, whose look of grateful freedom and barely suppressed glee most closely mirrors my own state of mind.

At the corner I make an abrupt right, away from my destination, curling back around my own block. I'm too distracted and the mechanical allure of work isn't pulling me today. I know already I won't concentrate on the editing, will have to read every sentence four times over instead of twice. My bag is digging into my shoulder and I give it a one-handed heave, curling my thumb in between to hold it. I pass a father and two children, little girls chattering as they skip along, peppering back and forth a piece of yellow chalk, leaping over it as it falls, ad hoc hopscotch on the run. The father, following them at several paces, left out of the game even as commentator, gives me a brief nod as I pass, and it hits me that I'm responsible for the silences in my house. A deep quiet has stolen in like the tide, insistent and stealthy, and, like any rocky shore, I've acquiesced. But however mature Quinn might be, however close in age we really are, it still falls to me to give the cues. Especially with this, with Sadhana.

When I burst in the door, I call out, "We're going to Montreal." And though at first I can't hear a response, in a moment there are his footsteps on the stairs, springing to life.

On the deck later, Evan clinks his glass to mine, scotch and water. For me, scotch and soda. Sadhana's drink. I don't have a taste for it yet, still tend to find the burn bitter as it goes down. Evan claims to have a nose for whisky, an interest he and a few cop buddies have been trying to cultivate with a couple of weekend classes and practice sessions before their poker nights. He swishes his glass, coating the sides, sips slowly, breathes through his nose as he swallows.

"Smooth," he says. "Biscuity." Then, "If anyone from my hometown saw this, I'd be locked in the trunk of a car." He's from a farm town in Saskatchewan with fewer people than my old high school. He's self-conscious about giving himself airs.

He slaps my knee from the next lawn chair, sets its springs creaking, my leg tingling from his hearty affection. He has changed out of his uniform, showered at the police station, as he sometimes does, slipping this time into jeans and a fitted grey T-shirt. His blond hair falls soft and flat without gel, which makes his face look sweeter, younger, rounding out the strong angles of his jaw and cheekbones. It is almost one in the morning and we are talking in low voices. He parked around the corner and met me out back, tapping on the window. Quinn's windows face front. I wonder how much longer I can keep things secret.

"So you're leaving for the weekend," he says.

"Yep."

"Quinn going with you?"

"Yes." I take a sip of my drink, and a lone cricket sounds loud and insistent from somewhere near the lilac bushes. A mating call. "The idea is for him to check out the university, see the campus. And it's been a while since he's seen his uncle."

"Your uncle, right? His great-uncle." These little moments of fact-checking warm me like the scotch. Each one like its own little promise: *I'm learning you by heart.* We've known each other exactly two months, have been dating just under that, though there have been fewer dates and more moments like this, of talking and sitting close. A few frantic afternoons at his apartment, where we wore down each other's deep needs until we became languid and still. Interludes. I like him very much, though in a tentative way, with a tremor of danger humming at its base. The danger, I think, is to my own heart, for he is both good-looking and seemingly very decent. A catch.

"Yeah, my uncle. Harinder." With Quinn almost grown up and seemingly still a credit to me, my relationship with Uncle has shifted, grown a new layer of sediment, like a softer sand washed back onto shore. Things moving, slipping away underfoot, some replaced altogether. Contempt on both sides giving way bit by bit to respect.

"That'll be good. It'll give you a chance to take care of some things, eh?"

I nod, avoid his gaze in my glass. Evan knows that I have yet to go through Sadhana's things. On one of our first dates, I had to explain the unexplainable—that my younger sister had died of a heart attack at age thirty-two. That she had spent half of her life starving herself, or trying not to. That after the funeral we had flung her ashes into the St. Lawrence River, and part of me had been scattered then, too. In his own way, he's been urging me to go clear out her apartment. Two weekends ago he offered to drive me to Montreal himself. "We could go for a nice dinner," he said. "Stay in a hotel. You could do some shopping."

Tonight he says, "It feels good to put some things to rest." He is being direct, and though my instinct is to shrink away, I'm grateful for his concern. Being younger, he doesn't defer to me as he might, except concerning Quinn. I know Evan wants to stop sneaking around, though only once has he hinted as much. Last night, one side of his mouth had twitched up, acknowledging the cliché, as he'd said, "He's not a kid anymore."

Now I say, "You're right about the apartment. I'm going to take care of it." But even saying the words spins me into a moment of distraction, a spilling out of my agitation, and my gaze drifts to the edge of the yard, where the bushes meet the fence in a perimeter of darkness.

"Good." Evan leans over and cups his hand on my cheek, startling me back to him with his touch. "You're in need of some rest yourself, you know, Beena. You're pale as a ghost."

A cloud passes in front of the moon, as swift and eerie as a movie backdrop, and the suddenness of its shadow makes the earth beneath us seem tired and old. I want to say that ghosts don't need to rest — or they can't, or they won't — but I don't know if I mean myself or my sister.

If Sadhana's a ghost, I haven't seen her. I haven't spotted any signs of her shading my footsteps or tracing my name across a rain-soaked window. In a way, though, I'm not surprised. I spent so many years watching her disappear, little by little, that it is impossible for me to believe that there could be any of her left over.

ONE

⤳ THE HUKAM ↝

Ghosts ought to have been my specialty. There were enough dearly departed in my family to haunt a dozen Gothic novels, and if I never stopped to listen for a telling knock or squinted through the darkness for a hazy outline, it was only because doubt flowed through my veins more palpably than the blood of any continent. My sister and I were skeptics. Angry and cynical as only skeptics who have waded (who have swum, who have been given water births) into belief truly can be. But that was later. At the beginning, there was me, and there was Sadhana. There were Papa and Mama. And there were the things that Mama told us.

Mama was a very theoretical woman. I mean, she was a real woman, who was interested in theories of all kinds. When she showed us the stars, she held my sister Sadhana on her lap and pointed up at the thin strip of night sky. What we could see from our balcony was bounded by the roofs of other buildings crowding up in one direction towards the slope of the mountain, the other sides shunting back our perspective with an excess of light, street lamps brightening the darkness to a grey glow in every distance.

"The stars that we see are in the past," said Mama. "It takes thousands of years for their shining to reach the Earth."

With her pale face as a guide, a moon in my field of vision, I struggled to make out the points of light, stretching myself flat on the wine-coloured rug. Mama's voice above the street sounds was solemn and full of wonder.

"There's a theory," Mama said, "that the universe is getting bigger. It will keep expanding, like a huge loaf of bread rising, like a great fat belly, until there's nothing left to make it out of, no more heat. It will be like a day that is so long it goes on forever, until time is a substance and it is made out of ice."

Sadhana was only four, two years younger than me, and she was falling asleep on Mama's skirt, her fat brown chin drooping onto Mama's freckled arm. Sometimes Mama would get started on something and she'd tell us all about it, even when there was no way we'd understand. I sat up to pay attention, to draw myself towards them. Mama pointed out a constellation that I couldn't see, the Big Dipper just a name for a stretch of sky between one wave of her hand and another.

"There's also a theory," said Mama, "that the universe is getting smaller. Millions of years from now it's going to start shrinking and heating, like fat and flesh melting into bone, because it is the destiny of things to come together. All that there is will get closer and closer until there's no space anymore between anything, even between the things themselves."

"Like soup?"

"Like cosmic soup," said Mama, "that boils away into nothing."

She pointed to a faint spot that was hard to make out. "My lucky star," she said.

I leaned my head on her knee and felt her fingers threading through my black hair, as she murmured more about the legacy of dying stars, their nighttime brilliance. It seems to me now that all my memories are like this—points of light in a dark field, now clear and now slipping away, and no matter how much I look, I still can't spot for certain where I should be joining them up in patterns, constellations of what a life could mean.

In theory, when a person dies, they're gone forever. At least that's what I think now. Before she died, Mama always talked about reincarnation, but it got to be too troubling for me and Sadhana, sizing up every cat and dog that looked as if it might be coaxed into following us home, the babies with blue eyes grasping air in their fists from their strollers. The hummingbird we spotted on the balcony, skimming forward and back before the feeder, its wings beating as many times per second as our hearts might in a minute. When I watched it, looking for signs of my mother, my pulse felt faster, as though the bird itself was skittering around inside and had taken up the place where my heart should be, where Mama told us she would keep on living forever and ever.

~∽☙∽~

My sister and I were born exactly two years apart at the same hospital. Named for a queen no longer revered, the hospital stood on the side of the mountain that was the volcanic heart of our island city. It had been more than two hundred years since the English took the city from the French as the spoils of war, but the battle was still being waged whenever people forgot that most of the time we all got along just fine. That the French were the true victors and had claimed an ancient gathering place in the name of their lord and kingdom was obvious in the hundred-foot cross erected on the top of the mountain—once a real wooden cross that Maisonneuve planted to thank the Virgin for saving Montreal from a flood, but by our time a giant hulk of steel that lit up the city's night skyline for a distance of forty miles.

In our little neighbourhood north of the mountain, it was just as common to hear Greek or Yiddish or Italian as it was to hear French or English. At our family's store, famous for making wood-fired bagels in an oven that devoured trees like the furnace of hell itself, nearly every day was brightened by the chime of tourists with the hard shine of American accents.

It would have been to our mother's perpetual regret, if she had believed in such a fruitless notion, that we were born at the hospital and not at home in our little apartment above the shop. Mama told us that Papa had insisted. "He said if anything went wrong, almost all he knew about was making bagels, which could hardly be of very much help. Same thing with pie crust."

Papa also thought that the bathtub was too small for such momentous events. He had been born in India, in the Punjab, and he had arrived with such admirable rapidity that he was very nearly delivered in the central courtyard of his village where they kept the livestock. As it was, the woman who helped bring him into the world had also attended at the births of the healthiest local cows, which was considered by his extended relatives to be a fortunate circumstance. But for his own children, there could be no greater distinction than to greet the universe in a hospital where the doctors were paid to look after human beings and nothing else. He wrote to his parents in India, announcing each addition to the family, but nothing ever came in return except for overexposed photographs of the young Indian daughters of their friends. All the women he might still be able to marry if he tried.

Our parents rarely spoke of how they met and fell in love, ignoring our questions with the same implacable front they presented to bedtime negotiations or fussy standoffs over unpalatable foods. Papa would get stern, his thick lips pressed together as he turned his back on us to indicate there were some things we had no share in. Mama, for her part, said we would be making our own love stories soon enough, that there was no call to get greedy for theirs as well. We found this ridiculous considering how often she talked to us about her lost draft dodger whom she'd followed to Canada, or the other men, presumably lovers, who had brought her important messages from the universe.

I tried to imagine her through Papa's eyes, a pale sprite at the gurdwara, the white of her turban setting off her fair skin to disadvantage, her pink eyelids and blue-veined temples standing out in the absence of any other colour. Her chin lifted at an angle, revealing an awareness of glances from the people around her. Papa said once, when pressed, that he fell in love with Mama's purity of soul before he cherished her as a woman, but I think it might just as easily have been that touch of defiance in her jaw—the rebelliousness that so often made my heart sink towards my shoes—that first caught his attention and lured him away from the traditions of his strict upbringing. Or it could have been the look of her nipples, just barely visible through her layered white cotton shirts, or her toes peeking out below her skirts, small and rounded like tiny pearl onions. Or her perfume of patchouli and musk oil, spicy like sex and old religions.

Or it could have been that Papa had always been different. He came from a place where the details of his birth might have constricted his life, his love, and even his thoughts. But they didn't. He followed the rules the way he followed a recipe: carefully, thoughtfully, and sometimes, at the last moment, with an inspired change.

But contrary to the opinion shared by his brother and the rest of the family back in India, Papa remained a believer. He wrote to his father about the equality of all human beings, both men and women, according to the very teachings of the holy gurus. He wrote to his mother urging her to reread the scriptures. Later, he wrote to apologize for his disrespect, but he was not cowed by his parents' fury into believing he had made a mistake by marrying a white woman. Instead, he prayed for them.

On the morning everything changed, August twenty-first, 1978, Papa announced his intention to take a *hukam* from the Guru Granth Sahib, the big holy book compiled in the age of the gurus. He often did this after breakfast, opening to a passage at random to give us insight into the day to come. Sadhana and I watched from the kitchen table with the near fanatic joy we always reserved for family rituals. I felt an unwarranted proprietorship over the practice: the first letters of our names were chosen from the first letter of special *hukams* taken after we were born. Sadhana, just three, loved it all without really understanding.

Papa was in his yellow cotton pyjamas. We were a family who breakfasted in pyjamas—another beloved point of observance for me and my sister. In his bare feet, he stepped over to the special shelf where the book was kept and unwrapped it from its silk covering. Everything that he did was gentle and deliberate. He read aloud the first line of the hymn, the *shabad*, he had turned to. His voice was quiet but resonant, even as he covered his mouth with one of Mama's embroidered handkerchiefs as a sign of respect.

He read it in Gurmukhi before translating it into English: "The One Lord is the Creator of all things, the Cause of causes."

Mama waited until Papa had replaced the sacred book before she got up to kiss him. When she dropped back down from her tiptoes, Papa smiled at all of us, and the smile travelled up to his eyebrows and all the way into his orange turban. "I don't want to be late," he said.

"You never are," said Mama. She cupped his face with one of her small hands before he went off to the bedroom to get dressed.

And after all that, after that normal, considerate conversation that might not have happened in exactly that way but probably did, my quiet, excellent Papa went down to our bagel shop and died.

~ THE FORECAST ~

On the day Papa died, the temperature in the bagel shop was a sweltering thirty-eight degrees.

"Hotter than Calcutta," said one ambulance attendant to the other. They spoke in low tones in French, and they had already given up. They were wheeling Papa's body on the collapsible gurney out through the back kitchen, where the employees watched with grief and awe as the Boss was taken past the stainless steel counters, the ancient metal shelving unit full of flour sacks, and the cords of wood stacked nearly to the ceiling behind the ovens. Somebody gasped as Papa was manipulated with difficulty around the industrial mixer before being levered out the back door and into an ambulance. He was so still that his soft cheeks wobbled above his floury beard. The apron tied around his sweat-soaked shirt was dirty from the fall to the floor as his heart seized. His own grandfather had died the same way, of sudden heart failure, working in the fields in the Punjab.

Mama, who had already rushed down to my father's side, felt a pity for the bagel workers that she did not yet feel

for herself, and while she rode to the hospital, an elderly cashier named Lefty came upstairs to watch us. When Mama
returned, hours later, she tried her best to explain, but for
once, her metaphors failed her. She told us what she had seen
(the flour sacks, the soft cheeks), and what she had heard (the
murmured French, the frightened gasp), and how Papa was
gone before she even got down there to kiss him goodbye.

We were sitting on the sheepskin rugs in the living
room, and when Mama finished talking, she rose and went
to the mantelpiece, with its purple brocade runner topped
with her collection of inspirational objects: a carved dolphin,
an orange pillar candle in the shape of a star, a jam jar full
of sand from a beach in British Columbia, where she said
she had "found her purpose." There was a horseshoe from
Galway, where she was born, and a braided ribbon from San
Francisco, where she'd gone next. There were cowry shells
and a conch, and stones of all shapes and sizes on a silver tray,
some with flecks of mica, others with the fossil shadows of
small creatures long dead. There were feathers, too, that she
had found, goose and peacock and one from a red cardinal,
poking up out of a green Plasticine turtle and fanning in the
breeze from the window. And there was a tiny brass cobra,
coiled upright at attention as though charmed or about to
strike. I could hear Mama breathing as she lit the candle with
unsteady hands, and when she turned back to us, she looked
girlish rather than serene.

"Stay awake with me?" She phrased it as a question with
a measure of hesitance. I could not remember her ever having
asked us for something in quite the same way. I held Sadhana's
hand and nodded as I squeezed it, waking my sister from her
light doze.

We sat up that whole long night with our mother, and the world grew black as we wept, which was right, and the stars winked on one by one, like cosmic comedians with unbearable mirth, and when the sun had not yet risen, Mama pulled out the mats and bent herself forward and back, stretching in silence from Bhujangasana to Parvatasana, her whole body seeming to collapse and expand in turn as she moved through her yoga postures like a dance with space. Then she began to chant, and I felt goosebumps spread over my skin. The chanting had no words I could recognize or understand, but as the pitch rose and fell in waves of rhythm it reminded me of a dream I had forgotten, in which I stood onstage and sang a song I made up as I went along. I knew they were the same sacred mantras Mama had sung every morning before sunrise since before we were born, but the sounds that came out were as worn and reedy as a tin whistle, as though all the air had gone out of her.

I remember the desperation of my sorrow in the days that followed as a terror of being alone. The phone rang and rang with condolences and I always ran to answer, just to hear a voice, any voice, not transformed by grief into something almost unrecognizable. Mama clutched my sister to her chest, her face flat and tear-glazed as she held out her other arm for me to take my own comfort if I could. Sadhana was too young to understand what was happening, and I was jealous of her ignorance. But her inability to comprehend that Papa was gone for good seemed to give peace to our mother. She held my sister on her lap like a worry doll, stroking her long black hair.

Six weeks later Mama asked Uncle for the name of an Indian astrologer. Though he frowned and narrowed his eyes, he was not a hard enough man to be able to refuse the request of a widow, even if she was a white woman he disapproved of.

"In Indian astrology," Mama said to us, "they use a different zodiac. Instead of only looking at the Earth and the sun and the planets, they calculate using the fixed stars, too."

We knew about astrology from the back of the newspaper, where the comics were, and from Mama always pointing out her lucky star, though she claimed not really to believe in it, or maybe just a little less than she believed in most things. I asked her what she would do if the astrologer gave her bad news, and for only the second time in my whole life, I saw her hesitate.

"It's just one way of looking and seeing," she said with a hint of apology. And then, "Like guessing how many jelly beans in a jar." She undid the elastic holding up her long red-gold hair and let it unwind and fall to either side of her face before twisting it to put it up again. "Or, if it's anything, it's just a weather forecast, liable to change at any moment."

I was worried about this explanation because she had taught us that the stars had paths they were bound to, their own places among the others that never changed. And if you couldn't be sure, why even bother to ask?

When she came home, she told Uncle to come and pick up Papa's clothes. Then she took all the silverware out of one drawer and put it into another.

"What did the astrologer say, Mama?" I was anxious to know. "What was the forecast?"

"He said nothing," said Mama. She looked surprised and a little blank. "Nothing that meant anything."

From then on, Papa's death triggered in Mama a deep storytelling urge. She had always been ready with theories, if not facts, to frame our experience, scooping them out like salves for all the little wounds and worries of childhood—but all at once she seemed driven by an urgency to form the stuff of our lives, of Papa's life especially, into something strong and beautiful before it cooled. Molten gold, fresh from the forge. The workings of these tales were so intense and profuse that we began to trip over them like guards in a Vatican storehouse. A coronet. A hammered bowl. A candelabrum with twelve arms reaching out towards the ceiling. Although later we sometimes pretended differently and at other times it was hard to tell, most of what we came to remember about Papa came from these stories Mama told us.

When November twenty-fifth arrived, and our first birthdays without Papa, she pulled a chair into the kitchen for me, sat Sadhana on the counter, and talked to us about him while she mixed butter with sugar for a cake. She told us that Papa had never intended to run a Jewish bagel shop. He had never wanted to be a businessman at all. That was where he and Uncle were different, one of a hundred ways they were different. Papa had wanted to be a baker, and he was a baker before everything.

"I fell in love with him," said Mama, "because he was an artist and a craftsman." She showed us the mixture in the bowl, and the sugar sparkled like stars in the creamed butter. Mama said, "He was also the only other person I knew who got up at five in the morning."

Papa was trained as a pastry chef, but when the opportunity came to buy the bagel shop with the money his parents had given him when he went to Canada, he decided to do it. Later, when Uncle came to Canada, too, he gave him a job as the manager.

"Uncle," said Mama, with great diplomacy, "is not my favourite person."

Uncle enjoyed everything that Papa had hated, everything that Uncle called the nitty-gritty: the purchasing, the ledger, the profits, the firings. Uncle even enjoyed the customers who were visibly surprised to be buying their Jewish bagels in a Hasidic neighbourhood from a big man in a huge blue turban. This was something he found amusing.

"Your Papa," said Mama, "liked nothing more than hiding out in the back and training boys in the ways of baking bagels."

When weeks of incompetence forced him into letting someone go, Papa was easily consoled. Every employee lost just meant another one to train, another boy to initiate into the midnight toil of baking bread.

Mama's baking was never as skilful as Papa's, but when we finished making the cake and sat down to eat it, it seemed to have a little something of him in it. Mama and I each had a second piece while Sadhana licked icing off her fingers.

"Papa always said you could bake love right into something," said Mama with wonder in her eyes, scraping her fork along the side of the flowered china plate. "He said you could taste the difference."

Other facts about Papa were harder to pin down. The strength of his hands or the way he used to smell were things Mama tried to describe when she was putting us to bed. "Like flour," she said, climbing between the sheets with us, "and eucalyptus, and the sweetness of chopped basil." On either side of her, Sadhana and I each had a cheek on the pillow as she closed her eyes to conjure Papa. "And sometimes he smelled like a raft in the ocean, just a few feet from shore, about to be pulled in by the tide."

We didn't always understand what she was talking about.

"Mama?" said Sadhana.

"Like seawater," she said, lashes curling down her freckled cheeks, "and fresh breezes. Like the most lonesome ship-wrecked sailor at the first sight of land."

Sadhana and I nodded, and nuzzled her neck, and threw our arms over her so that she would stay until we all fell asleep. When Mama called Papa's laugh a sneeze full of tulips mixed with a river of swans, it was hard to tell if we were already dreaming.

While we both gathered stories to carry forward, like explorers face to face with a vanishing tribe, Sadhana became focused on what was going to happen next. She did not like me to sit in Papa's chair at the table, and when Mama got dressed one day before breakfast, Sadhana wept and refused to eat. As for the *hukam*, which had stopped altogether in our father's absence, Sadhana insisted that it be reinstated, and Mama agreed.

At the beginning, Sadhana and I fought over who would do it, until Mama settled it by taking over. She read from the Guru Granth Sahib, and then sometimes from other holy books, the Bible or the Koran or the Tao Te Ching. Other times, she pulled the *hukam* from Shakespeare or George Eliot. On the longest and most silent of days, she would just close her eyes and point to a book and read from it, no matter what it was.

The mercy in interpretation, we discovered, was an excess of information. The more we took in, the easier it was to let go of the parts we didn't like. The eerie time we got "Meantime we shall express our darker purpose" from *King Lear*, or the unfathomable "Can a man take fire in his bosom, and his clothes not be burned?" from Proverbs. And whatever it was that the astrologer had told Mama. We let it all wash over us and pass away.

But the less we were concerned about specific omens, the more worried we became about all of them in general. A list of superstitions had been scared up from some of the employees at the bagel shop. Mama had been encouraging us to run down for visits, probably so we wouldn't grow to dread the place. We were small enough then that we could slip right by the customers and pass under the counter.

"Mirrors," said Jean-François, who had a beard like Papa's and rangy blue eyes. "Don't break them." He had been working there the morning Papa died. Jean-François, like the rest of the employees, was always willing to humour us. "And black cats, ladders," said Jean-François, his palms and fingers never stopping their rapid work of rolling thin slices of dough and joining them into circles. A loose fluorescent light buzzed above his head.

"What else?" asked Sadhana. She was looking at his face instead of his hands, paying absolute attention for once. I was flapping loose the front of my shirt where it was sticking to my stomach. The white-painted brick walls shimmered in the heat above the deep black openings to the ovens.

"Ask Lefty," said Jean-François. By then he was throwing the pale dough circles onto one of the long wooden oven paddles.

"Yeah, come here, kids," Lefty called from the front. Until he started working at the shop, Lefty had shined shoes at the airport. He loved it but quit because everybody started wearing sneakers. He told us to hunt for sweets in the pockets of his coat hanging on the rack while he rang through the customers. Then he leaned his elbows on the counter and started adding to our list. If he had guessed that our paranoid inventory would yield such sober and scrupulous results, he probably would have hesitated.

After that, walking around the corner to get milk turned into a twenty-minute trip as Sadhana and I high-stepped over the cracks, our solemn, anxious faces wed to the sidewalk. Ladders we shunned as if they were lepers, though we more or less agreed that doing much of anything outside was too perilous anyway, given the number of black cats in the neighbourhood. Instead, we played mostly indoors, or on our two balconies when the weather was fair.

We removed the salt shaker from the table and hid it in the cupboard. Mama, exclaiming upon finding it there, held it up and studied our faces. "Girls," she said, "I've been looking for this. Don't worry, I'm not going to spill it. Is that it?"

Sadhana shook her head until her braids started to come out, and Mama put the salt back out of sight. My job was to hide the umbrellas, which was easier, as we had only one. Mama was a great lover of rain. Mirrors were less easily disposed of, but we gave a wide berth to the dresser in Mama's bedroom, which had its own tilting mirror as well as a hand mirror that was part of an heirloom set she'd brought from Ireland. The mirrored medicine cabinet in the bathroom we handled only with something equivalent to a surgeon's careful touch.

If our mother noticed us becoming more worn and manic, she never said anything. She liked to leave us to our games and amusements. With Papa gone, she had her own shadow side in which she laughed a little less and did more yoga, and every once in a while, when the phone rang or the kettle whistled, I'd see a flicker of fear cross her face, and I wondered if she was afraid that something else bad was going to happen.

∽ THE HUNGRY FLAME ∾

The fire came in like a stray dog, slinking up the stairs as we slept, dragging its empty belly along the floor and blackening the walls with its great dirty hide. From where I lay in bed, it sounded like nothing so much as a large animal, sniffing and snapping as it prowled. I awoke to the crackle of it chewing on the thick green rug that Papa had stapled to the staircase when he and Mama first moved in. In the faint glow of the nightlight, I could see its hazy floating shadow in the hallway. I sat up and made myself scream to scare it away. Instead I only woke my sister, who kicked off her covers and, without opening her eyes, declared that this time she was sure we were going to melt before morning.

"A dog," I said, and it came out in a whisper. My throat felt ragged, as though I'd screamed more than once. The only reply from Sadhana was a grunt. She had probably fallen back asleep before her covers even touched the floor.

While I was still deciding what to do, Mama came running in. Behind her I could hear a beeping, as though she had decided to set her alarm clock for the middle of the night.

"Wake up! Wake up! Wake up! Wake up!" Her voice was a loud, strange singsong. She was carrying sopping wet towels she told us to press to our faces. I sputtered against the shock of cold water.

"Stop it," I said. "Did you see the dog?" But the sound had changed, and I wondered if I had been confused. "Are we going to look at the stars?" I asked. Once or twice Mama had woken us up well past our bedtimes to go and look at the night sky—the three times that Mars was in conjunction with Jupiter, and another time for a lunar eclipse.

"No, not stars," she said. "Wake up." Though her face was mild, something in her voice and eyes was fierce. She was naked apart from a wet towel that was dripping onto the bed. "You're dreaming. We're going to the balcony. We're holding hands in a chain and running to the balcony."

Mama hauled Sadhana out of bed and pushed her ahead as she pulled me behind, holding us by the wrists instead of our hands. Outside of our bedroom, the heat was immense, like a force field pushing us back from the front door. The dog's shadow I thought I'd seen was a black cloud of smoke that stung at our eyes.

"Duck down," said Mama, crouching with us, but she did not slacken her pace for a moment. Choking and gasping, the three of us flew through the cloud across to the kitchen, out to the large balcony through the sliding patio doors, and down the fire escape.

Mama didn't slow down once we reached the ground. She pulled us around the corner into the alleyway and then out front to the shop, to get them to evacuate and call 911. Uncle wasn't working, but Travis, the night manager, along with Carlos and Ajay, who had worked there the longest, came outside with big white buckets full of water. Mama shook her head at them as they approached our front door.

"There's nothing but possessions in there now. Sticks and stones. Please don't take a chance." And when they began to insist: "Don't you dare."

The fire station was just around the corner, so in almost no time at all there were wailing sirens and three red engines and a dozen firefighters in impossibly heavy-looking yellow suits hurtling into our apartment. Bagel customers arrived and stood staring with us on the sidewalk on the opposite side of the street. In half an hour, the fire was out, though in that time it had made its way up our front staircase and into the apartment, where it had begun to char the living room.

It was one of the firefighters who called us lucky. He came out and announced that the fire was out, and Mama threw her arms around him in a ferocious hug.

"Not everybody remembers to change the batteries in their smoke detectors," he said, patting her shoulder as she pulled away. His cheeks were dark with soot, and beneath that we could see the deep blush left behind by Mama's embrace. She was still wearing only her towel.

Mama told him he had no idea how lucky. "The girls and I, we can't smell smoke anymore," she said. "From living over the store with the wood ovens going all day and night. Like the people who live near Niagara Falls and don't notice the roar of the water."

The fire chief said the blaze had started with a gas-soaked towel stuffed through the mail slot, followed by a match. The shop itself had escaped unscathed, but our front stoop had been spray-painted all over with a symbol that made Mama gasp when she saw it. Nobody said they saw anything, though the shop had been open all night, as usual. Uncle, when he arrived later, began shouting for somebody to get the turpentine.

$$\sim\!\!\infty\!\!\sim$$

The apartment, when we got back from a stay with one of Mama's yoga friends, was no longer the spoiled child of fire and water. The green rug on the front stairs, soaked by the firefighters where it was spared by the flames, had been torn up and replaced by a blue one. The drywall all along the entryway had been patched up, and everywhere, as far as the fire had penetrated, had a new coat of paint. Sadhana and I were amazed that so much had come to pass during our absence. It was Mama's way to do most things herself.

"The wonders of insurance" was all she said about it. She touched her fingers to the new banister and looked at the fine dusting of white powder as she pulled them away. "Fixed up in broad strokes. Cleaned in a hurry."

At first, Sadhana and I were absorbed in discovering every little thing that had been altered. Mama let us do as we liked and unpacked all our bags by herself.

My sister stepped carefully around the apartment with her hands in her pockets, looking at everything as if she had never seen it before. "Everything's different," she said. She picked her way across the living room as though the charred debris from the night of the fire was still strewn in its wet piles, trailing from the front door.

"It does smell different," I said. There was a clean, chemical scent of fresh paint, and after our time away I could detect the persistent campfire smell of woodsmoke from the shop's ovens, the one Mama had said kept us from smelling the fire as it came. But I thought I knew what my sister was feeling: that it was strange and awful to be away from home, and even more strange and awful to have things transform on the sly without us there to stop them.

Mama let us stay up late. Between the new paint and the fresh enjoyment of being restored to the delights of all our belongings, Sadhana and I were much too excited to fall asleep. It was after midnight when Mama finally tucked us into our separate beds, each surrounded by toys or books from which we could no longer bear to be parted.

When I woke, the apartment was dark and silent, and I sat up to look out the bedroom door, remembering the woozy fear of the fire. I checked to see if Sadhana happened to be awake and was astonished to find that her bed, apart from an orderly row of stuffed toys, seemed empty.

"Sadhana," I whispered, in case she was hiding somewhere in the room. But there was no answer.

I was afraid to get out of bed, but more afraid for my sister, so I forced myself to swing my legs over the side. The feeling of my feet planted on the carpet was a comfort. Maybe Sadhana had had a bad dream and gone straight to our mother.

But Mama's room had only Mama in it, asleep on her stomach, naked except for a cotton sheet that covered her up to the waist. I stepped back from the doorway, both wanting and unwilling to wake her.

There were only so many other places Sadhana could be. The living room, emptied of the ruined yoga mats and the sheepskin rugs, seemed stark and unfamiliar, though the mantelpiece altar persisted with its determined parade of little objects. At a glance I could see the room was empty, but

I crossed to the fireplace to examine Mama's special items, as I had seen my sister doing the night before. Most were no worse for wear apart from a little soot. Only the feathers had really been burned by the heat. The quill of the former peacock feather looked like an oversized straw.

When I remembered my mission, I wandered into the kitchen, where I found Sadhana near the stove, her breath coming in quick little pants.

"What are you doing?"

"Checking to make sure it's off," she said. She was on her tiptoes, waving one hand in a kind of rhythm over the dials as she used the other to grip the stove. She was leaning in so closely I could see the oven handle digging into her stomach.

"We didn't even use it tonight," I said. "Of course it's turned off."

"No," said Sadhana. "No, no. We have to be more careful. We don't want another fire."

"Okay, so it's off," I said. I decided not to point out that the fire hadn't started with the stove, anyway. It occurred to me that Sadhana had been out of bed for a long time. "Let's go back to sleep."

Sadhana turned to look at me then, and I could see that she was crying, her cheeks streaked with the tally of her misery's duration. "I can't," she said. "Every time I try and leave, I start worrying that I've done it wrong, and I have to check it again."

With coaxing, Sadhana followed me back to bed, and her exhaustion seemed to make it easier. But my sister's strange behaviour in front of the stove made me uneasy.

In the morning, Sadhana seemed normal. She moaned about not wanting to get up, she complained that I'd taken the nicer piece of toast, and she almost fell off her chair laughing when I indulged her with my awful impression of Daffy Duck, which was performed only under circumstances of extreme benevolence or necessity. Though I watched her with unusual attention, my eight-year-old sister seemed as fun and annoying as she'd ever been, and as I didn't see her taking any particular notice of the stove, I decided not to mention our midnight wanderings to Mama.

But Mama had her own ways of knowing when something was amiss. Sadhana began dragging her feet every night at bedtime, always calling for one more story or glass of water, and once even asking to brush her teeth for a second time. While she was putting us to bed, Mama asked Sadhana about her new unease, just as if it were any other question Sadhana was capable of answering.

"My darling, what are you worried about? I can tell there's something fretting you."

Sadhana looked at me, probably thinking I'd betrayed her, but I shook my head.

My sister exhaled an emptying sigh as our mother's slender fingers ran through her hair. Mama was stretched out on my sister's bed, her tiny feet crossed at the ankles below her wide cotton pants. She was speaking softly, as though there were someone else asleep in the room with us she was afraid of waking. There was a pause so long that I could feel it like a belt starting to tighten around my waist, urging me to break it. But I could sense Mama's will, too, a force stronger than my own impulses, compelling me to accept the taut silence as part of the tonic for my sister's disquiet.

"Sometimes," said Sadhana, "I want to make sure the door is locked. And I forget if I've checked already." I could tell from her voice that she was very close to tears. "And the same thing with the stove, when I go to make sure it's off."

"Don't you think you can trust me to take care of all those things?" said Mama. She had her head tilted to the side, the way she always did when she was trying to process new information. "Don't you think that's my job?"

It was a moment between the two of them, and my role was to be invisible. To strive not to undo whatever magic Mama might be working.

"It's everybody's job," said Sadhana, "to keep us safe."

Our mother began to say something else, but Sadhana wept then, with her head pressed to Mama's chest, and when I tried to share a smile with Mama over my sister's silliness, my mother gave me a look that might have meant I wasn't turning into the person she hoped I would be. I always faltered when Mama's eyes were on me like that, the hungry flame of mild reproach catching in her irises. That she would always love and forgive us was as clear as the fact that we were bound to disappoint her again and again. The weight of her trust that I could be good would come over me like gravity's spell on a returning astronaut. It burdened my very bones.

From then on, Mama watched Sadhana the way she watched the balcony basil, the only one of our herbs in perpetual danger from the neighbour's seemingly Italian cat. Though I rarely caught her looking at it, she always knew when it needed water, when it needed shade, when it had been bitten ragged and needed to come back inside. For all the living things in our house, Mama's attention was the one and only sufficient condition for flourishing. Under Mama's watch, Sadhana's worries seemed to ebb away, as though they were jinxes or wishes that, once spoken, could only lose their power.

——— ———

The train is full, almost no empty seats. It seems that I was lucky to get tickets, booking only last night, just after supper. Quinn begged for the train, laying out argument after argument against the bus as he rushed through his meal, finishing two veggie burgers long before I'd even come to the end of my salad.

"The bus smells," he said, "for one. The bathroom is disgusting." He was straddling his chair, his dark denim jeans making a V on the turquoise vinyl. A retro fifties kitchen set Uncle had brought over when he decided to invest in new furniture for our old apartment above the shop. Probably something Mama picked up at a garage sale. Everything in our house tying me to the past.

"The bus is cheap," I said. "And we'll sit near the front, away from the bathroom."

"You can read on the train," he said. "You get motion sickness on the bus."

"I'll probably just sleep on the way there anyway, or look out the window." Trying not to think about what lay ahead. I speared the last remaining slice of bocconcini, pushed it through the dark, glistening pools of balsamic dressing beaded into discrete droplets by the oil. Letting the smooth slide combat the trembling of my arm.

"You can buy snacks in case we don't get up early enough to have breakfast." Quinn's eyebrows flickered up in the deliberate expression of somebody who has just turned the corner in a debate. It was a sign of my inability to wake up early that the snacks were actually a valid selling point.

I parried anyway. "If I want to pay a dollar fifty for bad coffee and an extra two bucks for a dry muffin. Which I can tell you right now, I don't."

Quinn couldn't offer much in the way of a defence of the food, but he could tell I was cracking. I almost always gave in, and though I tried not to show it, this time I'd been ready to opt for the train even before he started arguing. He was being playful, for the first time in a long time, and I could have let him go on and on. Shrugging over my plate, I hemmed with feigned indecision for another ten minutes, letting him work himself up to his drollest theatricalities, watching as he leapt to his feet to plead his case like an orator.

Now, as we shuffle down the aisle behind brighter-eyed travellers, he is morning Quinn — gruff, not cranky, more high-functioning than I usually am at this hour. Whenever I'm up to see him like this, when I get a call from the law firm to come in early to start proofing briefs or feel motivated to make breakfast before he heads out to school, I always get a kick out of it. He seems like Quinn in a time machine: older, set in his ways, benignly fussy. Shades of Uncle. Slow-moving but unapologetic. Frank.

"Have a seat, Mother," he says to me now, rolling his eyes at my intense visual scouting for the best spot — somewhere strategic between bathroom and exit, equidistant between a couple of nervy babies. He ushers me into the window side of the nearest two seats together.

"Let's get this show on the road," he says. He settles into his seat with a heavy sigh and clamps on his headphones, folding his arms as his eyes close shut.

We pull away from the station as the safety instructions and non-smoking announcements are read out in puzzlingly mechanized cadences, both official languages crackling over the loudspeaker. The snack cart is stuttering up the aisle with the light percussion of change clicking as quarters pile into palms, and I'm halfway through a watery coffee even before parting with my ticket. When I'm finished, I lean back my head and look out the window, where the city has disappeared into fields. It used to be a point of familial protocol that Quinn always got the window. Through a new gallantry or an assertion of maturity, he started giving it to me once he turned seventeen. Both our last two trips saw him sitting taut beside the aisle, held straight as a rod whether sleeping or reading, looking ready at any moment to lunge up to use the bathroom, grab some water, or do a head count of the pretty girls sitting alone.

It was winter the last time we went to Montreal, the city tense in the grip of an unseasonable deep freeze, two weeks of minus thirty-five, the Christmas lights strung everywhere downtown like determined lifelines to a cheerier outlook. Uncle had called with the news about Sadhana. He said, "Your sister has passed away. You need to come." He said almost nothing else, or nothing else I managed to take in. I hung up the phone with an overriding sense that there had been a mistake. I knew that she had been doing well for months.

Quinn and I didn't talk on the train that time, nor did we sleep. It felt strange to head straight to Uncle's, and Quinn had to correct me when I gave Sadhana's address to the taxi driver. When I went to pry open the car door to get out, I noticed my train ticket folded to an accordion, still gripped in my right palm. And now, grazing alongside the edge of this memory, I look down to see a wadded napkin tucked tightly into the same place. I reach over to the paper garbage bag hung under the window and open my fist to drop it in.

The time before that was in the fall. Sadhana had called us to request a visit. Montreal trips to her apartment were almost always by appointment of this kind, though she often popped into Ottawa with no warning. But Quinn and I had seen her only three times that summer, which was well below par, so both of us were excited and pleased. The official pretext, a play being put on by a friend of hers at the Friday Night Café, a tiny theatre at McGill University. Fifty seats, more or less, of folding chairs. It was a play that Sadhana thought was important for Quinn to see.

"It's called *Art*. It'll be good for him, no matter what the production's like. Very provocative dialogue." Her voice clipped along in the precise way she had of describing artistic events, as informative and promotional as a fringe festival program. She was in good spirits, and she seemed healthy. A turquoise pendant adorned her breastbone, and she was wearing a cap-sleeved top that showed her arms. Her brown eyes were sparkling. "I love one-act plays."

"Are you saying this production is going to be bad?"

"Of course not. This is Alex we're talking about."

Alex could be anyone. I was positive she'd never dropped the name before. Most of Sadhana's closest friends tended to be professionals in their artistic fields, not amateurs mounting plays with university students. This was an acquaintance upgraded to friendship for the purposes of this conversation only, to get us into town. I was sure of it.

But he turned out to be more of a friend than I'd imagined, though I found it hard to navigate through the effusive warmth of theatre people, one that didn't necessarily seem false to me, and maybe wasn't, but which to an outsider's eye seemed superfluous. When we visited Montreal, Sadhana was constantly running into people who upon interrogation turned out to be the vaguest of contacts. Someone she'd met once at a party. A friend of a dear friend of hers.

But Alex she greeted warmly; they'd embraced.

"Sadie," he called her. Sadie was her pet name among her dance and theatre friends in Montreal. It had surprised me the first time I heard it, but the hardened vowel suited her. They kissed on both cheeks.

"Al," she said. "I can't wait." She introduced me and Quinn, her hand a light touch on my son's arm, before leading us away to some seats in the second-last row. Quinn and I pored over our programs as my sister leaned forward and back, chatting with folks she knew, waving to a few others sitting on the other side.

When the lights dimmed, she spun to face front, leaning over to whisper us a stern warning: "Cellphones off, duckies."

That set off an indignant Quinn, who reached into his jacket pocket to prove we'd done it without prompting, but Sadhana shook her head, index finger to her lips in a silent shush.

After the play we went out for dinner near the university, where I watched Sadhana eat two slices of Blanche, the five-cheese pizza at Amelio's. She'd picked up a bottle of wine on the way, and she filled both our glasses as she leaned towards Quinn, prompting him for his observations on the play.

"I thought the guy who played Serge was a bit awkward," he said.

"Really? Did you think?"

I knew she was testing him. The actor in question was the show's clear weak link, visibly nervous though he'd tried to hide it, even build it into the character, but it didn't quite work. He'd spent the better part of three scenes inspecting a large ring on his clenched left hand, bringing it up to his face as though breathing in the scent of an invisible plucked blossom.

"I did," he said, after a moment. "Yeah."

Sadhana nodded, satisfied. "And what about the set? Did you like it?"

Quinn chewed, considering. "I guess it was . . . minimal? But I thought they used the stage well."

"Good direction, yes." Sadhana sipped her drink, the two sterling silver rings on her right hand clinking against the stem of the glass. One many-petalled rose and one eternal lemniscate, a sideways figure eight flattened to her middle finger, made by an artisan friend of hers. She looked over at me. "Alex worked miracles with those kids. I dropped in on some of their earliest rehearsals."

I sat back, watching Sadhana animate the conversation, expounding in her desultory way to Quinn, drawing him out, taking obvious pleasure, as she always did, in his quick mind, his willingness to listen. She had never stopped trying to show him things, never seemed to doubt that there were still plenty of things she had left to teach him.

Quinn is reading a trashy magazine that he found slipped into the seat pocket in front of him, behind the safety instructions. It looks well thumbed, as though it has made the rounds of the whole line, from Sydney to Prince Rupert, though this train runs only the same short route daily. I'm seized with longing for a book, bewildered that I didn't pack one.

"Interested?" asks Quinn, noticing my peering. He is holding out the magazine, nose wrinkling. It is a two-page spread of celebrity photos, of starlets caught out being human: picking their noses, scratching along the tight bands of their underwear. Criminally bad hair days.

"No thanks," I say, though if I were alone I would probably flip through. I sometimes have bizarre urges to prove myself to him, never knowing when one wrong move might lose his esteem. I remember Sadhana becoming steeped in judgement before she started high school, calling out Mama for never having gone to university and for believing in animal spirit guides.

"I don't believe in them exactly," Mama had said. She was perched on the sofa, knitting. She never flinched from Sadhana's attacks. "It's just nicer to think they exist than that they don't. Remember that thing with the grey cat last year?"

There had been a cat that followed her home, nestling itself into our recycling bin to sleep, its nose bunged into an empty tin of tuna. There was a lightning storm that night, the whole courtyard lit up and booming with it. In the morning, we found the green bin melted, all the cardboard cartons burned to soot, and the cat circling the perimeter, yowling. Its tail fell off a few days later. When it stopped coming around, Mama said it had come to bring us a message and gone back to its own people. What message, though, was anybody's guess. As Sadhana grew into her long legs and out of the fancy of Mama's worldviews, this was the kind of vague claim she began to despise. And though Quinn lacks my sister's sharp tongue, I can see his eye-rolling divisions between things, the implacable teenage discrimination between cool and uncool. I'm still hoping to make the cut.

Quinn is shoving the magazine back where it came from, out of sight. "Maybe I can buy you a newspaper," he says. "Would you like that?"

"Sure, if you can find one."

When he bounds away, I find my eyes closing. I think about what Evan said about me needing a rest, wondering how many times we've sat in a mutual silence I've found comfortable or a lull of my own creation he's merely endured. I wonder if I've been spooking him all along. Now and again it becomes clear that I've been relying on a mimicked peace of denial, letting my subconscious do the heavy lifting. The anxiety dreams I wake from daily, that I shake off with coffee and a paper run, a fast change of scenery: my sister always, turning away from me in blame. Her hand letting fall a piece of bread, her glare taking in a ringing phone, her black hair swinging loose to graze the stark rails of her collarbone. At first consciousness, I'm gripped with a sense of personal doom. Something that wants to linger, something gnawing. Whatever denial might be staving off, its ultimate gift seems to me to be mercy. Reprieve.

TWO

⁓◯ HIDE AND SEEK ◯⁓

We were strange little girls in our way. We had a hard time knowing where one of us left off and the other began. Mama said it was because of our shared birthday; we were almost like a special kind of twins. Sometimes Sadhana pointed to her cheek where she boasted of a brown freckle, but that was where mine lurked when it wasn't swallowed by my dimple. And every summer we forgot who loved strawberries and who was allergic. Once, after watching Sadhana finish an intricate drawing of a horse, I called Mama over to show her what I could do, only to be surprised by the awkward, rolling sensation of the pencil between my fingers. Other times, we would try to play hide-and-seek, but one of us would forget to look and instead we would both hide. When we realized our mistake, we would call out for Mama to find us.

"Why would I do that?" came her reply in her strong, clear voice. "I always know where both of you are, and you're always right here in my heart."

Separately but together, we groaned and pleaded, and within a minute Mama's hands would be on us, one after the other, as if she really had known where we were the whole time.

There wasn't much room for hiding to begin with. Our apartment was tiny, a second-floor walk-up over the store. There was a kitchen, two bedrooms, a windowless bathroom, and a long narrow room that tended to be given over to the game of the moment. There were two balconies: one larger, back balcony facing onto a quiet stone courtyard, and a smaller one on the side, overlooking the alleyway. For hide-and-seek, we usually tried squeezing ourselves into a closet or scrambling under a bed, or, in one hilarious instance that we almost always tried to repeat, rolling ourselves into Mama's yoga mats, with our heads and feet sticking out at either end.

The bedroom I shared with my sister, first in one bed, then later in two, was painted cream with green trim. In the high heat of the summer, with the perpetual fire of the wood ovens in the shop below, the paint on the walls would start to bubble. But our room was our headquarters. We called it that. *Headquarters*, or HQ. I was two years older than Sadhana, but it never seemed that way. We liked the same games and amusements. We read detective stories and spied on people and met there to take stock of our findings. There was never anything interesting to report, though we still made note of four of the five Ws in pink scribblers: *who, what, where, when. Why* was the one usually left blank. We sought out murderers—or kidnappers, at the very least—with the cheerful bloodthirstiness peculiar to children. We ached to free someone from a cruel captor or summon the police to a crime in progress, one where we had already trapped the thief inside, face sweating beneath his ski mask with embarrassment at being shown up by a couple of plucky kids.

Instead we saw the homeless man who begged outside the shop slip into the alley to drink mouthwash behind the dumpster. Ignorant, buffered as we were, we thought this merely stupid instead of sad. *Doesn't he know he's supposed to spit it out?* We saw the most ordinary of things through binoculars trained on people's windows. High drama was a man in a blue bathrobe open to the waist making a peanut butter sandwich. The curled dark hair on his chest, his slow chew below a blank stare into the sink. He was meticulous about washing his hands before and afterwards. The Case of the Very Clean Hands. It was inevitable that we came to spy on each other.

School was a good thing for curing us of our strange habits, for helping us let go of those reveries bit by bit. Sadhana befriended a girl named Lou Lou, who was the best rope climber in gym class and who had also exploded all parameters of superstition by walking under a ladder thirteen times with no ill effects.

And it was at school that some of the other things we took for granted started changing. Two grades below me, Sadhana got used to not having me around. At three o'clock, we would return to each other with a daily-growing sense that the balance had shifted. Bright, beautiful, and sharp-tongued, Sadhana quickly assumed a role of importance in the microcosm of first grade. Quieter and more hesitant, I was less gratified than my sister by the schoolyard experience. It was hard not to feel diminished as Sadhana chattered away to her friends while we waited for Mama, without once reaching for my hand as she used to or even asking for my opinion on anything.

One afternoon I was the first one to spot our mother, and I waved.

"Is that your mommy?" Lou Lou asked. Mama had slowed down, digging in her bag for something.

"Yes," said Sadhana.

"Really?" said Lou Lou. Her nose, crumpling up like a gum wrapper, communicated profound doubt. "You don't look like her."

"That's true," I said. Mama was white and we were brown. She sometimes claimed she was the teapot and we were the tea. Sadhana's lip trembled, but I went on, "You should probably mind your own business."

Unfazed, Lou Lou tilted her head and her blonde pigtails jiggled. "Touchy, touchy."

Sadhana frowned at me then, as though I was the one who had brought on the question, as though there was something about me that made her friends have second thoughts. She grabbed Lou Lou by the hand and pulled her towards the gap in the fence. "Come on," she said, leaving me behind. "I'll introduce you."

But in the evenings, as Mama cooked and we played cards or Chinese checkers or with the family of little toy bears that lived in the wooden dollhouse, everything seemed to return to normal. Sadhana listened to me and laughed at my jokes; she leaned her head on my shoulder when she started to get tired. Sometimes she fell asleep in my bed as we took turns looking through Mama's kaleidoscope, our faces fixed cockeyed to its shifting rainbow heaven of jewelled stars.

Report cards, though, remained pitiless messengers from the outside world.

"I'm excellent at swimming and running and dancing and dodgeball," Sadhana said, as though we didn't already know, while Mama donned her grasshopper glasses to take another look at the note stapled to the back. "I'm even better than most of the boys when we have gym."

I nodded. The change in her had happened almost imperceptibly, but my younger sister, though still not as tall, could by then easily outrun and out-jump me in every game. Like Mama, she was lithe and flexible, whereas I was one of the heavier girls in my grade. Not fat, but somewhere well beyond sturdy. Not graceless, but not quick either.

When Mama decided to put Sadhana into soccer, she asked if I wanted to start an activity of my own. "I'd really rather just read, I guess," I told Mama, who kneaded my shoulders and said how proud she was that I was such a good student.

Knowing my mother was proud of me didn't quite take the sting out of witnessing first-hand how much more excited parents seemed to be about sports. During dusky evenings on the sidelines, the bleachers trembled with the verve of parents shouting encouragement to their children, often to sets of siblings playing in simultaneous games in adjacent parts of the field. Other families brought snacks and sandwiches to these matches, even coolers of drinks, as well as a whole vocabulary of sport and exhortation with which Mama and I were unfamiliar. *Up the wing! Man open! Dig deep!* I could feel Mama bristling beside me when some aggressive strategic suggestion burst through the cool of the evening air towards children so small that just the sound of a harsh tone sometimes tripped them into the grass.

As the sun went down on Sadhana's last game of the summer and a chill set in, Mama gathered in her long skirts, heaping the excess up over her knees, and, opening her giant woven bag, pulled out crocheted shawls that we wrapped around our shoulders. Mama switched her cheering allegiances from minute to minute according to whichever side was losing. She always rooted for the underdog and didn't object to yelling as long as the messages were positive. Years of chanting and deep breathing had honed a considerable instrument, and I tried not to wince as her bellow threatened to drown out even the voices of the coaches and the referees.

When Sadhana came off the field, Mama held out her arms, her shawl sweeping back like green lacy wings.

"Did you see my goal?" said Sadhana. We were pressed together in our mother's embrace and I could feel the warmth coming off her cheek as Mama bent down to kiss us.

"Everyone saw it," I said, though I knew Mama had been cheering for the other side just then. "It was great."

"Good."

As Sadhana ran back to shake hands with the opposing team, Mama finally pulled out her camera. It was her favourite part of the game.

Walking home from the soccer field, I dragged my feet and looked at my family. Though my skin was lighter than Sadhana's and grew even paler in the winter, Mama said I was my father's daughter, since I had Papa's full lips and cheeks, his large brown eyes, his propensity for sweets, and a love of bread.

My sister was darker, smaller, bird-boned, her face angular where mine was round. We both showed signs of inheriting Mama's strong nose, but when it came to comparing ourselves to the girls at school, Sadhana never wavered in her conviction that we were as pretty as anyone else. Of the two of us, Sadhana was the best at managing to take the world in and judge it.

That kind of looking and thinking was something I did so rarely that I was always taken by surprise when someone did it to us. With Papa gone, we forgot that Mama's part in us couldn't really be seen, that people like Lou Lou would always be inclined to ask questions. That may have been when we began searching, hunting for more parts of ourselves that took after her, parts we could show the world to prove we were her daughters. Something to go along with everything from Papa that we couldn't hide.

When I got my period for the first time, Mama baked a spice cake of cinnamon and cloves, its batter tinted red with the juice of crushed beets. I was eleven and ambivalent, but it was a luxury to have a celebration of my own for once, something besides the usual mutual birthdays. I asked if I could have balloons, too.

"Of course, kitten," said Mama. She was in raptures, having long prepared us for the day it would happen. She climbed on a chair to reach the balloon stash and began tossing down red ones. "My mother called it the curse," she said. "Jokingly, maybe, but I think it's a sin to talk like that. It's a blessing to grow up and become a woman. Remember that."

When Mama began extemporizing about the blessings of blood, it was best to just sit back and take it. In truth, I had more horror than enthusiasm for my supposed initiation into womanhood. But it was also a chance to make my sister jealous, so I projected a mature contentment.

"I definitely feel a little wiser," I said, tipping the kitchen chair back on two legs. "Less hyper." My sixth-grade teacher was always fumbling in her purse for a bottle of Tylenol and complaining that our class was too hyper.

Sadhana observed me with some curiosity and a little more expressed distaste. "It seems icky," she said, "having blood come out down there."

"Life," Mama said, "is a messy business, pets."

"If you say so."

"I do. And it's going to be beautiful," said Mama, "watching the two of you grow up."

We grew up like sleepwalkers. We got taller in the night when no one was looking. Dark hair came up here and there like windblown crops clinging to fallow fields. One morning I caught my sister staring at the lumps under my shirt with a hurt fascination that made me wonder if something besides my body was changing. Between Sadhana and I, getting older was like breaking the pact between us, shattering the rapt fervour of our childhood games. We had been acting as though my red-cake party had been only an interruption of the status quo, an aberration rather than a signpost, but there were rumours of adulthood built into our very bones. Every now and again they would make themselves known, and we pretended, like anyone, to have heard what they were about, and it somehow became important not to let on to the other that we might doubt or dread what was starting to seem inevitable.

We took turns refusing to play with each other, and the word itself that had characterized all the best hours of our lives began to take on a taint that made my heart ache. *Play.* I would not be the first to renounce it, yet I could not allow myself to be the last. One day Sadhana had a friend over, who, upon discovering our dollhouse, asked witheringly if we still played pretend. And Sadhana said, "What do you think?" and her friend's eyes darted around before she finally shrugged. I felt angry and relieved and proud of my sister. It was how we all got by, on bluster and redirection.

Growing up seemed to mean that the only kind of pretending that was still safe was pretending we could do without it.

We woke up to the city. To the lights and its joyful sleeplessness and perpetual youth. We had seen enough of it under our window to find it less amazing than we might have otherwise, but to have it turn up right when we needed it, where it had rollicked all along in its lingual mingling and the easy lustfulness that by then was almost its birthright, was like another manifestation of the city's magic. Weekend nights we stayed up to spy out the front windows at the late-night customers as they caroused in French and English and weaved in and out of line with shuffling footsteps that would have fallen somewhere between dancing and stumbling if such distinctions held sway in the midnight realm of Montreal.

It was because of Sadhana that we discovered the hidden appeal of the balcony above the alleyway, the one that overlooked the bagel dumpsters. Positioned over the side door of the shop where the employees took their smoke breaks, the balcony was just large enough for the two of us to lie stretched out and silent on a couple of blankets, eavesdropping on the young men who worked the late shift. It had been more than a year since Sadhana had last showed signs of her bedtime nervousness when she asked Mama if the two of us could sleep outside.

"It's so hot," said Sadhana. "We'll sleep better." With my help she had already dragged two yoga mats and some blankets onto the balcony. I wasn't crazy about the bugs I thought might be out near the dumpsters, but it was so still and humid in the apartment it felt like the very air in our lungs might start condensing.

Even Mama, who tried to drink enough water to slake any heat wave, was looking flushed and a little wilted. She pressed her lips together for a moment and considered my sister in one fractional, holistic squint before saying, "That's a nice idea. Just be sure to put on pyjamas."

Sadhana and I shared a furtive smirk. Mama was under some misconception that the whole world liked to sleep in the buff.

When the bagel boys came out, we were stretched out on our backs with our eyes on the stars, nestled so closely I could feel my sister's hair standing on end where our goosebumped arms brushed together on the blanket. As the male voices rang out in French, English, Tamil, and Punjabi, we thrilled to the daring of our own concealment and to another feeling—one that felt connected to the great island of our city and everything it contained, to which we were still hoping to gain admission. An idea of getting older that did not feel altogether like loss.

When Sadhana got her period, she told Mama not to bother with a cake. She said it wasn't the kind of thing anyone else made a big deal over.

"Half the girls in my class have theirs already," she said. "And believe me, nobody threw them a party."

Mama had already measured the flour and the sugar into a bowl, but she didn't complain. "As long as you don't feel any shame," she said. "I want you to know that this is a beautiful, joyful thing."

"Don't worry," said Sadhana. "I get it." As Mama put away the cake pan and the measuring spoons and stood deliberating over the dry ingredients in the mixing bowl, I saw Sadhana go to the oven to check that it was turned off.

Mama said, "I didn't start it preheating." She took a step back from the counter and watched as Sadhana tapped the dial three more times before joining me back at the table. Though Mama and I had never talked about it, I knew my mother was worried that the strangeness that had afflicted my sister after the fire might have started to return.

"No cake is one thing," said Mama after a thoughtful moment. She was still looking at the oven dial. "But what do you say to the three of us going on a little trip?"

So, one weekend just before I started grade nine, Mama acquired the use of a cottage near the Gatineau Hills, through someone in one of her Westmount yoga classes. When she told us we were going, Mama said, "I want a weekend where I have my big girls all to myself." She'd started calling us her big girls that year, after the measuring wall beside the fridge had declared in faint but definitive pencil lines that we were both officially taller than she was.

Sadhana said, "That's every weekend," but I knew she was excited. Mama had an elusive way of being around when she was home. There were always people calling or dropping by for advice, or meditation sessions going on in the living room or sewing circles in the kitchen sustained by endless cups of tea. Mama always had us all to herself, but we didn't always have her undivided attention.

I liked seeing Mama at the cabin, doing things we didn't know she could do. Chopping firewood, lighting pilot lights, steering from the back while Sadhana and I sat astounded and life-jacketed before her like two useless orange peas in the pod of the red canoe.

In the afternoon, while Mama did chanting on the deck, Sadhana and I sat further down the shore on stumps by the edge of the water. Sadhana was bored, and the still water oppressed her. She cheered every time a motorboat passed, making waves that reached our shore as the smallest ripples. She waved at a water skier who didn't wave back. I took off my shoes and waded in, hunched close over the water, looking for tadpoles. With every step, I kicked up sand, no matter how softly I tried to walk. Every pace yielded a sandstorm, an underwater mushroom cloud.

"We should have brought a volleyball," Sadhana said. She was on the school's junior team, the Gators, who were the reigning city champions. In the final game of the year, she had broken her pinky setting the ball for match point and had become an instant school hero. I hated volleyball.

"No net," I said.

"No problem," said Sadhana. "I bet Mama could build one."

On the first night, there were bats, and I had never seen my mother so excited as when they swooped down close to our heads before gliding back out over the water. Sadhana and I shrieked and cowered, and Mama hushed us, urging us to open our eyes and watch them arcing and crossing each other and reversing direction mid-course.

"That must be how we look to someone on the outside," said Mama. "The way they fly, blind but sure." She held her hands out to the side like a scarecrow, as though she wanted to catch one or show us how well they could avoid her. Two came plunging over her head, but she didn't flinch.

"Careful, Mama," said Sadhana. "They carry rabies, you know."

Mama just laughed at us and stretched up to the sky, arching her back as if she was about to swing down into a set of sun salutations.

"Don't be afraid, kittens," she said. "Not ever." Mama was a specialist in impossible advice.

Then Mama got a fire blazing and led us in a dance around it, singing out a rhythm like a drum beat, *BOOM-bah-boom-bah-bah*, *BOOM-bah-boom-bah-bah*. Mama made herself small on the downbeat before springing up on the next one, her head bobbing back, her arms folding in and out like book covers falling open. I tried to imitate her but it turned into a chicken dance. Then we were all doing it, with Mama clucking out the song until Sadhana and I were laughing so hard we both fell down in the dirt.

The evening before we were supposed to leave, Sadhana searched the cabin up and down and came up with a bottle of tequila, a fifth full. It was in a cabinet, tucked away behind a make-your-own-stained-glass kit.

"Oh no."

"Oh yes." She put the bottle down on the table and went to the cupboard to get two small glasses. Mama was outside chopping more firewood, and we had promised to gather kindling as soon as we were finished our game of Crazy Eights.

"I think they hid the bottle for a reason."

"They won't even notice."

Sadhana poured us each a shot, and I wondered where she had ever even gotten the idea to drink. She was eleven and a half. When I was her age, in grade six, my friends and I were mostly into skipping double-dutch, with the occasional tame foray into Truth or Dare.

"I think you're supposed to mix it with something," I said. I was trying to sound disapproving but it came out excited.

"There's nothing."

We were clinking glasses when we heard the sound of the screen door. Mama was standing in the cabin, clothes and hair spiked with sawdust. She was an owl, with her eyes wide and the moon rising behind her over the lake. She drew her head back and then forward again as she stared first at our guilty faces, then peered at the bottle on the table.

"Mama," said Sadhana. "We just —"

She broke off as Mama strode past us, seizing the bottle, wood chips flying from her flannel shirt. Neither of us had ever seen her lose her temper.

Mama took a glass out of the cupboard and poured a double shot of tequila. "It's been seventeen years," she said. "Why not?" She held the glass up for a second, then downed it in one quick draught.

"*Buh!*" She made a face and looked as if she were about to spit. Sadhana giggled, but I was too shocked to speak. Mama put down the glass and recapped the bottle, keeping her palm tight on the cap as though the whole thing might explode. Normally, Mama didn't drink. She didn't smoke or eat meat. She awoke every day before dawn, had a cold shower, and did meditation and yoga for two hours. She didn't go shopping for clothes. She didn't hold grudges. She never once raised her voice to us that I can remember.

She was holy.

"You have to respect the power of a substance like this," she said. "You're curious, kittens, but you're too young." She picked up the bottle and held it to the light. "This has ruined people, ruined lives. Body and soul. I've met some of them. It's not worth the pain." She held the bottle up by the neck and shook it. "And look at us, we're stealing from our hosts."

"Why did you stop?" I asked.

"Drinking? I was never much for it, baby. It's poison for the body. But it was when I started yoga. And it's against what I've worked for my whole life. Choosing to confuse my mind instead of opening it up to the truth."

"What about meat? How long is it since you've had it?" Sadhana had caught on to my idea. Keep Mama talking until she'd forgotten what we'd done, what we still had sitting on the table in front of us.

"Longer. Since before I lived in California."

"Do you miss it?" Sadhana and I had had hamburgers once at a birthday party, though we'd made a pact never to confess. I'd gotten sick anyway.

Mama looked thoughtful. "I miss roast chicken like my mother used to make."

"What did it taste like?" asked Sadhana.

"Heaven," said Mama, closing her eyes.

"But you don't eat animals anymore."

"That bird," said Mama. "Maybe that one bird, I would."

"After all, it would be dead already," I said. Mama swatted in my general direction as she got up from the table. Heading back out to start the fire, she handed me the bottle. "Put it away, girls, and come outside."

The cabin, built by geography professors on sloping land, vibrated with each step she took down the porch stairs. Once everything had stopped shaking, Sadhana raised her glass. "And?"

I had to laugh. I picked mine up, too. "And."

We drank them fast the way Mama did.

~~&~~ CHICKEN ~~&~~

It was in spite of all this that we turned out normal. That's what Sadhana said, though her observation came about the time I was in grade nine, when she was just turning twelve and I was just turning fourteen and had more than a few ambitions about just how much more normal I was going to become. She meant Mama's strange philosophies, her uncanny enthusiasms. The way we'd battled over our lack of a television and how Sadhana used to beg to go over to her friend's place to watch *Punky Brewster* until she learned that a well-timed lie could avoid one of Mama's earnest eye-level interventions.

We were sitting around a table draped in bright red crepe, at our mutual birthday dinner. As Mama made flourishes on the cake in the adjoining kitchen, squeezing sugar roses from the pastry bag and singing Pete Seeger, my sister was explaining how miraculous it was that we had come out on the other side of our childhood with a passable claim to ordinariness, with no outward signs of outlandishness or zeal. We were both in high school now, in the other half of the cement-block building where we'd started in kindergarten.

In the green and yellow hallways of jostling, slouching, hollering teens, seventh-graders like Sadhana were reminded of what it was like to be the lowest of the low.

"Think about Emann," she said, "and Judith-Christianne." Sadhana regarded Emann, who wore a headscarf, and Judith-Christianne, a timid girl whose mother packed copies of The Watchtower into her lunch bag, with a strange pity. "We got off easy."

"I don't know," I said. Emann was sporty and smart, not to mention twice as popular as I was.

"Mama is not like other moms," my sister said. "I don't know if you've noticed."

We had made a pact that we would not invite anyone over because we were, just then, exceedingly embarrassed by our mother. There was the little white turban, for one thing, that she rarely wore outside anymore, but often still wore at home. And there was the time she was on a mono-diet of bananas and herbal tea and Jennica Moore came over and saw so many banana peels in the garbage she asked if we kept a monkey.

"It's a religious thing," I'd told her, while Sadhana glared. "I mean, a health thing," I amended. "Cleansing. You fast from one full moon to the next and eat nothing but bananas."

"That is super weird." Jennica Moore looked really shocked and was glancing around our kitchen as though hoping to find something worse. I saw her eyes pass over the bronze Nataraja statue of Shiva dancing and the Indian Buddha floating on a pedestal of lotus blossoms, both presiding over the room from a mint-green wall shelf. Laid out between them was a Tibetan prayer wheel on a wooden handle.

Sadhana said, "I know, right? Really weird." Jennica was her friend, and I just happened to be at home. Anything I said wrong could and would be held against me.

That was when Sadhana began talking about Mama as though her ideas were a kind of contagion, a viral pattern of thinking that would alter us, in obvious and irrevocable ways, into earnest, off-kilter versions of ourselves, wearing all white to strengthen our auras or writing down our dreams to decode messages from our unconscious selves. I was not altogether against these ideas, these versions of me that might be closer to my mother, but I could see Sadhana's point of view. Being like Mama in the world would be a bit like throwing yourself to the wolves.

In the campaign for normality, hair was the next frontier, and while we waged war against our unibrows, Mama was rooting for the other side. Though she no longer abided by all the pronouncements of the holy gurus, the practices concerning hair happened to coincide with her own wisdom. She was adamant that we not cut it and wept the day Sadhana came home with a shoulder-length ponytail. My sister kissed our mother's cheek before dropping the scissored end of her braid into Mama's palm. "Here's a little bit of God's precious creation," she said lightly.

There was a particular look of shocked horror on Mama's face that always made Sadhana laugh.

It was the same month that Mama discovered our bag of disposable razors in the cupboard under the sink. She brought them to the breakfast table with an attitude that was half-quizzical, half-disappointed. Mama had stopped shaving her legs in the sixties, even before she converted.

"I can't stress enough how unnecessary this all is," she said, regarding the pink plastic Bics with a degree of mournfulness. "Why do you think you need to do what everyone else does?"

I felt my cheeks flushing as I hesitated, while Sadhana said, too fast, "We don't. You're right." I gave her a quick look and saw that she was trying to finish the conversation.

But Mama was satisfied. "You're perfect the way you are, kittens," she said, cupping my face as she tilted it up with her cool hand. "It's what's inside that matters."

So we started concealing our stash in the bedroom. Razors, wax, Nair, tweezers, all stowed away behind a row of Nancy Drews on the bookcase. I had a qualm or two, thinking about what Mama had said to us, but Sadhana staved off any hesitation.

"She's a redhead," said my sister, shrugging. "What does she know about moustaches?"

That year Mama gave us each a blank notebook for our birthdays. "Stay in touch with yourselves," she said, without a trace of wryness, "if not with me." It was possible that she sensed how our idea of her had started shifting. Each notebook had a bright woven cover and delicate pages the colour of coffee stains.

Sadhana hugged hers to her chest. "I'm going to use mine to keep a journal," she said. "And you better not read it."

"I wouldn't," said Mama. "I wouldn't dream of it."

"I know, Mama. I meant Beena."

"Fine," I said. "Same goes for mine." I wrote DIARY on the flyleaf and announced that I was going to hide it in our room, though I thought it seemed like a chore to write about things that had already happened.

Mama bought one for herself that she was going to keep beside her bed for writing down dreams. Elise, one of her yoga-teacher friends, did dream analysis. Of Mama's strange recurring dream of brightly coloured parrots tumbling from the sky, Elise had said, "There's nothing waiting for you in heaven that you don't already have on Earth." As she related both the dream and its interpretation, it was clear that Mama was eager to hear what Elise might say next. She left us to rinse the plates from the birthday dinner and bid us an early goodnight, patting her stomach. "A full belly is better for dreaming," she said, laughing. "Wish me luck."

After we could hear Mama's light snoring, my sister dared me to hide Mama's turban. Sadhana had wide-open, mischievous eyes that spoke of a post-cake sugar rush.

"No way," I said. There were some things Mama could joke about, but that wasn't one of them.

But Sadhana wasn't to be put off. "Chicken," she said, and while I wondered if I really was, she ran and shoved Mama's turban into the bottom of the laundry hamper and returned to our bedroom in a fit of giggles. Although Mama had mostly stopped wearing it outside by the time we started school, she still wrapped her head before doing yoga. She said it helped keep the bones of the skull in place and channel positive energy.

"I wear it for all the reasons that your uncle wears it," she said as she scolded us the next morning. "And why Papa used to. For the reasons all proud Sikhs wear it. It is a very courageous thing to do when so many people around you despise you for it. Or even attack you. Or your business."

"Your business," I repeated.

"Do you remember the fire?" said Mama, and we nodded. "Well, that happened because somebody didn't like seeing Uncle behind the counter in his turban."

Sadhana raised her eyebrows. "I thought that was an anti-Jewish thing done by neo-Nazis who were too stupid to realize who was running the bagel shop."

"Really?" I said. For some reason, my sister and I had never talked about the people who had set the fire. Maybe because we were too afraid.

Sadhana tucked her feet up under her. "Yeah. I remember Uncle trying to wash off the swastikas."

"The swastika isn't just a symbol against Judaism anymore," said Mama. "It's a symbol of intolerance and prejudice against all kinds of people."

Sadhana said, "Bagel haters, then. Anti-bagelists."

I cracked up, and Mama looked severe.

"Do you think there was anything funny about the fire?" I fell silent.

Mama said that for most people there was a difference between claiming to believe something and actually showing you believed it by changing the way you looked. "It's different from wearing punk or hippie clothes, which are mostly just a fashion statement. A turban is anti-fashion."

When Mama showed such startling awareness, it only made me more worried for her. For it seemed that her way of living, of always seeing the best in us, was more precarious than I could ever have imagined.

～◌～

At a certain point, if you had asked my mother, she would have said that she was lucky. She had lost her parents and her husband, and her dead husband's brother regarded her as an interloper, and her world, which must have once seemed so open, so boundless and unpredictable, had soon narrowed to the domestic sphere of two inexhaustible little girls. Nevertheless, she considered herself one of the most fortunate people she knew.

"I have loved and been loved, and every day that goes by, I am grateful to be alive." She explained this to us with relentless patience over supper or during bathtime or while brushing out and braiding our long black hair. Before bed, she sometimes still pointed out her lucky star, that blinking repository of wishes we strained to see through the glass. "When you are all grown up, my own loves, you might find out how blessed we are."

In anyone else, it might have seemed as if they were trying to convince themselves. But Mama claiming her own good fortune was like a master artist declaring a work complete, one long, thoughtful pause after flinging the final blotch of paint at an abstract canvas. Saying it made it so, for who was there to say any different?

But I thought I knew better. The older we got, the smaller Mama seemed, not only because we had grown, but as we needed her less and less, she, in turn, seemed to miss Papa more. She didn't speak about him any more than she used to, but I could tell she was sad. Her narrative impulse had returned. Whenever she made her spiced tea after breakfast, she began to tell us stories about her parents.

"They were American," she said. "Did you know that? From a little town in Florida, so humid you could count the droplets as they hung in the air."

"But you're from Ireland," said Sadhana.

"I am. They visited Galway on their honeymoon and decided to stay."

Mama described how her parents had bought an old house in disrepair and converted it into a tiny hotel they named the Quarry, since the yard was choked with stone. Mama's father learned how to balance rocks, filling the backyard with virtuoso towers of stones, their massive weights improbably balanced end to end. Inside the hotel, the front and back staircases were lined with Mama's mother's clock collection. The floors were covered in multicoloured rag rugs she'd made during three Florida summers squandered inside by the fan.

"I bet you miss it," said Sadhana. She was better than I was at interjecting during Mama's reminiscences. Whenever sadness clung to Mama's voice, I became nervous and silent.

"I do," said Mama. "Almost as much as your grandmother's roast chicken." Mama never seemed to remember that we already knew everything about the chicken.

The chicken in its ideal form, the sense memory as described by our mother, might have loomed even larger than our grandparents in our collective mythology.

"At least missing something means you remember it," said Sadhana, and I looked at her in surprise.

Mama pulled her close and kissed her brown cheek. "My wise little kittens," she said.

Sadhana and I decided to make it. It was my idea. It was going to be Mama's cheering-up meal once she got back from a yoga retreat weekend she was leading in the country.

The checkout lady balked when she saw what we were trying to buy. "This is a little out of the ordinary, isn't it, girls?" Sometimes she teased Mama about how we bought vegetables she didn't even know the names of. "I have all the normal register codes memorized," she'd say. "You're the only ones keeping me on my toes." She wrapped the dead chicken in a plastic bag before putting it in our cloth bag with the other groceries.

"Yes, ma'am," said Sadhana. "We're doing a surprise."

"Be careful," said the lady. "A chicken is a different animal than a zucchini."

"Don't worry," I said. "We know all about salmonella." It was part of the latter dozen of reasons Mama recited when anyone asked her why we were vegetarians.

Mama's friend Deana was the one who drove her home from the country. I turned on the outside light so Mama could see to get her key in the lock.

"It smells so good in here," said Mama once she got inside. "I must be dreaming."

Sadhana had set the table, and we all sat down. Sadhana and I held our forks in reserve until we saw Mama eating.

"This is delicious," she said, after the first bite. But on the second bite she started coughing. She reached for her glass of water and took a drink. She started sputtering and coughing again.

My sister and I exchanged a glance. Part of me thought it was one of Mama's routines—pretending meat would poison her, that sort of thing. Her coughs became almost soundless. Little ghosts of coughs. I laughed. Mama shook her head, shoulders seizing up towards her ears. She waved at the door.

Sadhana ran downstairs for help. I could hear her footsteps echoing along the metal walkway that led out over the courtyard, and the door swinging closed behind her. I stayed frozen to the spot. Mama slammed the table with both hands. She pointed at me. I jumped to my feet and put the glass of water up to her mouth, but she refused it, shaking her head. She looked angry, her face turning purple. She pulled her plate of chicken off the table and it smashed. Her eyes were bulging. She staggered to her feet and threw herself against the wall. Her hands were at her throat.

"Here, Mama," I said, bringing her the water again, but she was sliding down to the floor. There was blood on her foot from where it had caught on a shard of plate.

We knew how to smudge sage, how to make dye from plants, how to strengthen our auras. We'd practiced chanting mantras and spinning wool and making Indian cheese. But we didn't know what to do if someone was choking. I'm not sure we even knew what choking was.

"I thought she was coughing," I told Sadhana over and over afterwards. "Just coughing." At the hospital they told us that a bone from the chicken had become trapped in her airway. They told us she was dead.

Sometimes I thought I could imagine Mama forgiving me for what I'd done or failed to do, but there was no way to explain this to Sadhana. In her, there was no absolution, for herself or for me.

———————

Once I unlock the front door of Sadhana's apartment, some of my dread subsides. The sun is at my back, and the long, curving staircase leading up to the third floor is stuffy and warm from the light streaming in all afternoon. At my feet and massed behind the door is a pile of mail, mostly in the lurid oranges and greens of pizza flyers. Gathering them to my chest, I climb the stairs, and the habit of feeling, the way certain places cause emotion to coast along familiar tracks, takes over. Sadhana is no longer here, but the motion of mounting these stairs still summons up the ghost of my usual anticipation, and the timid rattle of guilt for the way I know I am about to try to interfere.

The walls of the staircase are creamy white, the paint rubbed away on the top ridges of the wainscoting and chipped in places here and there where the fenders of my sister's bicycle banged the plaster as she lugged it up and down every winter and spring. The framed photos of Sadhana, the chronicles of her many stage roles, are dull with dust, and I wonder, if dust is mostly particles of human skin, whether this coating is Sadhana. Pieces of her left behind.

If my sister were here, the second door would already be open, framing her welcoming posture at the top of the stairs, usually opening a bottle of white wine that she would barely drink but press on me, as if keen for me to slip into an indulgent frame of mind, one less equipped to take notice of the state of her health. The last time I was here, in late fall, it had already snowed, and Quinn clomped ahead of me in his winter boots, ready to take over the conversation, pretending to swig from the wine bottle and thawing into a million questions for his aunt about how to pick up girls. When I got to the top, his boots were tipped sideways in a pile of melting snow, and he and Sadhana had already moved into the living room, voices raised and overlapping in the flush of reunion. I could never tell if it was something about her presence that brought out his talkativeness, or whether it was only his earnest desire to keep us locked onto topics besides her health, to keep us from fighting. It could be, though, that I have him backwards, that it is something about his serious-minded mother that makes him mild and silent.

I unlock the upper door with a quick turn of the key, and, pushing it open, I wait for a sound, a sign, something that will give me an excuse to leave again. I entertain a fantasy of a squatter, rude and violent, or a colony of birds or bats, some infestation that has taken hold in her absence. Something to give me an excuse to turn away and call a professional. But the apartment is still and quiet apart from the sounds of kids playing basketball in the back alley, thumps and crunching gravel and shrieked obscenities in French. It has been six months since anyone has lived here, five months and three weeks since they found my sister's body.

I can see at a glance that everything is as it should be. The worn oriental rugs unrolled along the narrow hallways. The four gold-framed bevelled mirrors, hung across from each other at staggered intervals, reflecting the deep purple of the walls leading towards the bedroom. The lone prickly cactus on the low living room table is still sustained by a shaft

of light where the drawn curtains are gaping. The horror
I expected, the shakiness of stirring in the place where she
died, is mostly absent. Every familiar object is a balm to my
twitchy gaze. Uncle said they'd cleaned everything up, but
when I asked what he meant, who had done it, he said none
of Sadhana's things had been touched. Then I gathered that it
was only she who had been cleaned up and taken away.

In Sadhana's living room, I tie back the curtains, dump
the pile of mail onto the coffee table to go through later.
There's a lot of sorting to be done, and the mail might be the
easy part compared to the other projects I have come here to
carry out. The clothes, the books, the furniture. The lease.
As I sit on the couch, the sun through the front window is
hot against my back, and I lean forward, as though pushed by
the light, to rest my head in my hands. The room still teems
with Sadhana: strands of black hair along the green couch
cushions, the magazines stacked underneath the table in
three proportional piles of fashion, art, and music. It is almost
easy to expect the sound of her voice from the other room, its
cackling high register and wilful low melodiousness. As an
actress, her voice was the most powerful part of her instrument, and here in the apartment it was mistress and conduc-
tor, beckoning us to listen or look, to play our parts a little
more broadly, or a little more to her liking.

The subscriptions to *Rolling Stone* and *NME* were mostly
for Quinn to leaf through on our visits, though Sadhana sometimes scanned them herself with an interested eye because
she liked to be up-to-date on those matters, the things that
people talk about at parties. She said it was the only reason
she hadn't thrown out her television, though I know she liked
to watch movies, the old ones, with the kind of actresses who

made legends of their own personalities. Her own CD collection never strayed far from jazz or the hypnotic lounge music that she put on when she was tidying up. The CDs. Something else to take care of.

Housekeeping, for Sadhana, was something manic. She would get up while Quinn and I were still eating dinner, taking an abrasive yellow sponge to the dishes she'd used, donning elbow-high blue rubber gloves and a severe focus. She'd rinse and stack any takeout packages or pizza boxes, refrigerate leftovers, and wash and moisturize her hands, all while Quinn and I sat eating, making alternating and desultory attempts to win back her attention.

"I heard honeybees are disappearing," I had said to her last winter, putting down my fork. "Nobody knows why billions of them haven't been returning to the hives."

Quinn nodded, but Sadhana made no indication she'd heard me. "That'll be a problem for pollination," he said. "And the food supply." He had his face to me, but his dark eyes were on her as she flitted back and forth in front of the sink. The dining room looked into the kitchen as though through a picture window, adjoined by a high-flung shallow archway.

Quinn raised his voice. "A lot of crops need the bees." He waited less than a beat before changing tack. "Auntie, I wonder if you would take a look at my French assignment and check the grammar. It's a paper on Toulouse-Lautrec."

Sadhana was draining the water from the sink, returning the dish soap to the cupboard below. She had cleared her plate before I'd had time to judge how much she'd eaten. "If you like," she said. At last she came back to the table, narrowing her eyes at the rest of my buttered roll. She said, "Toulouse-Lautrec paintings always make me wish I wore stockings more often."

It was hard to tell which came first between us: the scrutiny or the deflections.

There are photos in rows on the mantelpiece. A couple of the two of us, one of Mama. More of Quinn. Many of friends. I don't know all their names, though I have lingered in front of their images often enough that they are all familiar. Sadhana kissing her friend Rachelle on the cheek. Sadhana and the women in her knitting circle. Sadhana and the cast of *Hedda Gabler*. Sadhana and the men and women in her dance troupe. Sadhana posing with the other organizers at a fundraising gala for refugees. Sadhana and her friend Terence on Halloween, wearing matching nurse outfits and platinum wigs. There is only one photo I don't recognize: Sadhana and a young woman with long blonde hair, riding a merry-go-round. I run my finger along its fur of dust before tucking my hand into my pocket.

She had so many friends, so many people in her life. I can't understand how so many of us failed her.

There were dozens of actors at my sister's funeral. I knew them right off from the colours, or thought I did: bold reds, turquoise, a few shades of violet. One or two oversized handbags of canary yellow bobbing just below eye level like a meagre harvest of huge squash. I barely noticed, but if I'd thought about it, I would have put it down to flamboyance without too much deliberation. Later, though, I was told that Terence had sent around a group email requesting that nobody wear black. Apparently he and Sadhana had planned their funerals together one evening over buckets of sake and decided they wanted colour, an infinite palette on parade, followed by an Irish-style piss-up. A number of people mentioned the email to me, probably having second thoughts about their hot-pink blazers or orange ties, but my only feeling on the matter was a sensation of being underdressed myself, that I had misgauged the occasion entirely.

The ceremony was at a funeral home. Uncle had arranged things, though I remembered him asking me questions and me saying *yes, yes, yes, that's fine, yes*. It was at the place where Sikh families from the gurdwara held their funerals, though I did not think we were going to do it quite like that, chanting prayers to ease the deathless soul out of its cycle of reincarnation. But I did know there was going to be a cremation, and I had a vague terror that we were supposed to stay for that, to utter prayers as it was happening, for I knew this was what sometimes took place, though I could not remember ever having seen it done. I would leave, that was all. I would leave if it came to that.

Later, we would take her ashes to sprinkle them into moving water, since a soul to be reborn needs no monument. And that is what I waited for that day, for Sadhana to leave my hands. For it to be over.

Quinn was next to me, holding my arm as we came in to take our places at the front. I was suffering from a headache that added to the sense of unreality, a buffer of moderate pain between me and the world as it normally seemed. Anything in the head seems to undo me more than it should. Touching my fingers to just above my right temple, I could feel my pulse thudding fast and hard, like a current just breaching a dam. Physical pain always startles me with its intensity, its

immediacy and insistence upon being felt. The body's broad
signals. The way pain isolates and reduces and makes it difficult, if not impossible, to focus care outwards while it runs
its course.

"We're sitting now," Quinn said, pulling me down
next to him. I looked upwards to the ceiling, its decorative
wooden beams and clean spackled ceiling. Three large fans,
slowly rotating, hung from the central beam running down
the length of the room. It seemed that the funeral home was
hot even in December. I noticed the collar of my black blouse
clinging to the back of my neck, stuck like wet newsprint.

At the front of the room, just a few metres from where
we sat, there was a coffin, closed, which I tried not to look
at. Before it, resting on an easel, was a large photograph of
Sadhana, a colour candid of her somewhere outside, smiling
in front of a backdrop of autumn trees. It seemed recent. Her
left hand was up in what looked like a wave, but I had a feeling
it was caught en route from pushing her hair back from her
face, a typical Sadhana movement and one that she always
made before pictures. It was a good photograph, though I
thought Sadhana herself would have preferred one of her professional black-and-white headshots, which were perfect and
stunning. I supposed it didn't really matter. Likely someone
thought a headshot was too impersonal, though I had no idea
who that someone might have been. Surely not Uncle.

I remembered Sadhana at our mother's funeral, sitting
next to me in a flowing black dress of Mama's that looked
like spun cobwebs, outlandish, with billowing sleeves and a
long asymmetrical skirt cut on the bias. It was gathered at the
throat like widow's weeds, but the chest was pure lace from
neck to bodice. Uncle had not yet stepped in to take charge of

us, and though there were a few horrified glances, Sadhana's outfit seemed mostly to inspire pity among Mama's friends. We had turned into orphans, and though we were teenagers, we were really only children. Sadhana playing dress-up in a mourning costume.

Sadhana spoke at that ceremony. She speculated about how Mama must be happy in heaven with Papa, how badly she had missed him. She recited a poem by Emily Dickinson, something about Death stopping his carriage to carry her to immortality. Sadhana's chin quivered above the lace of the dress, her small hands flitting back and forth as she spoke. I had seen her practice elocution like this in front of the round mirror on Mama's dresser.

She talked about reincarnation, too, how Mama thought it was the most beautiful and logical way of looking at death. The funeral itself was held not in the temple but in the large landscaped backyard of a woman who lived up on the mountain, who'd taken private yoga lessons from Mama. There were red-winged blackbirds swooping in back of her when Sadhana said, "I'll be looking for her now, for both of them. Wherever they are, I know they're together." She had everyone in tears.

Then Quinn's elbow was at my arm, nudging me. His cheeks were wet, and I could hear that Terence was still talking, his British-accented voice low and resonant in a theatrical declamation about Sadhana's career.

"Mom," said Quinn, "pay attention."

The ringing of my cellphone breaks the stillness. I fumble in my purse to find it. It's Quinn, calling from downtown. When we got off the train, he'd asked if he could head up the hill to the university, and I said yes. I could tell, once the moment arrived, that he was almost as nervous and reluctant as I was to breach the vacuum of Sadhana's empty apartment.

"Hello?"

"Are you there?" he says.

"I'm here. Can't you hear me?"

"No, I mean, are you *there*?"

"Oh. Yeah. I'm here."

"And? How is it?"

"It's okay. It's weird. I mean, it is and it isn't. I don't know. It's hard."

"Do you want me to come?"

"No, it's fine. I just . . ." The temptation with my son, with his strength, is to lean on him. "I haven't started anything yet. I haven't been here long. Where are you?"

"The library. There's a ton of people here, even though classes are over." I can hear quiet voices in the background. He has seen the campus before, lots of times, but I imagine him now wanting to cut across the paths with an experimental ownership, scope out the cafeteria, rehearse an inner mode of feeling like a university student.

"Well, there are probably summer courses on."

"Yeah, it's great. There's a barbecue stand out here. I got a hamburger."

"Lucky you." I try to evaluate whether or not I'm hungry, probe the source of the strange feeling in my stomach. I wonder if there's still coffee in Sadhana's freezer.

"I know. So I'll see you later? At Uncle's, right?"

"Right. Call if you get lost."

"Okay. Bye."

"Bye."

After I click the phone closed, I put it down on the table, where it glints, smooth and alien, next to the potted cactus. Then I pluck the hairs off the couch, hold them up to my head to compare length. Sadhana's hair was shorter than mine is now, which hits well below my shoulders. An unfashionable length for a woman in her thirties. The couch is not as clean as it could be, and as I root around I find change, small pebbles of dirt, even crumbs. She didn't care about vacuuming or ironing, though she did both from time to time. She liked things she could put her hand to without much in between, so the tub was always scrubbed, surfaces polished, rips and worn patches mended within days. Outside of those kinds of things she was not very particular.

She liked having everything out where she could see it, trusting her makeup and jewellery to shallow pottery dishes and trays, her best-loved shoes and clothes laid out on wide shelves and dangling from wall hooks in the bedroom. Though in her way, I imagine there was an order, a system underlying what looked like simple non-conformism on the outside.

It is her meticulousness, along with an arts council grant, that has allowed me this six months' reprieve. For years Sadhana was in the habit of paying her bills in advance whenever she came into money, converting paycheques into rent cheques with just enough lag time to make sure they would clear at the bank. Acting gigs and her health were both unpredictable, but my sister liked to be in control of her life, though she was never good at saving. French television commercials were her financial mainstay, though she also taught drama at a studio on the Plateau after she gave up waitressing.

Her will was straightforward and left everything to me and Quinn. She'd never mentioned to me that she'd had it drawn up, but then, between us there were subjects we always avoided. Uncle paid for the funeral with an attitude that was almost grateful, as though he were getting off more easily than expected.

With pen and paper from my bag I make a list, leaning back along the couch that I can still imagine clinging to her form where she curled up on the farthest side of the L shape, a tiny S of one hundred pounds. What I begin to write, though, becomes redundant, an itemization of belongings, room by room. I scratch it out and write: *Everything.*

THREE

DEANA

During the first weeks after Mama died, Mama's friend Deana stepped in. Her phone number was stuck to the fridge on a stained and curling scrap of paper held by a ladybug magnet. She and Mama had a deal to take over each other's yoga classes if either of them ever got sick. They'd had the arrangement for a year, but Mama never bothered learning a phone number off by heart. She had more important things to keep in there, she said.

When Deana picked up the phone the day after Mama's accident, her voice was husky with sleep even though it was three in the afternoon. I started crying.

"Honey," she said. "Sweetheart. Don't cry. Who is this?" That was Deana all over. She was ready to comfort a heavy breather if he needed it.

"I woke you up," I whispered. "I'm sorry. It's me, Beena." Our names rhymed, so sometimes when I called, I said, "Deana, it's Beena." And then she would say, "Oh, I thought you were Tina." Most of the yoga ladies didn't share our corny sense of humour, but Deana was a hoot. Mama's word.

The news about what had happened slipped through my lips like bitter vinegar. I couldn't hold them in, but the words *accident* and *gone* seemed to scour my mouth as they came out. The vinegar burned through my heart and watered my eyes. I swallowed and asked Deana to go to Mama's class at the community centre. "You could tell them," I said. "Or stay and teach it. Whatever you want." I hated the thought of the students waiting there for Mama and getting angry with her, and then how awful they would feel later when they found out.

Deana drove right over in her boyfriend's car. We had all the lights in the apartment blazing. Uncle was working downstairs, because nothing could close the bagel shop, not even this, the end of the world, and Travis, the second shift manager, had come up twice to check on us. The first time he came up with his condolences. The second time he came up with a long face and a cooling glass casserole dish of cheese and noodles his wife had fixed for us. Sadhana was putting it, uneaten, into the fridge, and I was watching out the window as Deana parked the car in the tow-away zone in front of the store and tripped up the steps of the side door. I buzzed her up.

When she got upstairs, she was already crying, great black triangles of mascara bleeding down under her eyes. I was so numb I almost asked her what was wrong.

"I'm here, sweetpea," she said. She slung her huge shoulder bag onto the floor. "And I'm so sorry."

She held open her arms, lips trembling, then folded me into an embrace that widened to include Sadhana, who pounded over to us in her sock feet. My sister and I had stayed up the whole long night after leaving the hospital, weeping and dozing by turns, first on Sadhana's bed, then on opposite sides of the room after Uncle silenced a sudden screaming match. He'd spent the night on the couch, since it was too late to drive home to the suburbs. Terrified by the sudden emergence of his huge, angry face, Sadhana and I had stopped fighting and stopped talking, too. All morning we'd been fretting and weeping alone in different parts of the apartment. But squeezed together on the front mat by Deana, neither of us pulled away, and I was relieved. I closed my eyes and leaned in to smell Deana's scent of pears and powder and Sadhana's dirty hair. It didn't feel like Mama hugging us, because Deana was much taller than both of us, and Mama had been almost a full head shorter.

Deana let us go to wipe her eyes, and then she said, "I'm starving. Have you guys eaten? I have to eat when I get upset or I turn into a demon." She kept one arm around each of our waists and propelled us into the kitchen. When Sadhana told her about the casserole, she let go and rushed on ahead of us.

"Sit down, sit down," she called. "You shouldn't have to do anything. Do you want some? Are you hungry?" From the back she looked a bit like Mama, though she was younger, in her twenties, and her hair was a bit lighter, more gold than red. She was an extraordinarily pretty woman. She had fine, pale hands and a wide, hilarious mouth. I knew that when she subbed for Mama, the new students sometimes asked if she was her daughter.

Sadhana and I sat at the kitchen table watching Deana spoon noodles into a bowl to reheat. She was telling a story about our mother. I wondered how she could go so quickly from crying to talking to bustling around, when the pain of it all was stabbing me in the chest, in the throat.

She was saying, "I took my first yoga class from your mother. My first class ever. I'd just graduated from high school. Did you know that? She took one look at me and knew I was in pain. She invited me to stay afterwards for spiced tea with milk, and I told her all about Mike, my crummy boyfriend."

Deana turned on the oven and popped her bowl inside. I was worried that the porcelain would crack and looked over at Sadhana, but she was intent on Deana, or at least staring in her direction.

"I started training with your mother, and I left Mike." Deana sat down and reached across the table to squeeze Sadhana's hands, which were lying on the table, knotted in a hard knuckle lump. My sister barely blinked. "It must have been about seven years ago. And I've never looked back. Your mother even helped me quit smoking."

"How did she do that?" asked Sadhana. She was gazing past Deana now, at some indefinable point of interest in the direction of the refrigerator. It was calming, somehow, to watch Sadhana, the way she had of sailing forward into something but keeping herself separate. For my part, I was afraid to stir or ask a question. Anything that kept us moving ahead in time without Mama.

Deana shook her head. "I've no idea. I swear, she must have hypnotized me or something. I still don't understand it. She just told me not to do it, so I didn't."

She took her bowl out of the oven, though the food could not have been hot but only warmed. She ate while we watched. Every once in a while she would swallow and look up at us and smile, and Sadhana and I tried to smile back. I could guess what my face must have looked like by seeing my sister's, which was pale in the cheeks and dark in the eyes. Quivering and dry and too soft in the mouth.

If Deana saw the thinness of our rallying, she didn't show it. To me she said, "I'm going to stay as long as you need me." I nodded, and she went on, "I mean it. I'm not leaving you guys one second before you're ready for me to go."

"Okay."

She got up from the table, looking beatific in her blue jeans with the gold glinting in her hair, like an angel sent to save us. But then she was leaning over the counter with her hand over her face, tears flowing. It was as though once she had eaten she remembered why she had come, and she started breaking down again, just as she clinked her empty bowl into the sink.

We learned a lot about her in those weeks, about her father the pig farmer, her brother who was in the navy but wished he could be a pilot, her mother who taught piano to all the children in the neighbourhood. She talked and talked, and her voice became a thread that was pulling us along. It was nice to have her there, filling up the silence. We did not stop to wonder why her heart went out to us in our trouble, for to us our trouble was the whole world. It was only puzzling that the rest of the world was not there with us.

She slept in Mama's room, and we slept in there too, taking turns next to her and on a pallet on the floor piled with blankets. She breathed through her mouth while she slept, and I liked the windy sound of it, loud and even. In the night, she kicked off all the sheets and it was cold with the breeze from the window she kept open, but Sadhana and I didn't complain or give up our turns in the bed. We stayed up later and later, until it was normal for us to be waking up around noon. Sometimes Deana left while we were still asleep and went home to see her boyfriend Freddy, and then she would come back with another bag of clothes or a bunch of new records to play.

There was nothing to do, after the funeral. Deana and the other ladies divvied up Mama's yoga classes and cancelled some. Uncle still ran the store, like always. It was summer, so there was no school.

I was getting better at frying eggs. We ate a lot of fried-egg sandwiches. Sadhana took to heating up beans from a can and frying bologna that we dipped in mustard, small suns of yellow squirted on our flowered plates. I don't know where we got the idea to eat that way, as Mama's way of cooking had always leaned to whole grains and stews and lots of vegetables, but Deana seemed to think it was fine. When she cooked, she made spicy spaghetti or fish sticks. We ate a lot of bagels from the store, since they were free. My stomach started hurting most of the time, but Deana told me it was only because I was sad. In between telling stories and playing records, she seemed almost as tired and sorrowful as we were.

She got the idea one Friday night, from looking at Mama's box of candles, that we'd have a candlelight dinner. She'd found them in the cupboard when she was looking for clean towels. "Candlelight makes everything look better," said Deana. "Even food."

I was all for it, but Sadhana disapproved. She traced her fingers over the lid of the box, covered with lilac paper doilies and curling silver ribbons. A strange remnant of our crafty years, but canny enough to be obviously Mama's handiwork. Sadhana reminded me that we weren't allowed to touch the candles.

"I'm sure that was just for safety reasons, honey," said Deana, who was listening. "It'll be okay."

Sadhana shook her head. "No, it's not just that. These were our mother's meditation candles."

"Really?" Deana pried the top off the box. Inside was a jumble of white tea lights, tapers of every colour, and pillar candles in gradient shades of dark purple.

"Lovely," said Deana.

"She made those ones." Sadhana pointed.

Deana reached past the candles she'd indicated and took out two of the tall orange tapers. "These two will be perfect. Don't you think?" She was asking Sadhana, who nodded. Deana took them, and Sadhana carried the box to our room and shoved it under her bed. I followed her.

"They need to stay in a cool, dry place," she said when she turned and saw me looking. "They'll melt otherwise."

"I thought you didn't believe in meditation."

"That's not the point." Sadhana looked ready for a fight, but I didn't press it. She could get fierce about loyalties, and anyway, I knew how she felt.

Back in the kitchen, Deana had found two Christmas holders, sprigged red and green around the base with fake holly. She'd placed them on either side of a large serving dish atop the burgundy linen tablecloth, and there was ketchup in a little blue bowl with a tiny spoon beside it. She'd found the cloth napkins, too.

"See?" said Deana, putting in the tapers. "They match the Kraft Dinner." She lit the candles with a lighter in a beaded case she pulled from her pocket, then flicked off the lights. In the dimness, the pale wax matched the food, just like she said. Creamsicle orange. I asked her why she had a lighter if she had quit smoking.

"For occasions like this one," she said, as if it were the most obvious thing in the world, and I realized it wasn't only in her looks that she reminded me of Mama.

We all sat down, but then Deana got up to put on a Carole King record. She said, "I can't stand the sound of people chewing and swallowing. Even you guys. Even me."

As she came back, the end of her hair passed close to the flame, just as Sadhana bumped the candleholder reaching for the ketchup. The taper wobbled twice in its stand and connected with Deana's hair. In half a moment, the flame licked up the end of her ponytail as a dozen strands of red-gold hair sparked and blackened and shrivelled to dust. I gasped, but Sadhana quickly clapped the hair between her hands and it was out.

I stood up. "Oh God," I said. "It was an accident. Are you okay?"

Sadhana pushed back her chair from the table.

"Are you okay?" I said again. There was an awful smell, and Sadhana had her hand muffling her nose.

Deana was unruffled. She inspected the end of her ponytail. "Oh, I have a lot of hair. No big deal. But that was a close one. No more candles for us, I'd say."

I let out a breath. Deana smiled and patted the turquoise seat of my chair in invitation until the vinyl started squeaking. Then she blew out the candles. "Don't worry. It's safe now."

I sat and started eating, and Sadhana edged in a little closer. Deana tucked up her feet so she was sitting cross-legged. "Did you know hair is growing all the time?" she asked. She pointed the drooping end of her ponytail at each of us in turn. "It's dead tissue. It keeps on growing even after you die. Just like your fingernails."

There was a small noise from Sadhana, who let her fork clatter to the floor as she bolted from the table. I heard our bedroom door slam.

"Oh no," said Deana in a hushed voice. "Your mama."

Deana thought we should cry as much as we wanted, and she cried right along with us, at the table, on the couch, in Mama's room in the middle of the night. When Sadhana or I was racked by sobs, nose streaming, Deanna would weep silently, one arm around my shoulders, or one hand rubbing the back of Sadhana's head. Sadhana and I never cried at the same time anymore, except at night.

One night I woke in the dark from a dream about our parents, both of them alive together as I had never known them, except when I was very small and almost too young to remember. I barely breathed, trying to keep still and cling to the strange elation as it faded. I heard Sadhana cough and then sniff twice, and as I came back to an awareness of my body, I could tell without opening my eyes that we were alone in the room. Something about the weight of the bed I was lying on. Deana must have needed to drive home for something.

Sadhana said, "Bee? Are you awake?"

"I was just dreaming."

"I don't know what we're going to do." She sounded choked. "What's going to happen to us?"

"It was the most beautiful dream, Sadhana. Mama was there, and Papa, too. They were fine. We were going to a park, I think. I don't know. We were all talking. They were happy." Mama in her green pioneer dress with the high collar and Papa in his wedding garb, the embroidered white *sherwani* of the photo on Mama's dresser—and wearing a bowler hat. I wondered where my mind had picked that one up. Even as the glow of the dream faded, I felt as though I'd been given a message, or at least a bubble of peace we could enjoy until the air ran out.

There was a pause, and then my sister in a hoarseness, saying, "You don't know that they're happy. They're dead. They're dead, Beena. Wake up." There was a rustling as she rolled over in her sleeping bag, probably to face away from me, but I refused to open my eyes to check.

Uncle came by from time to time, but he couldn't look at us straight on. Sadhana said it was just that he didn't know what to say, the same thing that kept our friends away and made the clerks at the grocery store stuff our items into paper bags lickety-split, without any chitchat.

One time when Deana was out, Uncle came in and left his shoes on and stomped through to the kitchen where he began exclaiming over the dirty dishes on the counter. "What is this pigsty? Where is that woman? How did your mother raise you?"

"We were just about to do them, Uncle," said Sadhana. "See how we stacked them into piles?" I was amazed by the fluidity of her lies. We were no sooner about to do the dishes than we were about to wash the windows or clean out the rain gutters.

On Sundays he brought us cash for groceries. He always handed it over in an envelope with my name on it, with a warning to me to keep close track of the contents. "You and your sister," he said, "you go yourselves to the store. I am making you responsible."

"Yes, Uncle," I said, but every time after he left I gave it to Deana without even opening it. She was looking after us, and the money was her job. With all his business sense, Uncle should have been willing to accept a little collateral financial damage to keep us off his hands, but maybe he couldn't resist trying to hang on to such a good deal.

One day the phone rang and it was Freddy. He never said hello, only "Deana there?" but this time all he said was, "Put her on."

I could tell it was a bad conversation. Deana was backing up as she listened, shrinking into a corner of the living room. She started out loud, then got quiet. Sadhana and I were lying on the rug playing an endless game of Crazy Eight Countdown, and I had just changed suits to hearts, a killer move for me, when Deana noticed us staring. She covered the mouthpiece by sticking it close to her chest and told us to go to the store to pick up stuff for burritos. She fished a ten-dollar bill out of her pocket and handed it to Sadhana.

When we came back, she was in the bath. Sadhana took the groceries to the kitchen and left them on the table. Whole-wheat tortillas, a tomato, and a head of lettuce, because we weren't sure what burritos were. Then we heard Deana crying in the bathroom, little sniffling sobs like sneezes, and when I tapped on the door, she told us to come in.

The bottom of her hair was hanging down into the tub, below the water, but the top of her head was dry. It seemed wrong and disorganized. Her clothes were lying in a little heap on the bathmat, and she had a glass beside her on the floor, beaded with condensation.

"Hi," she said. She hunched forward, arms crossing, elbows on knees, brow resting on the back of her wrist. Her hair swung forward to either side of her face, like heavy drapes. "Don't be frightened. I'm just sad."

Sadhana perched on the edge of the toilet seat and I crouched on the little stool that Mama used to sit on when she washed our hair. Deana had more freckles on her body than Mama had had, a wide patch spreading down her back from the base of her neck.

"I wish your mama was here," said Deana.

This had become the usual refrain for us, more like a chorus to a silent song we'd all agreed upon than any longer a specific lament. Saying it was like a charm, or a secret handshake.

"Me too," said Sadhana and I at the same time. That was the amen.

It turned out that the car Deana had borrowed from Freddy had been impounded without any warning at all except for the growing stack of parking tickets pulled out from under the wiper and tossed into the back seat. But she was caught off guard and Freddy was furious, and there was no way to get to the impound lot unless she could find someone to take her and lend her the money to pay the fee. I wondered if she would ask me to try to get the money from Uncle, and I knew I would if she asked. But she didn't.

She paddled her arms up and down a bit in the water. "It's Deana soup in here," she said. "I feel like a boiled carrot."

"Limp and orange," guessed Sadhana.

"You got it."

She made a move to get up, and we handed her some towels that, though no longer clean, had been refolded by Sadhana, who had the best knack of the three of us for getting crisp corners. Deana rubbed herself dry until she was pink and wearing something close to the tired expression that passed for smiling in our apartment. By the time she had her jeans on, we'd developed a game plan. She had the towel around her neck like a prizefighter, but she looked dazed enough to seem like she'd already been punched out.

"You'll go straight home and apologize again, then kiss him until he forgives you." This was Sadhana's advice. "Wear something really sexy."

"Just tell him you'll make it up to him," I said. "However he wants."

We watched as she put on a tight black sweater, gold earrings, and a fine dusting of turquoise eyeshadow.

"Wish me luck," she said, kissing each of us at the door. She looked nervous. Her fingers were wrapped tight around the handles of her bag and her lips were almost white, like frozen raspberries left too long in the freezer.

"Luck," said Sadhana. We locked the door behind her and went to the window, where we watched her sally forth to the bus stop, her long stride barely reined in by her high wedge sandals. Sadhana and I spent the rest of the evening eating crackers and resorting to Monopoly after our card game was derailed. On a lark, Sadhana had tossed the deck in the air, and we decided we were too lazy to pick them all up.

Deana came back just after midnight with five garbage bags of clothes and a cardboard box containing what she called the rest of her life. I peeked in and saw necklaces tangled in with seashells and headbands, a curling iron, and a pack of pastels. I carried it into Mama's bedroom and set it on the dresser, pushing to one side Mama's matching hand mirror and brush set with the mermaid handles that had belonged to her grandmother. I looked up to see Sadhana's reflection frowning at me.

"What?" I said into the vanity mirror. "She has to put her stuff somewhere."

"Not there she doesn't."

I shrugged and left it where it was, keeping one hand on it. Sadhana waited for a moment, then left the room.

Deana herself was quiet and didn't say much besides it was over. Freddy couldn't forgive her because the car was his baby and he'd had it even before he met Deana. Sadhana was outraged and called him a pig, which made Deana flinch.

"But it's true," said Sadhana. "It's not like the car is gone, just towed. If he wasn't broke he could just go get it."

"But he *is* broke," said Deana. This was another way she was like Mama: never blaming other people for their feelings, even when the feelings in question were stupid.

I was glad about the breakup and said so. "This is so much better," I told her a few days later, when she was mostly done with sitting in baths and crying. I was curled up on Mama's bed eating cookies, in sheets that were starting to feel gritty. I brushed away the newest crop of crumbs and they fell to the floor where they blended in with the wooden parquet. "Freddy wasn't good enough for you. And now you don't have to go back and forth all the time."

"You're right," she said. "This is better." She sounded far-away, though, her words sagging as she rooted through a pile of clothes, looking for a clean shirt.

"Also," I said, "there are plenty of fish in the sea."

"That's what they say," said Deana, pulling on a T-shirt and shaking out her hair like a wet dog. "But what am I going to do with a fish?"

Around noon one day Sadhana got a call from a school friend, and when she was done being surprised, she managed to accept an invitation to go swimming. By the time she put down the phone, I could see her shoulders pushing back, her pride taking hold. Whether it was her elation at being remembered by her friends or her relief at the prospect of getting out of the apartment, everything about her seemed more defined, as though she was focusing her gaze until it was sharp enough to see her out of the soft fog of our grief. She dug into her dresser, looking for a bathing suit.

"Don't go," I said.

"Why not?"

"We haven't finished our game of crib." Deana had bought us an amazing cribbage board with a little plastic skunk that popped up. And her brother had mailed us a bunch of card decks from real casinos. All the cards had two of their corners clipped to show they'd been used, and we were cycling through the packs during our games, trying to guess which decks were lucky or unlucky.

"We can finish when I get back."

"What am I going to do?"

"I don't know. That's your problem." Sadhana's shrugs were somehow always elegant.

I left the room and considered complaining to Deana, but instead I went and lay down in Mama's bed, pulling the quilts and the sweaty smell of sheets up around me, even though it was the hottest point of the day. I turned over a pillow and found that both sides were equally strewn with long, clinging strands of red and black hair. Mama would have told Sadhana to take me along, oblivious to the fact that she and I didn't share any friends and that tagging along ought to have been well below my dignity as the older sister. But Deana was part of the real world in a way that Mama never had been. Deana wouldn't allude to the social hierarchy of teenage girls, but she knew enough to realize that if I wasn't invited, I wasn't wanted.

I didn't know what it was about Deana, how she could make the air around herself soft, so it was easy to move through it to her, to get close. Not as hard as it was with some people — with most people, really. She was like Mama that way, but maybe even more so, since she had no expectations of us, and no rules.

At some point I fell into a hot and tossing sleep, and when I woke up I went into the kitchen, where Deana was eating a piece of toast and staring out at the balcony. She looked at me and said, "Have you been sleeping? You should get out of the house."

"I don't have anywhere to go."

"Go for a walk. Pick up some groceries while you're at it. I'll make you a list."

"Okay." I stood by while Deana wrote out a list in her neat printing, then handed it to me along with some money.

"I have a yoga workshop to teach, so take your keys." I nodded. "And take your time too. If you don't get some exercise, I'm going to have to drag you to class one of these days."

It was the first time, apart from trips to the bathroom, that I'd been alone since Mama's accident. I knew where the store was, but it was strange to have to think about how to get there since I was so used to following. I walked two blocks in the wrong direction, out of habit maybe, or some secret mission known only to my feet, before stopping up short in front of a fish shop that smelled bad enough to snap me back to attention. At the grocery store, when I finally got there, everything went smoothly except for when I saw the sympathetic cashiers, whose look of open pity was almost too much for me to bear alone.

"You take care now, darling," said one of them. I almost started bawling.

When I came back, bags swinging from the crooks of my arms, I saw Deana sitting low on the front stoop, arms resting on piles of garbage bags to either side. She was wearing a backpack and a cap pulled low on her forehead against the sun. A queen on a black polyethylene throne.

I called out to her when I got close. "Deana!"

Her shoulders jumped, and one hand flew to her hat. "Goodness, honey, you scared me." She pulled me to her, and I toppled over onto the pile of bags.

"Mind the groceries," I said. I was worried the eggs were going to smash. "What's going on?"

A green Thunderbird pulled up, Freddy's car, rescued somehow from the tow lot in the far industrial reaches of the city. And it was Freddy, I guessed, behind the wheel, who passed his eyes over me for the briefest of moments before bending his head to pop the trunk.

"Sweetheart, I've got to go," said Deana. "I'll see you later, okay?" With a loud smack she planted a kiss on my cheek, just next to my ear, and started throwing garbage bags into the car.

"When?" I said. I glared at Freddy, who kept his eyes on the rear-view mirror. The Thunderbird was parked in the loading zone again.

"Tonight." She passed her hand over the top of my hair and squeezed my shoulder. "I'll see you tonight." She got in the car and waved as Freddy cut in front of a minivan and drove away.

I put the groceries away and went to bed, where I read and dozed and waited for Sadhana to get home from her party.

"Did you see this?" she said, when she came in the room. She held out her hand, and it was shaking.

It was a note, taken off the refrigerator where Deana had stuck it with a magnet. I couldn't understand how I'd missed it.

"She's not coming back," said Sadhana. She looked panicked. "She says she loves us, but she's not coming back."

~⊙ UNCLE ⊙~

After Deana left, Uncle was stuck with us. A friend of Mama's named Sylvia came by to check on us and, after seeing the state of the apartment, began a series of prodding conversations with me and Sadhana (how long before I turned eighteen, what were the exact provisions of Mama's will, who were our nearest relatives living in Canada) before embarking upon some able and unimaginable negotiations with Uncle. Within one week of her campaign of competence, our rightful guardian had rented his house in Dollard-des-Ormeaux and made arrangements to move into our apartment.

We didn't take to Uncle. For all that he was our only living relative on the continent, not to mention the only one we'd ever met, we were in the habit of regarding him as something of a stranger. Though he'd been working at the shop since Papa died, he had rarely visited. He had consulted with Mama on certain matters related to the business or the building, but when she asked him to stay for tea or for supper, he had always declined with a nod almost too decisive to be quite civil.

What we did know did not please us. Every change at the shop had been a change to something Papa had done, a kind of undermining. Never mind that between us we could scarcely remember Papa. We knew from Mama's stories that there had always been a bit of bad blood between her and Uncle, and Mama got along with everybody, so that was really saying something. The main thing we knew about Uncle was that seventeen years ago he had offered Mama fifteen thousand dollars on his parents' behalf for her to go away and leave Papa alone. The other was that he had pitied Papa for having daughters instead of sons. This was a fact that both outraged us and inclined us to regard Uncle as at least a little bit stupid.

Mama had looked pained when she explained that in India male children were more valued than daughters, that it was not at all unusual for someone to think that way. When we asked why, she said it was complicated. "It's beyond my own understanding," she said, "or I'd try. But your Papa didn't believe that. He told your uncle never to so much as suggest that he was not the happiest man in the world to have two little girls."

Uncle arrived with two matching Samsonite suitcases and a very modern vacuum cleaner with a see-through canister. He told us that one of the suitcases used to belong to Papa.

"Our mother bought them for us before we came to Canada. What do you think about that?" He swung one out in front of us as if it were a dog we might want to pet. With a feeling of duty, I reached out to touch its cracked blue leather, but neither Sadhana nor I made any reply. "So that would be your grandmother," said Uncle after a moment.

Papa's parents had not troubled themselves much with us after his death. A letter had come that Mama had read once and put away. And another, later letter had arrived while Deana was with us, inquiring about the terms of Mama's will, as if there were some final proviso her forgiving heart might have led her to include, something amounting to a conciliatory message from their dead son.

But there had been no unexpected stipulations, either rancorous or appeasing. Uncle was to pay for what we needed from our share of the profits of the bagel shop, which had passed to me and Sadhana after Mama's death. He was to continue to run it, as he had since Papa died, with his manager's salary and one-third of a share in the income. All in all, Mama's will was a standard legal document, which, when it was read out loud by her lawyer, seemed like a mistake. Not its contents, but the thing itself. We had always believed that Mama never did anything by the books.

Uncle frowned as he put down the suitcase. "I suppose your mother told you bad things about your grandmother," he said.

"Not at all," said Sadhana, which made me glad. I was too indignant for words.

"Ah."

He put both suitcases down and stepped around us on an appraising tour of the apartment that was over in five minutes. He pointed inside our mother's bedroom. "That is where I will be sleeping, if you would like to get it ready for me." He sounded imperious, but I could sense a hesitation to go in amongst our mother's things. I told him we would take care of it.

"Good," he said. "And it is almost seven o'clock, if one of you would like to start making supper."

There were two weeks left before school started, and Sadhana said later that it was a shame we wasted them being afraid of our uncle. Though he was cold and alien, he was not cruel, but his manner was so different from anything we were used to that we cringed and floundered when he told us what to do. Apart from asking us to cook and clean, he didn't seem to take much of an interest in us. We watched him sidelong whenever we happened to be escaping his notice, ogling the belly stretching his shirt out over his belt and the set look of his thick lips beneath the thick, black beard that fell three inches past his chin.

Uncle was as strange to us as a new kind of tree, a fir in a grove of maples, and he might have felt the same way about us, since he had always been a bachelor. He said things like "You must fight your feminine tendencies towards lasciviousness" and "You are in league with each other, I know," which baffled and insulted us but gave me the idea that we made him nervous. Taken with his tendency to leave us to ourselves, Uncle's remarks were like those of an armchair anthropologist, a Victorian studying the natives by virtue of reports and illustrations alone. Like the first attempts of the ancients to track the stars, he managed to get some things right, for who were we in league against if not him?

We did our best to keep house, though we had no experience and he was impatient with the results. When he was at work, it became a game, and though Sadhana usually took the lead, we both took pleasure in the measuring out of ingredients, the chopping of vegetables, even the wiping down of the counter—in all of the things that seemed to connect us to Mama. It had become possible to cook without thinking of the chicken we'd made, though we also did not buy any meat, keeping instead to Mama's few vegetarian cookbooks and the handwritten recipes she'd tucked inside.

Stirring a curry as Uncle finished a shift downstairs, taking turns performing elaborate taste tests between seasonings, my sister and I found ourselves laughing, and to have that feeling return so suddenly, when I thought it might never be given back to us, almost stopped me up short. It was more than I could do not to cry, which, since I was crying about a lack of crying, was enough to make me laugh or cry all over again.

I reflected, when she stood in profile to me at the stove, that my sister was very beautiful. She had always been pretty, but she had finally grown into her high brow and cheekbones. When she caught me staring, Sadhana smiled and handed me the wooden spoon to take a turn.

But when Uncle clomped upstairs in his steel-toed boots, our peace was shattered. Hunched over the bowl with focused scrutiny, he tasted the curry and declared it inedible, even as flecks of it caught in his beard and moustache as he bolted it down. "It is a shame your mother didn't teach you how to cook," he said between bites. "But then, I suppose she did not know herself."

As our routine shifted with the start of school, Uncle began flexing his authority like a long unused muscle. Accustomed only to the management of employees in the bagel shop, his preferred method of interaction was issuing orders. We soon discovered more than we wanted to know of his views on the evils of contemporary culture. There seemed to be no end to the list of things Uncle did not approve of: music, sleeping in, caffeine, movies, phone calls for any purpose besides making plans, bright colours, Hallmark holidays, novels, exhibitions of emotion. Our list was shorter and consisted only of him, and possibly culottes, an article of clothing for which our mother had had an odd fascination.

Weekday mornings were always a battle, for, like Mama, he woke very early, around five, and he could not understand why we did not spring out of bed and dash to the kitchen with the alacrity of hungry cats. "You are the laziest children I have ever heard of!" he would bellow from the doorway to our bedroom. "You are a disgrace!" He was impatient because he had to take a break from his early shift to wake us and ensure we were on our way to school. Sluggish and indifferent as we were in the mornings, he did not trust us to rouse ourselves. He cursed the gossiping he suspected of robbing our sleep, as if anything besides our separate unhappiness would have forced us to keep silent vigil throughout the night.

Besides the difficulty of pushing through tiredness that felt like six feet of water, I, for one, was not anxious to go to school. Everyone knew that our mother had died over the summer, and I could feel the pity and curiosity of my classmates like a stinging brand that singled me out with its fresh pain. Everything I said or did in the mornings was dilatory or cantankerous, and Sadhana likewise.

We were still in our pyjamas when Sadhana tried to tell Uncle about a blockage in his sacral chakra. I didn't think she believed in that stuff, and neither did I, except for how Mama had told me my heart chakra was strong and with Sadhana it was *vishuddha*, the one in the throat that controls communication. Anything Mama told us had a truth to it that went deeper than lucid belief. It was knowledge that came to us like melodies or the days of the week, information that was simply there rather than something up for debate. Mama had learned how to read auras from a guru in California, which she said was a Whole Other Story. So when Sadhana started talking to Uncle about the six-petalled chakra located more or less in the area of his groin, it was clear, to me at least, that she was trying to insult him rather than help him find his way to personal enlightenment. A blocked sacral chakra meant the inhibition of joy, enthusiasm, and creativity. But Uncle wouldn't even listen long enough to be insulted.

"Do you know about the kundalini, Uncle?" Sadhana was sitting cross-legged on the rug when she was supposed to be getting ready for school. Neither of us had tried much with Uncle, but sometimes she just talked for talking's sake. "We can teach you how to meditate so that you can raise the kundalini energy up through your spine. Right now I suspect you have a blockage in your *svadhisthana*."

Uncle was retying his turban, wrapping a five-metre swathe of maroon cloth with an intricate technique, as he held one end of it in his teeth, then pinched the fabric at the top of his forehead as he angled the folds of material. I slurped cereal at the kitchen table while Sadhana waited for Uncle to respond. After what felt like a long time, he took the end out of his mouth and tucked it in over his right ear, speaking to my sister without looking at her. "Can't you be quiet?" he said. "Good girls are quiet girls."

We were grateful yet sulky about the long hours he spent working at the shop. If anything he worked longer hours now that he lived right upstairs and home was no longer a place of perfect frozen dinners, cable television, and an immaculate lawn but a cramped two-bedroom apartment with no air conditioning and two bereaved teenage girls with cried-out saucer eyes who stared at him like a jailer.

Though at first we were united against Uncle, the fellow feeling that had sprung up between me and Sadhana seemed in danger of dissolving. One night after she snapped at me during dinner, I waited until she was taking a bath and slipped her diary out from where I had seen her hide it between her mattress and the box spring.

She had filled far more pages in her birthday notebook than I had, as though she had been writing in it steadily since Mama gave them to us. I flipped to the most recent page and, spotting my own name, was overcome with such mingled feelings of guilt and dread that I shut it at once and slid it back under the mattress. But knowing the diary was there made reading irresistible, and before the week was out I had looked at it four more times.

Each new foray into Sadhana's notebook brought with it more mortification. It was almost as if she suspected I was reading it and was creating ever more horrible observations as punishment. Far from being an inventory of crushes or a logbook of secret languages or anything that our childhood had prepared me to find, my sister's diary resembled most closely a catalogue of grievances with accompanying insults. I recognized the names of teachers, of girls in her class and in her soccer league, but the principal offender, appearing on nearly every page, was me. The time I hadn't stopped to help her find her headband in the morning, the way I finished my homework before she did, the style of my hair—all of these might as well have been crimes against humanity from the way they were described in the pages of my sister's diary. As a result, I was deemed a jerk, a show-off, a total fashion disaster. When I read *Beena's face is so fat it looks like a pecan pie*, I had to snap it shut before my tears could mar the ink.

With each successive furtive reading, the shame of looking drained away, replaced instead by a growing outrage for which there could be no expression and no redress. Even Uncle came off better than I did in the world according to Sadhana's diary. But though my sister and I had stopped confiding in one another, a slight hardness in her demeanour was the only clue that she might despise me.

"What's eating you?" she asked one morning as we walked to school. Sadhana had mentioned the upcoming Halloween dance, and I had not done much more than grunt in response.

"Nothing." The word came out with as much bile as I could squeeze into it. Sadhana stared at me, then shrugged. She knew I loved Halloween. She also had no patience for people who were mad and couldn't say so—a claim I was beginning to question, given the contents of the diary. We walked the rest of the way to school in silence.

If I could have told Mama, if she were still around to tell, I knew she would say that Sadhana didn't mean any of it. She would have reminded me of my own unkind thoughts and pointed out that Sadhana had never uttered a single one of the insults she had written down. Definitely, I would get in trouble for snooping. Mama might even have praised my sister for her honesty, explaining that it was better to purge those nasty thoughts from your system by writing them all out. It was possible that Sadhana would have gotten in trouble too, but far from guaranteed.

I said all these things to myself and I tried to believe them. None of them offered any solace for what I had read. The only idea I could fix on was that it was Uncle who was the problem, who had come into our house like our own misery made flesh, and in his blunt bulk had become the wedge around which my sister and I could no longer see eye to eye — even if, in the moment, we were united against him.

The lengths Uncle would go to in order to protect his peace and quiet became the battle lines of our domestic wars. He began with scolding, moved on to shouting, uttering threats, wielding punishments, and when all that proved to be ineffective in bringing our benign misdeeds to a close, he ended with a morose monologue cataloguing his woes and persecutions. He had unrealistic ideas about how quiet two teenaged girls could be within a confined space, and he was more or less right when he claimed we had no respect for him. "I should take in a couple of stray dogs," he shouted one night. "At least they would do what I ask."

After a time his bullying stopped frightening us. Sadhana and I steeled ourselves against his bellowing and he had nothing else up his sleeve. When Uncle tried to get rid of my white tape deck, he left it out on the street with the garbage and I just ran down and grabbed it. When he told Sadhana she wasn't allowed to go out after supper, she went out anyway.

Sadhana held herself apart. If anything she was rude to Uncle, and I followed her lead. It was only too easy to cast him as the enemy. I backed her up in the hope that Uncle might succeed me as the villain in her diary, even though I had stopped reading it.

A favourite tactic in Sadhana's arsenal was over-salting his food. Once we had served ourselves, she would add an extra teaspoon of salt or cayenne to Uncle's bowl before calling him to the table. This continued on and off for two weeks before even the sight of Uncle's sweating brow and the certain knowledge of his discomfort could bring us no pleasure, nor gratify our sense of vengeance for his attempts to control us. I pitied him, even as he banged the table and demanded we refill his water glass, denouncing us as the worst cooks and the worst girls anyone was ever unfortunate enough to have as nieces.

He sat unmoving at the table while we cleared the dishes, and remained there as I stood washing them while Sadhana had her bath. He was shaking his head with what looked like a fury precluding words.

"Uncle," I said.

"Are you trying to kill me?"

"No," I said, horrified. Though of course he knew about Mama's accident, Sadhana and I had never told him about the chicken, that it was something we had prepared for her. "What do you mean?"

"My heart," he said, and I blinked. It was something Mama used to call me.

"Uncle?"

"My heart." He touched his palm to his chest.

For a confused moment I wondered if he had given way at last to affection, but it turned out he was anxious about his blood pressure. Papa had died so young from a heart attack, after all, and Uncle said their own grandfather had died the same way. He had been to the doctor and he was on some pills, but he'd been advised to monitor his blood pressure and avoid salt and cholesterol.

"I am not sure," he said, "what is cholesterol and what is not." He went into the bedroom and came back with a stethoscope and a brown and black contraption he said was a blood pressure cuff. "My friend, Doctor Ernie Davidson got me this," he said, which surprised me. I had not thought of Uncle as someone who had any friends. Maybe an esteemed customer. "I need your help to put it on so that it is very tight."

I helped him wrap it snugly around his upper arm, pulling it taut with all my strength and relishing the crunch of the Velcro as it folded closed. As I did so, Uncle explained how it worked. The cuff had a dial on it that looked a little like a watch. I got the feeling he was talking so as not to look at me. We had never stood so close to one other, at least not since I was a little girl and Papa was alive.

"Can I pump it up?" I said. Uncle said yes, and the metal pincers of the stethoscope went into his ears as he placed its smooth circle on the inside of his elbow.

He nodded at me. I squeezed the black bulb shaped like a shallot until the cuff swelled like a balloon around his arm, and I returned the pump to his hand as he gave me a look that called for silence. Then he let it deflate, listening for something as he stared at the gauge. When it was over, he kept staring at his arm, seeming every bit as concerned as he had before.

"Was that your own blood you were listening to?" I asked. The idea was both interesting and disgusting.

Uncle looked at me as though bewildered. "Why can't you put less salt?" He sounded angry. "Why can't you both just be nice girls?"

I sit down on the steps outside Sadhana's apartment with the sense that I've locked a mystery behind me. The June sun glares down with a radiance that defies death, and I think about phoning Libby, the woman who left me the message about Sadhana, but I hardly feel up to talking to a stranger. Shielding my eyes behind the maple, I feel like I'm returning from another planet. Pulling out my phone before I can change my mind, I dial Evan's number.

"Good for you," he says, when I tell him where I am.

"Not really. I'm outside."

"Something's the matter."

The sympathy in Evan's voice almost makes me want to cry. Below me on the sidewalk, there are two girls giggling together on their way to the corner. Neither of them looks up to see me. "I just don't understand how it happened."

"You told me she was sick. For a long time."

"She was." But she had been better too, though I don't know quite how to explain it to him. All that back and forth between sickness and health. "I don't understand," I say, "how nobody found her for a week."

"It's bad luck, Beena." Evan sounds unfazed. I wonder if he has uncovered any corpses in the line of duty. "It's what happens when people live alone. It's not your fault."

I say nothing. My baby sister, come apart like that.

"Beena."

"It is." My voice is small and my stomach churns with an ache that might be hunger, but I can't tell. "My fault. I'm the reason she did this."

"I thought you said she died of a heart attack." Surprise makes him sound younger, less reassuring, as though there is a part of himself held back while playing the cool head in a crisis. "Are you saying she killed herself?"

"Of course I'm not saying that," I return, without conviction. Over the years, even as her body wasted and she refused food, Sadhana always claimed she didn't want to die. Mostly, I had believed her. "I'm sorry. Let's talk about something else. How are you?"

"Go back in there, Bee. There's nothing for you to be afraid of."

My scuffed shoes recede from my blank look as I partner up for one set of a recriminatory dance with my voice of reason. I know he's right, that the apartment is just a backdrop — neither an accusation nor an epiphany.

"Okay," I say. "I'm going." And after I hang up, my finger really does touch the metal of the key in my pocket. But when I get to my feet, they carry me the rest of the way down the stairs and out along the sun-baked sidewalk that feels firmer with every step taking me away.

⁓◦◦⁓

A few hours later, Quinn and I convene outside the shop. It has been so long that Uncle is almost pleased to see us. He greets us outside the apartment as though he has been awaiting our arrival, leaning from his chair to hear the whistling slam of the door at the top of the stairs. A walkway hugs the courtyard along its upper levels, and as we start across he is already padding forward to meet us, his wool slippers silent on the grated metal below the thundering racket of my rolling suitcase. At a look from Uncle, Quinn bends slightly to pick it up. My purse slips from my shoulder to the crook of my elbow, and with nothing to carry, my hands come together uselessly at the front of my waist, like anxious bystanders, for they do not know, have never known, what to do here.

"Hi," I say, and Uncle nods at me. He looks pale under the fading evening sun, and it occurs to me that I carry no image of him in the daylight, only one of him ruling us inside the apartment and another of him holding sway over the bagel boys under the fluorescent lights of the shop downstairs.

There is a moment as I fumble with my hair and look at Quinn, and he steps ahead of me to shake his great-uncle's hand in a sure move. The sky blue of his polo shirt is the same colour as Uncle's turban. "Hello, Uncle," he says.

My uncle scratches at a spot to the side of his nose, just above the start of his moustache. Nearly sixty, his beard is still uniformly black. Papa's younger brother by fourteen years, he was born the same year as Mama, and this might have been the start of their antipathy: Uncle's disapproval of Mama's full-blown love affair with his thirty-seven-year-old brother. Though she always told us it was because she was white, because Uncle didn't believe that she really wanted to be Sikh.

"Come in and eat," says Uncle. "You must be hungry."

Inside, we take off our shoes and carry our bags into my old bedroom. The apartment smells of curry and the campfire smoke of the wood ovens in the bagel shop downstairs. There is another smell too, of artificial pine, the strong perfume of the fabric softener sheets my uncle puts in the dryer. In terms of functionality, he has improved the place, with the laundry facilities he installed when Quinn was a baby, the metal grid frame hung from the kitchen ceiling for storing pots and pans, and the addition of sliding screen doors on the balconies to keep out the bugs. Mama's way was to keep pace with only the most pressing repairs alongside her own pet renovations, which tended towards the spiritual or the ornamental, like rearranging the furniture according to seasonal energies or sewing curtains out of old paisley skirts. In between, she squeezed caulking into the gaps around the pink toilet and tub and glued down the wooden kindling of our aged parquet floor as it scuffed away underfoot like a disintegrating jigsaw puzzle. When we were older, she took an upholstering class at the community centre and covered a yellowing armchair with a swathe of green corduroy.

Piece by piece, after we moved out, Sadhana and I carried away almost every item we could claim as our mother's, but there are still a few lingering signs of her, even so long after her death and a full fifteen years of Uncle's bachelor living. It is only his disinterest in decor that has allowed her choices to endure for nearly two decades: cream walls with mossy trim in the bedrooms, a rich buttercup in the kitchen, light brown in the living room like a dusty road. My old bedroom, mine and Sadhana's, and Quinn's for a while, is mostly untouched, even the furniture. I asked Uncle, once, why he had left it alone, and he said it was as good a guest room as any. But it could be that he does not have many guests.

"I was only planning a light dinner when you called," says Uncle, "so I picked up a pizza."

"You're kidding."

"That would be a strange joke, don't you think?"

"Pizza," I say. Never once had Uncle given in to our teen-age pleas for a pepperoni reprieve from cooking duties. "Great."

"Super!" Enthused, Quinn hurries to set out plates.

Uncle lowers his voice. "How did it go at the apartment?"

"There's a lot to do," I say. I decide not to mention that I lasted only twenty minutes in Sadhana's apartment. After calling Evan, I'd spent the afternoon at the library, walking up and down the aisles as though I were at a museum, with the same stuttering pace and spectatorly remove. Then picking up books with deliberation and putting them down somewhere else. Drifting from chair to chair.

"Nothing anyone else could have done for you," says Uncle.

"I know," I say. "I didn't mean it like that. Of course I have to be the one to do it."

Uncle eats with his forearms on the table, head lowered close to his plate. Quinn watches us carefully, rolling the handle of a fork between fingers and thumb before picking up his pizza with both hands. I can't tell whether it is only his aversion to conflict or some concern on my behalf that is making him uncomfortable. The rims of his ears are turning red, like peaches in the sun. "I'm looking forward to moving here," he says. "Do you think I'll like it, Uncle?"

"I imagine you will, yes."

"I'm going to start taking programming classes in fresh-man year," says Quinn. I look at him, and he tugs at the cuffs of his short shirtsleeves. "The whole curriculum sounds rigorous," he says.

Uncle nods. "That's good." He wears a look of full approval, his whole face altered from any usual expression. His cheeks filling out like Papa's in my parents' wedding photos.

I sip my water and bring my glass down hard. "Rigorous?" I say, snorting. "At least part of the attraction of the rigorous program has to be Montreal's reputation for beautiful women." It's like I am sixteen at this table, always. It's like Sadhana's at my ear, egging me on.

But Uncle only says, "I imagine your son is more sensible than you give him credit for." His tranquility unruffled, he continues eating, and Quinn shoots me a dark look, no doubt wondering, as I am, why I would choose to open him up to attack.

After supper, I make a pot of chamomile tea, while Uncle turns on the national news. Quinn holds fast in the kitchen laying waste to a fourth slice and, like one of the pigeons that flock outside the shop, to three of my untouched pizza crusts.

"A lot of Quebec headlines," I say from the couch. Uncle grunts and pulls his armchair closer to the television.

There is an update on the little Quebec town with the five-page, so-called welcome bulletin for potential immigrants, drafted by the mayor and town council. It is a text that has become infamous.

"It's embarrassing," I say. It is an all-white, all-French town. A tiny place with a population the size of a high school, they have made headlines around the world by deciding to take an ignorant stand. Among other things, the document forbids covering the face except at Halloween, belittles cultural dietary restrictions, and outlaws the public stoning of women.

"Private stoning's okay, though," says Quinn. He's out of sight of the television, but not out of earshot.

"This isn't funny. They're going out of their way to single out people of different religions and insult them."

"You're not crazy about any of those religions either," says Quinn. "Or the segregation of men and women, all the things they're talking about."

"That's not the point."

I can almost hear him shrug. "What's wrong with banning stoning? You like stoning?"

"Of course I don't like stoning."

Uncle has been frowning in concentration, trying to hear the broadcast. As the segment wraps up, he says, "I think probably they are only afraid of losing their own culture. I can understand that. Look at your son. Quinn probably does not even know what a kirpan is."

"I know what it is," says Quinn.

"Hmm." Uncle folds his hands over his stomach.

"Even if Quinn had one," I say, "he wouldn't be allowed to carry it to school there. Did you see that bit about ceremonial daggers? Never mind what the Supreme Court says."

"I saw, yes. But it depends what is in their hearts, the people of this town."

That Uncle could remind me of Mama is not something I would ever have believed. "Hate," I say, anyway. "Isn't it obvious? I'm sure there's a bit about turbans, too, for your information."

"Maybe not hate. Maybe only fear."

"Is there a difference? Are you saying we should be

tolerant of other people's intolerance?" I think about reminding him of the fire, the spray-painted swastikas out front that
took ages to remove, but I know he cannot have forgotten.

"Maybe," Uncle says again. "It depends."

Then there is a story about a refugee family claiming
sanctuary in the basement of Saint-Antoine Church, a few
neighbourhoods north. A man, a woman, and their one-year-
old son, who was born in Canada. The mother is Somali, but
a permanent resident. The father, an Algerian refugee named
Bassam Essaid, lost his appeal to stay in Canada on humani-
tarian grounds.

"The church is letting them stay?" says Quinn, as the
voice-over by an English interpreter patters around a clip of
an interview with one of the parish priests. Just out of view
of the screen, Quinn is straining to follow. "Why don't the
police go in there and get them?"

"It's a kind of tradition," I say. "Churches are considered
inviolate. A sort of sacred space, higher law kind of thing."

"Wow."

"Yeah."

"So," says Quinn, considering, "if I committed a crime,
I could just go find a church and nobody could arrest me?"

"No," says Uncle.

"It probably depends on the crime," I say.

They've turned to a picture of the family onscreen, a
father, mother, and baby. There's no telling why a flash of
longing or sympathy goes out to someone you hardly know.
What my mother would have called vibes and what science
sometimes calls pheromones. Sadhana would have said it has
to do with faces, with the bones in someone's face. The pro-
portions between eye and brow, nose and chin. The magical

ratios set out beneath our skin and underpinning our whole lives. I remember Sadhana having a theory that, however it might torment and elude those who seek it, beauty, and love of beauty, is what makes us civilized.

"I know that family," I say. And I do. I've seen the couple in the photo before. "Sadhana knew them."

Nobody seems to hear me. But I remember when my sister showed me the photo, a quick click of her mouse to another window, in illustration of a story she was telling me — the basics of her ongoing work with No Borders, the refugee activist group sprung from her women's knitting circle. She was working on emails on her laptop during a weekend in Ottawa, trying to finish something pressing to do with a Monday morning hearing in front of the immigration board.

"You wouldn't believe it, Bee," my sister had said, bringing her knees up to sit cross-legged in my swivelling desk chair. "What Bassam Essaid has been through to stay here. It's so bureaucratic and unfair. They're trying to make an example of him because he's an activist helping other non-status Algerians."

She'd pushed her hair behind her ears as her brown eyes blazed amber, and I remember puzzling over the composed nature of her outrage. Sadhana in a fury was usually either a tempest or a flash freeze. Clicking closed the window with the picture, she went back to work on her email, her fingers drumming the keyboard with an unhesitating patter as I wondered at my own surprise at the admiration I felt.

The story on television wraps up with a series of sound bites from neighbourhood residents. Midway through, Uncle makes a startled movement that draws my attention to a fleeting caption at the bottom of the screen: RAVI PATEL, LOCAL

POLITICIAN, MOUVEMENT QUÉBEC/QUEBEC FIRST. Without the clue, I doubt I would have recognized the teenaged boy I once knew. And even before I hear what he has to say, the knowledge is a whip to my racing pulse. The English translation dogs the words of the original, but with a modulated tone at odds with the sentiments expressed by Ravi Patel, local politician: "These people think they don't have to follow the rules, but they deserve the same treatment as everyone else, church or no church. And if they don't like it, they can leave."

"Harsh," says Quinn from the kitchen as the segment ends. He gives up on the pizza, puts the rest in the fridge, and comes to join me on the couch. He sits at the other end while I let out my breath slowly. I dart a glance at Uncle, but he appears absorbed in the screen. Taking a cue from him, I keep my gaze facing forward as I feel my expression dissolving into panic. Even if he looked, I doubt Quinn would notice the blankness of my mouth and eyes. I'm only his mother, after all.

~ FOUR ~

⌒ RAVI ⌒

Sadhana and I walked to school together every day, through a compact rooted somewhere between convenience and sentiment. We had always walked together. Even before Sadhana was old enough to attend, she and Mama had squired me there together, and my sister's wet kiss on my cheek had been no less essential than Mama's hug at the gate and their mutual, final waves from the corner when I turned once before going inside. These days Sadhana may have been harbouring a secret anger, of which only I and any other guilt-ridden readers of her diary would be aware, but I was at least a willing, if unresponsive, audience to her morning monologue as she geared up for school.

School was hardly a refuge from the home scrum, though Sadhana seemed to take it that way. My ears would still be ringing from Uncle's bitter epithets as we turned the corner of our street, as Sadhana began her transformation from sulky niece to sparkling high school freshman. Her glare fell away, her laugh returned. She skipped over sidewalk cracks in her pink and white sneakers as she gossiped to me about the girls in her grade, ignoring my affected boredom and the miserliness of my mumbled responses. Every story she told about her classmates was animated by a spirit of fun that made everyone come out looking better at the end. At the intersection, she applied lip gloss in the pause of the red light, while I reflected on the seething rage in her diary. I watched for the turn of the green and always stepped first off the curb, so that for a moment I could be away from her and the sham happiness that made everything harder.

Each wing of our high school had its own adolescent anthropology. My locker had always been on the third floor near the science labs, along with most of the kids in my homeroom, and Sadhana's was down the hall past the water fountain, in sight, if not within earshot. Her end of the hallway was the favoured hangout of the most popular kids in the tenth grade, as well as ninth graders, like Sadhana, in the know. Hot-and-heavy couples who wanted to make out had their lockers assigned to the end of the second floor near the French classrooms. Faun-legged freshmen usually had their lockers on the first floor, near the principal's office, as they didn't yet know enough to avoid the roving eye of Saul, the attendance officer, and his unpredictable coffee runs.

I had stopped eating lunch with the friends I'd had since grade school. If I might once have been surprised by how quickly things fell away, the past year had cured me. It had been five months since Mama died, but it felt like forever. All the time stretching ahead of me seemed like forever, too, but empty. There was a poster on the guidance office door with a picture of a hot-air balloon that said ENDLESS POSSIBIL-ITIES! Every time I walked by, I thought, *That sounds about right. Endless.*

I returned smiles and exchanged hellos in the hallway between classes, but as soon as the lunch bell rang, I ran to the cafeteria to line up for spicy fries and chocolate milk and a Styrofoam container with the hot lunch, no matter how disgusting. Then I took it down the hallway and ate sitting on the floor in front of my locker, which I'd had switched to the basement.

My new corridor in the basement was populated mostly by Chinese kids a grade below me, two of whom I knew a little from junior orchestra, where a battered viola had suffered the travails of my ambition before I'd dropped out. After a week of my silent spectating, they invited me to play cards with them. From then on, we spent the lunch hour playing Hearts in the basement hallway, an interminable game with an ongoing daily tally maintained by Hung Ma on the back of his physics notebook.

Once Sadhana passed by on her way from the cafeteria to the girls' bathroom and stopped in surprise to see me with people she didn't recognize. She had changed into a weather-inappropriate black tank top she definitely hadn't been wearing when we left home, and she was with Jennica Moore, who was acting as if we hadn't met dozens of times before.

"Hey, sis," I said. Since I'd moved my locker, it sometimes happened that we didn't see each other at all after we parted ways in the morning.

Everyone I was sitting with looked up. Vicky Chen stopped trying to fold her limp napkin into an origami box. Matthew Lee paused in dealing the cards.

"Hey," said Sadhana. She hesitated for a second, then turned and went into the bathroom. Jennica followed, already whispering in her ear.

Matthew was the school's best trombonist, or best boner, as he preferred to be known, and he was planning on becoming a virologist. In the meantime, he had become my main competition in the Hearts tally, which had scores already numbering in the hundreds.

"That's your sister?" he said, still staring after the door had swung closed. I saw Hung and Vicky exchange a look. Not many ninth graders were known throughout the school. Only the exceptional ones. Besides being pretty, Sadhana was on the track team and the volleyball team, and she had already starred in a school play.

"Yes."

"Cool." He turned back and started to deal out the next hand.

The best part about the basement hallway was that nobody was much interested in talking.

Sadhana met up with me after school that day, falling in step as I turned onto the corner of our street. She said, "What happened to Julie?" Julie Paysant and I had been friends since we were eight years old. One time, she had shown Sadhana how to take cat's cradle further than any of my sister's classmates in the first grade.

"Nothing happened to her," I said. I thought of Julie's peaked, devilish eyebrows and the beaded bracelets we'd bought each other out of the grocery store vending machine two summers ago. There was a space around the thought of her that seemed like it might quicken into sadness, but it didn't come. "Things change." Julie still smiled at me in homeroom and ate lunch with everyone near the soccer field. She had called steadily throughout the fall, but there was nothing I could think of to talk about, so I never called her back.

"Yes," said Sadhana. "They do."

We walked in silence for a while, past the Italian butcher and the good corner store with the milk that was never expired and the bench outside the Greek bakery where a toffee-coloured poodle had its leash tied up every afternoon around four.

"Beena," said Sadhana, and her voice beckoned from the thrall of our old games, urging me to play along. "Do you think we're going to be happy?" There was a young couple coming down the street, and the woman had a baby strapped to her chest, facing front. As the mother walked, one hand on his stomach, the baby's legs jiggled. His face was all wide-open amazement. The father was carrying bags of bagels, laughing at something.

"Yes," I said. Against my sister's hopeful smile, small falsehoods seemed like the safest balm. "I do."

Sadhana slowed as we passed the baby and stopped the parents to coo over him. After they moved along, Sadhana linked her arm through mine as we came into view of the shop.

"And do you think Mama misses us as much as we miss her, wherever she is?"

"Yes," I said again, though the conversation was bringing me dangerously close to tears. "Oh, here we are." I fished the key out of my knapsack to let us in, and I let Sadhana bound past me up the stairs.

The next time I checked her diary, my sins seemed to have faded from its pages. Only Uncle's misdoings remained.

*Yesterday when Uncle got home from the gurdwara, he complained
that the tub was clogged and ordered me to clean it out. But it was
probably all his stupid beard hair, anyway! All he needs is a pointy
hat to look just like a giant garden gnome.*

With a relief that felt close to happiness, I put it back,
vowing never to touch it again.

~⊙⌒

If Uncle was like a gnome with his long black beard, then
Ravi was like an Indian god. Krishna, maybe, whom we'd
read about in Mama's illustrated mythology books, the con-
summate lover who multiplied himself so he could dance in
the forest with each and every milkmaid at once.

Ravi had been working at the shop since before Mama's
accident, though he was just another one of the bagel boys, the
mostly teenaged males of mainly South Asian descent whom
we viewed as our own private stable of potential crushes.
We'd canter a passing interest around the block to see how
it felt before committing, then pick one of them and doodle
his first name (we rarely knew their last names without con-
certed investigation) over and over in a notebook before moving on to the next. Sometimes we both liked the same boy at
once, but it wasn't a problem since we never spoke to them,
just kept tabs on them from the balcony. We were lucky in
that way, to have so many distractions. It was probably what
kept us clear of any real boyfriends at school, what we per-
ceived as this multitude of options.

We'd been neglecting the bagel boys since Mama died,
but we'd picked up with them again after Uncle came to live
with us. If Mama had discovered our fascination, she never let

on, though I think she must have known by the way we were always lying stretched out on the balcony, so we could hear the boys chatting and fooling around outside during their smoke breaks. We kept our heads down so as not to be seen because we hadn't yet mastered the art of flirting. Ravi was one of the most prominent bagel boys since he was always out on smoke break. I'd started to pick out his voice before any of the others because he had a funny way of saying Rs, as if his tongue was just barely skimming the roof of his mouth and he'd cut out the roll altogether. Not so bad that Ravi became Wavi, but enough so that his whole manner of speaking sounded exotic and lazy and cool.

After supper was when Sadhana always went for her run, and, casting around for something to do, I would read or finish my homework. If Uncle was out when she got back, sometimes Sadhana would flop down on her bed after her shower and start talking, and it was easy again between us, now that I was able to leave her diary alone. We talked about people at school, the ins and outs of her group of friends, and the things we might do when we finally managed to get away from Uncle, though the last was hard to imagine. More and more, and maybe since it was easiest, we talked about boys.

We were reminded of Ravi on a night that Uncle was downstairs working, and Sadhana and I made a bowl of popcorn seasoned with nutritional yeast and a pitcher of iced mint tea and went out to camp on the balcony. We had things timed to be in position before the evening shift took their first smoke break at nine-thirty. I'd just lain down on my stomach, Sadhana settling down on her back to keep an eye on the stars, when the door below creaked open.

"Man, I think he wants me to quit." That was Ravi, talking about Uncle.

"He sure rides you hard enough." That was Carlos, one of the more long-term and upstanding of the shop's employees. He knew Sadhana and me, and Mama. He'd even been up to our apartment once, to pick up a late paycheque.

"He's had it in for me since I started. Can't figure it."

"It's easy." Carlos was chuckling in his low way that could sound like coughing if you didn't know better. "You don't say 'Yes, sir. No, sir' like everyone else. Don't you have ears in your head? That's all it takes. The boss is old-fashioned, so that's how you got to play it."

"Huh."

"Listen, I just gave you the best piece of advice you ever got. Nobody else wants to tell you because it's nice for us when he's got his whipping boy already picked out."

I wriggled to the edge of the balcony and peeked over. I could see Ravi, fingers idling in his lavish black hair, his face creased in contemplation of Carlos's bestowed wisdom. Carlos was tapping the ends of the cigarettes left in his pack, counting them maybe. They were both in their white bagel aprons, the ones that used to be printed with the name of the shop in red until Uncle switched the logo to a cartoon bagel with a face on it. It was safe to sneak peeks because the bagel boys never looked up. That ought to have been a clue never to get involved with any of them.

Finally Ravi said, "Ah, forget it. The old man can kiss my skinny brown ass." He tossed down his cigarette butt and crushed it with the heel of his boot, and Carlos chuckle-coughed so hard he really did start coughing.

"That's it, tough guy," he said once he could talk again.

"Keep it up so the rest of us can go on sitting pretty." They went inside then, and Sadhana and I had a lengthy tête-à-tête on the subject of whether or not Carlos would be a good kisser or if his stubble would be too itchy.

Occasionally, we'd prod Uncle for information on the bagel boys.

"Ravi?" said Uncle, after a not-too-subtle probing from Sadhana. "He's still there, though he's a bad, disrespectful boy." It had been a week or more since we'd last seen Ravi outside smoking, muttering his laconic complaints about Uncle to his co-workers. Uncle grunted as he got up out of his chair in the living room, a sure sign we'd disturbed his peace enough to drive him back to work. "But I know his parents a little, and I don't want to hear from them that I didn't give him a chance."

My first overtures came after Christmas and consisted of matches and diet Coke. I'd anticipate the evening smoke breaks and hurry downstairs and out the back door, offering a struck match or a beverage to the boys on shift like an assiduous smoking-room attendant. Some of the boys thought it was funny and a little cute, though Carlos and the older guys worried that my uncle would catch me out there and they'd catch an earful in turn for paying too much attention to the weird kid. Sadhana thought I was embarrassing myself, and stayed upstairs.

I didn't set out to make a play for Ravi. I would have been happy with anyone, any boy's attention. But Ravi was the first one to accept a match and then touch my wrist as he cupped his hands over mine, leading the cigarette between his lips to a kiss with the flame.

Up close, Ravi looked different, like he hadn't yet grown all the way into his face. His nose and lips seemed outsize for his thin frame, the way his hands and feet, too, seemed like buds set to burst from a narrow stem. Carlos, who was small and sturdy, with tattooed biceps, told Ravi he ought to bulk up. "Best way to get the women," he said. "Free weights."

"Seems like I've already got," said Ravi, with a tilt of his head to the spot next to the ash bucket. I was out there again, this time with ginger beers from the Caribbean grocery store, a treat even Carlos couldn't resist.

"Maybe," said Carlos. "How can you tell with the little flowers? They're so ripe they bring in all the bees." He looked me up and down, from my huge winter boots to my thighs as thick as bolster cushions and my blue and green plaid school skirt. My turquoise hair band. The down jacket I used to disguise my drooping belly and big breasts. I was getting to be a heavy teenager, though I went to the kind of school where nobody teased, only judged, and sometimes I had to wonder whether my group of friends was very select because I wanted it that way.

"You don't need to be bribing the boys, *chica*," said Carlos, after he finished most of his drink in one long slug. By the door it was warm, but he stamped his feet in the snow. He was one of the only guys who wore gloves out on smoke breaks.

"I'm not. But I know how hot it is by the ovens."

"And out here just the opposite." Carlos squinted up at the cloud cover before flipping his empty bottle end over end across the alley into the big recycling bin next to the dumpsters. It clinked like a round of celebratory toasts. "Stay warm, *chica*. Ravi, break's over."

"In a minute."

The door closed behind Carlos, and then Ravi and I were alone. He hooked his hand into the small of my back, pulling me to his chest in a quick, rough move. Then, my mouth still open in surprise, he slipped in his tongue, rolling it around and around in wet, silent circles. When he pulled away, my chin was wet and I wiped it with my hand.

"Later," said Ravi. He passed me his empty bottle, and after he went inside, I carried it up to the bedroom I shared with Sadhana and left it on the windowsill. Sadhana noticed the dusting of flour on my skirt and jacket from where I'd pressed against Ravi's apron.

"Which one?" she asked. She was propped up in bed reading one of Mama's cookbooks. Uncle expected us to make his meals, and he was getting tired of the sandwiches we'd reverted to after he complained about all the salt. Grilled cheese sandwiches, tuna fish sandwiches, egg salad sandwiches. *Witch food*, he called it, as though every one we made and served to him was just another hex.

"Ravi."

"Hmm." She wouldn't look up, as though finding a better recipe for rogan josh was every bit as interesting as my first kiss. I didn't care, because I was floating.

To the glass bottle on the windowsill, I added other mementos. Even before things got messed up, Sadhana started calling it the altar of my fallen idol. There was a button that had popped off one of my sweaters when Ravi was pushing his hand up under it. ("Your own button?" said Sadhana, unimpressed.) There was a pink ribbon he'd tied around a baggie of Hershey's Kisses. I wondered where a boy would ever find a ribbon and viewed it as an almost-proof of real love. There were the silver cigarette wrappings we'd folded into mangled origami creations, and stacks of bottle caps, evidence of time whiled away in the alley before it was dark enough to kiss freely. And a ticket stub from a movie that was our only real date.

"You really like him?" said Sadhana one day, as though she was considering taking an interest.

"Yes," I said. The truth was that I liked all of them. I wanted all of them in the way that a dissonant chord wants resolution, setting a vibration out into the world. In the way that a teenager wants her life to get started.

Ravi was tall, or seemed it. At sixteen, I was a full two inches shorter than I would be later. This meant that when we kissed outside in the alley, I had my face turned up to reach him, my head tilted back, and after a full few hours of it, a pain in my lower back that I had to treat with downward dog pose and a series of hot water bottles. Sadhana suggested that kissing shouldn't come with so many medical complaints, and that Ravi was probably doing it wrong.

When we finally did it, upstairs in my own bed while Uncle was working and Sadhana was out, I felt both triumphant and chagrined. I knew what sex was, but I didn't know that it could be so fast.

◡◠ THE DARK OF THE MOON ◠◡

My sister and I stopped bleeding at the same time. That was just how it happened. Both of us pretended to get our periods, but I discovered Sadhana was lying when I emptied the bathroom garbage and there was nothing in it. When I asked her about it, Sadhana said it was normal.

"Don't worry, sis," she said. She was rinsing her face, tilting up her chin in front of the mirror. "It just means I'm an elite athlete." She was running a lot, every day, sometimes twice a day. "It's a thing that can happen to athletes, you know. Not bleeding."

"If you say so." Under normal circumstances, we bled together at the new moon, according to one of Mama's schemes. In consultation with a lunar calendar, she'd pulled the blinds and left on nightlights until, through some sympathetic trick of hormones and her own iron will, all three of us had synched up our cycles to the light and the dark, to each other and to the sky. That was the way things used to be in the wild, Mama told us. There were rhythms and mysteries we could only observe, never understand.

"What about you?" Sadhana met my eyes in the mirror as I slipped past her out of the bathroom.

"Oh. Switched to tampons," I said over my shoulder. "Flushable."

I wondered if I had lost track of the days, or if it was just one more thing from our mother we were losing. I didn't want to be the one breaking the chain.

The thing with Ravi had been going on only a couple of months, but it was already wearing thin. And thin was part of the problem. He made no secret of his admiration for skinny blondes when they came into the store, more often in tow as the daughters of American tourists than as bona fide bagel customers.

"That one right there," he said on his break. There was a girl on the sidewalk next to a red Fiat, wearing tight blue jeans and a green, down-filled bomber jacket. She had her hands stuffed in her pockets and no hat. She looked cuter than I'd realized was possible in a Montreal winter.

"I'd take her for a spin," he said. I stared at him.

"In that car there," Ravi said, and laughed. "Nice car."

Unable to make any response, I stood there with him and we watched as she opened the trunk for her father, who was carrying two big brown grocery bags full of bagels. From the looks of it, at least four dozen. The girl noticed us staring, and as she got into the car, I was shocked to see her smile at Ravi. He nodded back as they pulled away.

"Ooh, ooh, oh," he said. Then he laughed and squeezed my ass, or tried to, through the padding of my winter coat.

Another afternoon, I caught him admiring Sadhana's legs as she slipped by us to go up to the apartment.

"Your sister, she's in pretty good shape, eh?"

"Don't even."

Every time he seemed to pull away, I'd ramp up my efforts
to the next level. I was already trying to eat less at supper
so I could lose a few pounds. And I started wearing makeup.
Deep carnelian blush and teal eyeshadow that Deana had left
behind. Sadhana mocked me when she saw me putting it on
before going out to the alley.

"Why bother? It's so dark out there, anyway."

"Not that dark."

"Well, hurry up. I need the bathroom." This was right
after supper, but I hadn't yet caught on to her routine.

I felt like I could make headway with Ravi if he'd only
agree to see me away from work. After our one trip to the
movies, where we'd groped in the back of the theatre, we
were back to smoke breaks and the odd half-hour after his
shift ended.

"It's not his fault," I told Sadhana, "that he has strict parents. They only want him dating Indian girls."

"You are an Indian girl."

"Not really. Not like they want."

It was always easier, for some reason, to know what I
wasn't.

One morning in April I woke up feeling fluish and decided
to sleep through breakfast. I could hear the clattering in the
shop downstairs as the firewood was delivered, and though
this was not a sound that could be slept through, I shoved my

head under the pillow until the stone heaviness in my stomach turned to a dizzy jig and I dashed for the bathroom.

"Hurry, please." I knocked on the door. I knew it was Sadhana in there because the newspaper was neatly refolded on the kitchen table, meaning Uncle had already gone downstairs.

"One sec."

"I'm going to be sick."

I heard the toilet flush and then the water running and finally Sadhana was opening the door and making way for me. She had her hair pulled back in a ponytail, her face washed and still damp.

When I came out, clutching my stomach, she said, smirking, "Hope it isn't morning sickness." Then her eyes got wide as we stared at each other.

"Oh my god," I said.

The day after Uncle found out, Ravi was gone. I waited out by the back door in the spring drizzle, my bare feet shoved into galoshes, a sweater over my pyjamas. Sadhana had defended me to Uncle during the long night of shouting, but when we finally went to bed, she refused to commiserate. It was plain she agreed with him I was ruining my life.

Carlos came out shortly before ten. "I heard the news, *chica*. A little sprout on the way? Ravi must have spilled the beans before he split."

"What?"

"Not me, but he told someone. And today his locker is empty." Carlos pulled out his cigarettes and shook the last one out. "I went looking for the pack he owes me. But *nada*. No joy."

Uncle took the news of Ravi's disappearance with a grim resignation. His view seemed to be that there was no use deploring the irresoluteness of a teenage boy. It was only critical that we should find him. Uncle paid a visit to his bank and then to Ravi's parents.

"He's going to offer them money to make Ravi marry you," said Sadhana, after Uncle had driven away in his best suit and turban. "Dowry."

"Don't be ridiculous," I said. Ravi was Hindu, not Sikh. But I wondered. I pictured myself in a red wedding sari or a puffed-sleeve white gown like Princess Diana's and felt less sorry than I expected. Perhaps Ravi would agree to a fire-walking ceremony, just like Mama and Papa had at their wedding.

Sadhana, sensing my reverie, was annoyed. "As if you're not getting into huge trouble for this." She was still smarting from the lecture Uncle had delivered after our last report cards, which showed her grades sliding below C level.

"Like Venice," I'd joked from the corner of the living room, and it had provoked another twenty-minute rant from our enraged guardian, who failed to understand that Sadhana's academic slump had very little to do with a disinterest in algebra.

Uncle had not even bothered yelling at me after that first night. Either he had already shouted himself out (doubtful, given his willingness to cause a ruckus over such calamities as burnt toast and unswept floors), or we had reached a new low in his estimation and were now deemed to be beyond remonstration, like birds or rocks. Sadhana was more awed by his evening silences than I was. I felt like I had already stopped listening, attentive instead to my new companion in the baby I was growing. Someone less likely to point out my faults.

Whatever Uncle's intentions in visiting Ravi's parents, they turned out to be thwarted. He came home and thumped his briefcase down in its spot by the door the way a more flamboyant man might smash a plate. There was to be no wedding (no dress, no fire-walk). Ravi had disappeared more thoroughly than he had yet done anything in his young life, and he had left not only his job but his parents' home, a fact I found baffling.

"Ravi is so lazy," I said to Sadhana later that night. I did not view this as a fault, but as something merely sensible, taking into consideration that Uncle was his boss. "Where on earth would he go?"

"Away from you," said Sadhana, reading in bed with her face turned to the wall.

If Ravi ever turned up, we never heard about it. It took a week or two before I realized that Sadhana's assessment of the situation was true: he had left me. Before that I had been thinking of him as trying to escape Uncle's wrath, or from his parents, whatever they were like. For three days, I didn't leave the apartment, expecting the phone to ring any minute with a repentant and reformed Ravi, calling to reassure me that he'd be back as soon as the worst had blown over.

Carlos became a comfort. He thought Ravi was the worst kind of coward, and he kept right on flirting with me during smoke breaks as if he felt someone needed to step in. It was little more than a few pecks on the cheek, some tickling squeezes. Every so often some longer kisses while he rubbed my arms to keep them warm. Whether it was because I seemed lonely, or only willing, Carlos seemed to like me more than ever. He even stopped smoking on his breaks because it was bad for the baby.

More than anything, Carlos's unexpected allegiance outraged Sadhana's sense of justice. "You got pregnant," she kept saying as if she didn't believe it, or as if she thought I didn't. "And nobody minds at all."

It wasn't as though Sadhana couldn't have boyfriends of her own if she wanted. But she could not or would not be happy for me. She ignored me at school and only raised an eyebrow when her friend Priya said I was getting even fatter than before. At home, she spent all her time on the phone or shut up in the bathroom. She rarely deigned to sit down with us for dinner, claiming the very sight of me put her off her food. When she did, she would pass me the bread along with a look of critical disgust. "Eating for two is just a figure of speech, you know, Beena."

At nights, when the lights were off, a truce was called. She would speculate aloud as to where Ravi could be hiding. "Maybe he's living with the mole people in the subway tunnels in New York City."

"If they'd have him."

"Maybe he went out to Alberta to work on an oil rig."

"He could have already lost an arm."

"Maybe he got picked up by a serial killer when he was hitching a ride out of town."

It always ended up with Ravi being dead. He had died in our bedroom in so many ways that I almost believed it, and really, there was not much practical difference as far as I was concerned. There was the mourning and the absence.

Once Sadhana had finished with Ravi, she could move on to other things. "Do you think Mama knows about the baby, wherever she is?"

"I think maybe," I said. "Maybe she does." I knew that this was what Sadhana wanted to hear, but I didn't believe it.

"But if she's been reincarnated, how would she even know about us?"

Though we liked remembering Mama's belief in reincarnation, it hurt to think about her as someone else. By then she could have been a baby herself somewhere, with her own new mother taking our place in her affections.

"I don't know," I said.

Sadhana rolled over so her back was facing me. "You don't know much, do you."

She was already starving then, but I didn't know it.

———————

In the bedroom I used to share with my sister, Quinn exhales where he lies on my old mattress, the rasp of the springs as he shifts his weight like the answering breath of a lover.

"We can't sleep," I say. In this room, the pronoun is always first-person plural. In this room, the air almost crackles with questions left unasked, and this time, it's Quinn I long to reach. *Did you see who I saw on television? How long will you blame me?* And our proximity just now seems to heighten our unease. My son is my idea of my son, who is made up of my past and his and all my memories and dreams for him and who he might become. But he is also himself and his body. The space he takes up in a room, the way he sleeps and eats. The things he wants to keep from me. The way parents and children slide from a physical relationship into something else, from contiguity to separation—it's continental drift, and it feels just as slow and significant. It feels stable, and then there's an ocean between you. It doesn't feel wrong. There will be an opening up to the world for both of us. But there is a desire for fixity, too. A bit of grieving.

Quinn's face in the half-dark is like a mask, his features at rest below eyes that seem to be retreating. The curtains are a pale striped cotton, a mere filter for light, and the shadows lying long across the room are tweaking my perspective. I think of the newscast, of Ravi onscreen, his declamation on the refugee family. It is impossible not to shudder at the inadequacy of memory to render a living face. Or maybe I shudder only at his refusal to remain in the past. I wonder through what trick of sympathetic physiognomy Quinn has managed to resemble my sister, with his strong cheekbones and wide, dark eyes. His father, for all his glamour, never had those cheekbones.

"Nope," says Quinn. "We can't." He rolls over onto his back and says, "Maybe I can move into her old apartment."

"What?"

"Why not? She always talked about how cheap it was. And all-inclusive, right? I don't want to live in residence, share a room with someone."

"You were lucky to get a spot."

"Not if I don't want to live there."

I try to think back to when we put in his application and made the arrangements. Was I the one pushing that through alone? Quinn was quiet, I remember, not too forthcoming, but that was at the beginning of the year, when two words together from him was something approaching chatty.

"Well, it's been rented, anyway, I'm sure. By now. There'll be a new lease."

"So I've missed my chance." There is an accusatory undertone there, and I retaliate.

"Well, you ought to have said you wanted to get an apartment. You ought to have said something before now." There is an expectation, in becoming a parent, of accumulating blame, but my tally is already so high that I judge it to be worth the effort of deflecting.

Quinn turns over to face the wall. I wait for him to say something more, but before he does, I am asleep.

The morning breaks grey and wet, with the hiss and splash of cars on slick pavement. Quinn's bed is empty, his pyjamas neatly folded on top of his zipped suitcase. I notice my clothes from the day before heaped in a pile on the rug. Being under Uncle's roof is bringing out the opposite of our usual habits. Even through the rain I can smell the garlic-and-onion bagels in the ovens downstairs, as I get up, make coffee, and, after downing a cup, return to the bedroom.

I pull out the number from where I've folded it in my purse. When a woman picks up, I ask to speak to Libby Carr.

The woman on the other end sounds flustered, then surprised. "That's me."

"Oh my goodness," she says next, when I tell her my name. "Just one sec." I hear a crash and then a rustling, as though the mouthpiece is being clutched to her body. Then her bold voice again, half breathless. "Just getting some privacy," she says. "Well, some quiet, really."

I wait. Then, after a beat, I say, "It's no problem."

"Thanks so much for calling me back. I know it must seem a bit crazy." Though her voice on my machine had been measured, she addresses me quickly, in rapid, almost musical cadences.

"It was unexpected," I say. My dread of whatever it is that she wants to say seems at odds with her ebullience. But then again, it feels like decades that I've been mixing up fear and hope. I hardly know what I feel.

"It's wonderful of you to call me," she says. "It's really terrific. So what do you think about getting together?"

"Well." I remember her strange declaration on my answering machine. *There's something else you ought to know.* I wonder if there is any way she will just come out and say it, whatever it is. "In your message —"

She keeps on. "I've been having a hard time making sense of everything. Sadie being gone." I can hear her breathing. "But . . ." She stops for a moment, and I can hear noises in the background at her end, a child talking. "I did offer my condolences at the funeral, but you probably don't remember. I'm not sure I even introduced myself."

Stretching out my legs from where I sit on my old bed, I knead my toes into the pile of the brown and orange carpet. A monarch butterfly pattern, a giant shag square that used to be in Mama's bedroom, left in here as a compromise when neither Sadhana nor I could agree who should have it. I am still in my bathrobe. I've chosen to dive into what I would have preferred to put off. Leaning forward, I rest my elbows on my knees.

I do not remember a Libby. There was a man with thick, steely hair and a wool coat, who pressed his pity into my arm with a leather glove. A group of women in quick succession whom I thought might be members of Sadhana's knitting group, albeit with radically evolved haircuts and outfits. A blonde woman with waist-length ringlets who told me she'd sent an arrangement of pussy willows. She had been Juliet in a dance show that Sadhana and I had enjoyed, had mentioned for weeks afterwards in appreciation of the lean, muscular body of the male lead. Romeo of the ropy arms. I hadn't realized Sadhana even knew her. There was a soft handshake, too, from a young man with rubber plugs in his earlobes who looked as if he had been crying. But I cannot recall a single name, even if one was ever spoken.

"You know, I can't say I remember much about anyone I met that day. But thank you for coming. I'm sure Sadhana — well . . ." I break off. No need to speak for the dead. "Anyway."

It seems clear that this woman wants to speak in person, and I feel ungracious declining. "Um, sure. Okay, let's meet."

"Wonderful," says Libby. She sounds both eager and exultant. "That's great. So, when's good for you? You live in Ottawa, right?"

"I do, but I'm here now. For the weekend."

"Aha, I see the area code." I hear a tapping, like a fingernail against a call-display screen. "You're in Montreal. That's perfect. I'm free today, if you are."

"I'm clearing out her place, actually," I say. "Finally. I've sort of been postponing it."

"Oh, that must be hard." Her voice thickens. "I'm sorry. God."

I close my eyes. Some emotion bristles between us on the line like static, but I can't tell if it is grief or sympathy. I let her suggest a time and place.

"I'll see you then," I say, scarcely believing it, and after bidding her goodbye, hang up.

~◦~

I am almost late to meet her. After waiting around for Quinn to return to the apartment, I finally give up, leaving him a note on the kitchen table. Then I head in the direction of Sadhana's place, stopping for a salad and a slice of quiche at a restaurant we'd often dined at. A block farther, when I pass a post office, I stop in to buy scissors and some rolls of packing tape. At every intersection, I notice, there are campaign posters affixed to telephone poles, and out of curiosity, I check along both main streets that Quinn may have taken. I count six different political parties, but I see no signs for Ravi.

At last, noting the time, I decide to take the long way around the park to meet Libby rather than get started with everything at Sadhana's. Although the café is only a few blocks from my sister's apartment, I somehow find myself almost out of breath by the time I get there, anticipation lodged like a stitch in my side.

"Beena! Hey," she calls, catching sight of me. Clad in loose jeans and a thin grey shirt, Libby Carr is standing behind a table laden with a pitcher of sangria and two wine glasses. She has her hand cupped over her eyes, watching for me against the dazzle of the afternoon sun. She'd described herself as "a skinny blonde with bad shoes." When I told her that didn't narrow it down much, she said she'd seen photos of me and not to worry. But I could have guessed who she was. Apart from her expectant posture, she has a complex, interrogative gaze and a long, pretty face tapering to a decisive chin. She looks like someone Sadhana would be friends with. Maybe even the girl from the photograph on the merry-go-round.

I walk to her quickly, aware of people's eyes on us after Libby's loud greeting. She is perhaps thirty, with dirty blonde hair that hangs well past her armpits. She gives the impression of height but sits before I can compare. Once I'm seated, she sort of laughs, then reaches out across the table for my hand and shakes it with what I think of as an American kind of vigour, a physical friendliness. I am aware of a tingling in my elbow.

"I'm so glad you decided to come," she says. "I hope you don't mind that I ordered for us. The waitress seemed totally frazzled, and I thought I'd better get something. But if you want something else, go ahead. I can finish this myself." She laughs again, a little loudly. There is a boldness to her voice

that seems self-consciously reined in, possibly for my benefit.
A hurricane losing strength over land. "I'm kidding, I think."
It occurs to me she might be nervous.

"This is fine, thanks." I draw my chair in closer to the
wrought-iron table. The café is popular and we are surrounded on all sides by other patrons, those of us unfortunate
enough to be only two people together all relegated to the
row of smaller tables placed down the middle length of the
patio. Waitresses in black aprons stream past on either side. "I
hope you haven't been waiting long."

"No, you're perfect. You're right on time. I got here
early." Libby takes hold of the two plastic stir sticks and swirls
them in the pitcher, looking at me. Slices of orange and lime
bob in the drink. "Oh wow, it's so freaky meeting people's
siblings," she says. "Seeing resemblances."

"Sure." I hope she doesn't say anything about whether or
not I look like Sadhana. The comparisons have always struck
me as unflattering, even when that hasn't been the intention.

"Good genes," is all she says, cocking her head to evaluate. "Both of you." She shakes her head then, waves her hand.
"Oh god, I'm sorry. I don't know what I'm saying."

"No, I—it's okay." In a blink, an image comes to me of
Sadhana, unmoving on the floor of her kitchen, and a quiver
seizes my back. The vision I'd dreaded at her apartment has
arrived without warning. I try to keep my eyes trained on
Libby's sober face.

"I've been having a hard time these past six months," she
is saying, pouring sangria into a glass for me. She holds the
stir sticks in a V, straining out the fruit, then in a neat motion
nudges in a few slices with barely a splash. "I've been wanting
to call you for a long time, actually, but I had to sort of work

up the nerve. I did call you once or twice before she died, but I hung up when you answered the phone."

"You did?" I feel as if I must have misheard something. Libby is talking mostly into her glass. "Why?"

"Yeah," she says, as though I haven't asked. The calls, I guess, were to do with whatever it is she wants to tell me. She goes on, "Sadie and I were very close."

I let the statement alone to see how it fills up, as Libby presses her lips together, and her eyelids flicker rapidly as I try to read her. There is a subtle defensiveness in her expression I can't quite account for. "I miss her, too," I say at last. "And I'm glad you left me that message. I needed a push to come back here to pack up her things."

"That must be hard."

"It isn't easy." An understatement, though I know now it's not the apartment, but me who's haunted. It will be a matter of throwing myself into the job without pausing to think. I take a long sip of the sangria and, over the rim of the glass, observe Libby looking miserable. I feel a vague pressure to say something. "So how did you meet my sister?"

Libby makes an effort to smile. "Through theatre stuff. I do lighting."

"For a living?"

She nods. "It's kind of amazing. I did a college diploma in it when I first came here because it was subsidized and it seemed artistic, but now I love it. I get to be around creative people all the time, and my little one, Mouse, is usually able to tag along."

"Mouse?"

"Christiane, my daughter. Somehow her given name hasn't quite stuck."

"Ah." I know so little about this woman, or what she hopes to accomplish by getting to know me. I had imagined a clearer direction to our conversation. "And where were you before Montreal?"

"Hearst," she says. "Way up north. It's in Ontario, but most of the town is French. It's a small town, so that was an adjustment, but the language thing was an easy transition, anyway."

"You speak French?"

She nods. "My husband is francophone. My ex." She shifts in her seat as she crosses one leg over the other. I see the shoes that she mocked on the phone, just regular black canvas sneakers with white laces. "Though he's bad news. A very bad dude, in the end. He's why I left."

"Good for you." I have a bizarre moment of envy. Better to be the one who leaves than gets left behind. I wonder what Quinn would think of me if leaving Ravi was a choice I had made for us.

"It's too bad, in a way, because his family is nice. But Mouse is really thriving here. She's seven and a half. Right now she wants to be an astronaut when she grows up. That or a ballerina." Her fingers drum the edge of the table as her eyes invite me to laugh along with her. I calculate that Libby must have married young, in her early twenties at the latest. "Let me top you up," she says then, gesturing with the pitcher. I slide my glass across the table. Libby says as she pours, "What was Sadhana like as a little girl?"

I remember Sadhana and me as children, performing a routine in Mama's gypsy skirts, a strange dance-pantomime hybrid we had made up to the song "Penny Lane." I couldn't stop tripping over my hem, but Sadhana had mastered the knack of keeping the skirt spinning out, away from her toes.

Even before she became a perfectionist, she was perfect.

"She was just like you might imagine," I say. "Fun, graceful. Though maybe less opinionated back then."

Tears spring to Libby's eyes, and she bows her head in a gesture that seems ancient and marked by grief. In a spontaneous move that takes me by surprise, I cover her hand with mine, but after a moment, she pulls hers away, holding her sleeve up to her eyes. When she takes it down, it is soaked. "I'm sorry. I thought I was ready for this."

"Oh," I say, startled. "But," I hesitate. "Wasn't there something you wanted to tell me?"

She bobs her head in a jerky nod. "Maybe another time?" Her glass clinks against the iron of the table as she sets it down. "Next time."

"I guess so," I say. "Yes, if you like."

"Thanks. I really am sorry about this." Libby motions for the bill, and once we have paid, she says she has to pick up her daughter from school.

"Mouse is my reason for getting up in the morning," she says, calmer now as we walk together to the corner. "My absolute all."

Beside Libby on the sidewalk, I find we are more or less the same height. She strolls with her hands in her pockets and gives me a two-fingered salute when we part ways. "Good luck," she says, which seems vague.

"You too."

Then, "Talk to you soon." And before I can reply, Libby crosses the street as the light turns green and is out of earshot, loping up the hill.

Watching her diminishing figure, I feel myself deflate. Whatever she wants to tell me, I badly want to know.

Whatever Sadhana said or did, Libby thinks it important, and my curiosity is piqued even as I anticipate disappointment. I'd never known my sister to confide in other people with any regularity. Beyond the pages of her diary, I'm not sure anyone was truly her confidante.

Her diary. It is a recollection to make me stop still. My eyes widen and water in the glare of the afternoon sun, and when I blink, I register something more than a mere physical relief. If I can find it—if she was still writing in it—it might have something to tell me. The truth of what happened in those last few days might be recorded there, or maybe even other, bigger truths. Whether she was sick again, or not. Whether she was happy. Whether she had spent most of her life really wanting to die and was holding off only for my sake. Whether she really did blame me for everything that had gone wrong. For leaving. For Mama.

I plod north towards St. Viateur Street with renewed resolve, the ranks of grey walk-ups on my left with their hand-lettered garden-fence signs reading *Pas de bicyclettes!* seeming like a cartoon backdrop, a small stretch of background spliced together on a reel stretching up to the horizon, a black dog and an old woman frowning into the sun appearing at paced intervals as I pass. Or so it seems. I try to blink away the tiredness. There is something about the angle of the light on the land that gives everything a hallucinatory shimmer. I check the street sign at the corner to make sure I haven't walked too far.

The liquor store surrenders a lucky yield of empty boxes, their former contents enough to flatten a fleet on leave for a week. I carry them as a tower, nestled one in the other, my arms looped beneath, fingers locked like a foothold at the bottom of a cheerleading tower. The top of the pile is about level with my head, and everyone I pass turns to give me a look, some sympathetic, some almost envious, as though my spectacle has reminded them that they ought to begin packing.

Less than three weeks until Moving Day. Mama always said it was the separatists who set things up this way, the lease system, everyone moving on the first of July and too busy to give a crap about Canada. A paraphrase, of course. But that isn't true, though I can no longer remember how it is supposed to have come about. Such a difference here from Ottawa on the first of July, that sea of red and white, the city's mild stuffiness replaced for one day with the brash pride of football hooliganism. It's cheery enough there until the drunkenness of the wee hours, post-fireworks. Here it's just the best day of the year to find a free couch.

At Sadhana's, the afternoon light has already begun to change, and I am struck by how much of the weekend I have already squandered avoiding the task at hand. I hurry up the stairs, then feel a sharp tug on my sleeve and almost stumble. Gripping the boxes, which tip forward but do not spill, I turn slightly to see a young man with a broad smile standing to the left of the staircase.

"Sorry, ma'am," he says. He has a clipboard and a royal blue bowtie knotted around the collar of a crisp white shirt. "Just trying to get your attention."

I frown at the cuff of my sleeve with pointed concentration.

"Could you spare a few minutes of your time?"

"No, I don't think so." I continue up to the landing and close the door on him. I don't want to give myself time for any more excuses.

I decide to start with the clothes, promising myself to make a dent in the work I need to do before any search for a missing diary. Without allowing myself time to reflect, I throw on a CD of house music, numbingly loud, and toss a few large boxes into the bedroom. The oversized closet has dusty shutter doors that fold up like accordions, a high, cluttered shelf, and one light bulb on a switch. I drag in a chair from the kitchen and flip on the light in the closet. When I get up to shelf level, I count three boxes marked *Photos*, but I decide they can stay for now. I climb down from the chair and set it aside. I daren't touch them anyhow.

I pull down the clothes quickly; no more than one sharp tug per item. A swift look before sending them into a box. No folding. No remembering.

The operation is a blur of colour: wool and linen in gem tones and greys and blacks. Deep dyes and Indian cotton. More handwash-only in the first five minutes than I've owned in my entire life. There are a lot of clothes, and more than a few things I've forgotten she had, things I haven't seen in years. Before long, the box designated for clothes to give away is virtually empty, the other verging on full. A dozen more items I've flung on the bed to make up my mind about later. She liked to wear loose things. It's possible some of them will even fit me.

I start pulling down the hangers themselves, clothes clinging to their wooden shoulders. A span of dresses I deposit wholesale in the box of things to keep, the weight of the wooden hangers compressing the bulk of the pile below. Then a bunch of sweaters and the job is more or less finished. Twenty or thirty hangers still line the crossbar, but I can't imagine a new tenant objecting.

At least the shoes covering the closet floor won't fit me. Two sizes too small. They can all be packed up for charity. Kneeling on the floor, I pull an empty box alongside me and pitch them all inside, until, leaning back on my heels, I feel the hot prickle of tears and force myself up. I don't know what I was thinking, starting with the clothes. I feel unequal to the task, utterly unprepared. It feels like a violation, more than anything. It takes me back to when we were teenagers. Sadhana yelling at me for borrowing her things without asking. It usually goes the other way, from what I've heard—the older sister tends to do the yelling. But Sadhana never wanted anything of mine.

The diary. Getting up, I check in Sadhana's childhood spot, between the mattress and the box spring, but finding nothing, I sit back down with a sense of disappointment soon yielding either to exhaustion or relief.

The things I used to hide under my bed. Items in heaps so extensive that one peek below the bedskirt and the piles would start shifting, slipping out. The only reason anything stayed hidden was that finding something specific would have been impossible. I used to keep notebooks under there, racy *True Confessions* magazines, the odd piece of clothing Sadhana might have fancied that I wasn't keen to share. There were library books, too, anatomy textbooks I was sure would betray my fascination with sex. To my sister, anyway. The librarian hadn't reacted when I'd checked them out.

I had always assumed Sadhana kept the same sorts of things down there as I did, and one day I violated her bed's implicit sanctity by getting down on my knees to rummage for a missing Beach Boys record. When I pulled up the ruffle of white eyelet lace, I found nothing more than a neat row of shoeboxes. Later, in therapy, Sadhana revealed that they had contained food in an elaborate configuration. Two boxes for uneaten food smuggled away from meals, rotting in a series of knotted plastic bags until she had a chance to sneak them into the garbage. Another two for chocolate and sweets, things she used to binge on until she gave up on eating altogether. I have no idea what I would have made of the contents of those boxes if I'd lifted the lids that day, but I have a feeling that Sadhana would have tried to explain them away, the horror and the strangeness of them, and I would have believed her. However improbable her story.

There is nothing below Sadhana's bed now besides a bit of fluff, though on the opposite side from where I've grasped the dust ruffle and thrust my head under, I see a metallic rectangle on the rug, joined to a cord snaking from the outlet behind the nightstand. My sister's laptop.

The contents, once I turn it on, are password-protected, and I feed the blinking cursor an array of talismanic possibilities. Our birthday. Papa's name, VISHRAM SINGH. Mama's name, KATIE BIRNAM. Our old address above the shop. Finally, one works. QUINN.

The picture on the desktop background is the same photo as the one on the mantelpiece, of Sadhana and a woman I can now identify as Libby. With the photo enlarged, I can see that the mouths of the carousel horses are open, their squared-off teeth huge and askew. Opening the documents folder, I click through the files but find nothing resembling a diary. Everything is well organized, which doesn't surprise me. Most of the documents are in a handful of folders marked "No Borders." Backgrounders. Media. Strategies. Emails— Drafts to Send.

In "Backgrounders" I open a file named "Bassam Essaid" and see the photo that flashed on the newscast. The same man that Ravi was denouncing as an illegal alien. It follows that, somewhere along the line, Sadhana would have caught wind of Ravi's opposition to Bassam Essaid's refugee claim, not to mention Ravi's political candidacy. I wonder exactly how long my sister was aware of what Quinn's father was up to, and how long she kept herself from mentioning him to me.

The Algerian civil war began in 1991 and claimed at least 150,000 lives before an amnesty in 1999 led many of the rebels to lay down their arms. Some refugee claimants fleeing the war were granted asylum, and some were not, and a ban on deportations to Algeria permitted a number of these refugees to remain in Canada without legal status. But the abatement of violence in that country after the amnesty left a number of these non-status Algerians in limbo after Canada decided Algeria was no longer a danger to its inhabitants. The decision followed closely upon a newly forged political and economic alliance between the then-prime ministers of the two countries.

There isn't a trace of my sister's voice in the document, nor is it the sort of thing that ought to showcase any personal style. It seems unlike her, to disappear into a cause. Yet the volume of work saved on her computer seems to give the lie to whatever prior notion of Sadhana I keep presuming is the real one.

As a conscientious objector and outspoken atheist, Bassam Essaid claims he will face deadly reprisals should he be forced to return to his country of birth, but the Immigration Board of Canada disagrees.

In his six years in Montreal, despite being unable to work or study, Bassam Essaid has fully integrated into Quebec society. He has also campaigned tirelessly to help other refugees seeking official status. He met and married his wife, herself a Somalian refugee,

in Canada, though unlike her husband, her immigration status is
secure. Together they have one child, born in Montreal, a baby boy
now less than a year old.

I spend a few minutes opening and closing other files,
wading through a wealth of these specific functional documents and little that seems personal. But there are hundreds
of folders and subfolders to dig through. Following the intricate architecture of my sister's organizational scheme is like
lowering myself through an ever-narrowing hole. It is tedious
and tiring, and when I turn off the computer, I feel calmer.

Moving the laptop aside, I pull back the covers and crawl
in between the egg-blue sheets. The linens, that's something
else to deal with. The bed, too. All the furniture. God. I'll
need a truck, not to mention somewhere to put it all.

I imagine Quinn in this place, the walls papered over with
Radiohead posters and Linux charts, if he were able to move
in. And, inevitable at the end of the summer, another packing
job. All of Quinn's books and clothes taped into boxes, too.
And with the thought of this packing, or in what I tell myself
is the terrifying thought of all the work ahead, my lips begin
trembling in earnest, and I let my tears leak out onto Sadhana's
pillow in a long cry that I lead myself out of only once I start
to hear the regular sounds of birds and cars outside. Against
this reassuring soundtrack, I begin a mental enumeration of
new necessities for Quinn when he leaves home, depending
on what the residence hall provides. A proper desk instead of
our old kitchen table, a bookcase instead of his planks-and-
bricks setup along one wall. Maybe a toaster.

Somewhere in the middle of this inventory, I fall asleep.

I am woken by a distant knocking that I decide is some sort of home improvement project going on in the apartment below. Picture hanging, or maybe crate assembling, something pointless and endlessly loud. I roll over onto my other side, away from the window, pull one of the cushions down over my ear. Then I hear the soft beeping tone of my cellphone ringing inside my purse on the floor. I fumble for it, bringing it to my ear.

"I'm downstairs," says Quinn. He sounds impatient. "Let me in."

When I unlock the door, he gives me a hard look, the entitled frown of annoyance of a person who has been kept waiting.

"Hey," says Quinn. "What were you doing?" He shoves a pamphlet in my face. "New political party," he says, and with a prescient fear I take it from him, my heartbeat loud in my ears. "It was jammed into the door."

And so I am barely surprised to see the three-fold glossy emblazoned with the words MOUVEMENT QUÉBEC/QUE-BEC FIRST, Ravi's affiliation that I saw on the evening news. Literature no doubt left behind by the man who'd yanked on my sleeve. The idea of Quebec independence not a recurring debate so much as a familiar refrain coming around after every new verse. A glance at the pamphlet shows me that it features only the party leader and key platform messages; Ravi's name and those of the other candidates have not been included. And a quick check of Quinn's face reveals no special interest or concern.

"Hi," I say. "You're here." I pull back the door to let him in, and the light from outside is dazzling. I can feel the heat coming off him as he squeezes by, taking the stairs two at a time. It isn't like him to push past me. I follow slowly. "What's the matter?"

"Nothing."

"Okay," I say, understanding, and my heart aches. But there is no way to take on this pain on his behalf. He is here now, of his own accord.

He pauses for a moment on the landing. I am standing two steps below, and I see the outline of his wallet in his back pocket, the lighter rectangle of denim on the right side. It's an image I associate with men I've known, their easy practicality. The way they move through time, happy to let it show in these little signs and markers. Shoes, jeans, wallets wearing out as a matter of pride.

"Go ahead," I say. "It's okay." And he steps into the apartment without looking back, as if not to acknowledge any hesitation. He looks to the left, where there is a brass umbrella stand with three umbrellas, a companionable number, and a straight-backed wooden chair, a favourite spot for shedding purses and coats. Then his head turns to the right, to the hallway that leads to the bedroom, then down to his sneakers.

"Leave them on," I say. "We'll be dealing with boxes and stuff." But he takes two squeaky steps inside before turning back, stepping on the heels of his sneakers to slip them off. He leaves them next to my own scuffed sandals, removed from force of habit.

"She wouldn't like it," he says, and he's probably right. It took Sadhana years of pleading to get her landlord to refinish the hardwood floors, and now they are shiny and perfect. So shiny I still half expect my bare feet to stick to the varnish, stopped in my tracks like a mouse caught in a glue trap.

I head back into the bedroom, and behind me, Quinn says, "It feels the same here. I thought it would feel different."

"I know." Though I'm not sure if he means because Sadhana is gone or because we know that she died here, that this is where she was found. My involuntary imagination has run through every possibility, but I don't know where exactly, which room. There are reasons to be grateful for Uncle's reticence.

"Have you been sleeping?"

The sheets have given me away, along with the scattered mess of clothing all over the bed, the things on the floor to either side. I pick up my bag and stuff the political pamphlet into it, together with Sadhana's laptop and some of the strewn items.

"A little," I say, though I have no idea what time it is or how long I have been asleep. This time of year, it stays nearly as bright as noon until past eight. Quinn ties back the double drapes so the whole room is full of sun, revealing the barest hint of lilac in the light paint, the zest of yellow colour fields in two Rothko-inspired canvases on the wall behind the bed.

"Where were you?" I ask, remembering how he left before I was up.

"Went for a walk." He is looking out the window. I can hear a family with small children walking by, high-pitched chattering over the lower murmurs of adult conversation. For the most part, it is a quiet block, just trees and walk-ups and on the corner a vegan café with two banks of washers and dryers.

I finish sorting the clothes on the bed and begin tackling everything else in sight, whatever I can see that can be packed. Quinn takes some boxes into the living room, and we work in silence for a while. There is no sign of a diary. When I start to get hot, I search on Sadhana's dresser for an elastic and pull my hair back in a ponytail. I can hear the plasticky shuffle of CDs as Quinn stacks them in a box.

"Are we keeping all this stuff?" he calls out.

"We can keep whatever we want." Or rather, we'll keep whatever we can't bring ourselves to give away.

When I check on Quinn later in the living room, I find he is more efficient than I am. The CD racks are stripped and disassembled, the books and magazines packed. He is working his way towards the kitchen.

"I guess we're taking just about everything then," he says again.

"I guess." I wonder if unexpected loss always breeds materialism or if it is only in our family. Sadhana and I divvying up all of Mama's clothes, and the accompanying screaming matches. There is one horrible scene I always think of, a yellow terrycloth robe torn seam from seam. And afterwards, both of us stalking off with our halves, tucking away the unwearable strips in our secret spots. Both of us reminding me of the bad mother before King Solomon, the one who had already lost everything that mattered. "Except the furniture," I amend. "Though it's a pity we can't sell it."

"Sell it?" says Quinn. "Why would we?" And then, "Why can't we?"

"We don't need it. Also, I wouldn't know how to go about selling it all. Not a lot of time to advertise."

"The internet," Quinn says with the merest shake of his head. "But I'm moving out. You don't want to have to buy me all new stuff."

I pause, considering the logic of this. "Maybe. We'll see. Maybe some stuff."

The light from outside is beginning to drop when I finally

finish up most of the bedroom, leaving one of the larger boxes untaped in case we want some of the clothes to wrap around breakables. Quinn has packed up the towels and linens in the bathroom, and I see that he has filled a tote bag with half-used bottles of shampoo and wrapped guest soaps.

"You're thorough," I say. I hope he has thrown out the toothbrushes, the makeup.

"I try." He steps past me to the wide windows behind the sofa, where square pillar candles on shallow ceramic dishes are ranged along the ledge. He gives me an inquiring look. When I shrug, he begins placing them in a box one by one.

"Someone must have been watering the plants," he says. As he carries the box back to where he has begun stacking them in the middle of the room, he stops by the spreading jade plant set on a low bookcase. His fingers graze a leaf, waxy and smooth. There is not even a wrinkle. "This wouldn't have made it. The cactus maybe, but only maybe."

"You're right," I say, though I'm unsure, wondering how my teenage son came to feel like an authority. We have the garden at home, but no houseplants. "Uncle, I guess."

Quinn puts on the radio in the kitchen and tunes it to the university station. Over the music, I can hear the muted bang and rattle of cupboards and drawers being opened and closed.

I am rolling up one of the long carpets in the hallway when I notice a shadow under the bookcase. Under the chair by the door and slipped halfway beneath the bottom shelf, where it looks as though it might have fallen, is a zippered leather agenda, scuffed along the spine. Not a diary, but Sadhana's planner. I drop to one knee to pick it up.

It is a Filofax-style agenda, with dated calendar pages, an address book, plain lined pages with personal notes, and coloured tabs dividing each month and section. A pocket at the back stuffed with receipts and business cards, and a wad of other slips of paper tucked in among the pages. Normally it was always in her purse, the purse that Uncle already took away, concerned as he was—as somebody had to be—about cancelling her cellphone service and credit cards.

"Mom," says Quinn, calling out. "Look at this. It was on the floor."

There is an urgent appeal in his voice, and I am at his side in a moment. The fear in my chest tells me he has stumbled upon something related to Ravi. I know I ought to have told him I saw his father on television, but I can hardly bear to face it. Guilt bruises into dread with the slightest touch.

"What is it?"

He hands it to me with the printed side up, an ATM withdrawal slip dating from the last week of November. "The other side," says Quinn.

On the reverse is scrawled a list in my sister's handwriting: *bread, bananas, tomatoes, penne, garlic, white pepper.* Each word has a line through it. A grocery list. The square of paper has a slight sheen, worn grey along the barest crease lines. I rub my thumb over the words before passing it back.

"I found her planner, too, just now," I say. "It was under the bookcase."

Quinn stands with the corner of the grocery list pressed between his finger and thumb, like a penalty card about to be raised aloft. "Did you see it?" he says. "Did you look at the date?"

"Yes." I think for a minute, but it is Quinn's face that makes me realize, the way the bottom of his mouth is scrunching up as it would when he was little and about to cry.

"Oh," I say. The end of November, the last days of my sister's life. Probably one of the last shopping trips she made, if not the last. In the same instant, I begin to fear the planner I'm clutching, as though it holds an image of Sadhana's final moments, a series of recordings, like the black box of an airplane. Even just the first blank page will be horrible. If I could throw it out of reach without alarming Quinn, I would.

"So she was eating," says Quinn.

"Maybe." I sit down on one of the wooden kitchen chairs, put the planner down on the table. I let out my breath. "Maybe not. Remember how she used to cook for us. Even through the bad spells. Maybe even more during the bad spells."

"But we weren't here. This wasn't for our benefit."

"It could have been for somebody else's benefit."

"Like who?"

"I don't know. Anyone. Other people who knew enough to be concerned."

Quinn turns back to packing the large pots and pans, and I can see he doesn't believe me. He has persistent doubts about whether or not Sadhana used to hide things from us, and I suspect him of having rewritten things in such a way that it was always me, doing my best not to see or know. He thinks that she talked to me in a way that she didn't talk to him, that I knew all her secrets.

"But if she was eating," Quinn says, turning back to me after wedging a handful of large cooking utensils around the edge of a stockpot. "That's what this list could mean."

"What?" I say. "It's a list. It's a piece of paper."

But it's more than that. It means that on November twenty-seventh, at three thirty-seven in the afternoon, my sister was still alive. When they found her body, it had been too long, they couldn't narrow it down beyond a stretch of days. In this I had failed her along with all her friends—none of us inclined to worry, or to worry, at any rate, about the right thing. For eleven days I thought she was reading my number on the call display and choosing not to answer. I put my elbow on the table, forehead pressing into my palm. Looking into my lap, I see streaks of dust covering my jeans.

Quinn says, "It shows that maybe there wasn't anything we didn't know."

I raise my head and see him looking at me, leaning forward across the box of pots, as earnest as I have ever seen him. He means that this time, maybe, she wasn't sick. That it wasn't anything we could have prevented or foreseen. I feel a tingling of hope.

"Anorexia weakens the heart," I say. "And she had it for a long time, since even before you were born. It doesn't mean there was a relapse." We knew all this before, the medical examiner had said as much, but I had not thought of it with any conviction, and, it seems, neither had Quinn. There was always a relapse. There had always been one.

"Maybe it just happened," says Quinn.

"Maybe."

We look at each other as the setting sun spills a reddish pool of light into the darkening kitchen.

"You know, it does feel different," he says, looking around. "Smaller."

~∽⌒∽~

When I get back, Uncle is still awake, sitting at the kitchen table over a crossword puzzle, an activity I find oddly benign for the time of night. Even the silver mechanical pencil he is holding strikes me as strange. Delicate.

"Hello," I say.

"Ah," he says. "You're back." He pushes back his chair, picks up a mug from the table, and carries it to the sink. He has a slow, tired look. A thought occurs to me.

"You weren't waiting up?" It is almost one thirty in the morning. I sent Quinn home soon after dark, while I kept working, wrapping up the dishes and other breakables I didn't quite trust him to pack. Working while I could, while it felt bearable. The planner I'd placed in my bag, shrinking from the moment I'd have to look at it. When I left, the bedroom was almost completely emptied. I'd only stopped because I'd run out of boxes. Then I walked, stepping out of line from the direct route between Sadhana's and Uncle's, veering first to St. Laurent, quiet on a Sunday night, and then over to the park, where I skirted the edges of a block before getting scared back to my senses by failing to notice a group of young men at a picnic table. I was nearly on top of them when first their eyes and then their faces emerged suddenly out of the darkness. Except for the tennis courts, the park was not lit up at night. I could not imagine why they were sitting there in silence, four or five of them together. One of them called out to me as I spun on my heel and walked away. "You just got here," he said. "We won't bite."

Now Uncle rubs his chin with the back of his wrist. He is wearing light green cotton pyjamas and his wool slippers. "No," he says. "Not waiting. Not at first."

"I'm sorry, Uncle. I should have called."

He just shakes his head, fingers smoothing down his moustache where it meets his beard. He doesn't seem at all angry.

"Since you're up, may I ask you a question?" I lower my voice as I realize I have been getting louder. Everything can be heard, I remember, across the breadth of this apartment.

"Yes, you may ask."

"Did you water the plants at Sadhana's apartment? Have you been taking care of them?"

Uncle nods. "Yes, I watered them from time to time."

"And the fridge. Did you empty it?"

"I did."

"There was food in it?"

"There was a great deal of food." There is a deliberate patience in Uncle's voice, whether because he is anxious to go to bed or because he expected me to ask this long ago, I can't tell.

There is no sign of Uncle when I get up in the morning, which likely means he is down in the shop. Quinn is still asleep as I make myself coffee, having developed a fondness for the squat red espresso maker in the spot that used to house a tiny filter machine. I am discovering that the apartment holds a number of these unexpected instances of luxury, fixtures geared mostly towards refining the everyday: microfibre towels, organic milk, a Waterpik toothbrush. I have Sadhana's agenda with me and a resolve fuelled by a restless, anxious sleep. I dreamed mostly of Sadhana, and every time I awoke and turned over I saw Quinn snoring on his back, his allergies making him wheeze like an old man.

Unzipping the planner, I hold it by its spine and shake it a few times above the table until some papers start drifting out. These I separate into piles: business cards, receipts,

other miscellaneous scraps of paper, then add to these piles
the neatly stacked items tucked into the pocket at the back. I
begin to see how many of the receipts are of the most mundane variety—groceries, toiletries, bus tickets. It dawns on
me that Sadhana kept all her receipts, possibly for sorting
later. As a self-employed artist, some of them might have been
important for her taxes. And perhaps for her the groceries
were not so mundane.

The datebook itself is no less meticulous. Flipping to
April, I see that every day has a list of appointments and things
to do, catalogued in two adjacent columns. On the far side of
every weekly two-page spread is a list of names, some of them
crossed out with a single line. Maybe people she planned on
calling. And periodically, in the upper right-hand corner of
the box for each day, a number, gone over with a yellow high-
lighter, figures like 1560, 900, 1290, 2400.

A truck starts backing up in the alley, its beeping like
a horror alarm clock, and within a few minutes I hear the
sounds of Quinn getting out of bed and moving around.
Before I lose my nerve, I turn to the end of November. The
last day with any amount of writing has only a partial to-do
list and nothing crossed out, no number in the top corner. And
so there is a date. November twenty-ninth, two days after the
bank withdrawal slip with the grocery list. That would make
it seven days before she was found, and only three days of
unreturned calls. The remainder of our last fight calculated
from the balance of my neglect.

Flipping back to the beginning to get away from the date,
I start to notice other patterns: people to call written in blue
ink instead of black, appointments almost always checked off
in red. Running my own life as I do, I am incapable of judging

whether these are signs of a well-ordered mind and system or of a bare, stripped-down obsessiveness.

Quinn shuffles into the kitchen with bare feet and mussed hair. "I smell coffee." His cheeks look flushed, and fuller somehow, first thing in the morning. It's as though a sweetness comes to him when he sleeps and clings to him after he gets up. I love him so much in these little-boy/old-man tired moments.

I grab his arm and tug him over to me. "What do you think about these?" I ask him, tapping the daily numbers. He takes a look.

"Calories."

I blink. He's right. Boy genius. I close the agenda and zip it shut.

"I'm having a shower," I say.

"Mmm." Quinn stares at the agenda but doesn't touch it. I see him moving in the direction of the fridge before I close the bathroom door.

Under the jet of hot water, the three walls of the shower and its curtain fluttering in the steam feel like a pink-tiled time machine. So many times I've stood in this same spot, letting myself think the same things over and over until the thoughts themselves are no longer ideas but only a kind of mantra. When I was younger, I used to instruct myself to keep my eyes closed so the shampoo couldn't trickle in. Later, after Mama's accident, I brooded about how she used to stand in this shower, how she used to scrub it, how even Papa must have stood here, even though I could barely remember him. And even later, a kind of squeamish disgust, thinking of Uncle washing himself, the bodily journey of the green bar of soap. He always bought Irish Spring. Sadhana and I had a separate liquid soap we shared. Sadhana once told me, jokingly I think, that when she was trying to make herself vomit she just thought of Uncle naked. And then that, too, got added to the shower litany.

When I get out of the bathroom, Quinn is gone. There is a note on the table: *Be back later.*

FIVE

∽ WAXING AND WANING ∽

At the beginning, it was like a curtain being pulled back. The heaviness we'd taken on under Deana's supervision started to drop away from Sadhana's hips like a melting candle. Sadhana ran and ran, and every day a little bit of her disappeared. As she lost the roundness of her face, her cheekbones came into view, and they were high and regal. Her arms became delicate and birdlike. She was coming out from under the cloak of her body, and I was jealous, so jealous I could barely look at her and her new, perfect self. I wanted her to show me how.

"It takes discipline," she said. "You probably don't have it in you."

Sadhana could wear anything and be anything, the way she started looking. She plucked her eyebrows and painted her nails and on the outside started looking just like any other pretty girl. Wherever the rest of her had gone, the sad part, I didn't care. I wanted to be like her and leave everything behind.

"I guess now's not the time, anyway," she said, deliberating in front of the closet. She held up a shiny silver top and pressed her lips together. "Soon you'll be as big as a house."

Sadhana's prediction came true. My belly swelled and my hips widened. My breasts, which had always been big, became enormous. I wore looser clothes, but even my face seemed fatter. At night, I felt for my chin to make sure it was still there. And as I grew with the baby, my sister kept shrinking. Not just the flesh on her bones, which seemed to melt away, but the girl who used to laugh at my jokes, who would have fought for me, who still knew what it meant to be a friend.

I had to stop going to school because I was starting to show. That was the unofficial rule at our school, so I wasn't surprised when I was called to the principal's office, where he kept his eyes glued to my opened file and suggested I'd be happier at home, where nobody could tease me. The administration actually seemed to fear that the very sight of a pregnant girl was enough to make other girls go and get themselves into trouble. Reproduction spreading faster than meningitis. As I stood in the basement hallway disgorging the contents of my locker into a plastic bag, I told people I was switching to the arts high school. But the truth emerged before the week was out, probably through the guidance counsellor's daughter, who was in my homeroom. Sadhana said people had asked her if it was true and she had told them to screw off, which was more or less a confirmation.

The third day at home by myself, I flopped onto the couch with my science textbook and longed for a television. I slapped my belly like a drum in time to a tune in my head. "Dum de dum de dum," I sang aloud. There was nobody to hear me. I listened to the refrigerator humming and the muffled roar of buses two blocks away, and I let the textbook slip off the couch with a thud. Boredom mingled with relief.

When the phone rang, I lunged at it, even though I could almost hear my sister's voice in my head. *It isn't him.*

It was the school. Sadhana had fainted in math class.

"Fainted? Is she on her way home now?" I asked. Once I'd had a terrible stomachache, and one of the secretaries had called me a taxi.

"No." The secretary hesitated, and in the pause I realized she knew who I was and why I wasn't at school. I wondered how much our files might say about what we had been through. "We called an ambulance."

At the hospital, Uncle and I sat in a crowded hallway while an ER doctor explained anorexia.

"She's not eating?" said Uncle. He had driven us over in a state of apprehension that seemed to be giving way to anger. He had seemed reluctant to let me come along, as though he agreed with the school that I ought to be kept out of sight. "On purpose?"

"She has been fasting, and possibly purging as well."

"She said that?" I asked. I tried to remember the last time I had actually seen her eat much of anything. "She's been running a lot." I felt an urge to defend her, though I wasn't sure from what.

"She was evasive," said the doctor. He looked young, but no less authoritative for it. Uncle's indignation had driven him to his feet, but the doctor made no move to get up. "However, her body is showing clear signs of starvation."

"This is crazy," said Uncle. "She made herself sick. That's what you're telling me."

"Essentially, yes. I'm telling you she is a very sick little girl. This is a serious disease, Mr. Singh, and Sadhana has dangerously low vital signs. We're going to treat her, but your niece is not going home with you today."

As the doctor kept talking, I could see it all happening. Sadhana going up to the blackboard, her head swimming even as her legs carried her to the front of the room. The horrible chalk in her hand. The pockets of dust in the guttered shelf of the blackboard. Vision blurring, she would have stared at the quadratic equation and understood the blip of the line and how it would taper down to zero. And her collapse, her sudden crumpling, would have been so quick and silent as to seem almost like an apology.

Nobody from our high school came to visit her. In a not very inventive piece of fiction, I told anyone who called that she was in the hospital being treated for headaches. A problem in her head—the barest kind of euphemism for mental illness. I only realized this after I had told the lie to four or five people, when it was too late to take it back.

"She's become very sensitive to sound and light," I said into the phone. "She can't have any visitors."

"Don't you visit her?" That was her friend Priya.

"Yes, but I don't say anything."

Sadhana had not given approval for the story I was putting out, but she didn't seem to object either. She lay scowling in her hospital bed, when she bothered to have an expression at all, refusing to acknowledge she was even sick. She made no comment on the feeding tube that went in her nose and snaked down to her stomach. Registering displeasure seemed to require too much energy, so she had begun resorting to a kind of shorthand—a dismissive wave administered in my direction whenever I said something to annoy her—while her face carried on as placid and remote as ever.

I found I had little to say. The words that did come got choked in my throat. *Blind. Negligent.* Her beauty had become deathly, and I had not seen it until it was shown up by the tube taped to her cheek. It was as if my sister and I had both been playing the same game of pretend, caught up in the same skewed vision. *I'm a fairy princess.* As for Uncle and his failure, I felt rage. But then he could never be expected to really see either one of us.

"I suppose it would be stupid to expect people to come visit when there isn't anything wrong," said Sadhana. "Wasting money on flowers."

I didn't say anything. I was angry at Priya and Jennica, her supposed friends who had failed her in the same way I had. I hugged my round stomach in a doting way, happy I had something else to look at. To look forward to.

"Do they think I'm really sick? Like, unconscious?"

"Why on earth would they?"

"Well, when Cora Davidson was in the hospital, she was in a coma. Nobody could visit except family."

"I don't know what they think."

Sadhana took so much perverse pride in her own lying that she never stopped to consider that someone else might be untruthful. She leaned her head back against the wall and started counting the ceiling tiles aloud. She would rather do anything than her homework, which was piling up on the nightstand. Uncle had threatened to stop picking it up.

Finally she got bored and fell asleep on her side, cheek

resting on her closed fist as if about to sock herself in the jaw. She always slept that way, as though ready for battle with a pack of sudden dream assailants.

The next time I visited, Sadhana complained about how they kept the bathroom doors locked. She wasn't allowed to go to the bathroom at all after meals, not until at least an hour had elapsed. "And sometimes even longer," said Sadhana. "Some of us here on the ward have metabolisms slower than evolution."

"That's good, then." She was still being fed via a tube, but maybe tubes had scheduled mealtimes.

"No, it isn't." She was almost pouting. "Neither the metabolisms nor the bathrooms." She motioned for my purse. "I know you still carry around that blush compact of Deana's."

Mirrors were another commodity on the ward. I handed over my bag and she excavated its contents with bony-fingered precision until she extracted the compact and flipped it open. Her face had so far escaped any obvious signs, which was maybe why none of us had grasped her illness. She looked normal and pretty, if a bit angular. Based on what I'd learned about her disease, I expected to see a sign of deep dissatisfaction as she looked at herself, but instead she seemed impassive, her eyes wide, her lips slightly parted. Almost surprised. She pressed her fingers to her temple.

"Sometimes I've just got to go, you know? God. Just because someone is in the hospital, it's not like they've agreed to surrender all their rights. I'm pretty sure habeas corpus still applies." Ninth-grade law was her favourite class—probably because she loved anything that could help her sound more sophisticated than fourteen.

"That's if you're arrested."

"Unlawful detention," said Sadhana, shaking her wrist with the hospital bracelet at me. "What do you think this is?"

"Nazi Germany, obviously."

"Ha ha."

"Well."

She had another complaint, that she could always hear a laugh track playing faintly in the background whenever she tried to fall asleep. Like in a sitcom. I found this worrisome.

"It makes me feel like we're all just actors. Like someone's waiting somewhere for me to deliver my punchline."

"Have you told the doctors?"

"I'm not psychotic, Bee." She waved her arms, the worst wasted part of her, and I flinched, but she didn't notice. "It's the televisions. And the walls." She tapped one. "Paper thin. Right, Laur?"

Laurel was her roommate. I liked her. She was a deadpan brunette who described herself as a misanthrope. I had to go home to look up what it meant. Most of the time she ignored everyone unless asked a direct question. Occasionally she offered a cutting but amusing remark.

"Shut up."

Janet, one of the other girls in the hospital, had short, bleached blonde hair with dark roots. Every time I saw her, the roots got longer, until her hair was half and half, the bleached parts and dark parts. Sadhana said she spent ages doing her makeup, the black liner around her eyes and her dark red lipstick. I saw Janet outside smoking sometimes, with one of the orderlies, and she puckered her lips in what I thought was a kiss, but it was pink bubblegum ballooning out in a sticky throb. I told Sadhana I liked her hair.

"Nobody likes that," she said. "Even Janet doesn't like it. But they won't let her out to get it done."

Getting out required a mix of weight gain and emotional stability that still eluded my sister and most of her companions on the ward. She would not take food by mouth, and once I saw her flail against a nurse who was trying to replenish her feeding bag. Reason seemed to have fallen away from her, like the hair that came off her head in clumps.

The longer she was in the hospital, the more questions she came up with. She wanted to know exactly how many parts of her were unique. Only her fingerprints and her retinas? Or the backs of her hands, the infinite web of near-invisible lines on her skin that dried out like an elephant hide when she got out of the bath. Toe-prints? What was there about her, about any one of us, that was special? That could only be once and never again?

"Surely there are similar snowflakes," she said. "Similar fingerprints." She splayed her hands next to mine and we squinted together at the whorls and dashes.

Then Sadhana wanted to uncover the meaning behind the saying "the world is your oyster." She wanted to know if it meant an oyster you could eat or an oyster that would make pearls. "Principally," she said, in an imperious and ridiculous manner, "if it is a culinary or a decorative idiom."

Presumably because, if it had to do with eating, then it was a piece of advice that could have no relevance for her, but if it had to do with shoving crap into a dark place and then forgetting about it until it had turned into something better, well then, that was something worth thinking about.

"That would be your style of things, Bee," was her comment on that when I told her.

"Very funny."

I looked up the oyster thing. "It's from Shakespeare," I said.

"Typical."

"It's about pearls. Just sitting there for the taking."

"Huh."

"I guess it means that getting what you want is easier than you might think."

I went looking for Ravi. It was in September, four months after he'd left his job and Uncle had gone to his house to find him. I was huge, on my way home from a visit to the hospital to see Sadhana. She'd glared and sulked and picked a fight over apricots, which she claimed were better than plums. She was always talking about food, and she was always querulous. It was becoming usual to leave visiting hours with an aching jaw from talking too much and the disagreeable sense of having lost a battle. If I were a better sister, maybe I would have managed not to get sucked in. But I could never resist. Looking at Sadhana's ragged limbs, the tart juiciness of a waxy plum seemed worth defending. While I was pregnant, my love for them was almost pious.

On the way down to the lobby, a pregnant couple got into the elevator with me. The man had his hand on the woman's stomach, which was the same size as mine. Enormous.

"Boy or girl?" he said. It took me a minute to realize he was talking to me.

"Oh, I don't know."

"You're not going to find out?"

"No, I don't think so." The way they were looking at me, I wondered if this was even allowed, to not find out. To not even be curious.

"It's helped us figure out what to buy." The woman smiled at me. "For our boy-on-the-way."

I nodded, trying to figure out what baby boys needed that could be different from baby girls. Maybe something to do with how they peed, different diapers or something. But they were still looking at me, waiting.

"Oh, a boy," I said finally. "That's nice."

They beamed.

"Names?" said the man.

"What?" It was as though we were running lines in a script I hadn't seen before. Every time I paused, they peered at me with a curiosity verging on concern.

"Have you thought about names?"

"No. Um, how about you?"

"Matthew," said the woman. "Or Lucas."

"That's nice."

The man had moved his hand from her stomach to the crook of her arm, to her shoulder, to her hip. He was never not touching her. Then the elevator doors opened at the ground floor and they said goodbye, wishing me luck before moving as an indivisible twosome towards the parking lot. I went out the other door, to the bus stop.

It was the first of a few conversations like that, at the hospital and on the street, with different strangers, some pregnant but mostly not. Outside our apartment, I never felt a moment's reproach or judgement for being a teenage

mother-to-be, just an earnest and sometimes intrusive interest in the baby. My extra weight, I was realizing, made me
look older than I was. I had decided to start wearing an old
gold ring of Mama's on my left hand.

I sat down on the wooden bench, reading graffiti
scratched into the sidewalk by an enterprising vandal who
had gotten to it while it was still wet. *Crystal and Jon V.
FOREVER 1987.* I kicked a pebble across the declaration. There
was something about the elevator couple. Their calm, their
utter absorption in each other, in the life they were creating.
Their love.

A bus was pulling up on the other side of the street, and I
surprised myself by hurrying across the road to catch it, even
though it was headed in the opposite direction from where I
needed to go. It was going to Ravi's neighbourhood.

I sat down next to an older lady who had a kindly look
about her. She was wearing a camel-coloured hat with a clus-
ter of pink flowers, and a heavy wool jacket. She offered me
some cheese. "It's good for your teeth," she said.

I hesitated a moment, then held out my hand. She shook
out some curds into my palm.

"Thank you."

"Good girl. Big girl. Too many skinny girls having babies
these days." She nodded at a little boy across the aisle, whose
mother was scolding him for wiping his nose with the back
of his hand. "Too many allergies." The little boy stared at me,
his upper lip still shiny with snot. I looked away.

The woman pulled out a Bible from the folds of her
jacket. It was a cheap one, the kind that people give out
on the streets, but small and light and almost ideally made
for carrying in one's coat pocket. I thought about this, the

appropriateness of the edition, and clung for one moment to the idea that she was going to use it to tell me something diverting and relevant and not at all crazy. She licked her thumb and flipped open the thin blue cover. "Have you heard about Jesus Christ?"

I nodded.

"I'm going to read to you from a part about the Resurrection."

She read aloud. I tried not to listen. The other passengers were staring, and the cheese felt like putty in my mouth. I swallowed.

"This is my stop," I said, and it was.

She stopped mid-word and put the Bible down on her lap, helping me out of my seat with a violent, two-handed shove against my lower back. "Consider the name Didymus," she said as I got off the bus. "Or Thomas, if you like."

Ravi's house was on the other side of the mountain from where we lived. I'd looked up his address in Uncle's files. There were a lot more houses in his neighbourhood than there were walk-up apartments. Some people even had lawns with little fences around them.

I stood on the doorstep and rang the bell. His mother answered, then looked at me and called something over her shoulder, and his father came, too. They were both very good-looking, and his mother was wearing an emerald sari woven with golden thread.

I felt abashed. "I'm looking for Ravi." I wondered for the first time if they had lied to Uncle. "Is he here?" The thought that he could be inside, watching television or even doing his homework, sent a wave of dizziness over me, and I grabbed at the banister.

His mother just barely glanced at my stomach. His father looked up and down the street and then over his shoulder into the house behind me, as though considering asking me inside.

"Go away," said Ravi's mother.

～ço~

My sister aimed to succeed in everything she undertook, and in being sick, she surpassed everyone's expectations. Where other people would have submitted to treatment as the path of least resistance, Sadhana fought to preserve her illness with an intense resolve, as if rescuing a child from a burning building. Though at first she had gained weight, she revolted against recovery just as she was nearing ninety pounds. Talk of outpatient treatment or of going back to school to see her friends had the opposite effect to what the nurses may have intended. The disease, the refusal, was the only companion she wanted.

Later, when whatever had been animating her had carried her past beauty, past intent and the possibility of stopping of her own accord, Sadhana told me not to feel sorry. The doctors had more or less given her up, or said they had, to try and frighten us. The progress she'd made into food and formula had regressed back to the feeding tube through her nose, until digestive issues and her own temper tantrums scuttled even that means of taking in calories.

Sadhana lay in her hospital bed on a pillow of stringy hair, worrying the tape around her nutritional IV. "Worst-case scenario, I'll see Mama and Papa again."

That made me jealous, too. She was sick, dying even, but she was as calm as a news anchor the way she talked about things.

She turned her head away from me. Her arms were laid out over the sheet as though they no longer belonged to her, tubes of bone and skin flecking pale and dry over every joint. "Tell your baby about me when it's born," she said. It was a week before I was due.

"What will I say?"

"Tell him," she said, turning back to me and wincing. Her neck was frail. Her fingers reached up to touch my belly. "Tell him I was pretty cool." Then she started laughing, and I joined in, and I knew because we had been happy for a moment that she would get better.

"You're going to live forever and ever."

"Whatever you say, Bee."

The nurses let me stay over because, according to her chart, Sadhana was in critical condition. But they didn't know what I knew. I set up two chairs to face each other so I could rest my ankles, and there were plenty of blankets because the skinny girls were always cold. We pulled the curtains around our side of the room and whispered all night, until the nurses came to shush us.

"If you can't be quiet, we're going to have to separate you girls."

Sadhana held tight to my sweaty palm in the cool of her slim grip. "Don't bother," she said. "You can't."

~ QUINN ~

The birth was not traumatic. My body was already a balloon through which my spirit seemed to wander. I'd been heavy before the pregnancy and had gained fast, which only added to the gap, the drift between who I thought I was and who I looked like from the outside. My thighs that chafed together, and the heavy bosom. My belly button that had popped out like the lid of a juice container, the kind that might have been tampered with. Something that had slipped open and spoiled. My toes were strangers to me. I felt as though I had flesh blooming everywhere. I wondered if it was possible to have fat ears, the extra flesh squeezing out the sound. Or maybe I had always been a bad listener and I was getting worse. The doctors and nurses kept saying the same things over and over as if I hadn't heard, and perhaps I hadn't. *Breathe, breathe. Push, don't push.* It seemed normal, in a way, to be prodded and poked, to feel the fingers of strangers slipped inside me, like oblique messages into an insensible letterbox. To feel like a tangential participant in a project we were all grappling with: the extraction of a small life from its shell. Of a painful growth from its host.

Nobody was there with me. I had called a cab and left a note for Uncle in the bathroom, tucked under a scented candle on the back of the toilet. He'd go in there sooner or later. When the cab driver didn't want to take me, I lied and said I wasn't in labour, though it must have been obvious. He was afraid, I suppose, of a mishap in the car, or an expensive cleaning bill. I shoved my money at him before he started the meter, as I backed in behind him, determined to keep silent. A plastic bag with a few things hung from my wrist, which, as I jostled myself in, spun itself into a tourniquet bracelet that bit at my skin.

I had put on my white nylon jacket that no longer buttoned. As a pregnant girl in 1989, I had lucked out, fashion-wise. At nine months, I was only at the very limit of things I already owned. That Saturday night it was a huge pink sweater and black leggings. I was making little moans that I tried to disguise as coughs, holding my fist up to my mouth, teeth digging at the side of my finger. I was wearing earrings, too, big black plastic hoops, because that was the kind of thing I did when I was home alone for hours and hours. Got dressed up, fooled around with makeup or different outfits. Stupid.

It was late on a Saturday when I called the cab, past midnight. I'd been pacing the length of the apartment, stopping here and there to clutch at a chair, press my forehead against the edge of a bookshelf as a contraction seized me. I'd drawn a bath but couldn't manage to get in. When I stood and then crouched, I felt a throbbing zip up and down my legs, lighting them up like neon tubes, like pain as a gas, as a substance that could be breathed in, that could fill up any space. And my whole body bent and glowing with it, a sign in a dark window spelling out I REGRET THIS. I felt like something might suddenly open up where it shouldn't. At one point, I found myself on all fours under the kitchen table, huffing like a dog, grit under my palms and the certainty that we didn't sweep enough. At last, a reason to care about hard-to-reach places. Uncle was down at the shop because he liked to show the staff how to handle drunk people, and I was trying to hold out as long as I could. I knew that I didn't want to go to the hospital too early. Be checked, dismissed, and ordered back home. I couldn't afford the cab fare.

When I arrived at last, having inflicted no injury upon the taxi driver's upholstery, I was ushered through reception with some urgency, more flurry than I'd expected. I had waited long enough, not too long, but long enough for things to be coming together, or, rather, apart. I tried to say something about my sister, that Sadhana was a patient who would want to know I was there. There was some confusion, a notion that she'd brought me and then wandered off, or was possibly in the bathroom.

"We'll page her, honey," a nurse told me. "What's her name?"

"No," I said. "No, no, no, no." I wondered why I hadn't called her myself before I left.

By the time I was checked into a room and had made myself understood, a nurse had been sent up to me to explain. I squinted at her face as she spoke, let the syllables drift towards me through the huff of my own breathing. Her jaw that tapered to a sharp point, dark feathered hair. She was telling me that Sadhana was asleep and they weren't going to wake her.

"Part of her treatment program is keeping her to a schedule. Eating, sleeping at regular intervals. And emotional stability." She shrugged in her mauve scrubs that still seemed new, that seemed to take a moment to follow her shoulders down. Her eyes, though, were worn, as though at the end of a shift. With my tear-streaked face, my stomach hard as a wall, there seemed to be no question but that I was a liability.

"I'm sorry," she said, and I nodded. I didn't believe her, but it was nice of her to say it.

When Quinn was born, I was staring at a tiny scar on one of the nurses' faces. It was at the side of her lip and curved up in such a way that it looked like a lopsided grin, even as she checked me, forehead wrinkling, barking encouragement with narrowed eyes. Where it was, as a cut, it would have bled a lot, and I was seized, in those dislocating moments, not with the betrayal of my own body into pain, for I expected no less of it, but with the utter vulnerability of the face. The momentousness of a change there, whether fleeting or permanent. People read reactions there, and character. Then I thought that sometimes even the look of a smile could be enough, as it was to me then. I was riveted on her, the point on my horizon, now far, now looming close, terribly close. It was because I was hunching my upper body, throwing it forward into every push. I thought about the wooden crib that Uncle had bought and the nurse that came to see me from Sadhana's ward, and I wanted to be able to be grateful for gestures, for the seed of a feeling behind a gesture, and also for whatever it was in me that might allow me to take this comfort even in something involuntary, like the nurse's smiling scar, that could be infused with meaning. To be able to exist in surfaces. Why should I demand anything more? I did not feel that I was particularly entitled. If I held out for something wholly real, for some secure certainty of authenticity, I might spend my whole life unhappy.

It was clear to me later that these thoughts were themselves a kind of coping mechanism, as was the idea I had then that the intensity of those labouring hours had given me a new insight into life, into experience itself. Pain was no doubt a factor, as were the drugs, and the memory of both, and of my accompanying strange descent into philosophy, soon faded. For profound thoughts, even or sometimes especially when they arrive by revelation, necessarily fade, and with the passage of time seem not only to lose their urgency but, by what might be in the end a wrong-headed logic, also some of their claims to truth.

Quinn, in my arms, was small, and intent on taking all of me.

When my sister Sadhana saw my son for the first time, she scraped the side of his cheek with her bony brown finger. He opened his mouth, fists working, the folds of skin on his face and hands voluminous and soggy, like something waiting to be blown up to full size. He kicked out one of his pigeon-toed feet and it brushed at the tape holding the IV tube in place on her hand.

"What a funny little raisin," she said. She was fourteen and I was sixteen and Quinn was the first newborn baby either of us had ever seen. Up where I was, in the maternity ward, I had heard a few more, from behind the curtains the other mothers kept drawn, where other people moved and snapped pictures and brought bouquets of flowers in glass vases from the shop downstairs.

"Can I hold him, Beena?" said Sadhana, and I was touched that she had asked with such politeness.

So we called a nurse, who propped up the pillows, cranking the bed so my sister could sit up without becoming exhausted. The nurse stayed a moment, with a tight smile, to watch me place Quinn against Sadhana's chest, helping us position her scrawny arms as though we were all afraid the baby might plummet through, like a set of dropped keys slipping through a grate.

"Don't you stay too long," the nurse said, and left.

"Can I look at his you-know-what?" asked Sadhana. "I've never seen one before."

We didn't know what to do with a boy. We could scarcely remember Papa. As for Ravi, I could hardly even summon the sensation of his fierce, darting tongue, though I often tried.

When Uncle came to pick me up at the hospital, he barely looked at the baby. "So your shame has been brought into the world," he said. "Congratulations."

Yet Uncle had already bought the crib and put it at the foot of my bed in the room I shared with Sadhana. He did not complain about Quinn crying, either, for just as he had ideas about the predilections of females, he had a notion of babies, as well. They cried, and were a nuisance, but there was no sense in grumbling about it as though it might be changed. So he told me, over and over.

So one of the surprises about Quinn was Quinn, how he was very much not like a doll or even a cat, which were my two closest points of reference. The other surprise was Uncle. There was the unexpected patience, and also a dignity that he began wearing around the house as though it were his work apron, talking to me as he might to a customer: his voice quiet and even, like that of a man who visits the public library and asks another man if he has finished with the *New York Times*. He stood straighter, as he did in the store; perhaps the bitterness implied in his slump was no longer the attitude he wanted to convey. I thought it must be Quinn, the possibility he offered of a legacy, a personality not yet turned to the bad.

Quinn was a wonder, a fullness. He felt like the precipice of every emotion I'd ever fallen into. I whispered secrets to him, things about Sadhana, about his father. About how he made me angry but it wasn't his fault because he was only a baby. At first I thought he looked like his father, then I didn't. I'd been trying to picture Ravi's face for months. I talked and talked, then felt guilty for exploiting his lack of language. I got out my French textbook and whispered to him in French. It was a story about a man who worked in a bank and bought baguettes on his way home to dinner. It felt like a poor world I was offering him.

Sadhana began calling after Quinn was born and I stopped visiting every day. Something about holding the baby had triggered a change, and from talking to the nurses, I knew that she had made progress. It made it easier to stay away, even if I'd been anywhere close to figuring out how to wrangle a baby out of the house to go visit. She'd call, and sometimes it seemed like I already had the receiver to my ear before the phone rang. I'd pick it up when she was just an angry pulse coming down the line, a second before she burst into sound.

I'd barely say hello before she launched into it. It was a long, ongoing conversation we were having. There were no pleasantries. She complained about the nurses, the doctors, a therapist she was forced to talk to who had called her a liar. If we didn't answer, she left messages that were accusatory and abusive. "I'd like to know what the hell you're doing that you're too busy to pick up the goddamn phone." She'd left behind all pretence of propriety. It was as if Uncle did not even exist, or she was past all thoughts of fearing him. I made no mention of the messages when I called her back.

One Saturday when Uncle was down at the store, I answered the phone halfway through the first ring.

"When are you coming?" she asked. "It's been nearly a week."

"It's hard for me to get down there, Sadhana."

Her response was icy. "Do you even care about me getting better?"

When I did arrive, Quinn strapped tight into a second-hand car seat I had carried on the bus, I was surprised to find Sadhana sitting up in her bed, surrounded by a group of girls I recognized from our high school. She was bright-eyed, strung up with vibrancy. When she was speaking, she did not give the impression that she was someone very sick at all. I could hear the laughter of the girls all the way up the hallway. Through her absence and ordeal, she had become a kind of heroine. And it occurred to me then that Sadhana had never needed me as much as she said she did.

~੭ᒧᕢ~

Not long after, Sadhana was discharged. Perhaps seeing her friends had done her some good, because at last she opened up her mouth and took in food, and if she did not relish it, at least she did not gag and weep and act as if everyone at the hospital was intent upon her destruction.

As I gathered her things into a knapsack, the nurses on her floor tried to give me advice.

"Watch her like a hawk," said a wry one named Helen. "She's trickier than most." She and Sadhana had a sarcastic kind of rapport.

Another nurse with dark blonde curls snorted as she stripped the bed. "See you soon," she said.

Sometimes it felt like death was something we were outrunning. It was hard to keep a baby alive. It was constant attention from morning till bedtime, and then, often enough, throughout the night as well. But Quinn's life in my hands felt secure compared to my sister's. Out of the hospital, she was losing weight fast, mostly to do with Uncle's haphazard guardianship. He yelled at her more often than not when it came to food, he had no patience, and for two months it wasn't clear whether it was her condition that was persisting or whether it was only a quarrel, a standoff with Uncle, that kept her from eating properly. Or at least that was how it seemed to me then. Now I know it was more complicated, that Sadhana was at least as helpless as we were. At the time, though, I was almost as angry at her as Uncle.

"It's stupid, you being here," I said. She was back in the psych ward at the children's hospital, and it felt like her eight weeks at home had been a dream. We were in a visiting room with chairs and tables, board games stacked on low side tables. The game boxes looked battered, but I'd never seen anyone playing them. I found it hard to imagine depressive teenagers wanting to play Monopoly. At least Sadhana never would when I asked.

"Stupid," repeated Sadhana. She was wearing a hospital gown over flannel boxer shorts, a concession to the nurses, who kept nagging her to put on clothes. With her legs tucked up sideways on the chair, the gown looked like a giant bib for a very messy eater. I was relieved that her legs were hidden. Even though I was used to them, it was hard not to keep staring at their scrawniness. I had Quinn on my lap, and he grappled at my plastic necklace while Sadhana made faces at him.

"Just try," I said. "Just try getting better. Then you can come home."

"I'm not coming home," said Sadhana. "Some people don't." She was in one of those moods when baiting me seemed to be her only pleasure. It seemed churlish to tell her to stop when she had so few opportunities for fun.

"What do you mean?" I asked, though I knew what she was getting at. Before we checked her back into the hospital, she was scared, she talked about death all the time. It was only a few days after she had been admitted that she started using it against me as a kind of threat. As a boast.

She had a notebook with her, and she pulled out a sheet of foolscap with writing on it. "I've started making my will," she said. She flipped it out to face me, and I could see *The Last*

Will and Testament of Sadhana Kaur Singh written across the top in fancy lettering, embellished on either side with vine leaves, clustering and veiny.

I knew this was bad, one of the warning signs, though I thought if she really wanted to kill herself, it would be easier to do at home. Still, it was possible that someone in the ward would try and help her, sneaking or trading pills. One of the therapists had warned us of suicide pacts, weight-loss competitions, dark things that girls did together. If Sadhana made any close friends, I was supposed to be worried.

"You can have my tape collection and all my books." This was half moot, as Sadhana didn't have any books, at least not any that I didn't already regard as being held jointly — children's books that Mama had read to us, two shelves of them on the bookcase in our bedroom.

"What about your clothes?" I said, and I thought I saw her flinch before she shrugged.

"Well, I promised Marie my purple Esprit sweatshirt. The rest, I don't care."

"Who's Marie?" I asked, suspicious.

"Just a friend. Quinn can have Floopy Bear." Floopy Bear was Sadhana's mustard-coloured rag toy that Mama had sewn for her when she was a baby. It was something between a bear and a monkey, with flowered patchwork paws and ear linings, tail like a fat thumb. After fourteen years of companionship, it was threadbare, disgusting, and much beloved. It was probably even more prized than Princess Puss, my mousy cat born out of green corduroy and a blue backstitch.

"Oh, come on," I said. She always went too far, she was always too thorough.

"What?"

"Well, what about your earrings, then? The ones that used to belong to Mama's grandmother?." Silver and amber, tiny and dangling. I couldn't remember how Sadhana had secured them for herself, but I was sure it was at the end of a long conversation with Mama, after which Sadhana came straight into our room and tucked them directly into her jewellery box. There were lots of things like that, little interests and pleasures that she and Mama seemed to share. Except that I was never convinced that they really did share them, that it was ever anything but Sadhana playing, flexing her skills. Trying things on.

"The earrings." Sadhana frowned at the will. It made a snapping sound as she flicked it with her pen, and Quinn flailed a fist in its direction. She held out her pen for him to grab and his fingers curled around it. "Fine, I guess."

Sadhana folded away the will then, as a very thin girl with limp blonde hair came in and sat in a chair by the window. She had a deep hollow below her brow bone, a face more wasted than my sister's.

"Hi, Cynthia," said Sadhana, cocking her head to one side. "Hi, Cindy."

Cynthia, or Cindy, stared. "Hi," she said. She was wearing a huge wool sweater, and the front pieces of her hair were held back with pink barrettes. She was pulling her fingers with their bitten-down nails in and out of the corner of her mouth, and she seemed nervous. I didn't blame her, as Sadhana didn't sound altogether friendly.

"Cindy, this is my sister, Beena," said Sadhana. "You remember me talking about her in group." Cindy nodded, her eyes trailing over to me. Then, "Beena, this is Cindy, another Ana."

"Pardon?"

"She has anorexia."

"Oh." Cindy and I exchanged hellos, and Sadhana watched, plucking with one hand at the fraying armrest of her chair. Cindy seemed tentative but friendly in a meek way. It was hard to imagine another reason for her to come into the visiting room besides wanting to speak to my sister. The windows only looked out to the parking lot, two acres of grey asphalt bounded by grey stone walls. Even with the windows closed, the sounds of the street leaked through, shrieks of cars braking as ambulances pulled straight out into rush hour. The air conditioning, too, was chilly. In the anorexia ward, they kept it turned down because the girls got too cold.

I took the pen from Quinn, beaded with spit, and wiped it off on my denim skirt. In protest, Quinn shook his foot until one of his baby shoes fell off. Cindy leaned down to pick it up.

"Cute baby," she said to me. She fitted the shoe back on as Quinn regarded her with open-mouthed curiosity.

"Thanks."

Cindy folded herself back into her seat. She had a thick rolled-up tube of papers in her hand. She looked over them at my sister. "I wonder," she said, "how long they expect us to keep choking down this crap they're trying to pass off as food? I mean, they know we're sick, right?"

Sadhana said, "Don't make excuses for your disease." She didn't crack a smile. It wasn't clear to me whether she was serious or just poking fun at one of their therapist's usual sayings. It didn't seem to be obvious to Cindy either, who made a small sound and looked away. The papers she was clutching unfurled in her lap, flattening into a glossy pile. She was just bending her head to them when Sadhana hooted.

"Did you catch your anorexia from magazines?" she asked, snatching the small stack and holding them up to show me. *Vogue, Harper's Bazaar, Seventeen.*

"Sadhana," I said. Quinn was fussing, wriggling on my lap.

"What?" She tugged with one hand at the edges of her blue gown, pulling it taut. Her knees poked up underneath like tent poles. "I'm helping. Leila says we're supposed to call people on their shit."

"I have a feeling this isn't what she meant."

Cindy's mouth tightened as she started up. She grabbed at the magazines Sadhana was waving back and forth, just out of reach, until she finally seized them and stalked out.

I turned to my sister. "What's wrong with you?" I asked.

"It's just so boring. Wanting to look like a model."

"And you're not boring?"

"No." Sadhana clasped her hands together behind her neck with false insouciance, stretching her bony legs out over the armrest. "I'm an orphan." She had a look of mingled insolence and rage, a grim scowl topped by a defiant glare. She was waiting for me to comfort her, but just then I felt that there was no room in her for my sympathy. Or my pain. For anything that I could try to share.

I stood up. "Well, I think you are. I think all of this is beyond dull. At least, now it is." And since Quinn was hungry and working himself up to a bawl, I carried him back down the hall to Sadhana's ward and to all the other skinny girls who didn't belong to me. I knew she wouldn't follow.

On the phone with Evan, after a long, silent bus ride back home to Ottawa, I mention Quinn's extended absences in Montreal. "He said he was at the library studying for his exams, but I'm not sure I believe him."

Evan says, "Maybe he's looking for his father."

"What makes you say that?" I've avoided mentioning to Evan the fleeting sight of Ravi on television, just as I've avoided thinking about it myself.

"He's from there, right? I would, I think, if I were Quinn. If I hadn't already."

As far as I can tell, Evan's relationship with his own father is one of admiration verging on awe. His father is a dairy farmer whose father was a dairy farmer. Evan's brother is going to carry on with the farm one day, but Evan says his dad always encouraged them to pursue their own interests.

"You think Quinn's already looked?" Years ago, when we first got the internet hooked up at home, I had tried to look for Ravi online. I typed his name into a search bar on the computer, and, after half an hour of clicking, to my great relief, there had been no real leads. Dozens of hits for Ravi Patels all over North America, but none that seemed any likelier than another. There were two hundred R. Patels in Toronto and more than fifty in Montreal. I wondered then if he had gone to India. There were more than a few hundred Ravi Patels there. Thousands, or at least too many to count. Not quite

John Smith, but almost. At the time, I thought maybe he had become afraid of me, after all.

"He could have. You say he's on the computer all the time at home."

Quinn is already up and eating breakfast in the kitchen, but when I come in, he stands and starts zipping up his knapsack. He hadn't wanted to come back to Ottawa in time for school on Monday, but I'd insisted.

"Only three weeks left of high school," I'd said. "Don't you want to savour them?" He had responded with an unequivocal no but failed to offer any more objections after Uncle weighed in against him.

"Morning," I say now.

As he slings his bag over one shoulder, he makes a wordless sound in his throat that might be only the swallowing of his cereal.

"Leaving?" I ask. It's early, just after seven, but the school is already open for business. There are orchestra rehearsals, Greek lessons, free tables in the art room before classes start at eight fifteen. Not that Quinn does any of those things. I wonder if he has started smoking and gets there before the bell to hang around the side the building to share cigarettes and flirt with the smoker girls. I stare at his baggy shorts and T-shirt and try to assess whether his fashion has changed from the slightly preppy standard of his friends in the gifted class to something else. I wonder if he still even has the same friends. He hasn't mentioned a name I recognize, or any name, in months.

"Mm-hmm."

"See you later then," I call with forced cheer as he legs past me towards the front door, but it sounds less like a patient reminder of my unconditional love than a vague threat.

After Quinn is gone, Evan rings the doorbell with his nose, hands full with two large cups of milky coffee.

"I have the day off," he says. His face as he hands me the coffee reveals an agenda of enjoyment. "Let's roll."

Parking the truck at the two-thirds mark, just off Elgin Street, we launch a downtown stroll targeting the Byward Market. Evan stops at a farmer's stall for a net bag full of green apples he vows to make into a tart. Taking one out, he raises it up to the light. "It almost seems a shame to bite into it," he says. "It looks too perfect."

I pluck it from his grasp and drop it back in the bag, which he holds opens for me. "I'm more concerned about this dessert you've promised to make."

Sadhana was never happy with surfaces. If new love was a drug, then she wanted to break it down to the chemical level rather than enjoy the high. She'd prod and poke and ask impossible questions to make sure things weren't floating by on appearances. I'd seen her do it at parties and on the few double dates we endured. We'd be at a dessert place after a movie, sharing two slices of cake between the four of us, all eating with absurd parity and pace, when she'd suddenly turn to her date and ask him where he'd rank her on the beauty scale compared to everyone he'd ever kissed. She'd tried to pass the habit along to me, but I was always resistant. There was no way I was going to pose to a new boyfriend some ridiculous moral or aesthetic quandary, such as whom he'd choose to save from a fire, me or his favourite first cousin.

Walking along the canal beside Evan, I can almost hear her at my back, whispering subtle sabotage under the guise of necessary truth. *Ask him if he has a hero complex and you just seem like the closest person who needs saving. Ask him if he's had bad luck with girls his own age and he's just moving on up to the next-most-desperate age bracket.* Questions that skip the investigation and move straight to accusation, the real root at the base of all her musings.

"You're quiet," says Evan.

"That's nothing new, is it?"

"I suppose not." He reaches to clasp my hand. With the other, I point out Quinn's high school, just a dozen yards away on the other side of a bank of trees and benches.

"That building there with the silver roof. And the one beside it."

"That close? And you're risking being seen with me."

"Well, it's early yet." Just past ten, before even the most unabashed slackers would begin skipping class.

"It doesn't seem fair to keep them in on a day like this. Pure gorgeousness." And it is. Fully warm without being hot, a clarity to the morning as the sunlight skims and dazzles off the surface of the water.

"And what are we doing with the rest of our fair day? You've been alluding to big stuff."

"I was thinking of painting my bedroom," he says. "And bringing you along to help choose the colour."

"And for grunt labour?" I shift my train of thought from picnics to renovations.

"For management of operations."

"Ah. But I thought you were planning on moving out."

Evan gives me a quick look. "Do you want me to?"

"No." Although if I think about it, I really do. "Your roommates are nice."

"They are." Evan is emphatic. "Good guys, and smart. I'd go crazy if I only hung out with cops all the time."

At the hardware store, a nightmare in orange and huge, towering aisles, I follow Evan as he leads us past hulking lawnmowers and gleaming light fixtures to the paint section. Though the scale of the place is alienating, the whole store has a warm, earthy smell that makes me think of food.

"It's the sawdust," Evan says. "Though I wouldn't recommend eating it." And then the rows of paint chips are spread before us in a rainbow grid and he asks me to choose.

"What?" I look at him in surprise. "I thought I was here for consultation. As in, 'Select one of these four nearly identical shades to which I've already narrowed it down.'"

"No way. I want you to pick."

I try to picture his bedroom, the colour of the walls as they are now, and I find I can't do it with any certainty. Grey maybe, or dirty white. Or maybe a clean, gleaming white that only looks shadow-coloured in the near dark of the late evenings I've spent there, the fading light dampened by the thick cotton blanket Evan hangs as a curtain over the room's one window.

"What's wrong with the way it is now?"

"Too unintentional. I haven't changed anything."

"I think it's fine." I make a slight move towards the closest section of green samples but pull back my hand as Evan leans in. "It's fine," I say again.

"I'd like it to be better than fine. As my dad would say, it needs a sprucing." Evan plucks a handful of paint chips, mostly green, but a few in scales of yellow and rose. He waves them under my nose. "You really hate choosing, don't you?"

"All by myself, yes. Anyway, it's your room. What makes me the expert?" I realize then that he hasn't seen the surfaces inside my house yet, the walls still the same colour they were when I moved in, all tans and taupes and flat cream, the generic palette of real estate. He imagines, maybe, a coordinated design scheme, something other than the cumulative effect of years of ad hoc acquisitions and very little removal. "You think I have feminine expertise on the subject," I say, with some accusation.

"Hoped rather than thought." Evan deals out the chips along the counter of an empty cashier's booth. "I'm going to build some shelves, too. Stain them a dark chocolate. Do you like the sound of that?"

"Well, I like chocolate." It's becoming more and more apparent that Evan's redecorating project is both a confession that he's staying in his apartment and an attempt to mollify me as to his decision. "But suit yourself." I find myself feeling irritated.

As Evan ponders aloud some imagined virtues of yellow over green ("Yellow flatters your complexion and green makes me look washed out"), he makes me laugh once or twice, until finally I stab out at one of the faint green blocks. "This one, okay? This one."

"'Verdant,'" reads Evan. "A fine choice, m'lady." Then, as I cock my head sharply to the right, he says, "What?"

"I thought I heard—one sec."

Doubting my ears, I walk to the end of the aisle and look around. And there he is. Quinn stopping for a moment, then disappearing around a corner, a sandy-haired girl in glasses at his side. They have their arms full of power bars and extension cords and a few other miscellaneous items I can't identify from this distance.

I hurry back and grab at Evan's wrist, his heavy wristwatch. "How long have we been here?" It's just after eleven.

"What's the matter?"

"It's Quinn. Oh shit. Shit."

"What about Quinn? Is something the matter?" Evan has his hand on my elbow, eyes scanning mine, peace-officer mode to my hysterical woman. "Did somebody just call you?"

"No, he's here. He's *here*. What is he doing here?"

"I thought he was at school," says Evan, letting go.

"So did I. Shit." I pull Evan into the next aisle, away from the exposed area around the paint-mixing kiosk and cash register. Leaning back against the hanging rows of sponge brushes and roller refills, I try to guess which way Quinn will be heading.

Evan puts one hand in his pocket and rocks back on his heels. He has an air of forced casualness. "So are we going to go say hello?"

"No," I say. "Not you. Not like this."

Evan nods. Then he says, "But I want to see. Okay?" He doesn't wait but strikes out towards the end of the aisle when I fail to object. He peers around the corner, then, perhaps remembering that he is still a stranger to Quinn, steps right out into the aisle and examines a display of stainless steel cookware, pausing once or twice to give a long glance in both directions, as though looking for a salesperson. I can guess when Evan sees him as there is a moment where his eyes pop a little before he blinks and looks away.

"He's tall," he says, returning.

"I told you." More than a touch of pride there, even in the midst of panic. "Is he coming back this way?"

"Yeah. What do you want me to do?"

"Get the paint. I'll meet you at the truck."

Leaving Evan behind me, I walk away towards the front of the store, trying to look absorbed. But I see Quinn right away, and he spots me at almost the same instant.

"Mom," he calls out. The girl at his side slows her pace before turning and melting into the crowd of shoppers clogging the area near the cash registers.

"Quinn," I say. "What are you doing here?"

"I had a spare period before lunch."

"And this is the new teen hangout."

"Reno's all the rage, Mom."

"Quinn."

He sighs. "I came with a friend," he says, gesturing vaguely, though the girl he came with is no longer in sight. "She drove. She needed to pick up some things for her dad."

"That's a lot of power cords."

"They're having some wiring problems at their new house."

"Where is she? I'd like to meet her."

"Do you have to?" There is a pleading there, as well as a slight edge of annoyance to his question.

Behind him, I see his friend now waiting in line, and I wonder if Evan has already checked through or is still waiting for his paint to be mixed and shaken. I let out a breath. "No. No, I guess not."

"Thanks." He turns and sees her and starts moving away. "I'll see you later." Then he stops. "Wait. What are you doing here?"

"Oh. I thought we needed a flashlight. One of those hand-cranked ones. Two, actually. In case of disaster." I fold my arms, hugging them in, adding, "I haven't found them yet."

"Right. Okay, bye." He joins his friend at the farthest cash register, where I watch until they both look up, no doubt to check whether or not I've left yet. I hold up my hand for a moment and smile, while Quinn glares and the girl gives a small wave in return.

Driving back to Evan's, four litres of paint stowed in the back and two new flashlights at my feet, I wonder aloud who Quinn's friend could be. "I'm positive I've never seen her before," I say. "And Quinn went out of his way not to tell me her name."

"You remind me of my mother," says Evan, and before I can verbalize my horror, he clarifies, "I mean your shameless curiosity about your son's business." He's amused.

"You think I should leave him alone."

"Not exactly. But he's grown. He's entitled to keep his own secrets. Just as you keep yours."

When I get home, I look for Quinn, intent for a moment on telling him about Evan. Evan has volunteered to drive Sadhana's things from Montreal if I ever finish packing them, and if I take him up on his offer, it will be difficult, if not impossible, to avoid introducing him to Quinn. It will be a relief to tell him about the affair. And after all, it is not even really an affair, since Evan and I are both single, and Quinn, I decide as I unlock the door, will probably not even find it interesting. He has known me to date a few men in the past, but after the first bungled romance he witnessed, he seems to assume that a breakup is not only a likelihood but an inevitability, liable to strike before any relationship of mine can cause him much personal inconvenience. A bit insulting, from my point of view, but I can see the self-preservation at work in his belief and have no better reason to object.

I call out for him as I slam the door shut and kick off my sandals, but there is no response. *How he must hate that* — this is the thought that occurs to me in the space of silence of him not answering. His mother hallooing for him the second she walks in the door. Do I always do this? I try to remember. I hope I am not needy. Children are supposed to need their parents, not the other way around.

No sign of Quinn's knapsack, but there is a pile of mail, the tidy white envelopes of bills splayed uniformly on the counter. He's here. There is a message still flashing on the machine. When I press Play, Libby's powerful, lilting voice comes blaring out of the speaker. Someone has turned the volume all the way up, and I hasten to turn it down.

"Hi, Beena, it's me again. Just wanted to say it was nice meeting you and I'd like to do it again soon. Hope everything went okay at the apartment." In the pause, I can hear the slight squeak of the machine's worn cassette tape. "Give me a call the next time you're in town and we'll have a nice chat." She ends on a bright note, though the promise of another meeting makes me anxious, reminding me of Libby's café tears.

I press the button to delete the message. If Quinn heard her leave it, the flashing light means he didn't bother to listen twice. Even if he did, I suppose, she didn't mention anything about Sadhana.

I find him in the backyard, kneeling on the grass, surrounded by wood and scattered papers, and the full assortment of our tool collection ranged along the edge of the deck. I squeeze onto the step, planting my feet to the left of a plastic tub of nails.

"Hey, Ma." He sits back on his heels and straightens his glasses. Then he pushes some wood out from directly behind him and sits right down on the grass, stretching his legs.

"Hi," I say, pleased that I rate a break. "What's all this?"

"I'm building a dolly. Trying to build."

"What for?"

"For a friend. A friend who needs it to help film something." The girl, it has to be the girl. That business about the wiring just a lie, like my flashlights.

"I see." I look out over the assembled materials with an eye for the stated project, but it isn't clear how it's going to come together. Then I spot some red wheels poking up out of the grass. "Oh, your skateboard," I say, pointing.

"Yeah, well, I don't really use it much ever."

"You know, you weren't that bad." He gave it a try the summer he turned eleven. One weekend when she was visiting, Sadhana bought him a deck and we walked him over to the remotest parking lot we could think of so he could practice out of sight of the other kids on our street, a few of whom were already alarmingly advanced. We stood around — Sadhana chugging club soda while I sipped a milkshake — and tried not to look involved. He got to the point where he could roll along just fine, if a bit stiffly, but I never saw him try his luck against a curb.

"I sucked," he says. "But whatever."

"I love the sound of a skateboard coming down the street."

"Want to try before I sacrifice it for the dolly?"

"Thanks, but no thanks."

I leave him to it, but I pop my head out later, remembering my plan to tell him about Evan.

The hammering breaks off into swearing, a string of expletives defaming our substandard Vise-Grips.

"How's it going?"

"Can you just leave me alone for five minutes?" This rolls out on the same exasperated stream as the cursing, and I decide to ignore it.

"I could call somebody," I offer. "I know someone with a lot of tools. Better ones."

He tosses the hammer on the grass and shrugs. "Sure, if you want."

"It's someone I'd like you to meet, actually." I step out onto the deck. "Someone I've been seeing."

Quinn ducks his head and kicks at the grass in the area where the hammer landed. He waves his hand in a dismissal. "Let's do it another time then, eh?"

"Why?"

"Because, okay? Because I'm busy. I want to finish this."

"But he can help."

"Whoever he is, I don't need his help." He looks up at me when I don't respond, and says, with an adult kind of firmness that takes me aback, "Another time. I'm going over to Chris's for dinner." Chris is an old friend of his whose parents I know, though it has been a while since Quinn has mentioned him. I wonder if my son is telling me the truth.

Next I see him hauling the whole mess into the shed, which he unlocks with a key from his key ring. He seems to have permanently appropriated it from the hooks by the back door, where all the extra keys and a couple of miscellaneous padlocks are kept hanging.

"Am I too needy?" I call out.

"What?" He backs out of the shed to cock his ear.

"Am I too needy?"

"What do you want me to say?"

"Forget I asked."

He says nothing, but I can tell from his face that he is already trying.

Later, in the back of Evan's truck, the blanket is chafing.

"We've had better ideas," I say.

"What are you talking about?" says Evan. "This is the only way to judge how much room there is, by using your body as a yardstick."

"You're the yardstick," I say. My hand is below his belt.

"Hardy har har."

I push gently on his chest and he rolls off me.

We're parked in Evan's driveway, alongside the grey stucco house he shares with three university students from northern Ontario. The sun is just beginning to slip below the roof of the garage, and the shifting leaves of the maple filter the light in quicksilver flashes that run along the battered eavestroughing. The drone from the Queensway has petered out, and apart from its scattered rumblings the street is quiet.

Evan is talkative tonight. Over a supper of spaghetti and meatballs, he navigated a conversation with me and his roommates, steering it from either shore of computer gaming or the remaining available storage space in my basement, where it was likely to founder. Instead, we spoke of Freud, of composting, of the impending obsolescence of my laptop—Don gave it six months, Brett a year. Nick declared it already dead, pretending to groan as I handed it to him to look at. He said, "You know these things are supposed to be portable, right?" But there wasn't much time to linger over a discussion. In their house of four young men, supper is cutthroat, the only dinner bell the cook shouting, "Wolfpack!" in tribute to the fast ravishment to follow. As with most meals here, Evan seemed focused on civilizing the conversation while never drawing out the time spent at the table. I can tell he worries that when I see him with his roommates I will think he is too young. It used to be that every time I came over, he would say he was planning on moving out.

"So, do you think one trip will do it?"

We came out here with the camping blanket under the pretext of estimating how much of Sadhana's stuff would fit in Evan's truck. I can feel the heat of the sun-baked metal coming up through the wool.

"Hard to say. I'm not good at visualizing. How much will this baby hold?"

"A lot, I'd wager." He inches back until the top of his head is at the cab, his feet pointing to the garage. He flattens one palm and brings his arm up against the side of the truck bed, squinting. "I'd guess this was, oh, about four point five feet by six point five, with a depth of eighteen inches. Packed tight, about fifteen cubic feet of volume."

"I'm not falling for that. You knew all along."

"Could be. Would you prefer a figure in standard two-cube boxes?"

"I don't have standard boxes. I'm eclectic."

Evan eases onto his side to look at me. "So how did it go?" After a moment, when I don't answer, he says, "But all packed up, right?"

"Just about. A little bit left to do."

"That's good," says Evan, lying back down. I follow his eyes up to the sky, cobalt now, with cirrus clouds moving south.

Evan says, "I remember going with my mother to help my aunt pack up my cousin's room." Evan's cousin Lissa, I know, killed herself by drinking insecticide when they were teenagers, apparently over a guy, a shaggy-haired boy who dumped her on their three-month anniversary. It is Evan's brush with tragedy, his reference point for unassailable grief. There was a frantic drive and then a helicopter, an airlift to the nearest hospital, and he's told me that he cannot erase the image of his aunt and uncle, each holding one of Lissa's cold hands and filled with superlative and already futile hope as the paramedics kept her heart beating with epinephrine. He wasn't there, but he overheard his parents talking about it.

Now Evan's own chest rises and falls in an emptying breath. His eyes flicker shut, and when he opens them again to the growing night, I think I see a whole prairie of sky looking out of his blue eyes. The depth and solidity of winterized pain.

"This was only years later that my aunt could bring herself to touch her things," he says. "On the advice of her psychiatrist. In the end, my mom and I went over and did everything while my aunt baked peach and rhubarb pies downstairs."

"That must have been hard on you and your mother."

"It was. But it made it easier, knowing we could help like that. And some of it was nice, actually. Remembering Lissa. I'd stopped thinking about her for so long. I was in university by the time we did this." He smiles. "She was so goofy. When we were kids, we used to do musicals at Christmas, and she always tried to teach me this pretend tap dance and get furious when I couldn't figure out what the hell she was doing."

"That sounds funny."

"It was. If you ever make it to Saskatchewan, you can see the videos." He gives me a quick glance.

"I'd like that." I let my eyes close, and I can feel Evan's fingers tracing the rise and fall of my hip. "What happened to the guy?"

"What guy?"

"The guy. The guy she was in love with."

"Oh. I don't know. You mean, you wonder what effect it had on him?"

"Yeah."

"I wonder." Evan sits up and pushes himself down past the tailgate. He holds out his hand to help me out, and the cool touch of his palms on the surface of my warm skin makes me feel both steadied and fevered. "But I hope he didn't let it ruin his life."

At home, I open my bedroom window and hold my face to the screen to feel the kiss of the cool air on my cheek. But almost nothing stirs. It is a hot summer night like the ones of my childhood. It reminds me of the slowness of being young, of all the time I spent longing to be older and for the happiness that would come from being free. And later, the time I spent waiting for Ravi. The lies I told myself in the meantime.

Leaving the window open, I slip into bed with Sadhana's laptop, enter my son's name, and continue going through my sister's files. Libby and Sadhana beam out at me again from the screen as I perform a search of the hard drive. FIND: RAVI. While the computer dredges its contents in a rapid, scrolling cycle, I dial Libby's cellphone number.

Her voice is languid, as soft as tissue falling.

"Did I disturb you?" I shake my hair out of my eyes.

"Beena. You called." She sounds glad, even surprised.

"I said I would, didn't I?" Even as I utter the words, I'm certain I made no such promise. I rush on. "Actually, I have a question."

"Shoot."

"What do you know about Quebec First? Or Mouvement Québec, in French?"

"Ah." Libby lets out her breath slowly. "The province's freshly minted fascists."

"That bad?"

"Worse. And already popular. Goes to show what money and novelty will get you. Have you been to their website?"

"Not yet." I look over at Sadhana's laptop, but it is still hurdling through my last request. The fan is whirring now.

"It's depressingly flashy," says Libby. There is a creak as of worn springs, as if she is in bed, too. "If the party gets votes at the rates they're polling at, there's going to be a new player in town after the upcoming election. Or so I've heard."

"So what's their angle?"

"You mean, what are they all about?" I make a small sound of assent and Libby continues. "Well, their platform is anti-immigration, or at least half of it is. They're careful, though, to have a fair number of candidates of colour, all with acceptable Quebec pedigrees and perfect French." The volume of her voice, which has been rising over the course of her explanation, drops back down. "The other half is tax cuts for corporations and privatization of medical services."

"They're up front about this?"

"More or less. It's all doublespeak when they talk to the press, of course. But I've skimmed through their platform in the original language. The French version is a little bit more explicit."

"It's hard to believe they're so popular."

"Is it? Maybe it is." Libby sighs. "I'm surprised you haven't heard more about them. Sadie mentioned you guys used to know one of the candidates."

"She said that?"

"Your old boyfriend, wasn't it? Or hers?"

"He wasn't my boyfriend." It comes out definitive. Automatic. "Or hers."

"I'm sorry." For a moment, it sounds like tears are strangling her voice. "I didn't mean to upset you."

"I'm not upset." Her overreaction moderates my own. "I'm surprised Sadhana mentioned him to you, that's all."

"She —" Libby pauses. "Well, he just came up. Maybe you don't know he's made it a bit of a personal crusade to get a family deported that Sadhana was trying to help."

"I saw him on the news." I close my eyes for a second, remembering. Those lips, that brow. The luscious black curls. A spell when we were teenagers, the thrall of his beauty has burgeoned into a kind of glamour. A face to put on posters. "And the refugee family."

"They miss her too, you know," says Libby. "The Essaids. I went to see them and they told me."

I let my head come to rest on the pillow. "Let's get together in a few days. I'll be back in Montreal."

"I'll be waiting." Her tone is a strange mix of jokey and solemn. "We never did have our talk."

I hang up. Sadhana's computer, when I pull it towards me, is almost hot to the touch. The churning seems to be slowing, and after one long moment the search box shrinks to show the list of findings. There is just one result, in a document titled EMAIL DRAFTS, dated November eighth. I click it open.

Ravi, you might not remember me. I'm Beena's sister. You might not remember your son either, but he is an incredible young man you don't deserve to get to know. But that's what he wants. Call me tomorrow or I'll call you. And I have a feeling you really don't want me to leave a message.

SIX

⌒ YES OR NO ⌒

She was not better. For a long time she was only worse.

The third time Sadhana came home from the hospital, Uncle said, "I hope you have learned your lesson now. You had better not try anything like that again."

Sadhana overturned her bowl and fled from the table.

Uncle glared at me as Sadhana's untouched supper oozed out over the tablecloth. "If your sister dies of this, it will be her own fault." He handed me his napkin to clean it up, which was as close as he'd ever come to an apology.

After Quinn was born, I did not return to high school, finishing instead by correspondence. This suited Uncle, who viewed it as fitting that I should continue to hide myself and my shame from the world. Due to her illness, Sadhana fell behind in her studies, which added to her hopelessness. In the evenings, she babysat while I attended night classes at the university. Most nights when I got home from school, she would be writing in her diary or watching Quinn sleep, her textbooks untouched on the kitchen table.

"You're never going to graduate this way," I said.

"I'm never going to graduate anyway."

"Yes, you are. Now get cracking while I make us some supper."

It was because of Sadhana that I learned to cook. I'd more or less stopped around when Mama died, and just after that was when Sadhana started poring over cookbooks. But afterwards, when she got out of the hospital for the first time, she told me it would be easier for her to eat if she spent less time thinking about food. So I shopped and cooked and put a plate down in front of her and talked her ear off until she'd eaten enough to leave the table. I got used to the sight of her crying and chewing, silently, as I made my efforts to distract her. I tried to plan meals for when Quinn was napping so my attention wouldn't be divided. Later, Quinn and I both learned to pace our eating, chewing and swallowing with a geological slowness.

Sadhana couldn't eat if anyone was watching her, and yet someone had to be there or she wouldn't eat at all. What turned out to work best was a stream of chatter at the table. I'd save up stories from the headlines, nothing too newsy or off-putting, and begin my recitation as soon as I put the food down on the table. The three-legged dog that learned to skateboard, or the giant boa constrictor that got loose inside a mall in Toronto. It was important that the stories have a happy ending.

At some point, we turned to crossword puzzles. Uncle had left one on the table one morning, and Sadhana's gaze drifted over it as I rambled on about the world's largest ball of twine. She put down her fork and reached for a pencil, which I grabbed first.

"I'll read out the clues and fill them in," I said. And that was our new system. We didn't always have to use it, but from then on we kept a puzzle on hand, just in case.

Eventually, we moved out, leaving Uncle on his own above the bagel shop. It was the summer before I turned nineteen, and we found an apartment together downtown. It was better with just the three of us. Sadhana was still sick and spent another month in the hospital, but before Quinn's fourth birthday she had crossed the stage and accepted her high school diploma. A little too thin still, for her usual grace, and not with the classmates she'd started out with, but recovered and good-humoured and humble enough to thank those teachers, afterwards, who had offered her so much leeway and extra help. The teachers had seen things that Uncle could not; namely, that things such as leeway and extra help were sometimes necessary. For Uncle, a thing either was or it wasn't. We did not tell him about Sadhana's commencement, and he did not show up.

For Quinn's fourth birthday party, we had a cake in the shape of a school bus, which was something from his favourite TV show. Our own birthdays we acknowledged but did not always celebrate. Mama's absence was always between us. The first one we spent in our new apartment, we put Quinn to bed before getting drunk on cheap champagne that had us weeping and recriminatory before midnight. Since then, we had been careful about how fully we dared give ourselves over to the occasion.

Quinn hopped around the kitchen in his birthday fervour. "Is Uncle coming over?" Quinn had the kind of appreciation for Uncle that was made possible only by seeing him very rarely.

"No," said Sadhana.

"We'll take you to see him at the shop tomorrow."

"Can he have some cake?" Quinn must have detected some tremor of our dislike, for he always acted as Uncle's advocate in this way.

"Okay, we'll save him some." I ignored Sadhana, who scowled as she went to the fridge to take out the icing.

For birthday meals, we started with the cake and worked backwards. There was no point in risking satiation. Quinn's intensity of cake focus, after an afternoon spent observing the process, was nearly evangelical. It made me worry how many of Sadhana's food issues might inadvertently be passed along.

He endured our final preparations from where we'd banished him in front of the television, his head swivelling over to keep tabs on our progress. The apartment was small enough that the remote control for the TV could be operated from the kitchen counter. Technically, it was a bachelor, with one large central room where we had our beds in a complicated arrangement with curtain dividers, as well as a mess of oversized cushions, a kitchen table, a desk, and a giant bin that never seemed large enough to contain all of Quinn's toys.

"That's my cake," said Quinn, when he could sit no longer. He came and stood on his tiptoes by the counter. The icing Sadhana had gotten exactly right: a virulent shade of orangey yellow.

"That's right."

"Is it almost done? I think it's almost done now."

"It's done. Go sit at the table."

Quinn closed his eyes after the cake was set before him and gripped the table with both hands as he began to wish in earnest. I was anxious about having taught him something that, strictly considered, seemed like a lie.

"What are you so worried about?" Sadhana had said, when I told her of my discomfort. "He'll figure it out. Didn't you used to wish for things that could never happen?"

"I did. I wished I could fly. I wasted a lot of wishes on that."

"Wasted?" Sadhana laughed. "Now you sound like you believe in it, too."

"I just don't like lying to my kid, that's all."

The wishing had been allowed to stand, for it was hard to argue with tradition, especially when he was going to other kids' birthday parties. In this, as in so many other things, I found myself trapped by convention. I wondered where Mama had found her resolve.

When Quinn had finished deliberating and had blown out his candles and sucked the icing off each of them one by one, he praised the cake as we began serving it. "Thank you, Mommy. Thank you, Auntie S. For my cake." He gasped as we cut into it and he remembered it was chocolate.

"You're very welcome."

Sadhana kissed him on the top of his head. "We love you, Quinny-pie."

Later that night, I watched her out of the corner of my eye while we ate the lasagna together in front of a movie Quinn and I had checked out of the library. I had served her a large piece, the same size as what I was eating, and she had not protested. Quinn sat between us, and I tried to give the impression both that I was not watching her, so she would be at ease, and also that I was in fact watching, so she wouldn't try to sneak any of her food into the garbage. Sometimes I wondered what it would be like to have a meal without thinking about it. No doubt Sadhana did, too.

She was often skirting the edge of decline. A week or two or four would go by and she would have a kind of lightness that made her seem free of it, and then a bad grade on a paper or a fight with a friend would return her to the sullenness and fatalism of high school. Somewhere along the way, in spite of everything we had suffered, she had lost the ability to accept disappointment.

I watched her carefully. She pushed herself in her studies now, and she pushed herself in her dance classes, which was where she had channelled her athleticism. There was a contradiction in trying to monitor her, for the harder she strived, the more danger I felt her to be in. Sadhana's illness placed her on a teeter-totter where she was sometimes up and sometimes down, but she had not yet taken herself off the ride. I had learned enough to know that the matter of her eating, or not, was always something under consideration. Hers, and, by necessity, mine.

Most of her new friends at university didn't know. She'd shed her friends from high school and spread a story about a rare stomach disorder, an illness that could plausibly keep her out of classes for a week at a time and wreak havoc with her weight. Or so I gathered in snatches from eavesdropping on her telephone conversations. She'd been keeping her friends away from me for a few weeks, after I'd shared her secret with a man she was seeing.

He was a business major, swaggering and wry, and she was both smitten and overworked, strained by her classes and the kind of self-induced pressure-cooker of perfectionism that could precipitate a relapse. Quinn was at a sleepover, and I'd gone to the library, followed by a late movie, because Sadhana had begged for some alone time in the apartment. The business major and I ran into each other in the kitchen on a late-night snack run as he was arranging apples, grapes, and aged cheddar on a plate. He had a pair of cute, small feet, and a sweaty bare chest swirled with hair. I'd already heard the sick squeak of Mama's old box spring followed by low laughter and then moaning. And now whistling. A Johnny Cash song.

"Hullo," he'd said. "Here for a snack? Want me to leave out the cheese?"

"Just make sure she eats some." I took the block of cheddar from him without a thank-you. "And don't jerk her around. My sister doesn't need another trip to the hospital."

I left him looking puzzled, but it was only a day or two before the seed I'd planted flourished into a bitter-leaved conversation piece. And after he had a talk with my sister about it, he was gone.

~∘⊚∘~

The moment I stopped being afraid, it came back. Or it seemed that way. It had been a year of calm, a year of finding our way. We became ourselves more than we had ever been. Sadhana joined an amateur dance troupe and, with arms flung nearly as high as the spotlights, leapt jetés across a scuffed black stage in a piece called *Treeline*. From the audience, the flash of her lean brown hands looked like bats pitching in the air, and

I felt like I was part of the lonesome story she conjured from the inclinations and contortions of her own body, as though I had somehow helped nurture her bravery and expressiveness.

She started her second year of university, taking an extra course in literary theory that spawned our meandering evening conversations on deconstruction that had the extra virtue of driving Quinn to bed early. I had finished my degree and was doing a bit of freelance editing, though we were still being frugal with the payments we received from Uncle. It had taken a while, but we had found a domestic rhythm in which the mountains of laundry and dishes that had eluded us for years suddenly evened out into clear plateaus we could see our way across. We divvied up what had to get done, and we did it.

We had just finished ignoring another one of our birthdays when Sadhana declared that she was going to reorganize the shelf with all the spices. I'd grouped them according to usual culinary pairings when we moved in, but Sadhana thought we should go alphabetical. Quinn had gone to bed after his favourite canned ravioli and a chapter of Narnia. We were lingering over white wine and a late-night asparagus risotto, a small treat in silent acknowledgement of the occasion. We were still eating when she jumped to her feet.

"I've been thinking about this forever," she said, gathering up all the mismatched shakers and bottles. She took down the Mexican spices and the ones for baking, and then she was brandishing the container of hing.

"Should I put this under A for asafoetida or H for hing or M for *merde du diable*?"

"Put it at the end of the row. Otherwise it ruins the symmetry." The hing was in a Ziploc baggie wrapped inside a yellow plastic bag, which in turn was stuffed into an airtight glass Mason jar. Mama had been a firm believer in its healthful properties, and it went wonderfully with lentils, but hing was like the world's final fetid onion stagnating in a ditch, determined to leave its annihilators one last harrowing trace of its existence. It smelled, pervasively.

"Hmm. System or symmetry." Sadhana passed the jar from hand to hand as she weighed it in both senses. "Crazy to keep it, when neither of us uses it much anymore." But even as she spoke, she put it back where we had kept it since we moved in.

"Maybe we should," I said, swallowing the last bite of risotto and patting my stomach. Mama always said hing was good for staving off indigestion. I had persevered a few bites past sufficiency, but exceptions could be allowed on holidays, even unacknowledged ones. I poured myself more wine before checking to see if Sadhana's glass needed to be refilled.

Her plate, next to mine, looked full.

I forgot the wine and watched her as she bent to her task of sorting. All at once, I became suspicious. She was washing and drying the outside of each spice bottle before putting it into place. The baggy grey sweatshirt she wore after dance classes or the gym had become a kind of uniform, over a pair of loose cotton pants. Lately, I had rarely seen her wearing anything else. Her eyes were bright and large.

I stood up. "Hey," I said, moving closer to her. "Let me help you with that."

I grabbed her and felt my fingers sink into the jersey until they reached the narrow rod of her arm, slender as a hanger. With my other hand, I pulled at the bottom edge below her waist and saw the top sweatshirt layered over two more below. Her hipbone protruded from her pelvis like a door jamb, and I gasped. Her fingers scrabbled at the edge of the counter.

"Sadhana." For a moment, I felt dizzy. "No."

She pulled away and her elbow swung up like the wing of a bird trying to take flight. "God, get off!" she screamed. "Get off me!"

I clung to her. "Not again. We're not doing this again." Her arm felt fragile in my grip, and though I worried about breaking it, it only fuelled my ferocity. Because of the brittleness of her bones, she had already had to contend with a hairline fracture in her wrist.

"Are you listening, Sadhana?" I could have been shouting or whispering—it felt like there was not enough air in the room to tell. But she heard me. My lips were right next to her ear.

"Tell me," I said.

She fainted.

She spent two nights in the hospital with a nutritional IV, but we decided to stick to outpatient treatment. She didn't want to lose the semester, even though it was her rabidness over her classes that had probably caused the crisis in the first place. She bargained her way into it by pledging utter commitment to getting better and absolute compliance with all my rules: high-calorie meals at the table under my watch, twice-a-day calls from the payphone on campus, no more than two dance classes a week. I had a little more time on my hands since Quinn had started kindergarten—more even than I would have liked, because everything that there was, every new surplus of time and effort, was turned only to my sister. All my spare solicitousness and every extra hour of listening ears.

Mostly, I agreed with her that it would be better for Quinn if she stayed home, as I dreaded the thought of taking him to the hospital to see her.

Of all things, it was the referendum on Quebec separation that pulled her out of the slump, like a bright lure dangled into placid waters. It caught all of us in the mouth, and none of us could stop yammering. Yes or no, *oui ou non*, or as on the billboards, *OUI* or *NON*. There was the currency issue, the question of the Mohawk lands. There was the press release to recruit Quebec soldiers for the army of their new homeland-to-be. There was nobody without an opinion, and for Sadhana, stuck in the new rut of only her and her disease, it was the perfect thing to help hoist her out. It was French or English, in or out, and even having no allegiance except to the great ideal of coexistence became hard with all the speeches and promises flying back and forth.

The thing with the referendum was that it was impossible not to care. Between our neighbours down the hall who glued a petition to their door (for what, exactly, we never could determine, but we knew it was something to do with Anglo rights after we saw our francophone building manager mocking them for their supposed oppression) and the blue and white flags draping the balconies of the building across the street, it was hard to stop thinking about it.

Not that Sadhana wanted to, anyway. "If Mama were alive," she said, "she'd support separation." Whenever I heard the word *separation*, I pictured the whole province cut adrift, floating off somewhere north to Labrador, the island of Montreal left on one long tether as a compromise for the city folk who hadn't wanted to leave. It made me panicky, because I wasn't a strong swimmer.

"Like you?" I couldn't quite keep the derision from my voice. My sister, the separatist.

"Yes, like me." Sadhana was ensconced in the papasan chair where she'd taken to sleeping among a complicated arrangement of cushions. When she got that thin, it was almost impossible for her to lie down comfortably with her own bones.

"Doubtful," I said. Mama was all for diversity, for inclusion. She used to say that every different language in Montreal was like tuning your brain to a different channel. The full cable package. It was a strange comparison, considering she'd never owned a television. "Mama hated all that *pure laine* stuff. You know that. And she loved Canada. All of it. French and English both."

Sadhana pursed her lips, an arrogant kind of expression, I thought, for someone who could barely hold up her own head. She looked older when she got that skinny, her hair sparser and duller, and it was hard not to defer to her when she had both the look and the grit of an old woman. "It's a whole different issue," she said. "It's self-determination. You remember how she supported the Basques."

"That was only because of that Basque mail carrier." A chatty moustachioed fellow who used to come up for Mama's mint tea, he was much beloved for bringing us fruit chews and cancelled postage stamps.

"No," said Sadhana. "It was the whole principle of the thing. Just think about it." She was in good spirits then, fuelled entirely by her perception of herself as inhabiting a moral high ground already sanctioned by our dead mother. She'd even gone back to working on a sweater she'd started knitting in high school during her first stay in the hospital, a project we used to joke was so tedious that she started getting well just so she wouldn't need to finish.

I was the one who realized we'd actually lived through the last referendum, when Mama was still alive. Deciding we needed to take a less speculative approach to current events than using bits of news overheard in the elevator as the launching point for hour-long quarrels, I'd brought up a day-old newspaper left in the lobby by one of our neighbours. Shoving aside a pile of Quinn's picture books from the library, I spread out the paper on the table with a great deal of crinkling importance and had just started reading when I spotted a sidebar with a mini history lesson.

"The last referendum was in 1980," I said, blinking with surprise, calculating. We would have been seven and five. Sadhana paused mid-stitch, mouth falling open. "We should be able to remember it."

But we didn't. To her credit, however much she wanted to retain the idea of Mama's support for separatism, Sadhana didn't bother fabricating a sudden memory. But the fact that we had no actual recollection of Mama's allegiances didn't stop us from fiercely debating them. Neither of us admitted aloud that our inability to remember Mama's position meant she had probably stayed well out of it.

"Did she bake a cake with a maple leaf on it that one time?" I asked, closing my eyes to try to remember. "I can picture something red and white."

Sadhana smirked. "I think that was supposed to be Strawberry Shortcake."

So Sadhana knitted and argued and got more cheerful every day. Then we disagreed again, as we watched the poll numbers going up for the separatists, and Sadhana started eating breakfast and the sweater had a full sleeve and even a cuff. And then we argued more, and she was eating twice a day and she was so merry and almost normal-looking that she rolled the one-armed sweater around both needles and the ball of yarn and put it back in its grocery bag in the closet. Neither of us had managed to produce a single definitive memory of Mama's allegiance. We were at a stalemate until it occurred to me that we could simply ask someone.

"Why don't we call one of her friends?" I said. We'd let Mama's friends slip away, all the ladies who used to look in on us. Deana, Sylvia, an older lady named Elise, and the one who used to bake us pineapple upside-down cake.

Sadhana shrugged. "You feel like looking them up?" She meant tracking them down, since in most cases we didn't know their last names. We'd have to try and feel our way to where they used to live. Ringing doorbells. We decided to forget it.

The day of the *"Non"* rally, the big demonstration staged as a love letter to keep Quebec in Canada, I dressed in my federalist best: jeans and a white shirt, topped with a khaki sunhat emblazoned with an embroidered red maple leaf. I hoped the message for unity was clear, but Sadhana, ever the mind/body dualist, thought the hat implied a kind of top-down dictatorship. At the last minute, we both changed into white dresses, the way Mama used to clothe us before we were old enough to start objecting.

We walked downtown together through a sea of blue and red. There was a kind of shared expression I kept catching on people's faces, people on both sides of the cause, of a mingled sense of purpose and exhilaration. On René Lévesque

Boulevard, the crowd was dense and we had to squeeze and wriggle our way through, murmuring our thanks and good-will to the people who let us move ahead. We saw a bunch of high school students carrying hybrid Canadian flags, with bands of blue on the inner edges of the red fields. As we got closer to the square, we passed a row of unfamiliar-looking red and white city buses, dozens and dozens of them, with Ontario licence plates. "Ottawa," Sadhana guessed.

My sister had tears on her face, which shocked me. "This is really something," she said.

By the time the ballots were counted, and Quebec had voted to stay in Canada by the slimmest of possible margins, Sadhana was out of danger.

◦ QUESTIONS ◦

It was my idea to have a talk with Quinn about his grandmother. It was the anniversary of the day she'd died, and I
was sick of the reefs these charted dates kept throwing into
our course as we tried to navigate the basic waters of staying
alive, of staying happy. I was going through a strange spell of
reading about mysticism and it made me feel closer to Mama,
as though dates and blood and ritual were things that mattered. I had an underlined copy of Rumi and a box of incense
and a new-found sense of wonder at the world that I thought
might be something like the way Mama used to feel all the
time. Sadhana was dubious but had agreed anyway, if only
because she didn't want to be left out.

Quinn had become very interested in our family since
he'd started the first grade. He was puzzled as to why his classmates had relatives like grapes on a vine, fat bunches of them,
the connections spreading and spilling out in all directions. A
girl named Penny had told the class that she could trace her
family back to Henry VIII. Another girl, Violet, was descended
from Huguenots. Sadhana and I were helpless to offer anything

in response to this superfluity of hereditary data. Quinn knew there were reasons why he didn't have more family members around, but he was frustrated by the gaps in our knowledge. He was always wanting more, more, more.

We had a summit meeting ahead of time, at the grocery store. "We'll tell him about Mama," I said. "Everything we remember and everything she told us about her parents."

Sadhana scooped up two handfuls of oranges as I pushed the cart ahead to the cereal aisle. "What about Papa?"

"Him, too."

"And Ravi?"

"When he's older."

Sadhana tidied up the living room, putting away the new yarn and knitting needles she'd brought home the day before. Skeins of wool in emerald, raspberry, goldenrod. She told me she'd joined a knitting circle.

"Do they know you've been knitting the same sweater for five years?"

Sadhana laughed. "They don't. But I'm going to start something new." Then she pulled out the photo albums, the Bhagavad-Gita, and a recipe for cheddar cornmeal biscuits, a treat Mama used to make—batches of soft yellow batter cut and baked into stars. "I don't want to cry my head off," she said. "Okay?"

I agreed. Every time I cried in front of Quinn, I felt like the goalie on a losing team, letting in points and sinking the game as my teammate watched. I wanted to be like my own mother, who never wavered in front of us. Before Quinn turned three, I'd comforted myself with the thought that he wouldn't remember. Now my recourse was to imagine that eventually every breakdown would start to meld together into a single memory.

We gathered in the living room, a Karen Dalton record on the old hi-fi, and sat Quinn between us as we showed him photographs of his grandmother. He'd seen a few framed ones that we kept out, and he likely thought of her, if he thought of her at all, as in those same few images, a woman who was only ever petting a goat or standing beside a giant redwood tree or waving from the end of a dock, with a squinty smile and the wind blowing her red hair like a flag over the water. I think that calcification had happened to me and Sadhana, too, because the albums hit us like a revelation. We were almost beside ourselves.

"Oh my gosh, look at her dress," said Sadhana. It was Mama as a girl in Ireland, in a dark, lace-collared dress, like a porcelain doll. She was posed on cobblestones in front of a Victorian house with ornamented eaves.

"That looks like a normal dress," said Quinn.

"It is," agreed Sadhana. "Just not for her."

There were other photographs that amazed us, mostly Mama's teenage sojourn back to Florida, her birthplace. There were pictures of alligators and cranes, of Mama grinning against backdrops of swamps and orange groves, and beaches stretched against turquoise strips of ocean. Then one from San Francisco, with her arm wrapped around the waist of another young woman, both of them in white summer dresses, and another showing a group of about twenty long-haired men and women in tree pose, their hands pressed together against their chests as though in prayer, a few leaning slightly as they tried to balance on one leg.

Mama was standing the straightest and was the only one laughing.

The last time we'd looked at these photos together, Mama had been showing them to us. We hadn't touched them since her death, afraid, maybe, of the kind of anguish they'd set off. A crisis spoiling our prolonged, sedate misery.

Quinn had to tug at the albums to get a proper view, so absorbed were we in looking and looking. Both Sadhana and I had lapsed in our explanatory narration; we were now speaking only to each other.

Then Quinn spoke up. "Are there any pictures of my father?"

I froze. "No," I said at last. I felt caught off-guard. "No, there absolutely are not."

"Oh," said Quinn. "Okay."

"Beena," said Sadhana. Her voice was gentle. Abnormal. "Maybe we should —"

"No," I said, though I did not know what she was about to say. "No." We were already at the last page of the album. "That's that." I closed it and got up to put it away. When I returned, Sadhana was watching Quinn.

"It's okay," said Quinn. "Don't worry. Are you sad?" He patted her on the back. Both of us would rub the small of his back when he got worried about things.

"A little bit." Her life, and mine, just one long mourning period. "But no, not really. I'm okay, baby."

"Promise not to be sad anymore?" said Quinn.

My sister and I looked at each other. "It's time for bed," said Sadhana.

That first time Quinn asked about his father, I had the unreasonable sensation of having been a failure. I confided this to Sadhana after Quinn was asleep, and she told me I was being ridiculous.

"It's not because you're not good enough. It's a natural thing for him to wonder about."

I supposed she was right. Quinn was six years old and in the first grade. If anything, it was surprising that he hadn't asked earlier.

The next morning, I discovered Sadhana and I had different tactics when it came to talking to Quinn about Ravi. I sat him down with a bowl of cereal and told him that his father had been very young, too young to be blamed for his actions.

"He panicked and ran away," I told Quinn. I focused on the corn flakes, softening in their sea of milk. "He probably regrets losing us." I sometimes believed that. I pictured Ravi, whenever I allowed myself to think of him, as trapped in an arranged marriage in which he was fond of a wife who secretly despised him.

Quinn blinked. The morning light bounced off his glasses. "Then why hasn't he tried to find us?"

From behind us in the kitchen, Sadhana said, "Because he's a shirking piece of crap who's too afraid to face up to his responsibilities." She turned on the blender and stared Quinn down as if daring him to cry.

"Okay," he said, nodding. But he was quiet on the walk to school, and as soon as we kissed him goodbye at the gate, Sadhana began defending herself.

"There's no point in coddling him," she said, as we turned back down our street. "Better to know the truth than to have your illusions shattered later. Some people are bad."

I let her words echo in my head and waited for them to land on something. "It's not that simple."

"Okay, how about this, then?" Sadhana paused to let a truck pass. "Some people aren't worth knowing."

Not being sure enough myself of anything to do with Ravi, I had a hard time when Quinn pumped me for details. He started asking again the following year, one evening while Sadhana was at her knitting circle. There was so little I remembered. I told him the basics about the romance that had blossomed outside the bagel shop. Though I did embellish ever so slightly, just enough so that I could use a word like *romance* at all. For some reason, it was easier to talk about while Sadhana wasn't around.

"He played hockey. He liked salt-and-vinegar-flavoured popcorn," I offered, remembering our one excursion to the movies and how Ravi had pulled a seasoning shaker out of his bag, wielding it with liberality. "And his father was a doctor." Ravi had spoken once or twice about his parents' anticipation that he would go to medical school and how he was already steeling himself against their disappointment.

"My father works like a dog," he'd said. "For me, business school, then management. One day I'll be a CEO. Either that or prime minister." I didn't know what a CEO was, but I didn't want to ask. I had a hard time picturing Ravi as a manager. He was my uncle's worst employee.

"Well," I said to Quinn, who was by then sitting on the footstool with as much straight-backed attention as a dog waiting for a treat. "He wanted to be a businessman. Or a politician."

"Okay. What else?"

"What can I say? We talked about the Pixies more than we did about the future."

"What else?"

I thought hard.

"He could blow smoke rings. And whistle through his fingers. And he didn't usually show his teeth when he smiled."

"What else?" Quinn's dark amber eyes were relentless behind his frames.

There wasn't much else. He wore white briefs with a red stripe on the band. The treads of his shoes had a pattern of swirls stamped into the rubber. He had a canvas bag he'd bought at an army surplus store. There was a trace of a cowlick on the crown of his head. Almost everything I had was a clue I could skim off the surface.

"That's it."

"Did you love each other?"

I decided to be truthful. "No. Not yet. We were just starting to get to know one another."

But as I lay in bed that night, I wondered. What had happened to the young man I had expended so much energy trying not to think about? He had been so cool, oh so cool, and so afraid. So irresolute. His large, curling lips and the languid way his bottom jaw would shift to the side in scorn. His parents, too, had been only too willing to allow him to keep shirking his duty, at least as far as I knew. They had never contacted Uncle, and we had never pressed them, either. But I remembered their dignity, their rigidity, that day on their doorstep, and I did not think they would have let him go so easily. He could have run off, and maybe he really did. But he would have come back.

The apartment seemed to hum, then pulse around me as I blinked in the darkness and struggled to follow the thought through to its end. Rolling over on my left side, I let the rush of my anxiety flow out until I could detect what felt like a conclusion circling, then knocking up against the side of a drain. Too consequential to slip through. Ravi was not gone, not vanished forever, as I'd begun to hope. He was probably even in Montreal.

∽ WATCHING ⌒

The next morning I stood on a St. Catherine Street corner, my heart racing as I dropped a quarter in the box and dialled the number I'd looked up at the library. There was still a listing for a P. Patel at his parents' address. But none for an R. Patel.

"Hello," I said, when someone answered. I toed a yellow McDonald's hamburger wrapper with my sneaker and watched it catch in the breeze. "I'm hoping you can help me." I found myself affecting an accent, something warmer and twangier than my real voice. "I'm trying to get in touch with Ravi. We went to high school together, and I'm in town for the weekend, hoping to get the whole gang together." I paused, and in the silence, ran on: "This isn't by any chance still his parents' house, is it? It's the number I have from all those years ago." Not the best story, but not the worst. If his parents really were afraid of me or of Quinn, they would have moved or taken themselves out of the book.

"Who's this, please?" This woman did not sound as hard as the one in my memory.

"It's Sarah. I don't know if you'd remember me." I stared

at the hard plastic casing of the payphone, the bright blue lettering of the company. BELL. "Sarah Bell."

"Ah, I'm not sure, dear. Do you have a pen?"

"Yes, I do." She dictated a Montreal number I could tell she knew by heart, and I took it down, double-tracing the digits with my pen.

"Thanks very much." I felt almost buoyant as this fake Sarah, who I was suddenly sure had gone on to do a degree in oceanography or social work or human ecology. She might even have joined a sorority. Pleasantries would be second nature to her. "What is Ravi up to these days?"

"Oh, he keeps busy. Very busy. He might not have time to come to your little gathering, though I'm sure he'll do his best. He's always helping out with a campaign, you know, getting all the experience he can." I heard a clinking sound, like a spoon in a teacup. "We still tell him he might just be prime minister one day." She laughed a little, but the pride in her voice was unmistakable.

The allusion to Ravi's ambition gave me a funny feeling. "That's the way to do it then, I guess." I could feel the fictitious Sarah ebbing away. "Thanks, Mrs. Patel. All the best now."

I walked home with a new wariness of the strangers on the street. Lots of people came downtown. The whole city passed through at one point or another. Scanning the faces of everyone I passed, I felt a keen desire to get away—even as I knew that from then on I would be watching for him, for this one person I wanted so badly to be gone.

Later that week I went to a phone booth and dialled the number his mother had given me. I listened to his voice on the answering machine, discomfited that he was in the city but relieved that there had been no change—that I knew exactly where he was to be found. Unlike his mother's voice, I recognized Ravi's, yet it still surprised me. Its slow syllables and deep baritone.

I returned home to learn that our next-door neighbours on either side of the hallway had been broken into. It was an affordable building, but almost anyone had things that could be stolen. It was drug addicts looking to make some quick cash, or so we speculated with our agitated neighbours, who stood gesticulating in the drab hallway on a Friday evening. The door frames had been split around the latch with a hatchet. Our apartment had escaped unscathed. We examined our lock, which was the same as all the others. It did not even appear to have been tampered with.

"They ran out of time," I said. Who could guess why the robbers hadn't conducted their business in an orderly fashion, one, two, three in a row?

"Maybe our luck has changed," said Sadhana. She touched our doorknob as though the brass had some fortunate sheen. Our neighbours stepped around us to commiserate, and as we unlocked our own apartment, I felt a pang for the suddenness of their violation. But, between us, my sister and I had already squandered so much feeling; we could not think about them again once the door had swung shut.

Mostly what had been stolen were TVs, and we probably had the newest television of them all, small as it was. We felt guilty before we bought it, because of Mama, but afterwards we were surprised by how quickly the feeling went away. I patted the flat grey plastic of its top, its rounded back. "I guess the old girl will be sticking around a while longer."

"Good," said Quinn. He seemed to notice my glance turn to a stare. "What, Mommy?"

"Nothing." I was seeing his full lips, the shape of them. It was too soon to say whose lips they resembled. But I was afraid of spotting reminders in him, as though likeness itself might be a bond forging before my eyes.

While I was boiling water for pasta, Sadhana said she was going out. I could see her yarn and needles poking out of her shoulder bag on the table.

"Knitting circle? What about supper?"

"There'll be food there. Really." Sadhana buttoned up her coat. "I promise."

I watched the pot and could feel the evening stretching out ahead, flat and dull as a toothless saw. "Why are you so into knitting now, anyway?"

"It's fun, making stuff. Going out. Having friends." She smiled at me as she picked up her bag. "You should try it."

That night after supper, once Quinn was asleep, I turned on the television and watched a program about missing children. The next day, while Quinn and Sadhana were at school, I turned it on again. It filled up the place wonderfully. I watched a game show and a cooking show. I watched a talk show with a family of brothers who had traded wives. I almost turned it off after that, but the news was coming on at noon and I waited to see the headlines, then the weather. I left it on while I made myself some lunch. Then there was a stretch where the only thing on was soap operas, so I turned it off while I went out to get groceries. When I came home and started cooking, another talk show was on. This time it was fathers who thought their teenaged daughters dressed too sexily.

The following day I turned it on again after I was alone, and every day after that for the rest of the week. It helped to keep from thinking about Ravi, doing whatever it was he did on the other side of the city. Sometimes I sat and watched, and sometimes I had it on in the background while I did other things. I had a bit of freelance work coming in, mostly editing high school textbooks, something a former professor had hooked me up with. Sadhana was in her last term before she, too, would graduate.

When Sadhana was home, I turned off the television and watched her instead. The incident in her second year of university had impressed upon me the need to remain vigilant, to hold on to my suspicion even in the face of all assurances. She wore her hair long, and it was darker and straighter than mine. That spring, she was wearing more eye makeup, two or three blended shades of shadow over her lids and brow bone, and clothes that left less to the imagination than the year before, though she still tended to cover her arms. She had expanded her focus, it seemed, from dance to drama, as well. She spent a few nights a week rehearsing for a play at the end of the semester, but she seemed happy and hungry, from what I could see.

But whatever I could see, there was only that. It was just one sense, one kind of knowing, and it left a good deal out. Maybe even most things. It made me anxious.

I watched Quinn, too. He was a happy kid. He spent time reading or drawing comics, and he had plenty of friends at school, though we tried, given the smallness of our apartment, to avoid having any of them over. In spite of his glasses, Quinn seemed less than other children to suffer from the bumps and scrapes that were the usual result of little kids putting themselves into the world. Sadhana claimed he had inherited her own coordination and agility. At the park, she cheered him across the jungle gym, as I stood ready to run in with soothing kisses that were rarely required.

He grew. He was growing all the time, though it was almost impossible to see. The constant rounding and lengthening of his face that I'd noticed when he was a baby, as he went in and out of growth spurts, was a process that had not stopped, only slowed down. Though I hadn't traced it happening, he'd been growing taller and stronger, increment by increment. He must have been, in order to have become the little boy who was my son, who ran and caught balls and would hurry over to pet strange dogs in the park. Who was six and then seven and then eight.

It was this realization about Quinn that made me wonder whether all the watching of my sister was not making it harder for me to see her, after all—as any shift, minutely observed, becomes imperceptible. You needed fresh eyes to see clearly. And mine were as worn out as our foggy old kaleidoscope, with that split piece of glass I could hear sliding back and forth inside.

Sometimes I watched Sadhana scouring the Dutch oven or peeling carrots with a knife, and I was not at all convinced that the anger she'd harboured when we were teenagers had gone away. She had a sharpness to her, not only her quick way of thinking and the straight angles of her body, but an edge to her opinions that meant you were more likely than not to find yourself cut down or sliced open or otherwise dismissed. She had the kind of mind that could take pleasure in its own severity. She was the very best companion for a movie you were already inclined to hate. Because it was so rarely bestowed, her favour was sought and valued by those who knew how discriminating she could be. And her forgiveness, whether of me or of herself, seemed to come at a premium.

I sat at the kitchen table over the prop of a day-old newspaper, pretending not to watch Sadhana as she scrounged around for lunch between class and rehearsal. Our apartment was just around the corner from campus. She was eating an apple, and it was a twenty-minute affair. She had woken up late that morning and had left the apartment without eating breakfast. And now, as always, I was watching her.

"Don't you have an appointment at Quinn's school?" she said. She was rotating the core of apple as she gnawed it down in a showy kind of consumption. But only an amateur would be taken in by an apple.

"The parent-teacher meetings don't start for another hour and a half."

She took a sandwich bag of cut-up celery out of the fridge and ate that, her manner seeming to veer between teasing and annoyance as I held fast at the table. Then she took a single piece of bread and made a toasted peanut-butter-and-jam sandwich. One tablespoon of natural peanut butter and one of raspberry jam. She poured a glass of milk and gulped it down.

She went into the bathroom and I heard the water running but no sound of the toilet flushing. When she came out, she heated up some leftover lentil soup.

"Is this fun for you?" she asked. She was half laughing, but her eyes flashed as she got up to rinse her bowl and toss her crusts into the garbage.

"That seemed like a good lunch."

"Yeah, well, you'd better leave soon if you don't want to be late." She sat down to lace her sneakers and I knew she would be stopping by the gym.

"I will." I waited until she had rolled her eyes at me and closed the door behind her before I got up from the table. There was a gnawing in my stomach, but I could no longer tell if it was hunger or worry. I double-checked the kitchen garbage and the one in the bathroom, but there were just the usual coffee grinds and wadded-up tissues. I returned to the kitchen, where I washed the dishes and swept the floor.

My own lunch I prepared with weariness, and I ate it without pleasure.

She came home late. I woke up to the sound of a coat rack falling over. It was three in the morning. I slipped out from under the covers to go check on Quinn, who was fast asleep in the moonlight behind his Spider-Man–patterned curtain. Sadhana was moving through the apartment in the dark. I heard keys tossed on the table, followed by the drop and clatter of one shoe, then the other. She closed herself in the bathroom, and I heard retching. I followed her in. The bathroom did not have a lock because I had removed it. She was sprawled on the bathmat.

"It's not what you think," she said. Her forehead was on her wrist, which was resting on the edge of the toilet bowl. "I had too much to drink. Me and my knitting ladies."

"You were out with your knitting circle?" I hadn't pictured her famous knitters as partiers.

"They're amazing, you know." She half raised her head. "They're really, totally radical. We've got some amazing plans." Dropping her head, she murmured, "You wouldn't believe."

"You can't do this," I said. The toilet was full of vomit and I flushed it.

"I'm twenty-three. I'm supposed to go out and have fun."

"Not like this you're not." It might start out with too much tequila, but it would turn into her old calculations. How much her body could bear to lose, which was always less than she was willing to part with. And then it would be every night.

"I'm telling you it's not the same thing." Her head ducked over the bowl as she shuddered with another bout of retching. Nothing came up except for water and bile.

I turned away. "It looks the same. It ends the same. From where I'm sitting."

Sadhana wiped her mouth with a square of toilet paper. "That's just because subtleties elude you."

"That's not true." I counted six strands of hair stuck with sweat to her temple, and the row of sterling rings on her slim fingers as they splayed on the floor. "That's not true at all."

"Yes, it is. You're like a hammer the way you come down, Bee." She seemed to be concentrating hard to get her words out. "It isn't always about whatever you think it is, okay? Sometimes it's just whatever, it's nothing." Sadhana lifted her head and held it in her hands before opening her eyes to meet my gaze. "It's just me being me. This is normal. There are twenty-three-year-olds vomiting into toilets at three in the morning all over the country."

"But they're not you."

"Lucky for them. You make me feel like a freak."

As her stomach heaved again, I turned on the tap. The choked, throaty sound of retching made me queasy. "I'm sorry, but that's what it takes." I took a glass from the counter and placed it under the water until it was two-thirds full. Then I put the glass of water next to her on the floor. "If you want to do me a favour and actually become invested in your own life, that would be great."

"At least I have a life." She spoke this into the toilet bowl. It irked me that she did not mean gratitude for the fact that she had not yet died, though she had come close. She meant, of course, that at least she lived for herself and not as a sorry extension of the lives of others. I waited for her to say something else, but there was only the dripping of the tap that had needed to be fixed since we moved in. My sister's eyes were closed.

I heard Quinn stirring, so I closed the door and left her to it.

⤳ CASTING OFF ⤳

The next morning Sadhana was cold to me. She declined to get up to join me in walking Quinn to school, and when I returned, she was still in bed, reading a magazine.

"Hungover?" I asked. There was real sympathy in my voice, or so I thought.

"Not at all." She winced as she spoke and I knew she was lying. "Like you care."

"Don't be absurd," I said. "I care more than anyone."

She flipped a page. "Well, consider this an invitation to stop."

I ignored her. "Are you hungry? We could go out for a greasy breakfast."

"Beena." My name came out heavy like an oath. She stopped to give me a cold look. "Obviously, I am *not fucking hungry*." The magazine landed with a flap at the foot of the bed, though she'd probably tried to throw it further. "Just leave me the hell alone."

I went to see Uncle, not so much for consultation as to see how he could help. Whether out of pride or complacency, Sadhana and I had never pushed the boundaries of the economy that had been set down for us. We did not really know how things stood financially. What he had given us when we left as teenagers might have been calculated to call us back, eventually, to where he thought we belonged. In spite of our mutual enmity, I knew that Uncle loved and missed my son and wished for his return. I touched the buzzer and with it the thought that we might even have been entitled to reclaim the apartment where we'd grown up, once we were old enough to take possession of it. Though it was a place of horror as well as happiness: leaving it had always felt easier and right. It had been five years since we'd moved out. It was astounding how little else in our lives had changed.

When there was no answer from the apartment, I went down to the store. The fire heat of the ovens permeated it to the front door, which was propped open. There was the usual crush of customers, and rather than pushing to the front, I let myself be carried along in the lineup between the regulars and the tourists, whom I judged by language and accent and how long they appeared to study the placard above the cash register listing prices and flavours.

"*Une douzaine de sésame.*"

"Six blueberry, six multigrain, six garlic and onion, and, well, what else do you recommend?"

Over the heads of the people in front of me, I heard a woman's voice answering and was surprised. There had never been a woman working at the shop in the whole time our family had owned it. Good for Uncle.

As I moved further inside, I could see condensation on the glass of the fridges lining the right-hand wall. Uncle stocked lox, cream cheese, orange juice, and, in perpetuity since the store's original owners, gooseberry jam.

When I got up to the front, I half expected to see Travis or Carlos, but there were no employees I recognized. Behind the cashier, a lean young man with a serious face used flat planks the length and width of two hockey sticks to lever circles of dough in and out of the oven. Another man, with his long hair in a net, cut slices from a huge mass of dough rolled into a cylinder. Two teenaged boys fashioned them into the bagel rings to be fired.

I asked the woman if the manager was in. "Harinder Singh. Can I see him, please?"

"Yeah, okay." The woman paused with her hand on the till. She had cropped dark hair and a nametag that read JESSIE. Nametags were an innovation since my last visit. "Is there a problem?"

"He's my uncle."

She turned to the bagel boys working behind her. "Call the boss man."

When Uncle came, he lifted up the hinged part of the counter to let me pass into the shop's kitchen. I took off my jacket and followed him back past the stainless steel counters and bags of flour and sesame seeds to the office door. I avoided looking at any of the employees as we passed.

Uncle went in ahead of me. There were more filing cabinets than I remembered. "Come in," he said, which reminded me that it was his office, and had been for twenty years, even though I still thought of it as belonging to my father.

"Thank you."

Uncle sat down behind his desk. It was covered with invoices shuffled into piles and a calculator with oversized keys lolling a paper tongue of figures.

"So what is this about?" If I wasn't mistaken, Uncle's gaze had travelled to my midsection, as though suspecting another pregnancy. I wondered if he could guess how cloistered I'd been since Ravi. Perhaps he could, since he viewed me as a ruined woman.

"I want to leave," I said, though I had not expected it to come out that way. "I don't want to live with Sadhana anymore." Uncle had never been to our place on St. Marc, so he could not know its impossible smallness or the prison its lack of privacy created. I thought about framing it in a way he could appreciate. "I think it would be better for Quinn if he and I could live on our own." I watched his face to see what he made of that and thought I saw his moustache twitch. From the other side of the wall I could hear the clattering sound of firewood being loaded into the oven. "Healthier," I said, louder. "Can you help me?"

Uncle leaned back in his chair. "You should never have left. Two young girls like you."

"That may be." I knew this to be a safe concession, as he did not actually want us to come back and live with him. "But it's done."

"True."

Behind him on the wall, there was a calendar with a picture of the Golden Temple in Amritsar, in the Punjab. Through the window, I could hear the indistinct sounds of bagel boys in the alleyway. I sat up straighter.

"I was wondering if there's any more money. From the life insurance, or from the store."

"Not much," he said. "What there is I have been putting away for the two of you. For your marriages."

"Things don't work that way anymore, Uncle."

"They do work that way. If you marry a nice Indian boy."

"I think that's up to us. Also, I don't think you should be holding your breath."

"What do you mean?"

"I mean the traditional ship has sailed. For me, anyhow."

I saw him weighing it.

"Real estate," he said, "is a good investment. I will put you in touch with the man at the bank."

I made plans quietly. Sadhana finished her last semester and was about to graduate. Between the end of term and convocation, she performed in a contemporary dance production of *Red Riding Hood* that brought me to tears in the front row. Though the company was amateur—just a university club, really—Sadhana's performance had an intensity enhanced by irony, a complexity of expression that she brought to every movement. She was an actress right down to her bones, and the pas de deux between Sadhana and the wolf became something more about the deliberate refusal of carnal knowledge than a simple tale of innocence falling prey to experience. Most of all, I could see from her strength that she was in good health, slim but muscular, and this knowledge bolstered me in my decision.

But the more certain I felt, the more I put off mentioning the move. If Sadhana was doing well, and she appeared to be, I didn't want to upset things any sooner than necessary. But then I would remember Ravi, living and working in the same city as his son, and the idea of his having any part of Quinn's affection made me almost nauseated. His known presence in the city filled me with disquiet. In my mind, Quinn and his father were like magnets turned the right way round again. Instead of pushing apart, it was only a matter of time before they would come together if we stayed.

I spent a week rehearsing the words, as though finding the right combination would soften their meaning. Not *abandonment*. Not *selfish*. I practiced in my head and bolstered my resolve by anticipating her anger in order to heighten my own. *I'm sick of it all*, I mouthed. *I want my own life*. I got so worked up I would catch myself muttering, and then Sadhana would be at my elbow, telling me I'd finally gone bonkers.

On a night when Quinn was staying at a friend's house, Sadhana invited her knitting friends over. By the time I got home from dropping off my son, there were young women nestled into every nook in the living room.

"Everyone, this is my sister, Beena."

"Hi." Shrugging off my coat, I nodded to the girls in turn as they introduced themselves. Mel, Cherise, Tara, Rhiannon, and Anne-Marie. To look at, they were not exactly the women I'd pictured in all the months my sister had been spending time with them, though I'd always had a hard time getting a handle on Sadhana's friends. There were paisley skirts, nose rings, and dreadlocks. There were crocheted shawls, striped legwarmers, and canvas bags covered with protest pins and rainbow flag patches. They seemed unlike anyone I'd ever known Sadhana to hang out with. My sister invited me to sit down, and Anne-Marie, a petite woman dressed all in black, poured me some tea. She had a cherry blossom branch tattooed on the inside of her wrist.

With the warm cup in my hand, sitting on the rug in the midst of so many women, I was reminded of my mother. I remembered that she had had a sewing circle of her own.

"This is nice," I said.

The girl named Tara smiled at me. She was wearing an orange T-shirt that read HUMMUS IS YUMMUS. "Thanks for letting us into your space."

"No problem." I could tell that Sadhana had done some tidying and rearranging of the apartment before the gathering. Both our mattresses had been transformed into daybeds via the prodigious distribution of cushions. The television was concealed beneath a purple sarong. And arranged beside the teapot on the coffee table, she'd prepared a tray of snacks. I leaned forward to take some bread and cheese on a napkin.

"Do you knit, Beena?" asked Rhiannon, who was sitting near me on the floor. Covering her lap, what looked like a deep red blanket was being worked up on two large needles.

"No," I said. "I never learned." Ever since Sadhana had cast on her first stitches at the instigation of the hospital's art therapist, I had merely listened to her complain about it.

"We could teach you," said Rhiannon.

"That sounds fun," I said. I looked to Sadhana, but she was busy counting stitches in the bodice of a dress she was making. An ambitious project.

"We'll teach you our other tricks, too," said Cherise, a girl with spiky blue hair and a tongue piercing.

"Cherise," said Anne-Marie. She was laughing.

"What? I like to pretend we're edgy." With her round face and blue punk hair, Cherise was like a Campbell's Soup kid in the midst of a playful rebellion. Mel, who seemed to be her girlfriend, pinched one of Cherise's apple cheeks before kissing her on the lips.

"What tricks?" I said.

"No tricks." Sadhana spoke up. She was seated on the corner of the mattress on the other side of Mel and Cherise. "We've been evolving, as a group." My sister lowered her eyes before meeting my gaze, and I recognized it as a look of both admission and conciliation. A pre-emptive apology for what had become our separate lives.

"In what way?" I wasn't surprised that Sadhana had been keeping secrets, but it reminded me of my own hidden news. I thought of the list in my purse I'd already begun of what to take to Ottawa and what to leave behind.

Tara held up a purple toque-in-progress, hanging off a set of circular needles. "Rhiannon got us started knitting hats and mitts and baby stuff for a women's shelter, and then we found out this woman we were helping was in danger of losing her refugee status."

"We're going to knit a kind of peace blanket for her," said Cherise.

"Crochet," corrected Anne-Marie.

"We're going to try," said Rhiannon. She was soft-spoken but serious. "That's all we can really say right now."

Anne-Marie leaned forward and helped herself to a cookie. "It'll be kind of an art piece, something for people to rally around." The others nodded.

"Basically," said Mel, sounding wry, "we're a revolutionary knitting circle now."

I was impressed. "That's great." It seemed like a useful outlet for Sadhana's obsessive tendencies. Outwards instead of inwards.

"You should join us," said Cherise. "We'll teach you crocheting first. It's easier."

I looked at my sister and her face seemed veiled. Her

hands had fallen still in her lap.

"Well," I said, when it was clear no endorsement was forthcoming. The room felt quiet, and I got to my feet. "Should I put on another CD?" I went to the stereo, which was on the counter near the kitchen, conscious of the puzzled stares of a dozen eyes. I chose another album and pressed Play.

"Beena's pretty busy," said Sadhana behind me. "She has a kid, you know. My nephew, Quinn."

After a chorus of interest and probably feigned surprise, given the stack of kid's toys in the corner, I returned to the living room and the question.

"Actually," I said, reclaiming my spot, "I'm moving to Ottawa with my son just as soon as the school year is over." It was almost a physical jolt to say it out loud, as though my whole body were vibrating.

"Really?" said Cherise. "Why's that?"

"More jobs." I dared a glance at Sadhana, who was looking at me now, her eyes cold. "Plus, you all probably know by now, if you're such good friends —"

They were all looking at me with expectation.

"For a long time, Sadhana's been sick . . ." I paused and heard a choked sound from my sister, and I waited another beat, long enough to make her panic. "Of me," I said. "Totally sick of me." I flipped my expression into a grin, to turn it into a joke, and Sadhana was forced to laugh. Her friends were watching us tentatively, and the room felt tight. All knitting had stopped.

"Not true," said Sadhana, recovering herself. She got up and gave me a peck on the cheek before pouring herself more tea. "I'll miss you. And Quinn. It'll be the end of an era."

We got through the night. After everyone went home, my sister went to bed without speaking to me. The next morning, she went out early and stayed away all day, while I reorganized all my papers and Quinn's books and clothes. I made lunch, played eighteen games of Yahtzee with Quinn, cleaned up the kitchen, cooked supper, and worried about how Sadhana was coping with my decision.

Late in the evening, Sadhana returned and agreed it was for the best. She was flushed and sweaty and looked like she had come from the gym. "It's not easy to have a love life with a little kid sleeping in the next room, you know," she said. She was talking about herself, her new freedom. Relieved, I didn't rise to the bait, as I knew she would miss having him as an excuse — the little boy warm with sleep whom she always kissed with delight when she came in after another bad date. "Never another psych major," she would say. "Remind me, sweetheart." And Quinn would sigh as he slept, wriggle up further on his pillow.

"Thanks a lot."

"You know what I mean."

"Plus," I said, "I'm twenty-five and I've never lived alone."

"You don't need to keep convincing me. I get it. It's time."

Quinn was asleep as we spoke, passed out on my bed after finishing his hot chocolate. Sadhana and I sat across from each other at the kitchen table, swirling our cups, exchanging small wondering looks over the world we were opening up.

It was raining the day Quinn and I left Montreal. I set the alarm for an early start so we wouldn't drag out our good-byes. I had taken Quinn over to Uncle's for their farewell the night before, and Uncle had made it plain he was unhappy with my decision.

"Independence is not the same thing as neglecting your responsibilities," he said, while Quinn was tearing open his new Lego set. "You said nothing before about moving to another city."

"Sadhana is a grown woman," I said. "And she's doing fine right now. Plus we're going to do a lot of visiting."

Uncle had muttered about modern families and eroding values, but he insisted we take two dozen bagels away with us. Quinn threw his arms around him before we left, and when I saw Uncle's big hand patting his shoulder, I tried to repress the jealous satisfaction I felt in separating them. Uncle had long ago forfeited his right to be involved in our lives. The chill of his coldness to Sadhana and I had not yet worn off, and I had unworthy moments when I thought he should not partake in our only consolation.

"Time to split, huh? Hit the road?" Sadhana was being brassy because that's how we had become around topics that upset us. We had already wept ourselves brittle. It was easier to try something else.

"Pretty much." We hugged. Sadhana kissed Quinn before helping us down to the cab stand with all our bags. She kept waving as we pulled away, though I knew it was for Quinn rather than me. She looked slight, as always, but also not as tall as I remembered as she fell out of view behind us.

Quinn was sniffling as we waited in line for the Greyhound. I wanted to be the redheaded girl who was sitting on her own suitcase, reading a book, with a pillow under her arm. Then the line was moving, and she stood and picked up her suitcase just as Quinn yanked his hand away from mine and sat down on the floor.

"I'm not leaving," he said. He was eight years old. "You can't make me."

It always made me feel bad to see a kid hazarding autonomy against all odds. I struggled to pull him up by the elbow, my hands slipping against the slick of his blue raincoat. A giant muffler with his name on it, a farewell gift made by the women in Sadhana's knitting circle, was knotted around his neck and making him sweat. After I got him to his feet, a man with a military haircut helped carry our bags as I frog-marched my son onto the bus.

Quinn's nose was running down onto his lips so he could taste his own sorrow, and as I tugged down his zipper and held him, stiff and unwilling in my arms, I wanted to tell him that emotion was like a carnival ride: its heights and depths might stagger and astound, but after the first time, he would know he could walk away when it was over, legs shaking but still alive. But it was a non-transferable kind of truth, in both conveyance and meaning. I couldn't bring myself to say it. And not everyone, I supposed, was able to walk away.

I wondered what he was so sad to leave behind. His teachers, his friends, the shape of our apartment, the sloped floor that made tiny cars speed up before the roadblock of the door frame. I thought I would miss fresh bagels, speaking French, the heat and bullet speed of the Metro. I ended up missing cheap lattes, the Greek man who worked at the post office, a giant electric cross on my horizon.

I did not tell Quinn, *This isn't what it's like to feel bereaved.*

~⟨◦⟩~

Ottawa, the closest major city to Montreal, was really the
capital of another nation. A smaller capital of a larger nation.
Queen Victoria's choice, Canada's diminutive ruling city.
It was going to be my solace and escape, that sleepy place
holding the country in check. Getting away from Sadhana,
it seemed like the only option—close enough to visit, far
enough for separate lives. Everything in Ottawa was going to
be what we made it, not what had been given to us. I hoped it
would be a place for Quinn to spread out and dig in. It seemed
like the kind of place where it would be possible to believe
that what we wanted could make a difference.

We already had ties to Ottawa—little, mythical ones.
The city had been Mama's second stop in Canada on her great
trip of destiny from California to Quebec. After she went
north to B.C. with her draft dodger, she'd gone to Ottawa
for six months, then to Montreal at last in 1970. Mama's
sojourn in Ottawa had always been a source of speculation for
Sadhana and me, as she rarely mentioned it. When we asked
her what she'd been doing there, her answer was, "Gathering
my strength." Which seemed favourable enough to recommend it in any case.

When we first arrived, the place seemed huge: smaller in
an obvious way than Montreal, but large in its newness to us,
its unexplored streets and unknown citizens, a place where
every inch of ground wasn't choked with recollection. After
a pine-scented month in a furnished apartment, we bought a
little one-and-a-half-storey bungalow near LeBreton Flats. I
signed Quinn up for school and started handing out résumés.
I dragged us to yard sales and to the Salvation Army to pick

up furniture, though nothing I could say or do would persuade Quinn to become excited about our new life. He took the move badly, hurling up a stony wall of silent protest for several weeks, making it clear both that he was unhappy with me and that he'd picked up our tactics of passive aggression. He was a nightmare until school started and he made a friend and scaled back his offensive. He missed Sadhana, but I let him dial her number every night and pretended not to listen while they talked.

A week after we left, my sister decided to stop speaking to me on the grounds that I'd abandoned her. For my part, I pretended to be too occupied with cleaning up after dinner, or folding laundry hauled back from the laundromat, or other carefully timed household tasks that required both hands and prevented me from coming back to the phone. I hoped to hide our fight from Quinn until it blew over. But one night he hung up the phone and refused to go to bed, accusation all over his face.

"Auntie S said she never, ever wanted us to leave, and you tricked her into letting us move away."

There was no point in calling her a liar, since whatever Sadhana said became the truth anyway. The truth for all intents and purposes. She believed it, Quinn believed it, and sooner or later so would I.

———————

The next few days pass unremarkably, if uneasily. Evan calls to tell me his room is painted green and that I ought to come see it. Instead, I spend too much time visiting the website of Mouvement Québec.

On Thursday, Quinn and I return to Montreal. His classes are over, and his exams are spread out over the next two weeks. In my pocket, I have directions from Libby, but I am spared any need to divulge my destination once Quinn shrugs me off at the bus station.

"Give me some lunch money," he says, holding out his hand. "Please? I'm going to go to the library to study for my physics exam."

Out of habit, I try to stare him down, but my teenaged son merely blinks over his contacts until I place a ten-dollar bill on his palm. and his hand snaps shut like a trap. "À bientôt, Maman," says Quinn. "See you at Uncle's." Shouldering his knapsack, he runs down the stairs to the Metro without a backward glance.

The temporary campaign headquarters for Ravi Patel is the other address I have brought along, and the office is tucked into a little row of stores between an antique shop and a taekwondo school, just two steps away from the church sheltering the Essaid family. A few minutes early to meet

Libby, I promise myself one look, and I cross the street to take full advantage. A barber's pole, rusted at the cap, is still mounted outside as a relic of the site's last incarnation, but the office proclaims its new allegiance with six large identical campaign signs mounted in the windows. Ravi Patel, poster boy. I freeze with the sudden fear that Quinn will have seen them, but I remind myself that where I'm standing is two neighbourhoods north and a little east of the bagel shop.

A bell jangles as I open the door. Inside, there are five workstations with people making calls and a black folding table supporting a large coffee machine and an open box of doughnuts. Everywhere there are pamphlets and information brochures, some emblazoned with Ravi's face, others sporting the party logo and photos of the leader, a blond man with enough brilliance to his teeth and hair to make him at least as qualified for modelling as he is for political debate.

"Can I help you?" The woman who addresses me seems guarded, as if she can tell just by looking at me that I'm not going to be interested in supporting the campaign.

"Maybe. I hope so." I scan the room for a door behind which Ravi could be concealed. I have no way of knowing if Sadhana ever sent him the note I found on her computer. She often composed drafts of emails using word processing software before going out to find a café with an internet connection. But thinking of the two of them meeting behind my back makes my mouth dry up. I clear my throat. "Is the candidate here?"

"Oh no. He's usually making the rounds. He's so committed to the neighbourhood." The woman smiles at me as she starts getting up from behind the table. "I think he might actually meet every single voter before election day. Do you know much about Mr. Patel's vision?"

I grab for a pamphlet. "Just wanted one of these," I say, realizing I'm not interested in hearing the spiel. I don't think I could stand to hear Ravi described as an upstanding citizen. "Thanks a lot." I stalk out.

The very sidewalk is a comfort when I get outside. The trees. Anything without red and blue logos and Ravi's grinning photo. A little park across the street sets off the church from the drone of traffic. Libby is waiting for me on a bench, carrying a large shopping bag.

"The church keeps them fed," she says, after kissing me hello. She hauls the bag up over her shoulder, and I hear the dull roll and clank of cans. "But they can always use help."

"I should have thought of that."

"I do because Sadie did," says Libby, shrugging. "She was always cooking for them and bringing them food." She notices the pamphlet in my hand. "Wanted a souvenir?" she asks.

Ravi's face is creased hard under my thumb. I toss it in the nearest trash can. "Something like that."

The church boasts verdigris spires in limited heights — its size meant to accommodate a goodly sized parish and elevate their spirits to a modest degree. Once, when these roads were still dirt, it might have held all who could hear the peal of its bell. Now the faithful tread to its doors on a shell of concrete, the second great crust of the earth.

Libby leads the way inside, between newly polished marble pillars flanking graceful steps sloped through wear towards the centre. A plaque on the duller outside wall dates the church's consecration to 1858. Inside, approaching footsteps echo in the nave as our eyes adjust from the summer light. A figure like a moving shadow approaches us, but once he is close at hand, I take in a vital older man dressed in black clerical clothes. His Roman collar is the same white as his hair. It looks like silk.

"Father Cavanagh," says Libby. Her voice is loud in the still church. "This is Beena, Sadie's sister."

"Hello," I say, as he clasps my hand first, and then hers.

"It is grace that has brought you here," he says, "just as it brought me to them."

Leading us past a row of empty confessionals, he ushers us down a set of worn stone steps to an unfinished basement with stone floors.

"Through here," he says, taking us down a hallway. At the end of the hall, a narrow corridor leads west.

"That takes you over to the rectory," he says, "where I live." Turning right, we appear to enter another, more recent era of construction. A closed door is set into a newly framed wall that sets off part of the church's immense underbelly.

"Well," he says, turning the knob. He pauses for a moment while his eyes search mine, but he seems to find something in them he can accept as a guarantee. "Go ahead. I'll give you some privacy. We can talk later." His fingers run up and down the ecclesiastical edges of his dowdy black shirt-front. "I like to stay upstairs. Keep an eye on who's coming and going."

I step back to let Libby take the lead, then follow her into a long, narrow room with couches on one side and a tiny kitchenette near the entrance. The middle of the room is taken up with chairs and large meeting tables. "We're here," she calls out. "I brought her." Libby drops the bag of food on a counter near a little sink.

A tall, dark-skinned woman unfolds herself from a wooden chair in the corner, carrying a baby on her hip. Clad in a plain white T-shirt and well-fitted blue jeans, she has tightly curled hair pulled back from her forehead. A cloud of it puffs out behind her headband, in a black corona that dips and bobs as she kisses Libby in greeting, before turning to me. "So you are Beena, Sadhana's sister," she says, holding out her hand. "I'm Marwo. This is Léo. I am happy to meet you."

"Me too." Her palm is cool to the touch. Baby Léo has his mouth hanging open, his little lips glistening wet. His eyes focus on me with moderate interest as he grips his mother's T-shirt. "It's a nice space," I say, though almost at once I wish I hadn't.

"I am glad you think so," says Marwo. "We are grateful to be here."

She offers us tea, and when we accept, she moves to the corner near the sink and takes up a large thermos sitting next to a hotplate.

"Cool tea," she says. "No real stove. We have adapted." She pours a little into a cup for me to taste, and it is sweet and milky. It reminds me of Mama's spiced tea except that I can taste pepper.

"It is okay?" asks Marwo. "You like the taste?"

"It's very good. Thank you."

Libby pulls out some chairs for us and we all sit down at the table. I can feel Marwo studying my face.

As I sip the tea, my gaze drifts to the edges of the room. I notice two bedrolls with sleeping bags and a metal rack draped with drying clothes in opposite corners before I check myself and turn back to my host, who is watching me look.

"I'm sorry."

"Please look. It's fine." Her response secures my consent for her own careful observation of me.

"I understand you knew my sister."

Marwo puts her cup down on the table, out of reach of the baby stirring on her lap.

"She was a good friend to us. We were very sorry not to go to the service." She gestures to the spare walls of the modest room. "The safety Father has given does not protect us outside of here."

"Your husband could be arrested," I say. "Is that it?"

"And deported." She makes a sound with her mouth like the call of a bird, and a man enters from an adjoining room, through a door concealed behind a curtain. Marwo introduces him as her husband.

"Hello to you all." Bassam joins us at the table, taking Léo from Marwo and holding him on his lap. He has a fine profile, with a smooth head and a prominent, straight nose.

"Welcome to our country," he says to me. He has a soft voice, and I remember reading on Sadhana's computer that he was a conscientious objector before he fled Algeria. "For us, this is Canada," he says, kissing his son. "This room. This is Quebec." He looks up to meet my gaze. "It is smaller than yours, maybe."

Libby says, "You never know." She sounds subdued, but she has a rueful smile. "Maybe not."

"Can I ask how it happened?" I ask. The Essaids in person are an even unlikelier group of fugitives than I could have imagined.

"Like a dream that became strange," says Bassam. "Like papers that turned into daggers."

The story of his threatened deportation is surprisingly banal once he explains it, having more to do with changing addresses and technical negligence than anything that seems to merit the punishment. "I failed to present myself at the correct time," says Bassam. "I moved and didn't get the letter until too late."

Marwo takes up her tea now that her hands are free. "But it is more complicated, too. They want to get rid of him especially. He organizes for the other Algerians trying to stay. He helps them how he can, and he does a good job with the forms and money and times and places. But for himself, it has not been so easy, even though he always does everything right. And now we wait. Wait for an appeal."

I can do nothing but nod. My contact with Sadhana's friends has pushed me well beyond the bounds of my own introversion. Before carrying on with their story, Marwo offers her husband some of the tea, which he declines with a shake of his head.

"How did you meet my sister?" I ask.

"No Borders," says Bassam.

Marwo says, "It is a group she belonged to. They wanted to help us."

"I'm part of it now," says Libby. "I joined after she died."

Marwo takes Libby into the warmth of her expression. "All of them helped us, but Sadhana especially. She said there was a man who helped bring us trouble. It was a man she didn't like."

"Ravi," I say. It is still almost unbelievable to me that Ravi had simply turned up on the wrong side of what my sister was working towards, and yet, I am hardly surprised.

"Yes, Ravi Patel. The man who made speeches before we had to come to this church. The man who is still making speeches to turn the people against us and Father Cavanagh. A man who had hurt her family, too, she said."

"Yes," I say. "That's right."

"But you're safe now," says Libby.

Baby Léo pounds the table with his two soft, crooked fists. "We hope so," says Bassam.

"We pray to God," says Marwo.

On our way out, we pull the door shut behind us. Father Cavanagh meets us upstairs. A man and a woman have come in and kneel in separate pews. I see the glint of a rosary hanging down from the woman's fingers. Libby and I follow the priest back to the front entrance, where we speak in a low whisper.

"I think this is the most important thing I've done in my ministry," says Father Cavanagh. "In my forty years of serving the Church." Outside, the sun is sinking behind the mountain, and the colours from the stained glass pool at our feet. In the failing light I see that his eyes are shining. "They are truly children of God."

"But what if they didn't believe?" I say. "In any religion?"

Father Cavanagh just smiles. "My brethren have rarely been discouraged by the absence of faith in the practice of good works. It's usually quite the opposite."

"You mean missionaries."

He spreads his hands with an apologetic air. "And so forth."

Libby reaches out and touches his elbow. "It is good work," she says. "It's wonderful. It's good and brave and righteous."

"And so are you, my child."

She shakes her head, and the priest seems less startled than I am to see tears spilling out. "I'm not, Father," she says. "I wish I was."

By the time we reach her car, Libby is back to normal. She jangles her keys, asking how she can help with Sadhana's apartment.

"I need more boxes before anything." I want to keep her at my side, to coax her to explain her tears, to return to whatever it is she wants to tell me. "Do you think—would you have time to drive me?"

Libby holds open the passenger door with easy gallantry. "Let's go then," she says.

In the car, it takes only a question or two to throw wide the floodgates.

"So how did you and Sadhana start spending time together? You said you met at the theatre."

Libby lets the fingers of her left hand curl out the rolled-down window, cupping the breeze. Though the back of the car is immaculate, the front seat is littered with newspapers, chocolate bar wrappers, and empty bottles of iced tea. There are even a few paperback books soiling between my feet and the rubber floor mat.

"She was my first real friend in Montreal," she says. "For a while I was raving about her to anyone who would listen. Well, mostly to my mum, back in Hearst."

She shares remembrances of my sister as we drive across the city, but though Libby is forthcoming, her stories have a narrative quality that casts Sadhana as a character I no longer recognize. There is Sadhana the gourmet, who had Libby over first for drinks, then sushi, then cassoulet, and later for dinners lasting late into the evening. There is Sadhana as comedienne, launching into a bumbling bit of comedy at the playground when Libby asked her as a favour to pick up Mouse—Sadhana pretending Libby's daughter was too short to see until Mouse was jumping up and down and shrieking with a giggle fit that took hours to subside. And diva Sadhana, pleading for red licorice and a can of San Pellegrino when Libby visited her backstage during the intermission of one of her performances. The incidents themselves are plausible to a fault; I could have invented them or supplied my own, identical in nearly every respect. But the thing I realize as she goes on is that, for Libby, Sadhana is one and the same as the woman in the stories. Whereas I've always known that my sister existed apart from all her charming and destructive behaviours. All of that, the stuff people would remember, was just embellishment or disguise.

Libby says, "We were friends. New friends, just a year or so, but very close in the last six months. Do you know what I mean?" She pushes up the sleeves of her loose cotton blouse. She seems to relish driving. "When you have a new friend, they're almost dearer to you than an old one. There's so much possibility in the air. No flaws."

I glance over, but she does not appear to be talking about me. Her eyes are on the road.

"Yes, I know what you mean."

We pull into an alleyway behind a lamp store, where we find a heap of pristine cardboard boxes. Libby helps me pack the trunk with about a dozen, but when she pulls up to the curb in front of Sadhana's apartment, she shrinks from getting out of the car.

"Maybe I won't come in," she says, craning her neck to peer up at Sadhana's windows. "Mouse will be finishing school soon, and I should go pick her up. I'll swing by later and we can both help." Popping the trunk, she waits in the car while I unload the boxes. Then her pale hand darts twice out the window in a fluttering wave as she drives away.

While Libby is fetching her daughter, I make another pass at the apartment, filling up the new boxes and searching for the diary. The air is stale, so I prop open the kitchen window. I check my watch every few minutes, anticipating Libby's return, but the afternoon is dragging. There is almost nowhere left to look, though there are still piles here and there of miscellaneous items or things to give away.

On a hunch, aided in no small measure by the fact that they are the last untouched items in the apartment, I check the boxes in the closet marked *Photos*, and in the third, I find a pile of old journals. None of them, however, proves to be recent, and with an uneasy forbearance I can hardly believe, I seal them all into a new box without reading anything more than the dates at the top of the pages. Besides wanting to discover the truth of what happened in those last weeks — if she was sick or angry or both — I have no desire to relive the fights with Sadhana. I remember all too well the way that a single exchange could never be isolated but hearkened back irrevocably to other fights, old resentments spoken and unspoken. The deep trenches of our relationship that other people recognized only once they'd fallen in. It's impossible to count how many friends and lovers we cost each other over the years, though I never stopped being sure that I had lost more.

Moving into the kitchen with two of the boxes, I do a final inspection of the cupboards and find only a cast-iron skillet and a cheese grater. Although Quinn left his boxes untaped, he seems to have done a thorough job. There is a box waiting to be sealed shut that is full of cooking oils and spices and four Mason jars of rice and grains. With staples and dry goods that could last for months in her cupboard, it was always hard to take stock of how Sadhana was coping. But Uncle's assurance that there was food in her fridge is a comfort to rely on, even if I still can't find her diary.

The buzzer startles me from my kitchen reverie, and though I press the button to let them up, the persistent silence from the stairs leads me down to the street, where Libby and a child who can only be Mouse are waiting by the car.

Libby rests her hand on her fidgeting daughter's shoulder. "Mouse, this is my friend Beena. Sadie's sister."

"Hi," I say. Mouse is huddled at her mother's side and slinking behind her so that I can barely make out the little girl's face beyond two pink patches of flushed cheeks popping in and out behind Libby's hip.

"Ice cream, we thought," says Libby. "Do you mind?" Over her daughter's head she adds in an undertone, "Mouse wouldn't be much help in packing anyway."

So we walk to the other side of the park, listening to Mouse chatter on about some new kind of skipping game, suddenly voluble at the promise of a treat. Then, with two scoops of chocolate ice cream in an outsize waffle cone in hand, I reintroduce the subject of Sadhana.

But this time, Libby balks at the idea of talking about my sister. "It's still painful for me," she says, her face getting tight. She is picking at her own cup of butterscotch ripple with a miniature spoon. "You don't understand."

I press. "You seemed fine earlier, all those stories you were telling me."

Libby has another morsel of ice cream, turning over her pink plastic spoon to scrape the treat against her tongue. She blinks, and a lone tear runs down her cheek. She swallows and says, "Please. Don't interrogate me."

But I am determined to pull it out of her, even as I dread what she has to tell me.

"She wasn't eating, is that it?" I grow cold, remembering what Libby said earlier about all the food Sadhana had prepared and taken over to the Essaids. The food in her fridge that Uncle mentioned might never have been for her at all.

Libby doesn't appear to hear me. She has her face turned away, brushing at her eyes with the cuff of one sleeve. Oblivious, Mouse puts down her emptied cone and announces she's going to go play with a doggie. She stands up and points to a spot within our sightline where some other parents and kids are petting a leashed black lab puppy in the sand near the small children's play structure.

"Okay, honey," says Libby.

When her daughter is out of earshot, she says, crying openly now, "I loved Sadie. We loved each other."

My face crinkles in surprise. "You mentioned you were close."

"We were. We were together."

I take this in and find it is not unexpected. I only wonder that it did not occur to me earlier. In the ten years we'd lived apart, Sadhana had cultivated discretion nearly to a religion. I suppose we both had. There had been other women, I knew that much. Once my sister told me about a girl, a crush, and I said to her, "You're just like Greta Garbo, aren't you," and she was mad at me, even though in my head it was a compliment. I knew she loved Garbo. She had a *Ninotchka* poster up in her living room, and Garbo had had affairs with both men and women. But Sadhana thought I meant she was just acting out. "This is my life, Bee," she said. "I'm not playing."

"We're all playing," I remember answering. And again she was mad. But I didn't mean play-acting, and I didn't mean she didn't love whom she loved. I just meant there was no way to tell the difference between what we were doing and what we should be doing. We all had an idea of who we were or wanted to be, and we could only be in the world in such a way that was an approximation of that ideal—in that sense, it *was* a game, and some of us were better at it than others. It was an attitude I was trying to adopt in order to stop taking life so seriously. But I thought it might be embarrassing to explain. Instead I said, "So tell me about her."

But the moment had sped by. Sadhana had decided I was squeamish or prejudiced, or she was punishing me for my breeziness by pretending she thought I was. And now it was just another thing I had done wrong.

"Do you believe in heaven?" says Libby, abrupt.

"I don't know. Not really, I guess. Do you?"

She shakes her head. "I have to. I don't know what else to believe in instead."

Before I can think of how to respond, Mouse is back with us and anxious to leave. As we start walking south, Libby starts talking about the weather. "I was sure it was going to rain," she says, wiping her eyes and looking around at the sky in all directions. Then, like Mouse, Libby has her eyes on the sidewalk, seemingly taking care not to step on the cracks. I want to ask her if that was it—if the fact she has just shared is what she has wanted to tell me this whole time. But I am afraid of pushing. Or of saying the wrong thing, the way I did with Sadhana.

We end up walking down my old street, my feet leading me homewards, back in the direction of the bagel shop. Libby is weeping again, silently but intermittently now, pausing every once in a while to make a commonplace remark upon brick-work or graffiti, to which I respond with equal nonchalance. Mouse looks on, frightened but determined to carry on as if everything is normal, which perhaps it is. She has very pale skin, as white and translucent as a layer of onion, which looks even paler below her dark curls. With one hand she grips the side of Libby's jacket, and with the other she worries the buttons on the smocking of her dress. When we reach the bagel shop, Quinn is just unlocking the door to the upstairs apartment.

"Mom," he says, with what seems like inordinate sur-prise. He pops the last bite of a bagel into his mouth.

"This is my son," I say, pulling him in step with us. Libby nods at him. "And this is Mouse." He gives her a little wave.

"Walk with us a while," I say to him. "It's too nice an evening to go in just yet." The desperation I might have com-municated with my eyes is thwarted when he won't meet them with his own, but he seems to detect something in my voice. He hesitates just a moment before pocketing his key and falling in with us.

"What's up?"

"Mummy gets sad," says Mouse, with the air of someone repeating a familiar refrain.

"Oh," I say, alarmed, looking at Libby, but she appears not to have heard, ambling ahead to a bench to tie her shoe-lace. "Oh, I see."

"She gets jealous, too. But people don't belong to each other," Mouse says, chattering now. "People are always free. That's why slavery is wrong."

"Did you ever hear about the Underground Railroad?" Quinn asks her.

Mouse nods like a jack-in-the-box. "Yes. Our teacher read us *Underground to Canada* in my class at school, and we heard about all these slaves and what it was like for them and how much it cost to buy a slave and all about how to find the North Star."

"When I first heard about the Underground Railroad," says Quinn, "I thought it meant a subway."

Mouse's laugh is like her mother's, long and loud.

After we say goodnight to Mouse and Libby, Quinn accompanies me back to the apartment. He is still carrying a crumpled paper bag from the bagel shop, sesame seeds caught here and there on the front of his T-shirt. When I was growing up, the seeds got everywhere, the sesame bagel being our shop's foremost commodity. Seeds in the treads of our shoes, mashed into the rug, mixed up in a batch of laundry fresh out of the dryer. Sadhana once even claimed to find one up her nose.

"Where were you before we ran into each other?"

"Nowhere. Here. I went down for a snack after I got back from the library." But his boots on the mat are encrusted with mud and the apartment is dark until I switch on the light. Before I reply I make sure there is enough of a pause to convey my dubiousness.

"Thank you," I say, "for the stroll." With Quinn along, the walk had taken on a feeling of normality, a family outing rather than a dissipating crisis.

"She seems like a sweet kid." His way of telling me it wasn't a personal favour. He turns his back on me and heads straight for the bathroom—another sign he's just getting home. I sag onto the couch and reflect that wherever we are now, it isn't better than where we were before. That new ease between us I'd thought I'd started noticing was either imagined or cancelled outright by asking him to meet Evan. The subject of his father is still a sore spot for Quinn. And a man around, any man it would seem, is enough to aggravate that wound.

That Quinn's fixation on his father was turning into a real problem was something that only Sadhana, in her typical, fearless way, had been willing to address. I would have put him off with more evasions, more refusals, and shameless, blubbering guilt if I had to. Indefinitely. But Sadhana seems to have been prepared to find a way to put all his questions to rest.

Later, Uncle and Quinn drink tea in the kitchen. Quinn, studying for an exam, holds firm at the table, even when I come and join them. I try to enjoy the close quiet, but whenever I look up to see him biting his lip over his notes, I can think only of his father.

Sadhana and I had our secrets, but they told on the body. Ravi escaped his past without a trace. Though he is a poorer man for his choices, I know that. He lost Quinn, years of Quinn that would have made him better, as they have made me. And I do not think he deserves Quinn's forgiveness. He will never have mine. All he has coming to him is some bad luck. That would only be fair.

The more I think about this, what Ravi has coming to him, the truer it seems to be, until it is like a sudden doctrine animating me, and I know from the force and simplicity of it that it has to be a kind of lie. And just as clearly I feel as though I know what must have passed between him and Sadhana. The offer she would have made him, given his involvement in politics, to either acknowledge his son willingly or face public exposure.

Uncle goes to bed, then Quinn, and I bring the computer to the table and turn it on. I navigate to the website for Quebec First, then to Ravi's profile, and scroll down to the contact information. I am signing into my email account when my cellphone buzzes.

Evan's voice sounds warm with whisky. "What's up, buttercup?"

I talk to him about the work I've done in Sadhana's apartment, about Libby and her revelation. "So my sister had a secret relationship, too," I tell him. "Or she didn't get around to telling me. I think you'd like Libby." Especially if he has a thing for damsels in distress. News about Ravi doesn't make the cut, in case Quinn is awake and listening. And because of what I'm thinking of doing.

"What about coming home?"

"Soon enough," I say. We both say goodnight before hanging up.

Ravi, I write. *This is Beena. We need to talk about some things. Tell me when we can meet. I have a reporter asking me a lot of questions and I'm not sure what to tell her. Does your wife know you have a son?* Then, before I can change my mind, I hit Send.

The response is almost immediate. Ten minutes later his message pops up: *Don't say anything. I can meet you six days from now, next Thursday night. Do you know a restaurant called Bombay Palace? 8 p.m.*

And just like that, the real Ravi, the one who is more than a poster or a memory, is back.

———~———

SEVEN

∼ HOUSEWARMING ∽

Sadhana threw a party when she moved into her new place. She'd stayed on alone for another year and a half at the St. Marc Street apartment we shared after high school, putting out the call to anyone and everyone that she wanted a place in Mile End. She missed the neighbourhood, the comforting grid of the streets where we grew up, the routes she used to jog every morning before we moved downtown. In her mind was the idea of digging in her heels, making over an empty space into a home. Finally, an acquaintance from a dance class turned his lease over to her when he decided to move to New York City. At that point, according to Sadhana, she'd already looked at more than twenty-five different apartments.

She was excited. When we spoke on the phone, I could hear anticipation as well as relief in her voice, the veiled elation that she finally had a place all her own. Somewhere new. The place we'd shared had never really lost its flophouse feel, the haphazard aesthetic of two young women and a little boy sharing three small rooms. The rock posters and gritty floors, curtains slung for walls, a musty smell that never dissipated.

She sent us an invitation in the mail, on stiff, cream-coloured cardstock, neatly handwritten in the feathery script she could only produce with her fountain pen. Turquoise ink. The envelope was addressed to Quinn. Sadhana liked the idea of sending mail to kids. It read, *Your presence is requested in the warming of my new home. Bring someone or something you love.*

She'd waited until she was settled, until she'd spent four weekends in a row painting and a good chunk of two paycheques on bar glasses and a set of large platters. She was still low on furniture, but in a way that was better for a party with a lot of traffic. When I arrived from the bus station with Quinn in tow, hauling backpacks stuffed with sleeping bags, Sadhana was making hors d'oeuvres. There was Bebel Gilberto on the CD player, mulled wine on the stove. A huge impressionistic canvas of a nude woman, painted in hues of green and yellow and reminiscent of Modigliani, hung on the wall in the living room. I recognized almost nothing from when we'd lived together.

She threw our coats on her bed, showed me a spot in her closet where we could stash our things, then set us to work on a food-assembly line at the small kitchen table. A rectangular table that could comfortably seat ten was draped with a white cloth and pushed up against the wall of the dining room, edged with a string of tiny white Christmas lights. I skewered morsels of cantaloupe and prosciutto while Sadhana spread toasted slices of baguette with an artichoke purée. She pushed them across the table to Quinn, who crumbled goat cheese over them like clumping snow. Sadhana praised the way he added the garnish of chopped parsley.

"Nimble hands you've got there, Q," she said. She began plucking the hors d'oeuvres off the cutting boards, sliding them into symmetrical formations on a couple of white plat-ters. "Child labour is where it's at, Bee."

"Why do you think I had one?" I said. Quinn tried to shoot me a dirty look but couldn't quite pull it off. His dark eyebrows dipped and knitted behind his glasses, his expres-sion more puzzled than annoyed. He was ten, skinny as a rake, obsessed with spiders and comic books. I grabbed his wrists, then pulled back until I was tugging on the ends of his small fingers. "I had some very delicate needlepoint projects I needed to get done."

"Mom," said Quinn. He snatched his hands away.

People began showing up at dusk, which came early as it was the tail end of winter, the kind of season that unfurls along a slow spool, every thaw hiding yet another snowfall behind it. Through the closed windows came the sounds of dripping and thumps, ice sludging itself off a roof or balcony and crashing to the ground below. Inside, Sadhana turned up the heat as the windows beaded with condensation. As the apartment filled up, people began shedding layers of clothing. Quinn and I had been living in Ottawa for only eighteen months, but Sadhana's world had expanded like a budding universe.

I went to add my sweater to the pile in Sadhana's bed-room. Standing by her dresser was a man slipping out of a dark blue pea coat, peering at the framed photographs propped in front of the mirror. Observing me, he said, "You're the sister."

"I am."

"Younger or older?" His head was cocked to the side, his dark curls long enough to flop loosely off his forehead. He was wearing a peach-coloured shirt with a collar, a brown cardigan, wire-rimmed glasses. A stubbly beard over a weak chin. He looked to be in his early thirties. I tossed my sweater into a corner.

"Older."

"I wouldn't have guessed."

"Thanks." At twenty-six, it was hard to say whether being judged younger was a compliment. It was Sadhana's confidence and polish, her Montreal stylishness, that gave her an edge. I had the scrubbed face and comfort clothes I'd favoured since pregnancy, round cheeks that looked almost plump next to Sadhana's leanness. We had some features in common—our mother's strong nose, something about our eyes when we smiled—but overall we did not look much alike. I looked past the man into the mirror, wondering if I looked as childish as I felt. My straight dark hair was parted in the middle, as it had been since I was a little girl. I pushed it behind my ears and felt a trace of sweat there with my fingertips.

"Sorry. I suppose it's considered indelicate to comment upon a woman's age."

"It's fine."

There was a click and we both turned and saw Sadhana leaning her back to the closed door. Next to her was a blonde woman with dark eye makeup wearing a flapper-style dress. Each had her arm clinging around the other's waist.

"Someone in here," said the man. He looked amused.

Sadhana saw us, and her right hand travelled up to her loose chignon. She tugged at it until her hair fell free, past her shoulders. The blonde woman leaned her chin into the dip of Sadhana's collarbone.

"Pete," said Sadhana., "Are you hitting on my sister?"

"Trying," he said, shoving his hands in his pockets. "Not coming along very well."

I stared at him.

"We're taking a break," said Sadhana. She sighed and sank onto the bed, shoving the coats up and pulling her friend down in front of her. "It's getting pretty hectic out there." Leaning forward, she reached in a ballet stretch towards each of her toes in turn, her legs parted in a wide V with the blonde woman in the middle. "Why don't you guys finish off the gin? I hid it under the sink."

I felt dismissed. Lingering with my hand on the dresser, my reflection inclining away from the scene, I waited for a minute to be introduced, but when Sadhana didn't or wouldn't look at me, I left. Pete closed the door behind us and followed me into the kitchen.

"Your sister is rooting for me to get a girlfriend, I think." He was crouching beside me to keep his voice at my ear as I opened the cupboard. I found the gin, stored between the dishwashing soap and the garbage bags, and straightened up.

"Oh, yeah?" I was irritated by his easy familiarity with Sadhana, by her familiarity with all these strangers, most of whom had barely glanced at me. I edged my way to the fridge through a pack of young men dressed in white shirts and black ties. One of them, taller than the others, had long blond dread-locks that fell below his waist. Elbowing one of his friends, he prodded him away from the swing of the fridge door and gave me a nod. I nodded back. A single magnet, for what looked like a video rental place, clung to the outside of the door. The inside was crammed with beer and other booze, a handful of lemons and limes, and an opened box of baking soda. I couldn't help but notice there was no trace of food besides the leftovers from the hors d'oeuvres. I took a lime and a can of tonic water from the fridge door and moved out of the way. Over at the counter, I pushed aside a family of emptied beer bottles that chimed as they rattled against one another, their labels worried and peeled, hanging in strips. I mixed two generous drinks into coffee mugs, but Pete stiffened his before picking it up.

"She keeps inviting me out. Sweet of her, really."

"How do you guys know each other?"

"She took a philosophy class with me, a long time ago. Then I saw her in a play last year and hit on her shamelessly afterwards."

"She didn't go for it?"

"No. Professorial cachet is not what I was led to believe it was in grad school."

We hovered in the kitchen, where I was conscious of Sadhana's absence from the party, listening with one ear in the hopes of hearing her call out to someone across the din of music and conversation. To our left, out on the balcony, smokers were huddled close to the doorway, stamping their feet and clutching drinks in gloved hands, their faces obscured by clouded exhalations of smoke and freezing breath. I wondered what time it was and whether Sadhana was worried about her neighbours complaining about the noise.

"You're distracted," said Pete. He was looking glazed, emptying the remaining gin into his glass with a motion usually reserved for stubborn ketchup bottles.

"A little. I just want to talk to my sister." As I said it out loud, I realized how much I had missed her. And how little it appeared she had missed me.

We leaned against the counter, and I kept my eyes on the men with the white shirts, who were still with us in the kitchen. I had come up with the idea that they were in a band together as the reason for their outfits. The blond man with the dreadlocks had rolled up his shirtsleeves, and I could see prominent veins in his forearms, longish fingernails on his right hand. A guitarist, maybe. I gave in to the swim of the alcohol in my head and pictured his tie slipping to the floor, his shirt unbuttoned to the waist. It was like trying to shake off a deep sleep, the effort to sidestep that longing. The same heavy pull on body and mind. And there was another, halting feeling there, like what I thought might be a lingering dread of bad dreams. I was drunk, obviously. When my eyes flew open, he was looking at me, chin raised, drink held steady at chest level. A friendly look.

I turned around and put my mug down, nudging Pete, who was getting into Heidegger. "Back in a sec," I said.

As I passed through the hallway, I felt a hand on my arm.

"Is that your kid?" A young woman with magenta hair pointed to the living room, where Quinn was wandering through the partygoers with a set of smelly markers and scraps of paper. She flashed me her forearm, which was streaked with purple. "Maybe you should take him home now."

Quinn was wary as I approached. He capped the marker he was holding out for someone to smell and thrust it behind his back.

"That lady," he said. He was blinking slowly, and I could tell he was both excited and overtired. "It was an accident. She fell on the marker herself."

"Oh yeah?"

"Yeah," said Sadhana, appearing behind us. She was wearing a different outfit from before, a green linen dress and black ballet flats. Her bedroom door was closed, and I didn't see her flapper friend around. "She's at that stumbling stage where objects may be closer than they appear."

Sadhana put her hand on Quinn's shoulder. "Come on, kid. Let's get you somewhere where the adults will stop bothering you." She steered him towards a door off the dining room that I had taken to be a closet, which opened to reveal a small area lined with empty shelves, just wide and deep enough for the air mattress she'd slipped inside. There was a small stack of blankets and a pillow just inside the door, as well as a flashlight and two Encyclopedia Brown books.

Quinn flopped down on the mattress and bounced a bit. Over the music, I was sure I could hear the hiss of air escaping.

"It's a pantry," Sadhana told me. "At least I think so. But I haven't started using it yet. He's not claustrophobic?"

"No. Is it hereditary?" A shudder ran through me. But I was too big to be relegated to that narrow place. "Thanks."

"You hadn't thought about what we were going to do with him once it was four in the morning and there were still people here?"

I shook my head. The party rang around us, as though we were in a bell with Sadhana as the clapper, and whether it was the alcohol or just shyness, I felt pressed in and shaken, out of step. Compared to the monotony of my Ottawa apartment, the brightness of her world was jarring, and I felt like a swallow in the wrong sphere, blown off course from my usual haunts. Or like parties themselves were something that had flown south in a season too long ago to be recalled.

With Quinn settled, Sadhana pulled me by the arm to the kitchen, where she searched the cupboards and eventually poured a glass of wine into a plastic cup. "A few more people than I thought," she said, handing it to me. She bumped her hip up against mine. "Who do you want to meet?"

I couldn't help but look over at the band members, who were intent on a loud discussion I couldn't follow about the drummer from the Grateful Dead and the one from Sly and the Family Stone. "It was the Black Panthers, dude," said one. He had red high-top sneakers and a studied-seeming drawl.

Sadhana tugged me out with her to the balcony. There was a manic verve to her as she introduced me to friend after friend. I stood dumbly at her side, a poor magician's assistant, watching the eyes of her audience flicker over to me at the intro, then, after a moment, flicker back. There was no keeping the attention from Sadhana. And I was no better that night, for I wanted to talk to her and no one else.

"I'm cold," I said.

She pulled on the sleeve of my cotton shirt, as though about to suggest that I put on a coat, but a girl popped out her head to coax Sadhana back inside, to help resolve a burning question on the chronology of abstract expressionist painters.

"Pollock calls," said my sister. "Be right back."

I felt awkward on the balcony, so I went inside and sat on one of several chairs set up along the wall near the bathroom. I hoped to catch sight of her friends in the knitting group whom I'd met before, as Sadhana had mentioned they were coming.

Then Pete appeared and gestured with his drink towards the bathroom door. "It's unoccupied at the moment," he said. "Hope you haven't been waiting this whole time."

I shook my head, and he sat down. I was glad of the company. I was susceptible to the kind of mild solitude that deepened into its own dread entity, a psychic blot keeping others at bay.

"You're watching her," he said. He was looking through the crowd, as I was, as Sadhana filled glasses and laughed and stopped to cast the deciding vote on what would go next in the CD player. Then she was in conversation with the flapper girl again, raising and lowering herself on her tiptoes as she spoke and listened in turn.

"Yes," I said.

"You worry."

"Yes." I looked over at him, wondering how much he knew about Sadhana, of the myriad reasons for worry, or if the remark was just intuition or even small talk.

He slid his hips forward in the chair until his head was level with my own, his legs sprawling out before us. "Hey, is that your son in the closet?" He was laughing now.

"Yes. So?" I felt my cheeks flush and stepped across the room to the pantry door, which was an inch or two ajar. Peering in, I could see Quinn, fast asleep on his stomach in his usual pose: one leg drawn partway up, as though drowsiness had overcome some other sudden venture. His mouth was open as he slept, his hand still resting on the flashlight.

"He's fine," I said, returning. "Asleep."

"Sure. Kids can sleep through anything." He shook his head, patting the seat of the chair I'd been sitting on. "I didn't mean anything. I like that you brought him along. He gave me the opportunity of proving I could tell the difference between the smell of artificial apple and artificial grape. He's a cute kid." Pete looked at me in a sidelong way, as though with intentions just as oblique of offering some inept praise for my genes.

"He is, yeah." When comments about Quinn came to me dressed as compliments, I felt a moral urge to deflect them. It was one thing when he was a toddler, busy and clever and calm, when I was worn out and liked to think I ought to be praised. But the bigger he got, the more convinced I became that I was merely lucky. If people wanted to congratulate me on my luck, then I could only agree with them.

Then, without any warning, or maybe with the kind of look he had been giving me all night but that I suddenly chose to understand, Pete turned his face to mine and we kissed. His beard scratched my face, but his mouth was loose and wet, and I gave myself over to it.

Around noon, Quinn woke me by tugging on my sleeve. I'd passed out on the couch during the last wave of departures, around the time the birds got started. Pete had finally left after a very long session of kissing, followed by a stark, whispered entreaty to relocate somewhere more private, and, at the very last, a good half-hour during which I locked myself in the bathroom, crying in a stupid way for having been seen kissing a man who was nice enough but whom I didn't want, not even a little. I came out after his quiet tapping had subsided and found I had shed my invisibility, instead registering among the guests the signs of a general acceptance. Whether it was because the evening had passed its peak or because in my public tryst I had established myself as an integral player—the party's requisite figure of inebriation and humiliation—people nodded at me, addressed me, and I felt my anxiousness ebbing into congeniality. I spent the rest of the night in the living room, chatting a little with anyone who happened to come in. Two of the knitting women, Rhiannon and Anne-Marie, had turned up after another party, and I'd surprised us all by remembering their names.

Quinn waited as I sat up, wiping the side of my cheek, which was moist with drool. The living room was a minefield of empty glasses and bottles, red cocktail napkins dropped here and there like spatters of blood. As I moved I caught a whiff of some leftover rye in a plastic cup and felt sick. It was the wrong place to have brought my son.

"I'm hungry," he said. "And bored." He had a way of conveying his needs as plain facts, a kind of reportage that wasn't petulant, and when I already felt guilty, it was more effective than a tantrum. He had put his shoes and coat on, his hair still mussed into odd peaks along the back of his head.

I lifted my hands to smooth my hair and reached out to do Quinn's. Then I blinked and rubbed at the corners of my eyes. Sleep's markers and remainders.

"Eye crud," said Quinn, nodding. "Let's go."

"Okay," I said. "I'll just grab our stuff."

The door to Sadhana's bedroom was closed, though it had been open around the time I fell asleep, the bed a court full of stragglers as Sadhana sat tucked up by the pillows with her particular friend, the flapper girl. Wafts of cigarettes and marijuana floated out of the room, followed by clouds of spicy incense. When I'd first begun to doze, I found myself in a dream of Mama in our old apartment, lighting patchouli-fragranced joss sticks over a shallow bowl of sand.

With Quinn behind me, zipping and unzipping the pouch on his knapsack, I knocked lightly on Sadhana's door, then, hearing nothing, opened it. Sprawled on top of her mauve comforter was the man with blond dreadlocks, wearing only a pair of boxer briefs, his long hair spread out like fibres of thick cable all untwined across the spread of his muscled back. Sadhana lay next to him on her side, facing him in her sleep under the covers. I stared for a minute at my sister with this beautiful man, then tiptoed in and gathered up all our things. As I stepped away from the closet door, I caught my breath at the sight of a bare ankle on the floor, and tracking with my eyes up along a pale leg, I found it belonged to the nude flapper girl, asleep in a nest of throw cushions just to the side of the bed. The flapper dress, I noticed, hung from a padded hanger looped around the closet door handle, the brilliance of its turquoise sequins muted in the darkness created by Sadhana's double-lined canvas curtains.

I closed the door behind me, then donned all my layers, shouldering my large knapsack. As we left, Quinn said, "Are we going home now? Should we say bye to Auntie?"

"She's asleep," I said. "We'll talk to her later."

RELAPSE

Sadhana claimed it wasn't about the guy, but it was. That time, anyway. Unless her assertion was some kind of acknow-ledgement that that time was linked to all the previous times, and to the fundamental adolescent unhappiness that had gummed up the works of the rest of her life.

After three unanswered messages followed by one breezy and unconvincing call from Sadhana to solicit advice about the best brand of rice cooker, I picked Quinn up from school on a Friday afternoon with a knapsack straining each shoulder and ran with him to catch the four o'clock bus. He unzipped his bag when we got on board and was dismayed to find I'd packed only half the Lego he wanted.

"Where's the booster? I need the booster rockets if I'm going to play Space-Time Continuum." This was a game Sadhana had helped invent years earlier, to my continued frustration, in which a woman and a young boy travelled back to the past to meddle with history, with the noble aim of creating a future with the most possible candy. The sound they made as they leapt through time had to be provided by their human counterparts and sounded something like a drill crossed with a siren.

"You'll make do. And I think you left some Lego there last time, anyway."

"Not the booster."

"Well, you'll have to pretend." It came out sharper than I intended, and Quinn gave me a semi-fearful look.

"Oh, don't be so dramatic." And then he was mad, too, and played on his Game Boy with his back half-turned to me for the next hour, until he got tired and fell asleep against my shoulder.

When he woke up, he jolted upright. "What if she's not there?" he asked.

"We've got keys, remember?" The deep weariness I felt whenever Quinn showed his practical side was rivalled only by the tiredness I felt when I tried to beat him to the punch.

She didn't answer the door when I rang the bell, and after I used the key to let us in, she didn't get up to greet us, just turned her face to the doorway and blinked in our direction. I turned on a couple of lights after taking off my shoes and went down the hall to her room. Quinn followed.

"Hey," I said. "We missed you, so we came for a visit. I hope that's okay."

"Hey," she said, and it came out in a half-croak, in the voice of someone who hadn't spoken in hours.

Quinn stared.

"Hi, Q."

"Hi."

"Honey, go sit in the other room for a little while. Auntie Sadhana's not feeling well."

So Quinn amused himself with Lego in the living room, while I let Sadhana do a poor job of pretending she was okay. I sat down at the bottom of her bed. In the light coming in behind me from the hall, I could see that her room was spotless, her bed made up so tightly that her weight on top of the covers barely creased them.

"What's going on?" I asked. "Is it something to do with that guy with the dreadlocks?" On the phone, she'd mentioned him a few times, but only by the awful moniker of Mr. Wonderful. Now she was drinking green tea under two afghans and her eyes had a blank look that I knew meant she was both cold and tired. It was her look of retreat.

She shook her head and leaned back against the wall in a slump that seemed equal parts standoffishness and exhaustion.

"It's happening again, isn't it?" I said. "Back to the races."

This was during one of my periods of bare insecurity, when she could dismantle me with even the beginnings of an arch look. It got to be that my concern was befrilled with as much gloss and scorn as a pageant contestant, and considerably less grace.

"No," she said. "It's not."

I was annoyed that she couldn't even rouse herself to offer a vigorous denial.

"No? So why are we sitting here in the dark listening to Nico?"

"I like Nico."

We sat there in the semi-dark, and I traced my finger along the seams of her comforter. It was a kind of standing staring contest I had with Sadhana, where losing meant being the one to cry first. We were like soldiers in a war against sentiment, with no idea why we'd enlisted. Over the music, I could hear the sounds of Quinn narrating a Lego adventure at top volume in the living room, likely for our benefit.

"I don't see the purpose in lying to me, of all people," I said at length. Then after a pause, I pressed again. "It's something to do with what's-his-face, isn't it?"

She flinched.

"I mean the guy," I said. "You never told me his name."

"Jack." Sadhana closed her eyes. "No. He's seeing someone else now, though. Exclusively."

"I'm sorry."

She shook her head and jerked up one shoulder in a curt shrug. "Please don't," she said. "It's not. It's not what you think. It isn't anything."

I got up and walked over to the window. The curtains smelled like cigarette smoke and lavender. I pulled them apart and Sadhana sighed.

"I was keeping them closed for a reason," she said. "I have a headache." She added, "I think I ate something that disagreed with me."

"Don't even try to pretend you've been eating properly."

"Fine, then." This was as close to an admission of her illness as I was likely to get anymore. I'd attack and she'd agree in the manner of someone conceding a point in an argument only because she could not be bothered to do otherwise.

"Take it easy on me, Beena," said Sadhana. "Okay?" Her plea took me aback. It was unlike Sadhana to accord herself mercy, let alone ask for it.

I imagined that at first it felt like slipping back into an old coat, shabby but comforting, all folds and worn patches. The swaddling effect it could throw over your whole life, like the way a bad breakup would send me to a stack of Agatha

Christie novels and chocolate mint ice cream. A pattern reassuring in its very sameness, even if it offered only temporary relief. I wondered if she was as scared as I was.

"Get up," I said. "You're scaring Quinn."

At the table, I was regretting having forced her up, as her face was drawn, and Quinn kept putting down his spoon and shooting little looks over at her that she either ignored or didn't notice. The oatmeal was watery, and the cream and maple syrup I'd poured in as enticements only pooled in swirls around one another. Quinn used his spoon to stir and stir. I tasted mine and found it sweet and clumpy. I let the lumps roll over my tongue, as if I were savouring them.

"I think we should all change our names," said Sadhana.

"What?" I said.

"To what?" said Quinn.

"To whatever we want. To whatever suits us."

I frowned, but Quinn was intrigued. "Last names, too?"

"Sure." Sadhana turned to me. "Don't you remember Mama told us we could change our names if we wanted? When we turned eighteen?"

"No."

"Yes, you do. Of course you do. As I recall, you were obsessed with the idea. You had a list, a long list."

I did have a list once. She had a memory like river rock, my sister. Our history had worn her down, written itself on her.

"Maybe I did, at that."

"They were all very glamorous names," Sadhana told Quinn. "Gwendolyn. Ariel. Susannah." Quinn smirked. "Oh, and Pilar."

"I thought you liked that one. You had a list, too, didn't you?"

"Oh, very likely." She shrugged.

"But you thought it was a stupid idea back then," I remembered, and it came out accusatory.

"Well, what if I did?" Sadhana was laughing now, not her genuine laugh but her cocktail one. Light, tinkly amusement. "You have to admit it was a bit ludicrous. Although I have a much better sense of where she was coming from now. Initiation rites, self-transformation. Magical names. Mama seemed nutty, but she always knew what she was talking about, didn't she?"

"You were so hard on her," I said, thinking of Sadhana's entreaty to me in the bedroom. "You were so hard on all of us."

"Do you really think it hurt Mama's feelings that she raised a skeptical daughter? She wasn't naive, Beena. She accepted people for who they were. She was happy when we questioned her. She didn't set out to raise little clones."

I didn't say anything, and when Sadhana spoke again, it was with the lilt of conciliation. She had her hand on her spoon as though she were going to pick it up. "What I'm trying to say is that I think at this point I would fare better as a Katie or an Amy or a Liz. Something simple to start over with."

"How about Jennifer?" asked Quinn. "I like the name Jennifer."

Sadhana went back to bed after choking down some oatmeal, an exhausting interlude involving tears from both of us, after which Quinn began orbiting me, whining that he was still

hungry. I looked in the cupboard and found a package of Fig
Newtons and a can of tomato soup. Nothing else.

"Which one?" I asked, holding them both up.

Quinn furrowed his brow and pointed to my left hand
holding the cookies.

"Never mind," I said. "You're getting both."

After Quinn's snack, which I shared with him, I went
into Sadhana's bedroom and sat with her until she woke up.

"Still here?" she said when her eyelids fluttered open. She
followed me back into the living room, trailing along some
extra blankets. It was only a little after eight and the sun was
just starting to sink, but Quinn had taken it upon himself to
start closing all the blinds and curtains and turning on the
lights. A ritual inherited from visits with Uncle. When he was
finished, he went back to the large rug, where he was mustering a fleet of Lego rockets.

I tried to get some news from Sadhana apart from the
stuff to do with Jack, which she refused to talk about, but she
was stuck in shrugging mode, the marionette strings at her
shoulders wielded by a tremulous puppeteer.

"Are you working on any plays right now?"

She shrugged.

"You don't know?" I said. "How can you not know?"

"I auditioned," she said. "Haven't heard back."

"What about..." I groped for the name of one of her girl-
friends in town. "Marie-Josée? How's she? And Rachelle?"

She shrugged again, then said, "Fine."

"How about work?" I asked. She had a job as a waitress at a Greek restaurant near her apartment, and another
as an usher at a French theatre, where she wore a smart
black vest and cravat and handed out programs before

sitting at the back to watch the plays.

"Quit." As I opened my mouth again, she said, "Both."

"What for?"

"Sexual harassment."

"What?" I asked, aghast. "At both?"

But she was kidding, a dry chuckle catching in her throat. She said, "Actually, I just stopped going."

She fell asleep then for a while, her head drooping onto the arm of the couch, and I paced through her apartment, trying to stave off panic. I attempted to recall how we'd brought her back before, but without remembering any of the awful details. Quinn had been too young to retain most of the really bad stuff, and the worst of it had been right around when he was born. After the last big relapse, when she was in second-year university, there had been only a couple of slips, a few small precipices where she'd tumbled back into her old habits, but only for a week or two at the most before I'd noticed and forced a confrontation. And once she had come to me herself. A golden coin of hope I'd pocketed to rely on later.

When I announced we were all going home together to Ottawa, Quinn set off such a ruckus about leaving that even Sadhana was surprised and as a result may have scaled back the protest I'd been anticipating she'd make. He stood up and yelled, stamped his feet, and even cried a little before collapsing back onto the rug with sniffles and soggy shirt cuffs.

"Quinn, you are way too old for this," I said. "Sit up." To Sadhana, I said, "Just for a little while, okay?" She nodded.

"You know, it's very confusing for me to be moved around so much," he said with such deliberation and malignant confidence that I immediately suspected a conspiracy with a meddlesome guidance counsellor. Someone who had mistaken my son's quiet gravity for trauma and made special appointments to ask him leading questions about his inadequate single mother.

"Oh, you're confused, are you?" I said. "About what exactly? Where are you getting this?"

Quinn shoved at the black hair falling in his face and looked down to his Lego. He pushed one of the mini-rockets back in line with the others. "Where I belong," he said. "Who I am."

"Oh, precious," said Sadhana, hooting before she started laughing. "Sounds like Quinn's the one who needs therapy. Our kid is having an existential crisis."

I looked hard at my son, trying to figure out if he knew what he was saying, whether he intended to hurt us or had just hung on to the phrases as a likely bludgeon, sensing their power if not their meaning. I'd discovered children often possessed a knack for this.

"Don't laugh," he said, scowling. He flinched away from Sadhana's fingers on his shoulder.

"Easy there." Not taking him seriously for a moment, Sadhana talked Quinn down from his wounded-child story to the truth, which was that his Game Boy was just about out of batteries and wouldn't last the whole ride home.

"Easily remedied," said Sadhana. "They sell batteries at the bus station. Now stop pouting."

Quinn scurried around when we got home, grabbing blankets and pillows from both our beds and piling them onto the couch in a heap. He was skidding back and forth in his grey sport socks, planning a reorganization of the house along the lines of our old apartment and accompanying all his movements with verbalized comic-book sound effects.

"*Zing!*" he said, as he slid to a stop at the edge of the living room rug. "Remember? Hey, remember how I had my bed behind a curtain?"

Sadhana and I exchanged glances. What to us had been squalor had become Quinn's lost utopia, apparently.

"I remember," I said. We had played up the caravan aspect of things, all the scattered mattresses and floor cushions instead of proper furniture. But in truth the sight of Quinn's and Sadhana's curtains surrounding their beds had always reminded me of hospital rooms, with their feeble partitions between one agony and another. It had been decided that my bed didn't require a curtain, since I had privacy by default from the other curtains. Also we had run out of ceiling hooks.

Quinn spun around on one foot, arms out. "*Whooosh!* And the posters, all the posters along the wall by Mom's spot, under the light-up bananas." One of my rare decorative touches, those plastic party lanterns I'd found on clearance while buying Spider-Man paper plates for one of Quinn's birthdays. The lights had gotten lost when we moved, and Quinn, it seemed, had never forgiven me.

"Yes, whatever happened to those posters, Beena?"

Sadhana had seized Quinn in a hug on his last lap past the couch, skinny arms tightening around him like a lasso. He tried to wriggle free, but Sadhana, however exhausted, was still too strong for him. When she kissed the back of his head and let him go, he sprung from her to the basement door.

"I'm going to go look for some of that stuff." The basement was a repository of things I couldn't bear to look at or throw out, stacked in storage bags on old doors laid across bricks in case of flooding.

"Put your shoes on first," I said. "Put everything back where you found it."

"We should have a talk with him," I said to Sadhana when he was downstairs. "Explain that this is just temporary." He was running around in a state of such obvious glee that I was starting to feel bad.

"I'd rather not." Now that Quinn was out of sight, she was closing her eyes again. She could rally for him, but not for me.

Quinn came back up rubbing his dusty hands on the front of his sweatpants. "Too much stuff down there," he said, kicking off his shoes. He ran back to the living room. "If we make this into Auntie's bedroom," he said, pointing to the east side of the room, "we can hang a sheet between the bookcase and this part of the window."

"Auntie might want a real bedroom," said Sadhana. "If I'm going to be staying for a while."

We stared at her, then Quinn offered first his room, the little loft that was the whole of the second floor, and then mine, before I could utter a word.

Sadhana said, "I think your mother would prefer me to be down here."

"That's right. We'll get a cot."

But we didn't. Instead it was me and my sister, sharing a bed like old times, like the bad times. When she rolled over in the middle of the night, I could barely feel the bed creaking. When I opened my eyes in the morning and watched her sleeping, turned away from me, she didn't look any different from when she was fourteen years old. Long, ropy legs and arms like spaghetti noodles, clumps of black hair flocking on the pillow.

She wavered between a livid mutiny and a genteel convalescence. When Quinn was around, she submitted to the pizza and cookies on offer without much fuss, though she warned that I was in danger of making us all fat, that Quinn would never be weaned off a taste for junk food. She meant me, too, but she didn't say it. During these periods she could pass for a sufferer of a lingering flu, or at any rate Quinn seemed to believe that's what was wrong with her. It was only after Quinn went to bed that she became a roving menace, snaking through the house in a foul temper, complaining about my shoddy housekeeping and screaming at me when I followed her to make sure she wasn't throwing up.

I had a new boyfriend then, Andrew, and he recommended therapy after she snapped at him for parking too far from the curb. She had been watching through the front window. He came in, slinging off his jacket and calling out hellos as she struggled to a sitting position on the couch. "If you're going to pollute the environment with a car," she said, cheeks flushed, "why don't you learn how to drive it?" His white Toyota was slung between two green hatchbacks, nose to the curb, with its back end not quite tucked in. Sadhana could channel road rage even when she wasn't behind a wheel, which she rarely was.

Andrew snorted. He was growing used to her barbs, and he'd heard reports of her mood swings, but I could tell he was stung. He tossed her the car keys from his pocket, and she flinched away from where they landed on the couch cushion. "Feel free to park it yourself," he said. It sounded measured, but for Andrew this was a fury.

Later, at the Portuguese restaurant on the corner, he betrayed his irritation by suggesting that I not only ought to force Sadhana into therapy but that I should consider joining her there.

"This has been going on between the two of you for long enough," he said. He lined up the salt and pepper shakers along the edge of the table touching the wall. "Why do you let her talk to you that way?" We were waiting for two orders of chicken and fries. At the end, they would bring us a third order, boxed up to take home to Sadhana where I could watch her eat it.

"You mean, talk to you that way."

He ignored that. "It isn't healthy."

"I'm making her healthy."

I knew the guidelines, the list of dangers. You had to re-nourish a body slowly or it could throw off the levels of electrolytes, a phenomenon I didn't understand but knew enough to be afraid of. One of Sadhana's doctors once told me, "Swelling, heart attack, seizure, coma. Be careful." Then he handed me a stack of nutrition charts. His warning became my morning mantra, the one that ran through my head as I blended milkshakes and buttered toast. It came and went at other times, too, whenever I felt my own stomach grumbling or found my stride hitting a particular rhythm as I walked.

When the chicken and fries arrived, grease-slicked and salty, Andrew and I ate quickly and in silence, each turned to the privacy of our abashed consumption. Backsliding dieters as we were, our pacts to indulge in guilty pleasures tended to yield more guilt than pleasure. Andrew's girth was slightly outsized for his build, the product of years of late-night computer programming buoyed by solitary drinking. There were always moments when I shared my sister's revulsion for food but knew it could live alongside a dictatorial appetite. Andrew caught my eye as I replaced a drumstick on my plate, then looked away as I used my fingers to strip away one last piece of meat and put it in my mouth. Pulling the paper napkin from my lap, I covered the remains of the meal as it shifted before my eyes from something delicious to something vile.

After dinner, Andrew decided not to come in. He said, "I'll be glad when she's better." It was a declaration of exasperation rather than concern, and it was a feeling I knew so well that I was ashamed.

"Goodnight," I said, and I gave the door a firm close that was just shy of being a slam.

One afternoon I came home from a Saturday shift at the law firm to find Quinn and Sadhana digging in the garden in front of the house. Most of the houses along our street were equipped with only the gesture of a garden, an abbreviation delineated by salvaged railway ties leaking creosote into the packed soil. Ours was no exception, and when we moved in, the rectangular beds buffering our front porch from the sidewalk contained a weedy mix of delphiniums, columbines, and bushes of bleeding hearts, a tall, swaying mass of cool colours. It looked intentional, if less impressive than the neighbours' gardens, and I'd never gotten around to changing it. The tiny backyard, with its privacy and the circling embrace of lilacs I was coaxing up from shrubs, was my first priority.

As I came along the sidewalk, I saw Quinn perched on the edge of a garden bed and Sadhana crouched low beside him, digging with a hand trowel. The back of her grey shirt was dark with sweat, and when she turned in my direction, I could see her face shining with moisture. She looked exhausted but wound up, her legs trembling as she got to her feet. Quinn's T-shirt was spotted with dirt, and both of his shoelaces were untied. When I got close, I saw a pile of root-strong weeds laying twisted and clodded on the paving stones, and my sister and my son staring at me with the same brown eyes, pupils dilating to liquid black.

"What about Christopher Papadopoulos's birthday party?" I said. There had been a lengthy telephone RSVP with Chrisopher's mother earlier in the week, during which I'd enumerated Quinn's food preferences, his swimming abilities, and his comprehensive lack of allergies. I'd surrendered two emergency phone numbers, and bought and gift-wrapped two packs of *Magic: The Gathering* trading cards, which Quinn had assured me Christopher was bound to love. I'd even bought Quinn new red swimming trunks, after finding the waistband fraying on the old ones.

"We forgot," said Sadhana.

"You forgot."

"But look at all the work we've done!" said Quinn. "See? Doesn't it look terrific?" He took hold of my hand as he pointed out the dark patches of earth they'd cleared free of weeds.

"And Auntie says we can go get some seedlings tomorrow, maybe, if you're okay with adding in a, um, a border here?" He looked at Sadhana, checking his facts, and she nodded. "Oh, and fertilizer."

I eventually admitted my approval of the transformation, avoiding Sadhana's gaze just as she was avoiding mine. When I got inside, I called Christopher's mom, who chided me about the extra food she'd prepared. But when I sounded suitably remorseful, she confessed that she couldn't help but be relieved to have one less kid running around. I could hear the sounds of shouting and splashing in the background.

"I'll have Chris bring Quinn's loot bag to school for him on Monday," she said before she hung up.

Loot bags. It brought back memories of my own childhood. I couldn't remember the last time Quinn had been invited to a big birthday party at a classmate's house. He'd always had friends, two or three close ones, but my impression was that all of them were always just on the outside of the rest of their classmates. For whatever reason, he'd been more popular in Montreal.

Sadhana leaned against the fridge, blinking her long lashes as her eyes adjusted to the relative darkness of the kitchen after hours in streaming sunlight. "I really am sorry, Bee. I totally lost track of time."

I believed her. Her concentration was a brute force, a combustion propelling her like a torpedo towards her objectives. "It's okay," I said, and I stepped aside to let her get to the sink to scrub the dirt from her hands.

But the next weekend, it was the same thing. Quinn cancelling plans with his friend Keith to do something with Sadhana while I was stuck at work. Quinn was already too

solitary, too inclined to prefer the company of adults. Keith
was a brat, in my opinion, though I supposed he might grow
out of it, but I still thought it preferable for Quinn to make
his way by negotiating the vagaries of bad jokes and video
game supremacy wars with his peers, rather than spending
an afternoon running lines with his perfectionist aunt—no
matter what the quality or educational content of the play.
This time it was *Richard III*. I wondered how convincingly he
could play a conniving hunchback, and whether it could possibly be useful for Sadhana's craft or only to feed her ceaseless
need for attention.

When I spoke to my sister about it, it turned into a fight.
"You're just jealous." She could say cruel things casually, the
things other people normally say in a temper. "You're jealous of the bond between me and Quinn. That's why you
moved away."

"That's not true."

I'd left because I was sick of her sickness, sick of looking
after her, of worrying, of fighting, of being tossed from one day
to the next on a tide of fear. But I didn't say this because I was
looking after her again. By some miracle she was letting me.

I retaliated instead by training Quinn, giving him an
edited version of the recovery plan and continuing to sup-
press the facts of the actual illness. "It's very important for
her to eat in order to get well," I said. "She needs her vita-
mins. I want you to tell me if she's eating or not when I'm not
here. Okay?"

Quinn accepted the mission with his typical ten-year-old
gravity. "Okay," he said. "I'll keep track in here." He waved
a little yellow spiral-bound notebook that he'd been carrying around, spinning it around a pencil so it flapped like a

noisemaker. I could see pages filled with tiny printing and things that looked like cartoons.

"Thank you," I said. "It's a very important job."

It worked for a day or two, Quinn pulling me aside every evening to whisper what he'd seen, one sandwich or two, one banana or nothing but cereal, until the afternoon I arrived home to find Sadhana waiting for me alone in the living room, beating the notebook into her open palm.

"Did you think I wouldn't notice? You turning Quinn into a spy?" She seemed tearful, but when I tried soothing her, she sprang back into anger. "You know, it's humiliating enough having you watching my every move, let alone a little kid."

It amazed me that Sadhana could still take things personally after all these years of my working to prop up her recovery. Every relapse was like a train on a collision course, and there was nothing I wouldn't throw in front of it to try to slow it down. Even Quinn.

"He's not stupid," I said. "He's going to figure it out eventually."

Sadhana had screamed at him, it turned out, flying into a rage she'd been ashamed of when she saw how it frightened him. But she had apologized with humble sincerity, as well as with a new Nintendo game. After that he seemed to hold me exclusively accountable for the whole incident, as did she.

Both of them were ambivalent about recovery if it meant she would be going back to Montreal, back to her regular life.

∽ LAST WORDS ∽

We lasted two weeks in family therapy. It was Andrew who urged us to go, and Quinn was excited. After Sadhana's outburst, we had to explain to him the nature of her illness.

Both Sadhana and I still had memories of the group sessions from her teenage hospitalization. At those, we'd sit sullen and silent until prodded by the facilitator, but once provoked, we'd dominate the rest of the session with our sniping. With ten years of maturation under my belt, I thought I would be better equipped to handle myself, but everything about group therapy still worked to provoke me.

"Make her stop rolling her eyes," said Sadhana to Melinda, our new facilitator. It was as if we were sixteen and fourteen all over again.

"I'm not," I said. "Stop being paranoid."

"You are. You're doing it right now."

Melinda inclined a shoulder and rotated slightly to face me, clipboard held tight to her chest. "You were. But maybe you didn't realize."

"Give me a break."

"Mom," said Quinn. "You were. Just listen."

He was only ten going on eleven. I had to remind myself of this, or I wouldn't believe it.

Sadhana said, "Bee, stop trying to have the last word."

It was all I could do to stop myself from making a face.

My sister got sentimental about candy bars after we went back to therapy, and Melinda regarded it as a breakthrough.

"A Mars bar," Sadhana said one day in group. "I haven't had one of those in ages."

I could picture a Mars bar, the black packaging and the red-lettered logo. I associated them with older people for some reason I couldn't pinpoint. "I don't know that I've ever had one," I said. "Are they good?"

Melinda, who always got exasperated by unhelpful remarks from family members, shot me a look to be quiet. Quinn looked like he was thinking about telling me the same thing.

"Oh no?" said Melinda to Sadhana. Everyone else was acting as though I hadn't spoken. "When was the last time you remember having one?"

"When our mother had to go to the hospital," said Sadhana. "The night she died." She was looking at the floor, where she was drawing an arc around her chair leg with the toe of her black flat. "I got it out of the vending machine."

"What else?"

"Well, we weren't allowed to have candy normally, but we were so hungry and we'd been there for hours. I remember it was the best thing I had ever tasted, and I felt so guilty that I cried when I was finished."

"What did you feel guilty about?"

"Breaking the rules. And being glad about it."

"You saw it as a betrayal of your mother's values."

Sadhana nodded. "Maybe." She talked at length about unwrapping it, the crinkle of the paper and the smooth brown form of the bar, which made me smirk. And about the first bite, how she expected it to be heavy but it was light, how it melted on her tongue. I couldn't stand listening to her. She was talking as though she loved food, like she wanted to do more esoteric things to the Mars bar than just eat it.

"And was that the first time you purged?" asked Melinda. She thought she was really on to something. I tried not to show on my face that it was pointless to waste time on purging when Sadhana had mostly given that up years ago — after her first time in the hospital, when someone had explained how bad it was for her teeth. Throwing up was something she only tended to do at the beginning of a relapse.

"No, no. Nothing like that. I couldn't even have told you how many calories were in it then. All that came later. I wasn't sick then."

From the corner of my eye I saw Quinn, intent, as though tangents about hospitals and candy could really fix anything.

"What about Wunderbar?" I said, keeping my eyes away from Melinda. "That's a good one. When's the last time you had one of those?"

Melinda believed in the healing power of journals, and she encouraged all of us, even those of us who were not sick, to start keeping one. I stiffened at the first mention of the idea. The sting of Sadhana's original diary was a memory that had not lost much of its potency.

Sadhana raised her hand to speak. "I've been keeping a diary for a long time," she said. "It helps."

"Good." Melinda was encouraging. "It's a safe place to be honest with yourself, isn't it?" Sadhana agreed.

I put my hand up.

"Yes, Beena?"

"Well, here's my sister, who has been pouring her heart out to diaries almost daily for, what, ten years? Eleven?" I looked to Sadhana for confirmation and she nodded. "Okay, eleven years, and she is not one bit better because of them."

"I'm not suggesting a diary is going to make anyone better—"

"In fact, eleven years is about how long she has had this disease. What do you make of that? Coincidence?"

Discomfort settled over the group like a wool blanket, and Quinn was fairly writhing.

"I think it would make sense if the events precipitating Sadhana's illness might also have sparked other changes in her life. Including the need to start keeping a journal."

Bella, another one of the starving girls, chimed in. "Yeah, maybe she didn't have anyone she could confide in."

Until she spoke, and I heard the rest of the group's murmured agreement, I hadn't realized how very thoroughly I was disliked.

Another family in the group, the Pearsons, ended up talking about Christmas a lot because their extended family didn't get along and the holidays always seemed to bring them to a crisis point, like Mrs. Pearson's binge-drinking of special eggnog, which led to dish smashing or Fiona Pearson's cutting (wilful but cautious, with a butter knife) or little Angie Pearson's beheading of all her plastic dolls, in alphabetical order according to first name. How Mr. Pearson escaped this misery and mania was unclear, though he seemed as wretched as the rest of them in his wrinkled polo shirt, the kind of shirt that shouldn't even be able to wrinkle, as he sat in a red plastic chair alongside them, talking about his feelings and trying to describe his regret about the Christmas Eve argument that led to the destruction of his mother's heirloom crystal gravy boat without resorting to blaming words. This led Melinda to ask us about our family Christmases, which led me into another session of involuntary eye-rolling.

"I'm sorry," I said, when Sadhana pointed it out again. "But what makes you assume we even celebrate Christmas?" I was fairly sure my sister saw someone else as part of her regular therapy; Melinda knew her only from these family sessions.

Sadhana broke in as Melinda started to look worried, assuring her we had always celebrated it, in spite of not being Christian. "Our mother had a universalist kind of spirit," said Sadhana. "We celebrated the solstice, the birth of Christ, the hunt, the harvest, Saturnalia, what have you."

"We have the best Christmases," said Quinn. "We still do."

It was true. When Sadhana and I were little, our main celebration with Mama was something of an amalgam of Indian, pagan, and Christian traditions. We even had a special day picked out for it: December seventh, a kind of midpoint between Christmas and when Diwali, the Indian festival of lights, tended to fall.

The Christmases Quinn was remembering were the ones when we baked frozen tourtière and opened presents stacked beneath a hideous gold-tinselled tree we had sworn to use forever, after Quinn picked it out at the drugstore, calling it the "beautiful fairy tree." Late on Christmas Eve night, we had a huge meal with three desserts, and at midnight we opened presents before going to bed with full stomachs. In the morning, Sadhana and I had mimosas with breakfast, and then we all went to a movie in the afternoon. Quinn had reported that his grade two classmates found this shocking. His teacher kept prompting him to remember when we went to church.

Quinn shared this memory with the group and Melinda asked him to describe to everyone what his favourite part of Christmas was.

"Umm," he said, pushing his black hair off his forehead. He looked so strangely adult sitting apart from me on a black folding chair. "Being together. All the time."

Being together had become less of a fond recollection and more of a hard consequence. Sadhana had come, and with the exception of a few brief excursions to Montreal, she had stayed. Like Deana, she returned every time with more and more belongings. Bags of her clothes flowed out of my closet. Her makeup littered the dresser and the shelf in the bathroom. The weather had turned cold, though there was no snow yet. She had been sleeping in my bed with me for more than five months.

Those days she used to get out of bed with the greatest reluctance, as if sleeping were her only pleasure in life. She'd stretch up first one long arm and then the other, like a zombie hearkening to its master, and then, after this showy concession to her alarm clock, she'd let them drop one by one before turning on her side, nuzzling and shrugging her shoulder against the sheet as though tucking herself back in under sleep itself. I took it as a good sign, that she had at least reached a point where she could sleep comfortably, that her body could still give her some satisfaction.

"I need to know you're up before I go in to work," I said. It was another Saturday shift at the law office, a month after Andrew and I had broken up. We had mutually given up on each other after he acknowledged he was sick of the situation with my sister and I admitted it had no foreseeable end date. But a partner at the firm had taken a particular liking to my style of drafting correspondence, and I had reacted by taking every opportunity to work weekends with him, showing up in the nicest outfits I could manage. It was probably nothing, yet still nice to have something to think about other than the two people who depended on me for every little thing.

"I'm up." She spoke these words into the pillow.

"I don't want Quinn to get his own breakfast."

"So you feed him."

"I'm late."

"You should wake up earlier. This always happens, and you always get mad."

By the time I left, Quinn was eating cereal in the kitchen alone, asking me in a stage whisper what Sadhana should eat when she got up.

~ ○○ ~

And then she was better. One week, we weighed her, and she was only a little light, and she was still eating. The next week, she was heavier and cheerier. She packed up her clothes, and before we even realized what was happening, she left. Quinn missed her, but it was manageable. It was calm.

We didn't know how, or why, but mostly it went away. Her illness, or her sadness, if they were in fact different, seemed to dissolve into the other elements of her life, where they were absorbed or transformed.

Quinn and I visited her often in Montreal. She was acting and teaching workshops and helping run the box office of one of the larger theatre companies. When she was low on cash, she waitressed at a couple of upscale restaurants on the Plateau. We went to see all her shows, sometimes more than once.

I made a life, friends. Nothing that could approach the all-consuming intimacy of what I had had with Sadhana, but it was better that way. Quinn kept up in school, almost without trying, it seemed. I had to work to find out what he needed, and it was a challenge to challenge him. Finally, an offhand remark about hockey fuelled an idea about what he might be missing, and with Sadhana's help I encouraged him to join a league geared towards kids who hadn't started playing the country's favourite pastime as wobbly-kneed toddlers. He had always been good on skates, right from our first winter in Ottawa when I took him down to the frozen canal. I walked him over to hockey practice and watched him learn to skate backwards faster than anyone else. It took longer, though, for the stick in his hands to look like it might belong there.

One night not long after he started playing, I came home and found him calmly going through my papers. He was twelve years old.

"What do you think you're doing?"

"Looking for stuff about my dad." He said this carelessly and without bitterness, as though his father was only a chum he hadn't met yet.

"He's not your dad. Don't even use the word."

He didn't turn from his task, but pushing one desk drawer closed, he moved on to the next. "You sound like Auntie S."

"Well, maybe she's right about this."

He took all the file folders, the bills and the half-written stories and the newspaper clippings, and dumped them on the desk, spreading them with his hands like pieces of a jigsaw puzzle.

"Stop it."

"No."

I came up behind him and grabbed both his wrists, then held them together in my right fist. I pulled him away from the desk.

"Ow."

"I don't go through your stuff, do I?"

"I don't know. Probably." He sounded so angry. I had never seen this anger in him before.

"No, I don't. And there's nothing here." I let go. "Everything I know, you know."

"I don't believe you." He shook his wrists free. "You never talk about him."

"That's because there's nothing to say."

Whether or not he believed me, something in my manner made him let it go. It was three years before he mentioned his father to me again.

Quinn's birthdays, our own birthdays — these were the markers of how far we had all come, how long it had been. There was a wave-pool birthday party, a bowling-alley birthday party, and a laser-tag birthday party, and then Quinn was in high school and parties were verboten, and I was allowed to bake a cake but nothing else. Every one of his birthdays brought a visit from Sadhana, and every year she was still fine. I didn't know what Quinn wished for every year, but I was superstitious enough to start baking my own birthday cakes. We were not the kind of family that could squander wishes.

For his fifteenth birthday, Sadhana and I woke up before the sun and baked chocolate layers cut into the shape of a lightning bolt. While Sadhana finished putting on the yellow icing, I went upstairs with a glass of orange juice and shook Quinn awake. Between the floor and the desk I counted three empty cereal bowls.

"Mom," said Quinn. "It's Saturday."

"So? You used to love getting up early on Saturday."

Quinn rolled onto his stomach and pulled the sheet over his head. His voice was muffled. "That was for cartoons. I haven't wanted to get up early on the weekend since I was ten years old."

"We're going to celebrate your birthday at the actual time you were born." There had been that whole, long night of labouring alone before the morning came, with Quinn.

After thin slices of cake, we went around the corner to Ned's, the diner we visited so often that Ned had added "The Quinn" to the menu: an all-dressed sandwich on rye with pickles and spicy Hungarian salami. Of all meals, breakfast the way it was served in a diner bore the least connection to anything we had grown up eating. It was nourishment without attachment, merciful food. Every piece of bacon was like starting over as someone else. We ordered our eggs soft-boiled, and it was not hard to imagine that we were like any ordinary family eating together in a restaurant, dipping toast triangles into yolks with calm enjoyment instead of pretending not to watch each other with the strained truce of animals around a watering hole.

We all held out our mugs for coffee refills as Ned passed by. Quinn paused in his routine of pouring in six packages of sugar. "Do you suppose," he said, "my father thinks about me on my birthday?"

Sadhana looked to me to respond, and for all her misery, I had rarely seen her appear so openly sorrowful.

"He doesn't know when your birthday is, Quinn," I said. "Unless he made some special, secret effort to find out from somebody."

Sadhana said, "He probably thinks about you a lot, all the time." Then she caught my warning look, which must have been mixed with surprise. This was a new tack for my sister when talking about Ravi. She amended. "Maybe even when he doesn't realize he is."

I tried to get us out of the house when Sadhana visited. Quinn spent so much time inside on his computer or doing homework. After breakfast we rambled downtown to the Parliament Buildings. We stopped at the Centennial Flame, flicking in pennies for wishes, and watched as a small group of protestors mustered on the lawn, their signs demanding BETTER PENSIONS FOR VETERANS! Leaving them, we strolled around the back of the imposing buildings, taking in the cat sanctuary and the statues of queens and former prime ministers. We were surprised to find a gazebo behind the Centre

Block, and Sadhana got up and danced for us before pulling Quinn up alongside her to try teaching him how to pirouette.

When Quinn had resisted long enough that Sadhana finally gave up, we walked down to the fence and looked out over the escarpment to the Ottawa River.

"It's beautiful here," said Sadhana.

"Montreal is beautiful," said Quinn. He was always loyal.

Once we had finished our circuit and had come out on the other side of the Parliament Buildings, Quinn begged to be allowed to run ahead to the mall, where we had told him he could pick out a new video game. "I'll meet you there, and you guys can keep strolling."

"Sure," I said, and he hurried off. Sadhana smiled at me as the sun came out, and we let it warm our hands and faces as we passed the War Memorial and the Rideau locks and the great clean, landscaped centre of the city. It was early November, but the little snow that there was hadn't stayed, and downtown was filling up. Everyone we noticed seemed to have the same grateful, reckless look of wonder at a beautiful Canadian Saturday as we headed into the winter.

On the streets of Montreal, people stared at each other. In Ottawa, they looked away. My sister liked this. "Except that when people look at you in Montreal, it makes it okay to look at them."

"True." We had already been staring a little too much for other people's comfort.

As we approached the mall, Sadhana said, "He's not going to let it go, you know. Asking about his father."

I said nothing.

"Maybe we should all go back to therapy together so you can figure out how to talk to him about it."

"You're kidding." I looked up at her. "I thought we decided therapy was a disaster."

"No, you did, Beena. You did. That's so typical." She sounded peeved. "But you know, I've been back to see a therapist once or twice," she said. "Alone, I mean. The first time, when it started happening again."

I didn't need to ask what she meant. In spite of the sun, I felt cold. "When?"

"A couple of years ago now. When I was training for the marathon. But it's fine."

I remembered now that she had not run in the race, citing some kind of minor ankle injury. I could not focus on what she was saying about Quinn, for I was panicked that her illness had resurfaced and I had not known.

"Fine?" I said.

Sadhana touched my arm. "This is a good thing. It started, and I stopped it, and you didn't even have to know."

~∽◌∽~

Sadhana was right—he didn't let it go. It came up again during a hockey game. I was sitting in the stands and enjoying the crispness of cold air inside and the makings of a hundred Slush Puppies scraped up by hockey skates. I had a hot dog from the canteen. Quinn had played all through his gangly phase, and though he still spent hours learning programming languages on his computer, he was showing an interest in getting stronger and being competitive. He said I ought to come see.

"The games are getting a lot more interesting," he had said, shouldering the huge hockey bag it had taken me both hands to shove out of the middle of the kitchen where he'd left it. "I think you'll enjoy it if you come." I promised I would. I thought that this was sometimes why people had children, to send a little part of themselves out into places they wouldn't ordinarily go. Like casting a line. A new trajectory.

Quinn scored a goal with two minutes to go, and I jumped to my feet with the other home-team fans, spilling crumbs down to the cement floor. The feeling of being one with the crowd was electric, something I hadn't felt in years. I hoped someone would start the wave.

I sat back down. A man next to me said, "That your boy?" Quinn was the only brown kid on the team.

"That's him."

"He's coming along well," he said. "A real sniper."

I hoped that was a good thing. "I'm glad," I said. "He practices a lot. I'd hate for it to be for nothing."

The man had a close-cropped beard and a navy wool coat. He said, "If you keep coming, you'll find you get into it." He looked down at the space between us on the bench, where I had laid my gloves as I ate my hot dog. I wondered if he spoke that way because I was a woman, until I realized that he must come to all the games and knew I didn't. Although I had, at the beginning. I wasn't sure when it had gotten away from me.

"I'm going to try," I said.

On the ice we heard a pounding and a slamming of boards. Shouts and a whistle. People were booing before I realized it was Quinn.

"That's a penalty!" called out the man next to me. Other people were yelling. To me he said, "Go. It's all right."

I ran down the steps. Quinn had already skated off to the bench. He'd taken a hard hit into the glass. With one hand, he held an ice pack up to the side of his jaw.

"Quinn," I said. In case moms didn't do this, I tried for discretion. But everyone was watching the game. Thirty seconds left on the clock. Our team winning but out for revenge.

Shifting in his seat, Quinn turned to me. There would be a black eye, some swelling. His nose was fine, thank god. Through a mouthful of blood, he said, "I want to meet my father." Then he leaned over and spat on the ground.

~∽∘∽~

The last time I saw my sister alive, she was standing in my front hallway in her grey wool coat, calling me an idiot.

I had come home from work to find a rental car with Quebec plates parked out front on the street, Sadhana and Quinn inside the house, deep in discussion, so absorbed they did not hear me unlock the door and approach.

"So you'll help me?" Quinn was saying. His voice sounded fervent with gratitude.

"Of course, baby, if that's what you want. It might not be a good idea, but I understand how you feel." I heard a clink like a cup being set down on a saucer. "If I had a way back to my Papa, to get to know him, I'd do anything I could."

I turned the corner of the hallway into the living room. "What the hell is going on here?"

Quinn looked terrified, but Sadhana was composed. "Bee, I was just telling Quinn I'm going to help him find Ravi. He wants to meet him, and I think he's old enough to decide for himself now."

"No," I say.

"You don't have to be involved," said Sadhana. "If you're worried about seeing him again."

"I'm not," I said, indignant, though fear was clutching at my stomach from the back of my spine. I let my purse drop from my hand to the rug. "You're the one who always said he's not even worth knowing." Having Sadhana firmly in that camp had given me the magnanimous freedom to blame Ravi's shiftlessness on his youth, to keep up the appearance of giving him the benefit of the doubt.

"And I still think that." Sadhana looked over at Quinn. "I definitely haven't changed my mind on that one." From habit, I examined her neck as her head turned in profile, and the lines were not the sharp, rangy contours presaging danger. "But you're the one," she came back to me then, "who said he was just a kid. And people do change." She picked up her cup and put it down again, looking thoughtful. "I'd like to think that people might change with the right kind of encouragement."

Quinn, still looking spooked, dropped his hands to his knees, as though trying to brace himself or clamp down his nerves. "Mom," he said, with a peacemaking air, "we didn't want you to have to find out about any of this." I caught Sadhana shooting him a warning look.

"Excuse me?"

"We," he said, and faltered. "We weren't going to worry you."

"So you were going to lie to me. That's nice."

Sadhana sighed. She stood up and paced to the kitchen, turning on the tap to run water into her cup. She twisted the faucet closed so tightly the pressure in the pipes gave a little gasp. "I didn't come here to start a fight."

"Just to conspire with my kid behind my back?" I felt the shadow sentiment of how I might be feeling if I hadn't caught them in this dialogue—if I could have just relished the pleasure inherent in a surprise visit from my sister—and the lost enjoyment made me even angrier. She had visited just the weekend before, for Quinn's seventeenth birthday, and of her own volition had eaten an entire piece of tiramisu. We had toasted Quinn with champagne, and we had stayed up late, laughing on the couch. In the past year, I had felt myself letting go, little by little, of the feeling that I was in charge of my sister's illness. It was beginning to feel possible to reclaim an uncomplicated, or less complicated, friendship. If the fight wasn't happening, we might be making supper, or debating which restaurant to go to. Or maybe Sadhana and Quinn would have decided together before I got home, and they would each have taken one of my arms and turned me right around and marched me back out the front door towards our lovely evening together.

"Can't we talk about why you're so against this?" Sadhana was taking refuge behind the counter, and Quinn was rotating in his chair so he could keep us both in his sightline. I felt a pang to see how invested he was in the outcome of this discussion. A pang and then a stab of betrayal.

"No. *We* can't. This is between me and my son. *My* son." I wanted to hit something. Instead I yanked off my coat and tossed it on the couch where Sadhana had been sitting. "I'm the only one who knew him," I said. I hated saying his name. "So it should be up to me."

"He's my father," said Quinn with hesitation.

"He's a sperm donor," I threw back. "He's nothing."

"Then why do you care so much?" said Sadhana.

I yelled then. I swore. I told her to mind her own fucking business, and Quinn got up and tried to intervene. I shook his hand off my arm.

"There's a reason I moved away, you know," I said, taking a step closer to the kitchen. My voice was raw from screaming. "To get away from you. And it's about time you took the fucking hint."

Sadhana put her palms down on the counter, rings clinking. "Q-baby, do you want to get out of this madhouse?" she said.

I snorted. Quinn shot me a guilty look that was half fearful. I glared back. After that he kept his eyes down.

"I think I'd better stay here with my mom."

A minute later she stood at the doorway in her grey wool coat, which was hanging open. She was wearing a yellow top patterned with purple, brushed silver earrings shaped like birds, dark blue jeans, brown leather boots. She had the keys of the rental car looped around the first two fingers of her right hand.

"Fine," she said. "I'm leaving." She was angry, I could tell, angry but calm. I was the one with tears running down my face and collarbone, soaking the neckline of my sweater. My body was tensed, shaking, beyond my control. It always gave way when I tried to be strong. She shook her head at me. "You're being an idiot, you know."

"Don't come back," I said, reckless, and her eyes hardened, and she was gone.

Ten days later she called on our birthday and asked to speak to Quinn, and I hung up on her. And that was the last time I heard her voice.

~ EIGHT ~

⌦ GATINEAU ⌫

"Good morning," I say to the red-headed stranger passing by in the other direction. He has already said "Good morning" and "Beautiful day." His wife beams and nods. Evan makes a kind of salute with the brim of his black baseball cap. There is a charming etiquette to hiking. We are all friends because we are together outside. As we crest the rise, I can just see a flash of orange T-shirt in the distance. Quinn has charged ahead on the path.

Evan has his jaw set tight, his hands shoved in his pockets in an effort to seem casual.

"I put it off too long," I say. "Is that it?"

Evan inhales deeply through his nose, exhales, and says, "Could be." He's being short with me today. It isn't going how he planned. He picked us up at home in his truck and Quinn soon made it clear he was only coming along under extreme protest. He managed to shake Evan's hand without obvious rudeness when I introduced them, but afterwards he slumped in his seat, grunting responses during the drive over the river, his face glued to the window, knee up against the dashboard.

Quinn's bad behaviour makes me nervous and guilty, as if he has somehow discerned my secret meeting with Ravi, now looming just five days away.

"It's normal," I say. "Best to take it slow with these things. He's always wary at first."

"Always?" The tip of Evan's shoe makes contact with a rock, which skitters ahead and bounces off a tree trunk. "How many boyfriends have you introduced him to?"

I'm careful to make eye contact. "Two. Three counting you." Three, anyway, in recent memory. A few when Quinn was small, all regrettable. But however bright and large Evan looms in my life at the moment, I won't let him start shining into all the corners of the past. A new man can only try to reach back so far.

"Don't worry," he says, catching my look and scratching at the neck of his shirt. There are a few mosquitoes out here, close to the lake. They seem to hang in the air as though suspended by the humidity. "Interrogation over."

"I'm supposed to be happy I have a guy who can read my mind, right?"

"You got it." His hand is on my hip for a moment until the path narrows and I take the lead.

My ex-boyfriend Andrew brought bribes to his first meeting with Quinn: a chocolate rabbit, since it was close to Easter, and a package of hockey cards, a gift I found almost laughable, given our family's almost complete ignorance of sports, but which Quinn tore open with enthusiasm and began carrying around in his pocket to show people.

Andrew teased me that I had managed to raise a jock in

spite of overwhelming efforts to the contrary. "You should take him to some local games," he suggested, "or at least sit him down to watch some hockey on television. He's going to be hopelessly out of touch with the other kids."

I'd shrugged, but I let Andrew wrestle with the rabbit ears on top of our battered television set to get decent reception for *Hockey Night in Canada*. It became something we did together on Saturdays, all three of us ranged on the couch like benched players, Quinn and Andrew taut and edgy, as though they might actually get tapped for the ice. After Andrew and I broke up, I tried to keep watching with Quinn, but he quickly became exasperated with trying to elbow my nose out of a book.

"That's a penalty," I'd say, when I felt his fists battering the cover. "That's two minutes in the box."

But he just sighed in a theatrical way and exhorted me to at least pretend I was paying attention. "If you don't, I'm calling Andrew and telling him you want him back." He used his hands to lever himself all the way back on the couch, and his legs stuck straight out as he kept them from touching the floor. He had his arms folded in a posture of severe concentration.

"You're way too cynical for an eleven-year-old," I told him.

Another man, Toby, a predecessor to Andrew and a six-week placid mistake, met Quinn by accident when he was dropping me off after our date. Quinn had fooled the babysitter into thinking he was asleep, then sprung himself on us at the front steps as soon as her car pulled away. "Hey mister," he said, like some ragtag urchin about to plead for change. "Do you want to stay and play Go Fish? It's better with three."

Toby had been well informed of Quinn's existence but still seemed shocked by the sight of his small, bouncing person. He handed Quinn the Styrofoam-packed leftovers of our meal in Little Italy. "Sorry kid, I've got to head out right away. Here's a doggie bag, though."

I plucked it from Quinn's hands before he could go on a midnight tear. We were night owls, both of us, and it was bad enough contending with my own sleeplessness, let alone that of an eight-year-old fuelled by spaghetti and meatballs.

"Goodnight, Bee," said Toby, waving, backing down the path to the sidewalk before we'd had a proper farewell. Sadhana would have said he was running scared. After that night, things tapered off decisively, and I felt so relieved that I considered instituting a policy whereby any gentleman caller would meet Quinn on the first date, just to root out the weaklings. But when Quinn wouldn't stop asking about Toby, even after those unremarkable few minutes, I gave up the idea altogether.

Evan pauses from time to time to crouch at a bloom or a fern or to tap the side of a tree. He doesn't volunteer a speech but I oblige by asking, not so much because I want to know but because I love to hear him say words like *sap* and *canopy* and wrestle with his natural reluctance to speak more than two or three sentences at a time. I wonder whether this reticence is straightforward modesty or just the quietness of being in the woods, or maybe even someone before me who tamped down that eagerness with her disinterest.

"This here's a grey birch," he says, pointing. "And a Canadian hemlock. This is fun, all these different trees out here I'm not used to. East versus west." Then he looks a little sheepish.

"No, it *is* fun," I say. I look for a way to join in and am surprised to find one. I grab his arm. "There's a trillium." We stoop to it, and it looks like a winged white tongue in the maple shade, its three pale petals bent open in a shrug. A ghostly thing, Ontario's flower.

He says, "I once picked a western red lily for my mother. A gorgeous bloom, just like the one on the flag."

"The flag?"

"The Saskatchewan flag. Of course, you're not supposed to pick them. She told me, and I felt like a criminal. Just utterly miserable."

"Poor kid."

"I think she felt bad telling me, but she knew I would have run out and grabbed all I could find if she'd been nothing but pleased."

As the path leads up to higher ground, the air around us gets warmer. Watching Evan turning brown in the sun, his flesh that I want to press to my lips, I wonder how much of love is a simple hunger. The desire to take something inside ourselves. "You and some olive oil," I say.

"What's that?"

"It must be time for lunch."

I'm pinning my hopes on lunch, since food is the one thing that might keep Quinn at hand long enough for Evan to speak to him. Evan is so steeled for disappointment that the only thing that might catch him off guard is a lack of opportunity. Quinn has been outstripping us since we first set out from the truck.

We stop at a spot near a cliff face with picnic tables and brown garbage cans wide as rain barrels. It is a perfect day and we are all terribly flawed. The sun on my face as we come into the clearing feels like a reproach for my bad humour. A family at a table nearby has a brindle boxer that circles the rest area, ID tags jingling. Every time it comes close, it lets Evan grab hold of its jowls and listens, tongue lolling, as Evan assures him he is a good boy, such a good boy, in his absurd affectionate doggy voice.

"Did you guys ever have a pet?" asks Evan, as the dog wheels back to its family. He holds out his hands and I splash out some of the contents of my water bottle as he rubs them together.

"No," I say. "Quinn wanted a dog but I wasn't convinced we were responsible enough to look after one." Quinn says nothing, watching the family with the boxer. There must be six or seven of them, adults and children, all crowded around the table, the smallest kids getting up now and again to run with the dog before being called back in French.

I pass around the food, and over the egg-on-pumpernickel sandwiches there is some frank appraisal I can hardly bear to watch. Quinn is giving Evan what I can tell is meant to be a highly aggressive stare, though as a cop Evan has surely seen worse. Evan, for his part, is meeting Quinn's gaze and eating even more slowly than I am, perhaps suggesting that he is more than willing to drag out the meal past its natural conclusion.

"Gorgeous day for this," I say. "Hiking, I mean. Isn't it, Quinn?" He shrugs. The conversation from the other table is so boisterous, so unflagging and punctuated with obvious warmth, that it is an embarrassing contrast to our staid lunch. Evan's chewing is the loudest sound, rivalled only by the twitching of Quinn's boot against the wooden leg of the table.

Finally I say, "Another sandwich?" I have everything in my knapsack on the bench beside me, doling out the food to keep Quinn from rushing. They both reach out and I give Quinn his sandwich first, Evan's a second later.

Evan takes a couple of contemplative bites, one elbow on the table, then says, "So your mother tells me you're heading to university next year."

"Sure am."

"Looking forward to it?"

"Hell, yeah." Quinn crumples the wax paper into a ball. "I guess you didn't do the whole university thing, being a cop and all."

"I did. Criminology." The dog traces another wide loop around the clearing, and Evan's eyes move to it for a moment as it flashes past. "You're right, though, you only need high school, but I'd like to be a detective."

"When you grow up, you mean?"

"Quinn!" I am so alarmed I look at Evan, not my son, but Evan seems calm.

"Sure," he says. "It's still what I want to be. But it isn't as easy as just saying you want to solve crimes. You've got to put in some time first. But a degree helps."

Quinn grunts, and Evan finishes his sandwich. He holds out his hand for Quinn's wax paper, which I end up handing to him, and he carries our garbage to the nearest trash can. I start hissing at Quinn when Evan is a few paces away.

"Please. Please be nice. Would it kill you to be nice?"

Quinn has his arms folded on the table, and he lowers his chin to his wrists. It's hard for him to slump so far, given his height. He's putting in a real effort. "Maybe. Would you risk the life of your only son?"

I'm huffing my way into a lecture when Evan comes back and cuts me off. He touches my shoulder. "Let's not worry about it now, and just enjoy the rest of the afternoon, shall we?" He nods at Quinn. "Maybe we can save the getting-to-know-each-other stuff for another day."

Quinn says, "That's okay. I don't expect I'll be seeing you again."

The hard line of Evan's mouth betrays a moment of anger, but he shrugs it away as he moves his hands to his hips. His broad shoulders are square, like a drill sergeant's. "Right," he says. "Time to walk it off."

With Evan shooing us, we start single file along a new trail that should close the circle and bring us back around to where we parked on the other side. It is an easy trail, but long. We are working our way through the wedge of land that is Gatineau Park itself, the rugged shoulder of the valley. Across from Ottawa, just over the river that marks Ontario's border with Quebec, the park is a place that seems both in and out of time, an effect that fluctuates as we pass in and out of view of other hikers. There is a liminal sense in its silence, an indifference grown right into the trees as to whether their roots are buried in land that at different times might be described as French or English.

"Is that how you are with your young offenders? Mr. Nice Guy?"

Evan seems more relaxed since Quinn sniped at him. Quinn is still ahead of us, maintaining a lead that almost has me at a jog as we try to keep him in sight, though Evan, with his long legs, is still at an easy stride.

"I just keep trying to put myself in his shoes," he says. "If it were my mom."

As far as I can tell, his mother bears little resemblance to me. A farm wife with a wall of county fair blue ribbons in baking and quilting. With four children. A woman almost from another era, by the sound of it.

"You'd probably punch the guy's lights out," I say.

"No, I'd just strongly suggest he take a hike."

"So this is a good idea, then."

Evan gives a one-note laugh. "I'm not sure I'm winning any points today."

We hike up dusty slopes and down tracks crisscrossed with trailing roots, past fallen trees mossed over in scaly grey and a beaver dam near a still pool, where we linger looking for furred heads cresting the surface of the water. Quinn has stopped to watch, too. We stand in silence until we start to hear even the small splashing sounds of water insects.

"They must have done their beaver warning sign," I say. "Tail-slapping Morse code."

"The-humans-are-coming, the-humans-are-coming," says Quinn.

"We could wait," says Evan. "We could keep perfectly still."

Quinn kicks some pebbles into the pond with the tip of his sneaker, and they arc and splash. "Nah," he says. "They can stay under for ages." He hurries back to the path, leaving us again with the sight of his orange T-shirt and the flapped back pockets of his long khaki shorts growing smaller in the distance.

I sigh and we fall in step behind him, but this time it only takes a few minutes before Quinn is pulling so far ahead that we are in danger of losing sight of him.

Evan says, "Let him go. We'll catch up to him at the end of the trail."

I slow down. There is a fresher smell along this part of the path as we move up and away from the water. I breathe deep.

"I didn't know you wanted to be a detective."

"A lot of police work is like a carousel. Picking people up, booking them. Then they're back on the street."

"You want more," I say.

"I always want more."

When we come out at the end, where the path meets the parking lot, Quinn is nowhere in sight.

"Where is he?" I say. "What on earth?" I walk to the other side of the lot and look over at where it joins the road. There are lots of cars but no people.

"Quinn!"

Nothing. Then Evan is next to me, one hand cupped over his eyes to cut the glare from the setting sun as he scans in all directions. He checks the truck, but the flatbed is empty, as we left it.

"There's nowhere else to go," I say. "What is he doing?" I turn back to where we came out of the woods. "Maybe he had to find a bathroom or step off the trail for a minute."

"What's his cellphone number?"

"He doesn't have it with him." I saw it on the bathroom counter, of all places, as we were getting ready to leave. I almost mentioned it until it occurred to me that he might use it to avoid talking to us.

"Where's yours?"

I pat the blue fanny pack clipped around my waist.

"Is it charged?"

"Yes." I pull it out to be sure.

"Stay here." He is already moving away from me, holding up a hand when he sees my expression. "No, you have to. One of us has to stay. I'm faster. Just sit tight. I'll call when I find him." Evan flashes his cellphone at me after checking its battery level and hurries back down the path.

I sit on one of the cement blocks marking the parking spots, arms around my knees, waiting as the sky grows darker. I keep my eyes on the ground after too many false starts of spotting pairs of hikers emerging from the woods only to see them move towards their respective cars and drive away. One of the hikers, a woman, only notices me when she is about two feet away, and her hand travels to her chest as she gives a soft cry.

"I'm sorry," I say. "I'm waiting for someone."

"Sorry, I didn't see you there!" She calls this out loudly enough that the man who is with her looks over as he unlocks the car. He grips the top of the open door and peers at me over the roof of the silver Jetta.

"I'm sorry," I say again. "Just waiting for my son. Have a good night."

They wave goodbye as their car pulls away, and as the sound of the motor fades, the breeze picks up. The treetops flag to the west, leaves brushing leaves in a swishing sound that unsettles my stomach, as though the parking lot is all at once at sea.

Years ago, Quinn got lost in a department store, where Sadhana had dragged us to buy some mixing bowls. Caught up in a debate about the respective merits of a nesting set of spouted cream bowls and a moulded set in baby blue, neither of us noticed Quinn, bored out of his mind, edging away to the bath department and its patterned forest of hanging shower curtains, and from there to housewares, to electronics, and finally onto an escalator going down, in a quest to find the toys. When at last we found him, he was looking for help and just beginning to whimper. Sadhana was angry at me for not watching him, and I was a sobbing wreck. Then Sadhana said to forget it, because it came out all right in the end, so what was the point. She was wonderful at forgiving me, as long as it wasn't on her own behalf.

They are so very much themselves when they come into view, tall and broad-shouldered and, in Quinn's case, lanky to the point of awkwardness, that it makes every eagerness at a stranger's sighting seem ridiculous. They're walking side by side, but seemingly without conversation. If there is a new kind of truce between them, neither seems very excited about it.

"Where the hell were you?" They both slow down when they catch sight of me, so that I'm the one hurrying across the lot to meet them.

"I'm sorry. I got distracted picking up garbage," says Quinn, swinging into view a plastic bag stuffed full of litter. He still looks draped in shadows in spite of stepping out under the parking lights. After a moment I realize it isn't darkness but dirt clinging to his clothes from top to bottom.

"Since when are you an eco-warrior?"

"Since the glaciers started receding."

I squeeze his arm above the elbow. "Good answer." I give him a hard look to make sure I can see repentance or the trace of a reasonable facsimile. His mouth is drawn in tight as a knotted thread.

We head back to Evan's truck, and I make Quinn sit between us, a passive warning of my annoyance, a hint that he will not be getting off so easily. But I shift over to make room for him to stretch his legs under my side of the dash.

"Where was he?" I ask Evan.

"I'm sitting right here," says Quinn. "I was just off the path, maybe ten minutes back. Maybe a little farther." Evan nods.

"Radio?" Evan asks then, reaching for the knob. I shake my head.

There are leaves stuck to the bottom on my shoe, yellowing oak leaves, halfway to mulch. I kick my heels together, then start scraping my boot against the side of the truck door until I hear Evan say, "Don't. I just cleaned in here."

"Sorry," I say. "I didn't think."

Quinn says, "I scraped mine off before I got in." He sounds almost eager, or maybe it's a touch of that old instinct he had with Sadhana, turning himself into the monkey in the middle. The distraction from a fight.

"Thanks," says Evan. He turns on the radio, to a loud nineties rock station, letting the bellow-voiced singer rule out the need for any further conversation.

Libby calls early in the morning, before I'm out of bed. The cordless receiver remains on the pillow where I left it after hanging up with Evan, once I had finished uttering reassurances that Quinn, no matter his reluctance, would eventually come around. I projected more certainty than I felt. I could hardly even vouch for Quinn's goodwill on my own account.

Libby's voice resounds in my ear as I kick the comforter off my feet. I move the receiver another inch away from my eardrum. "I visited the Essaids yesterday," she says. "They said to say hello."

"Hello back."

"They're feeling a little down. Quebec First took a hit in the polls after the debate, but not as much as we'd hoped. And Ravi might actually win his riding."

"That's terrible," I say, sitting up. I don't know which is more awful, the repugnance of their political ideologies or the mere prospect of Ravi's career ambitions fulfilled. I wonder if he will seem triumphant when we meet at Bombay Palace. Public approval must be a powerful confidence booster.

"It really is. I'm afraid some people think they're the new hope. Maybe we'll go visit the Essaids this weekend? You are coming back, aren't you?"

"I am." Despite Quinn's best efforts and my more haphazard ones, there are still heaps and shambles at my sister's place. Boxes everywhere and the uncategorizable items still lying around in piles. All the things she touched that are impossible to jettison. I get up and go to the window to pull back the curtains, and for once it is overcast. "I guess I'm only half finished. Maybe two-thirds." There are puddles in the road from an overnight rain.

"It can't be easy," says Libby, growing quiet, "dealing with her things."

It is nothing she hasn't said before, but for some reason, hearing the tenderness in her voice, I am seized with an animus of blame — an opportunity to reapportion my own guilt. "You say you and Sadhana were together."

"Yes." Into the growing silence, Libby asks, "You don't believe me?"

"I do believe you. But . . . why weren't you worried when Sadhana didn't answer her phone for days on end?"

There is a quick intake of breath and then a pause. "Look," says Libby. "Sadie was a very independent woman. Sometimes I wondered if she needed me at all. So I tried to be the same way."

I long to see her face as she says this, but she sounds every bit sincere. "Okay," I say. "I'm sorry."

"Don't worry," says Libby. "And I'll help you. With the apartment. I promise."

In the kitchen, Quinn is hunched over a bowl of cereal. "You don't need to hide," he says when he sees me emerge from my bedroom and replace the phone on its charging base.

"I'm not."

"Oh, I thought you were talking to him."

Quinn's philosophy of not hiding has been in effect exactly twelve hours. After a tense drop-off from a gruff Evan, Quinn apologized for his behaviour before calling a friend from the phone in the kitchen. Speaking loud enough for me to overhear, he issued an invitation for dinner at our place the following night.

"Are you cooking?" I asked, when he hung up.

"Ha ha."

Before going in to shower, he left his laptop sitting on the kitchen counter, open to a website for someone named Caroline Henderson. There was a little bio and five or six short films that could be clicked on and watched. Based on the picture in the left-hand corner of the screen, it was the girl with the glasses from the hardware store. Our dinner guest, I surmised.

Now as I finish my cup of coffee, I caution Quinn as I prepare to head out to the grocery store. "If I make supper for you and your friend, it means you have to be nice to me tonight."

His response is more complacent than I would have guessed.

"I know."

Quinn's friend turns out to be less serious than her black-and-white website photo suggests. She shows up in a checkered skirt with red suspenders, carrying a pecan pie.

"Thanks for having me over," she says, handing me the dessert in its aluminum plate. "It's not homemade or anything. Did you know that people smile at you if you carry a pie on the bus?"

"No, I didn't know that."

"I think I'm going to start carrying one around indefinitely."

Behind me, Quinn thunders down from his bedroom to intervene. "Mom, this is Caro."

We shake hands over the pie.

"Caroline. But everyone calls me Caro."

We sit around the table and Quinn and Caro pass each other the salad while I serve portions of vegetarian lasagna from a glass casserole clutched in an oven mitt. Quinn has fiddled with the lights, turning down the dimmer, and there is a quiet CD playing on the stereo. Leonard Cohen. I'm tempted to make a comment on these unusual efforts, but I hold back. The music is a nice touch.

"I'm a vegetarian," says Caro. "I think it's so great that that's how Quinn was raised. My parents are still hoping I'll come around."

"I can't really take the credit," I say. "It was how I was raised, too. I'm not a vegetarian anymore, though. I just don't like cooking meat."

"My mother's a bit of a hypocrite," says Quinn.

"Quinn."

"Kidding."

"This is really great, Mrs. Singh."

"Not Mrs.," I say. "Beena is fine."

"Quinn says you're from Montreal. You both are."

"That's right."

"My grandmother lives in Montreal. I spend a lot of weekends there."

"You two should meet up the next time we're all there."

"Actually, we already have. Quinn's been helping me with one of my movies." She shoots him a quick glance. "In between his studying."

The scramble of looks passing between us in pairs is like the breeze on a windmill, spinning us and stirring up something new from the current. Apology and panic between Caro and Quinn. Guilt in my direction. I ignore it.

"What's the movie about?" I ask.

Caro pauses a moment. "Mostly just about my grandmother. I record her talking about her life. Then I kind of take the camera on a walk around the neighbourhood for local colour."

"Sounds interesting."

"I hope so. I'm trying hard to learn a lot." She is very earnest, extremely self-possessed for a seventeen-year-old. "I really want to make serious political documentaries. Poverty, immigration, environmental devastation. The works."

She takes another mouthful of the lasagna and chews quickly. "And I'd love to learn how to make this, too, if you'll show me some time. I need to figure out how to cook before I graduate from high school."

Over dessert, Quinn and Caro start talking about film, and the fluidity of their discourse feels like a window into Quinn's adulthood. I can see my sister strong in him, her tastes and opinions. She had taken pains with his artistic apprenticeship, in a way that sometimes seemed vain, but watching Caro incline her head and laugh and touch his elbow to interrupt makes me wonder if this was the kind of outcome Sadhana had imagined.

Any weekend with Sadhana meant a minimum of two movies, always handpicked to conform to her diagnosis of Quinn's burgeoning aesthetics and to further his cinematic education. As a formality, I might be consulted, but I was not the intended audience. One visit it was *What Ever Happened to Baby Jane?*, *His Girl Friday*, and *Strangers on a Train*. Another weekend it was *The Last Picture Show* and *Written on the Wind*. They were great films, and they knit a thread between the three of us, a second history of narratives and images. It was easier for us to hold on to other people's stories.

One time she showed up on our doorstep with a VCR under her arm, plugs trailing down to her boots. "They only had *All That Jazz* on tape." She waved the plastic case under my nose.

I worried she was trying to make Quinn into some rarefied thing, that she would be disappointed if his gifts didn't tend that way — as hers did, to art. I wanted us to leave the world open for him. It was only a matter of time before a rebellion, and Sadhana wouldn't be the one standing in its way. But by then Quinn was almost fifteen and still nothing but a good kid, somehow unencumbered. He had his dumb jokes and his own music that he played too loud every night in his room, until I bought him a pair of headphones, but he was present and not at all closed off. He crawled back behind the television and hooked up the VCR, genial and easy, and I wondered if there was anything of me in him, if it was the kind of thing I was too close to trace. Then I saw him bounce back to the couch with the remote controls, breathless, waiting for my sister to open the proceedings, energized by her presence, and I knew we were exactly the same.

I get up from my seat on the pretext of making tea and leave them to talk that has been skimming past me since I brought the pie to the table. Caro says something and Quinn's laugh comes out throaty, commanding attention. Sadhana's laugh. I put the kettle on to boil, wondering as usual whether I should have changed the water or whether boiled water always comes clean. While it begins to bubble, Quinn and Caro start talking themselves into a movie at the theatre downtown, and I do what I can to encourage them. I give Quinn twenty dollars, and he takes it from me with hesitation, wary of a bribe for goodwill extending beyond tonight's truce.

"Take it. Don't worry. Have fun." I want the place to myself for when Evan finishes his shift. Quinn shoots me a grin as they head off to the bus stop, and my gratitude is so unreasonable it's a relief to hide myself behind the door as I swing it shut.

When he arrives, Evan pauses in the doorway as though listening for something.

"I told you, he's not here. Don't be nervous."

"I'm not." Evan sounds disgruntled, but his expression changes to one of interest as he comes in the house. It's the first time I've invited him over to somewhere other than the back porch.

"I'm sorry about all that yesterday," I say. I pour us some whiskies and bring them over to the couch.

"No problem." Evan is studying some of the framed photos on the wall, but he sits down when I hand him his glass. His gaze lingers over one of me, Sadhana, and Quinn, taken by Terence at one of her dinner parties last summer. I am reminded by our outfits that there had been a lengthy and spirited debate about Terence's sweater and whether or not an ironic fashion choice could be considered legitimately chic. Sadhana and Terence had pounded the table until my wine began to leap from its glass and assault the tablecloth. The argument had petered out only after Sadhana called Terence a "bingo grandmother" and, falling into a fit of giggles, had to push back from the table, clutching at her left side below her ribs, where she was starting to get a stitch.

I change the subject to something I've been wanting to ask. "Do you think the stress of a fight could kill someone? Give them a heart attack?"

"Like a physical fight?"

"No, a disagreement."

Evan takes a small sip of his drink and a moment to consider. "Maybe? I guess it has to do with blood pressure. Maybe in the heat of the moment it could be too much for someone."

"That's just it," I say. "People don't die of a heart attack for no reason. They get angry or they're shovelling snow or playing football or something." As I say this, I realize I am giving voice to something I have been thinking for a long time. "Even people with weak hearts."

"What are you trying to get at, exactly?"

"I'm saying something happened to my sister." Evan's point about the heat of the moment helps me discard my own role in the theory, so even as I say this aloud I feel the possibility of absolution. Our fight, however it may have broken Quinn's heart, did not break Sadhana's. The hope almost makes me want to cry.

Evan puts down his glass. He reaches out and clasps my arms below the elbows with a light touch. "What about all the startling things that happen every day?" He is offering alternatives as though my guilty conscience is still hanging in the balance. "An alarm clock going off or an ambulance driving by with its siren. A mouse running across the floor."

"I wonder." I imagine an argument with Libby, or maybe with a downstairs neighbour. I remember there was a woman who once made a noise complaint after a party. Our fight may have been old news by the time of Sadhana's death, but what else could have happened in her life in the meantime?

"It could have been anything, Beena," says Evan, as if I'd spoken aloud. "She could have carried too many groceries up the stairs. If her heart was really that bad, it could have given out. They call it a ticker, don't they? Sometimes they run down."

"That's what her doctor implied."

"And she was sick for how long with her eating disorder?"

"Eighteen years, on and off."

"So."

"Yeah." I see his point, and for once, I feel it to be true.

Evan checks his watch. "When is Quinn getting home?"

"Soon."

While my silence still leaves room for him to imagine that I accept his analysis, Evan finishes his drink and urges me to give him a tour of the bedroom.

Later, when I'm alone washing the dishes, I remember what my sister said to me that last time, before I hung up in her ear. Not her last words, but her last to me in this world: "This is the kind of thing that gets followed to its end, Bee. Ravi is the answer to a question and Quinn can't just leave him alone. You can't ask him to." This logic is less hateful to me now, or I am. I was someone else then, I must have been, to have hung up like that, to have harboured that fury. At least, this kind of rupture is the only path I have found to mercy: if that was me, it isn't now. I dry each tumbler by hand before replacing them in the cupboard with the mindfulness of a person forging new habits. Now a call only ends once I hear the click and the dial tone in my own ear.

Speaking the words to Evan has given them purchase in the world, and the bare assertion is no more than simple truth. Something did happen to my sister, a mental illness at the very least. But the way that she died, the heart attack, suggests something more.

Fetching my purse, I pull out Sadhana's day-planner, which I have been carrying around since I found it. I turn to November, looking carefully now for some confirmation that she followed through on her pact to help Quinn find his father, despite our argument. Knowing Sadhana, she wouldn't have stopped just because I asked her. Once her mind was set on something, she rarely swerved. For all I know, the email draft I found might have been sent by Sadhana long before our fight. But if she knew what Ravi was up to, the kind of beliefs he'd adopted, and it seems that she did, then why would she have been so eager to help Quinn?

Unless that was her agenda all along—to show Quinn exactly the kind of man his father was.

The longer I think about it, the likelier it seems, though I can only guess that it was my aversion to his very name that led her to avoid explaining things. More and more, regret has simply become the shadow I would cast if I stood in the sun.

I open the planner on the counter. I've been avoiding it. It isn't the diary, and maybe that's why, or maybe it's the heart-rendingly precise scrawls under every date or the futility of the empty pages, but I can see once I finally look that the planner is full of information for the fearless biographer. It contains nothing so blatant as *Help Quinn* or *Call Ravi*, but there is more than one instance of *Call R* with a line through it, which I stare at until I remember her friend Rachelle Dupuis. Then, on November thirteenth, a note, *Meet RP*, next to the words *Bombay Palace*. This, too, has a line through it. And on November twenty-ninth, below the cryptic mention of *Juniper Berries*, a note to *Call RP*, with no location. That last hateful day with nothing crossed out.

I put down the day-planner, pace from the kitchen to the living room and back before once again taking it up. The notion that she'd talked to him, met with him. It bewildered as a possibility, but now it wounds as a certainty. The mention of Bombay Palace, his chosen location for our upcoming meeting, leaves no room for doubt, and even though I now believe Sadhana planned to expose him either to Quinn or to his constituents as a moral fraud, there is a sting of betrayal in the realization. Growing up, there was so little in my life that was separate from Sadhana. Ravi may not have been someone worth boasting about, but at least, when he was around, he was part of my story alone.

Getting changed into my pyjamas, I wonder if Sadhana ever made that last call to Ravi. If she was really trying to undermine me, yet again, in Quinn's affections—by helping him where I was unwilling. And what she would say if she knew my jealousy extended even beyond death.

∽ TRAJECTORIES ∾

In order to see Ravi, I have to lie to everybody. Quinn, Uncle, Evan. Even Libby. Quinn and I are back in Montreal for another long weekend, and when Libby calls, I find myself making excuses to avoid another invitation. Her friendship still takes me by surprise, but I better understand her loneliness now, her loss. And maybe she senses the same kind of loneliness in me.

The way I leave it, the only people with any interest in my whereabouts think I'm going to meet Sophie, an old friend from high school. But Sophie doesn't exist. I remember, as I walk at dusk from the bus stop the precautions one normally takes when meeting strangers these days: a busy, well-lit public place. Tell someone where you're going.

It's a small neighbourhood restaurant, just six tables. There is a large wall-hanging printed with elephants. Two televisions are suspended in opposite corners, showing the same soccer game. The commentary is in a language I don't understand, and one of the sets is turned up too loud.

The waiter at Bombay Palace seems to be seething in his own private fury, showing me to a table in silence that seems about to be broken any minute with a harsh word. He drops a menu on the table, and when I say I am waiting for someone, he gets another from the counter and tosses it on top of the first. I cast around to see if I can detect the source of his anger, but I seem to be the only contender. There is a host buffing silverware behind the counter, but he, too, seems to have his own grievances, which may or may not be related to the progress of the soccer game.

Ravi comes in, and I stand up. The surprise I thought I would feel in his presence is absent. He looks like his poster, without the beaming.

"Hi Beena," he says. I find I cannot greet him, my mouth fixed in as grim a line as the waiter's.

He breaks into politician mode then. He steps behind me and pulls out my chair. "Have you tried this place before? The food is delicious."

I recover my voice, stepping away from the table. "I don't understand what we're doing here. Do you expect us to sit down and have a meal?"

For a moment I see him waver, as though he thought his polish and bravado could carry him through this. "Do you want to go outside?"

"No, on second thought, I feel safer here." I sit down and spread my napkin across my lap. He stares for a moment, then jerks out his own chair and drops into it.

"What have you told the reporter?"

"There is no reporter. Not yet."

"So what do you want?" This comes out heavily, as if the question itself is a concession.

"The refugee family you're going after. I want you to back off." I am surprised that this is what comes out.

"God, what is it with you and your sister?" He takes hold of the menu but doesn't open it. I keep my hands on the edge of the table, afraid to disrupt the flow of information. "The man is here illegally."

"And what have you done to deserve to be here?"

"I was born here," he says in all seriousness. Even indignation.

I laugh in his face. "According to you, being born doesn't count for much."

His face startles into something like shame before he turns it into a frown. "That was a long time ago."

"I know. Your son is almost old enough to vote."

Ravi flinches, and I see creases line his forehead. He is older than me, I remember. I wonder if he has a career apart from politics, anything to fall back on. The day I visited the campaign office, Libby had said something about Ravi's wife being wealthy. Political careers need money at the back of them. I wonder how far a man might go to hide a child if he thought he might lose everything.

When he says nothing, I say, "So you saw my sister."

"Yes," he says. "That bitch."

"You know she's dead, right?" I get to my feet. "I guess I'm calling the papers."

"Hold on, hold on. No, I didn't know." The dour waiter finally appears, and Ravi waves him off. "Another minute, please."

Ravi lowers his voice so I have to lean in. "I'm sorry. Look, I had no idea. What happened?"

"Like you care. Just keep going. You saw Sadhana."

He is starting to look nervous. "Sure, I met with her. We met a few times, actually. We talked. She seemed a hell of a lot more interested in me than you do."

His narcissism hasn't changed. I sit back down. "And?"

"Then she gave me a piece of her mind."

I'm picturing the way she would have done it, soothing his wariness with a few polite questions before lashing out with a torrent of vitriol. She would have enjoyed it. She would have done a better job than I was doing.

"Probably not enough of it," I say.

"You're entitled to your opinion. And once she was done abusing me, she let me ask about my son."

"Your son, right." My scoffing nearly makes me spill my water. "And what do you mean, you met a few times?"

"Just twice. She told me so much about him, I asked her if she could bring some pictures the next time."

"Pictures?"

"Photos." Ravi's voice is soft but even. "I think he seems like a fine young man. There might even be a little something of me in him."

I ignore this. "And?" Sadhana's secrets were truly unfathomable.

"She brought them. We looked at them together. Then she said she thought that it was time for me to meet him."

"And?"

"And I told her it was impossible."

"You're sure you haven't met him?" I say. And then, "Why impossible?"

"Of course I'm sure. And it's impossible because I have a career, Beena. A family. A whole lot of people depending on me to be someone they can trust."

"So you'd prefer to keep lying to them?"

He starts to answer, but I cut him off. "Were you supposed to talk to her again on November twenty-ninth? Did she say anything else to you about Quinn?"

"No. The twenty-ninth? I don't know. I don't think so." He scowls as he turns the menu over in his hands and slides it back onto the table. "As far as I was concerned there was nothing more to say. She flipped her lid, and I left."

"What do you mean, flipped?"

"She threatened me about going public. But I could tell she didn't mean it. She told me to change my tune about the Essaid case, too."

So I was right. The commentary on the soccer game has been accompanied by jangling music almost as loud, and as Ravi's gaze keeps drifting above my head I wonder if his eyes are straying to the screen behind me. Both Bombay Palace employees are watching the other television from behind the bar.

"She didn't call you? You know that's the day she died, right?" I picture Sadhana screaming at him over the phone and her heart seizing. I watch him carefully for alarm or confusion, but there is only the continuing aggrieved air of ruffled conceit. He sighs and brings his eyes back to meet mine.

"No. And I didn't know that. I didn't even know she passed away, remember?"

I get up and grab my purse from the back of my chair. "Well, there's a new deal now. One week for you to support Bassam Essaid and his family and Father Cavanagh, or everybody finds out. And stay away from Quinn." I wait until he nods, then I push in my chair and walk out.

There is nothing in his face, or our history, to trust.

―∽◯∽―

The next morning I wake at eight and Quinn's bed is already empty. Uncle is sitting at the kitchen table in his apron with his coffee and newspaper. He began work before the sun and it is already his first break of the day.

"Your boy is intent on catching the worm," he says, when he sees me poke my head into the kitchen to check for Quinn. "You just missed him. Off to the library."

I sink into the nearest chair. "The city seems to energize him."

Uncle spreads out a page to read below the fold. "Young men have a lot of energy. Always it is the way."

"Well, at home he sleeps in."

"Mmm." As Uncle scans the columns, his whole face angles downward, his beard coming down to tickle his neck. He has reading glasses now, little half-moons. He lowers the paper and peers at me. "Have you had a chance to look through your sister's mail?"

"No. Not yet."

"I wonder if there is something from the tax people, the revenue agency. She was worried about being audited."

"Really? I don't know. I'll check."

"It isn't urgent, Beena. I'm only curious. I've already sent them all the papers they need now. For the estate and so on."

I stop halfway into the kitchen, one foot on the linoleum. There are so many things I haven't thought of that Uncle has already taken in hand. "I appreciate everything you've done," I say, at once feeling and sounding awkward. "You've taken care of so much."

"You're welcome."

I am reminded of a fact once confided in us by Mama, that Uncle had spent the better part of his youth before he came to Canada taking care of his ailing mother, who by all accounts had been a difficult woman to get along with. Papa, as the elder brother as well as a trained pastry chef and perpetual disappointment, had felt sufficiently disowned to more or less stay away. I wonder how Uncle must have felt when we were thrust upon him as teenagers, the rest of his life consigned again to duty.

Uncle gets up from the table. "Quinn said to say he wouldn't be home for supper. He tells me the university library never closes and they have a cafeteria there."

"How convenient."

"He's a good boy," says Uncle. "I was thinking—while you're here, if he needs something to do, I could use him in the shop. And if he likes it, he could work in the fall, a shift here and there."

Quinn as one of the bagel boys. The idea is disagreeable. "We'll see, Uncle."

"We have a computer program for the books, but there are other things he could set up for me. Something for the inventory and the schedule."

He, too, is worried about Quinn's day-long sojourns from the apartment. We are to become conspirators in constraining him.

I watch Quinn carefully after he gets back, but there is no sign of a change in him. There is also no way to ask him point-blank without giving myself away. *Did you see your father today?* Ravi's denial doesn't carry much weight with me. And though Quinn has never been very up on current events, I know it can only be a matter of time, here in

Montreal, before news of his father penetrates his consciousness—if he hasn't already been following his career. But my
son seems as he ever does. Calm and quiet. For all our silences in Ottawa, our lives were still running alongside one
another. There was a comfort in knowing most of the basic
facts. At Uncle's, a space has opened up; the hours Quinn
used to spend on the computer or at his friends' houses have
now been turned over to the city and whatever he does out
of the apartment all day.

"Good day?" I say.

"Decent."

If I don't ask him what he's been doing, he can't refuse
to tell me, and the fragile balance of our truce doesn't have to
be dissolved. He drops his heavy knapsack on the floor before
he starts scrounging for leftovers. At the table with a bowl
of curry and rice, he pulls out an unfinished crossword pil-
fered from Uncle's recycling box, but stows it when he sees
me looking over his shoulder.

Then he gets ready for bed, brushing his teeth and
washing his face in a comprehensive ritual almost as long as
Sadhana's. His long black hair flips back from his forehead
like a coxcomb after he buries his wet face in the orange
towel. In the bedroom, I lie under my blankets and face his
side of the room as he takes a thick paperback from his bag,
reading with the front pages curled back like a magazine,
hiding the cover. Then, exhausted by my watchfulness, he
sleeps, his body turned away from me. It is only nine-thirty
at night.

But when Quinn's breathing becomes even and he has
fallen into sleep, he rolls over to face me, his back nudging up
against the wall as his mouth falls open. And when I get out

of bed to turn off the overhead light, I pull the quilt up over his shoulder, and in his sleep he makes a pleased sound like a kind of thank-you.

The next morning I keep my eyes closed as I hear him getting out of bed. He is almost silent. He must have put on his socks before swinging his feet to the floor. It is only the building itself that betrays him, the floors and doors responding in their faint language of creaks and screeches. Quinn himself is soundless; he is sneaking. Feeling like a mother indulging some elaborate game of make-believe, I let him slip out of the apartment without breaking the illusion.

I count to ten before leaping out of bed and grabbing a black shirt and jeans and an elastic from my suitcase. I get downstairs in wrinkly, clinging clothes, hair knotted in a messy bun, just in time to see Quinn turning right on St. Laurent. The weekend bagel lineup is already snaking down past the ice cream shop, and I turn sideways to pass through the crowd. When I round the corner after him, I have a quake in my step, one knocking knee that might be trying to jar loose the guilty feeling from the part of me that can't ignore what I'm doing. I breathe deep to let it go, but it roots there, somewhere under my ribcage.

A block ahead, Quinn is already at the intersection, scratching the back of his neck, that sunburn from the lawn mowing, or its cousin. How someone so tall could come out of me—it's mystery physics. It's Russian dolls in reverse.

I slow down in case he turns around, and I don't pick up the pace until he's crossing the next street. His walk is enough to help me spot him from a distance, and this early on a Sunday there isn't too much movement on the Montreal streets. The city's long Saturday nights take their toll.

I don't know that I've ever made it clear to Quinn why there isn't more I can tell him. It's just that it happened so quickly. With all I've told him about sex and love and trust, I think I've let him imagine that Ravi was a boyfriend. But it was just a few weeks when Ravi was eighteen. I can barely remember his face as it was, only glimpses of it in relation to me. The side of his chin against my cheek, his thick bottom lip and those two days it was chapped. And now Quinn is the age his father was then. It is enough to make me stumble and check my shoelaces, still double-knotted. He is his father. He is the place where Ravi's face ends in my memory.

I still remember that awful feeling when Ravi disappeared, like the slow curdling of a stagnant pool. Without Quinn, who knows how long I might have stood still. And since then, all this time and carefulness, this scrupulous steering away from any allusion to that first rejection. But I am safe now. Safe from him. I don't know how or when it happened. Maybe only when the hurt was replaced with a new one.

Quinn goes into a shop, comes out with a newspaper. He seems so casual I have a surging moment of confidence when I am sure Evan must be wrong about my son looking for his father. But then Quinn tucks it tight under his arm, and in the slight motion of his head—as he bows down to check its snugness before snapping back up to look ahead—I think I recognize an old mannerism I didn't even know I remembered. It's an almost-march. Up ahead of me, he's parading into battle in disguise as a regular teenager. When he was very small, Sadhana used to give him drills when he was afraid, an umbrella for a rifle, a blazer for a uniform, and three stomps around the apartment to conquer Brussels sprouts or trips to the doctor or twelve times twelve.

He is still a block ahead, at the corner, when a bus pulls up to the curb and he climbs aboard, emptying a fistful of change into the cash box. It is a bus that could take him north to Ravi's riding, though there is no way of knowing if that's his trajectory. He might be going to meet his friend Caro if she's here for the weekend. I turn my back as it drives past before it makes a right at the next street, watching its reflection in the glass front of a store, looking for Quinn. He's staring out the window, and for a moment I could swear we lock eyes except for the lack of recognition on his face. His image in the glass is faint and brooding. Almost a stranger if I squint.

⟡ SANCTUARY ⟡

It begins to rain as I leave the bus stop, and the pink and purple impatiens in city planters are bowing under the deluge. The rain streams behind my ears and down my back, but the water is warm. Heading back to Mile End now, to Sadhana's place, I pass a soccer game in the park where the players' white and red uniforms are splattered with mud. In the newspaper boxes, I see headlines announcing that a second French-language school has kicked out a student for wearing a head covering that hides most of her face. NON À NIQAB: ÉTUDIANTE EXPULSÉE ENCORE.

Inside, I shrug out of my wet shirt and do a lap of my sister's apartment to see what might have been overlooked. The place already looks a little less like hers, which is as much of a wound as a relief. I go around unhooking the frames and canvases from where they have been hanging, leaning them against the walls. I put on a dry black T-shirt from one of the unsealed boxes in the bedroom. The sealed boxes I begin grouping in the centre of each room to get a better handle on what is left to pack. The only way to deal with Sadhana's

things is to pretend they aren't hers. Or that I am a professional mover and I have never before laid eyes on this set of
blue dishes with the white flowers, this grey wool coat with
the pink lining, the wall hooks shaped like four little silver
birds. I'll have to bring a screwdriver to take those down.

Anxious for a distraction, I pour myself a glass of water
from the tap. I turn on Sadhana's radio loud, out of habit.
Sometimes when I was younger, I would make noises just to
hear them stop. I used to rattle a pot full of cutlery in the sink
or turn on the worst kind of talk radio, spinning up the knob
until I could feel my shoulders squaring against the sound, my
whole skin burning to get away. There was a point at which
too loud became something physical, a horror. And then I'd
stop, and for a second a real kind of relief would flood through
me. I'd breathe slowly through my nose, in and out, like in
one of Mama's yoga classes. It was a trick, the sound and the
silence. A physical shortcut to the most fleeting peace, like
finally giving in to a sneeze after trying to hold it back. When
Quinn was a baby and Sadhana was in the hospital, making
and breaking a racket was one of the only ways I could get
calm. I did it only when Quinn was awake, for fear of waking him, and he seemed to understand with a baby's ancient
wisdom that it was the kind of thing best left alone, a bit of
private insanity between new mother and child that could be
safely and tactfully ignored.

When I switch off the radio at the start of the hourly
news break, there is no release. The thing that ends up startling me out of my agitation is a phone call from Libby.

"Did you see the news? The police raided the church."

"No," I say. At once, I wonder whether Ravi was involved,
though I've no idea if he has that kind of influence. "No, that's

awful." I think of peaceable Bassam in handcuffs and oblivious baby Léo in his mother's arms, and a quake runs down my back. "What's going to happen now?"

"I don't know," says Libby. There is a trace of excitement in her voice. "They didn't find them."

"What?"

"They weren't there. And Father Cavanagh was gone, too. He left word with one of the other priests that he was going to visit his mother."

"But are they okay?"

"I don't know. But I know who might."

～⟨∽⟩～

I meet Libby in the late afternoon, outside the bakery of the large outdoor market, and as she approaches I try to remind myself that I still haven't brought her around to talking about Sadhana's last weeks. She is pulling an old-fashioned metal grocery cart in one hand and Mouse with the other. Two loaves of bread in paper wrappings are peeking out of a cloth bag looped around her shoulder.

"I hope this isn't too embarrassing," she says, indicating the cart. "I know we're on a mission, but the fridge is empty and we live just down the street. It really is the best way to carry things." She pulls it along a few paces, the metal rods chattering in their frame. Mouse covers her face with her hands. "You see?" says Libby. "It makes my own daughter want to disown me."

"It's practical," I say.

"It necessitates a certain system," says Libby. "Root vegetables first. Bruisable fruit and other crushables at the top. Bread, you know. And eggs, god forbid."

We wind up and down the rows of stalls, Libby push-ing the clattering cart with one hand, still holding tight to Mouse's sleeve with the other. The little girl seems desperate to get away from us, bobbing out from her mother to sniff at flowers or gawk at other children. Watching her, I remem-ber a compulsion I had when I was her age to touch every unusual-looking object in the grocery store. Artichokes, yel-low crookneck squash. A raw trout that gave up its iridescent scales to my sticky fingertips.

Sadhana and I never went to the market much after Mama died, the place was too full of her, the flip of her orange hair over her shoulder as she looked back at us before leaning in to choose a tomato. The tomatoes them-selves, even: the fresh, sweet fullness of them, with a lit-tle salt jiggered onto them by the vendors. There were no ripe tomatoes left in a world without Mama. The touch of her hands on every vegetable felt like an initiation into her secret world where ordinary objects could be infused with a kind of goodness based on how well they fulfilled a par-ticular function. A leek resting upon her palms became a thing to marvel over. She got us to hold our fingers up to it, to compare the circumferences. We agreed that any leek that looked as thick as Papa's fingers was truly a magnifi-cent vegetable. Every time we went to the market there was something new to enthuse over: peaches as firm as tennis balls, onions that could make your eyes water from across the room, Indian mangoes the colour of the sun.

And Mama made us smell everything she bought. One time, when I exclaimed over an apple, she told me to take a bite. "Whenever you eat," she told me, putting one into my hand, "you should remember to be happy to be alive."

Now, to Libby, I say, "What else do you need?" So far the cart contains only a giant cauliflower and six cucumbers. "I thought we were going to talk to someone."

"We are."

We continue wandering, and with successive exchanges that never feel anything less than haphazard, the cage of the cart fills up with carrots and peppers and watermelon. Romaine lettuce and grapefruit and brie. Then Mouse asks for some pears, and an immoderate bag of at least fifteen pears is the last thing added to the pile.

"We're going somewhere, right?" I say as Libby tucks a handful of change into the pocket of her jeans. "This isn't just a shopping expedition."

"Multitasking. Don't worry."

A row of handicraft stalls lines the northern end of the market. Artisanal honey, lavender soap, foie gras from only the finest force-fed francophone ducks. "Lobsters!" screams Mouse. Dodging two families and a strolling couple, she darts over to the *poissonnerie* on the opposite side. "One sec," says Libby, dashing after her, leaving the cart.

The cart and I have paused in front of a booth full of knitted wool handicrafts. Tags penned in jewel-toned calligraphy are pinned to some of the items on display: *Mission Mitts $16, Gloves for Ghana $22, Truce Toques $18, Sanctuary Scarves $24.*

"Why do they need gloves in Ghana?" I ask. Two women are working in the booth and they both look over at me. I bite my lip. "Just wondering."

The woman nearest to me responds as she pins another pair to the back of the booth. Her burgundy hair is cut close to her head and comes to a shaved point like an arrow at the nape of her neck. "Gloves for Ghanaians in Canada. It's to welcome new immigrants who won't be arriving with winter gear."

"Ah." As she turns and steps closer to refold one of the scarves on the table, I see the larger sign affixed to the display behind her: ALL PROCEEDS SUPPORT THE ONGOING ADVOCACY WORK OF NO BORDERS.

"No Borders," I say aloud. Peering at their faces, I recognize them, or the people they used to be. The women I wanted to know. Sadhana's friends. "You must have known my sister."

"Who's your sister?" asks the woman with the short hair, and though the line of her jaw is sharper now than it was, I remember her name. Anne-Marie.

"Good," says Libby, reappearing at my side without Mouse, who remains immobilized in front of the lobster aquarium. "You found them." She introduces me to Anne-Marie and Cherise, who exchange a look.

"This is where we were going," Libby says to me, as though answering a question my puzzled face seems to be asking.

Cherise says, "I remember you. You went to Ottawa with your little boy."

I nod. "We were wondering about the Essaids," I say. "If they're okay."

"They're somewhere safe," says Anne-Marie. She begins pairing the mitts so that the price tags face upwards. I see her thumb stroke one of the striped cuffs.

"We were hoping to stop by," said Libby. "Let them know that our thoughts are with them."

The women exchange a look. "We'll tell them," says Cherise. Her smile, when it turns up, is familiar. Cherub cheeks.

"Where are they now?" I ask.

"Somewhere safe," says Anne-Marie again, running one hand through her cropped hair and crossing her arms. "Bassam mentioned that you visited right before the raid."

"We both did," says Libby.

Anne-Marie nods but studies my face. "And you know Ravi Patel."

"Used to know," I say. The implication dawns on me. "Trust me, I had nothing to do with it."

"It's better," said Anne-Marie, "if we don't have to trust you."

I feel my indignation rising, but Libby takes the bag full of bread from her shoulder and presses it into Cherise's hands. Then she adds the cheese from the cart and some of the pears, piling the food into the woman's arms.

"Give this to them," she says, and Cherise nods. "What will happen to them now?"

Cherise leans closer over the counter of the booth. "Well, there's an appeal —"

"Everyone knew what church they were at," I say, worried now, replaying my conversation with Ravi. "It was on the news."

"We know," says Cherise. "We know it's not your fault. But we're not telling anyone about the new location. Not even everyone in No Borders."

Libby touches her hand to my arm. "So what happens now?" she repeats.

"There's a judicial review. Bassam's lawyer filed an appeal, and there's going to be a hearing in front of a tribunal with the immigration board. On Monday." Cherise pauses to put down the food on one of the chairs behind her. "They think he's not going to show up. That's why they wanted him in custody."

"We're planning a demonstration," says Anne-Marie, "to show they're not alone."

Though I feel mortified by their mistrust, there is something comforting about looking at these women who were friends with my sister for so many years. I find myself wanting to memorize their faces. "We'll be there," I say.

Libby calls out to Mouse and grasps hold of the cart, which screeches in response as she starts to push.

"We will overcome," says Libby, half laughing, as we both fall in step with her.

The day of the big move of Sadhana's belongings, Evan runs a fever. I get up at eight to meet him at my sister's apartment. The night before, I'd reserved a parking spot outside the building, using two of Sadhana's kitchen chairs spaced out along the street with a length of masking tape running between them.

"You're sick," I tell him when he arrives. His sluggish descent from the truck is accompanied by the slightest of groans, and his hands on my back are hot paddles.

"It's not nice to tell a man he looks like shit before he's even had a cup of coffee," he says. He turns his head and rubs an arm across his shining forehead.

"Let's postpone it."

"We can't. This is my only weekend off before the lease is up."

"I know."

Quinn comes a few minutes later, hair still wet from the shower, and puts the chairs up on the sidewalk while Evan parks the truck. The pitch of Quinn's overt resentment seems to be lower than it was on the drive to Gatineau, unless it's just too early for him to have turned it up to full force. Or maybe his anger is wearing out, like a shirt that's been through the wash too many times, letting the real Quinn show through bit by bit. Courtesy by way of exhaustion.

"Where's your uncle?" asks Evan, checking the rear-view mirror as he shuts off the engine.

"Coming," I say. "He's probably just checking in at the store."

Upstairs, Sadhana's apartment strikes me again with its warm silence, its thick-as-a-fog emptiness, and the faint somnolent hum that makes me want to curl up in her bed. I poll Evan on its palpable morbidity while Quinn is in the bathroom.

"It's the humidity," he says. "That's all." He rubs the small of my back.

"You're one to talk. You're hot as a grill. Sit down."

Uncle arrives with a minimum of fanfare. When I introduce him to Evan, he surprises me by reaching out his hand, which Evan declines with a wave at his sweating face, which at this point most closely resembles melting tallow.

"Don't want to get you sick, sir, if I can help it."

We fall into a rhythm in which I drag the smallest boxes to the top of the stairs, then Quinn ferries them down the stairs and passes them off to Uncle. My uncle works the truck bed like a game of Sudoku whose emergent solution is apparent only to him, arranging the boxes in an ever-shifting puzzle to maximize the space. Evan readies what he can of the remaining larger boxes and furniture pieces in line near the door.

In the end, what we thought would take two trips can be managed in only one. My sister's whole life in fifteen cubic feet. I scoop up the mail and drop it into my purse along with the keys.

"One final cleaning and I'm done," I say. "I'll come back tomorrow."

"Is all this going to fit in your house?" says Uncle.

"Uncle, I'm sorry. Did you want anything? I didn't even think of it."

He shakes his head no, then mentions the larger left-over furniture. "Whatever we can't sell, I'll give away to my employees."

Evan calls to me from the driver's seat, already buckled in. "Let's go before I pass out."

"Why not let Quinn drive? He passed his test. He has his licence now."

Evan shakes his head no. The rattle seems to pass down his body and I see the muscles of his right leg jumping.

"I wish I could offer," I say. Neither Mama nor I ever learned how to drive.

"It's okay. Let's just go."

Uncle seems ashamed of us both for letting a sick man drive, but he looks on with approval as Evan holds one hand up in a wave before driving away.

The drive is uneventful. I sit squeezed in the middle as Quinn listens to his iPod and Evan drives one-handed with desperate concentration. When we arrive in Ottawa, Evan's roommates meet us at my house and make short work of the unloading, while I go down to Ned's Diner to pick up an order of six Quinn sandwich specials.

~⊙~

When everything has been unloaded and his roommates have left, Evan accompanies me down to the basement to point out which boxes have gone where. He motions from the far corner near the water heater to the space below the stairs.

"We started piling it there, and we tried to keep it in the back third of the room, but it didn't quite work out. The last of it stops here." He points to the area near the skates and toboggans.

The place is a reliquary now, a storehouse filled nearly to the brim. If clutter really reflects a scattered mind, mine is beyond saving. Haphazard, clogged. Disturbingly fixated on the past.

"There's too much," I say, sinking into one of Sadhana's armchairs. "I don't know what I'm going to do with all this."

Evan leans onto a sturdy tower of boxes just higher than his waist. His fever seems to have broken, though I noticed him popping a couple of Tylenol mid-morning. He puts up his elbows. "Leave it here probably." His tone is light.

"Thank you again, by the way. And thank your roommates for me."

"Sure. It was no problem. It took less than an hour to unload it."

Evan cocks his head as we hear a footfall upstairs. Quinn out of his room, likely prowling for a snack while I'm still feeling full from lunch. "So is that it?" says Evan. "Are you finished?"

"Finished?"

"Yes, as in done. Packed up. Finished."

"Not quite. I have to make one more trip to the city to clean the apartment."

He drops one hand into his pocket. "And what was her girlfriend like?"

"Nice. Interesting."

"Interesting how?"

"Good question." I feel exhausted rather than evasive at the prospect of describing Libby, her impetuousness and strange sensitivities, but there's no way to convey this to Evan. And even in the midst of my odd interactions with her, there is something intangibly familiar about Libby. "I'm not sure how to explain."

"Oh."

"Maybe it just hurts that Sadhana thought she needed to keep her a secret."

Evan nods. "So I want to help you finish." He stands straight and stretches his legs. I grab his arm to pull myself up. I feel in the back pocket of his jeans until he starts to laugh, and I fish out his car keys.

"In that case, come and watch me scrub the floor. You can help me fill the bucket."

It's more of a joke than an invitation, but I see him weighing it. Moving Sadhana's things was a task where Evan's help was essential. He might be checking to see if I can lean on him when things are less dire.

"I'll come if you really want me there." He cups my face and kisses me once on the cheek, as if to show his restraint. "If you really need me, I'll do whatever you want."

~∽⊙∽~

Having Evan in Uncle's apartment throws off the scale of everything. I look at him and bump my shin on a coffee table that has been in the same spot for more than thirty years. I see his shoulder next to my ear and catch my hip against the side of the fridge.

"It's cozy," he says, his fingers on the door frame of my old bedroom. He ducks his head a little to come in.

He is here now in the place where I grew up, where all the best and the worst things in my life happened, and he is handsome and he is my boyfriend and he is saying it is cozy. I sit down on my bed as lightly as I can, as noncommittal as a sit-down can be, with my fingertips gripping the covers, the balls of my feet pressing into the rug. How to countenance such a word. Cozy.

"Less now than before," I say. "We took a lot of stuff away when we moved out."

He sits down on the edge of Sadhana's bed. He can sit down only one kind of way, comfortably and definitely and with his legs spread out in a V that manages through the pitch of the angle to be at once masculine but still polite. The angle is about thirty-five degrees. I love that he cannot equivocate with his rear end. If he told a lie, his whole body would become the polygraph, all blinks and jerks and quivers.

"You can't stay here, you know."

"I know. Quinn's here."

"Even if he wasn't."

"Okay." He has arrived almost without warning, after first saying he couldn't make it. Quinn and I caught an afternoon bus, then Evan called from the road to tell me he'd changed his mind: he missed me and was coming to visit, whether I liked it or not. So far I'm not sure. I'm not used to someone looking out for me. Looking so closely.

He says, "I like picturing you here as a little girl. Hair in pigtails."

"Braids."

"Okay, braids. Either way, cute, I bet." He gets up. "Are there pictures up anywhere?"

I pull him back by his sleeve. "No."

"You're lying."

"I told you we took everything."

He shakes his head as though still convinced I'm not telling the truth and gets up to take the measure of the room, crossing it in two steps. Two beds, two nightstands, two desks. One formerly hotly contested and overstuffed closet.

"I knew it," he says, spotting a shelf with high school yearbooks. "The goods." He reaches out for one with a wicked flourish, ignoring me as I try to bat his hand away.

The shelf houses a motley and incomplete collection, one that neither Sadhana nor I cared to take away with us when we left. There is my own shortfall of yearbooks from when I dropped out at sixteen next to Sadhana's staggered volumes, each missing year a reminder of months of struggle with her illness. Anything from that time after Mama died is like an evil talisman. I haven't opened one since we moved away. Some of the books, I remember, have mean epithets or sly digs scrawled in them by classmates who knew us mainly by reputation. A yearbook being passed around was like a spinning bottle, in that there was no telling where it might end up. The comments in mine were for the most part unremarkable apart from some fat jokes, but I recall a number of block-lettered exhortations to *EAT!* across Sadhana's pages, and some stick-figure drawings that were supposed to be likenesses. It is possible there were not that many unkind students at our school, but those few have had a long and upsetting reach through their offhand graffiti.

"Give it."

"I'm sorry," says Evan. "But come on. I bet you look cute. A little peek? I'm still trying to figure you out."

"I'm not a puzzle," I say, grabbing the yearbook from him. Unexpected tears spring to my eyes. "There's nothing to figure out."

He sits down next to me on the end of my sister's old bed. He touches my shoulder and pulls the yearbook out of my grasp, tossing it back onto the pillows.

"I'm sorry. Really. I don't know what I was thinking."

He's watching for a sign that the crisis has passed. That attentive, forbearing look that never fails to prompt my own guilt and unease.

"You're waiting for me to get over it," I say with a slow carefulness, "but I might never get over it."

"Okay."

"And you're fine with that."

He puts his hand on my knee. "Yes. But I think you will."

"I thought she was mad at me. I was mad at her." I have both hands on my face, to the sides of my cheeks and temples. Blinders.

"You had a fight," he says. "That's normal."

"Is it? She was dead for a week, and I didn't know."

Later he says he wants me to show him Montreal, my Montreal. He doesn't realize how tiny it is. There is a lack to my life: it has been small and concentric. I had ascribed this in part to my son and my sister, but when I try to imagine my life without them, it is an invention that feels feeble, like the flap of an atrophied muscle. It is not clear what will be left for me once they have both passed out of my care. But I say nothing about this to Evan.

I take him to a dépanneur, where we buy a bottle of white wine from the fridge and take it to a tiny Thai restaurant down the street. We steer clear of the subject of Quinn and his father, Sadhana and her long illness. The waiter brings us an ice bucket, which he places right on the tablecloth.

I mention the Essaid family and their struggle to stay in Canada. Their evasion of Bassam's removal order, the police raid on the church, their flight to a mystery location under the protection of my sister's friends. The tribunal scheduled to revisit Bassam's appeal. I leave Ravi out of the story.

"What's going to happen to them?" says Evan.

"I don't know. They hope his appeal will be granted. I'm not sure there's much point in claiming sanctuary in another church. I might go to the demonstration."

"You could get arrested." He looks strained, almost embarrassed. "Oh, Beena."

"Don't worry." I am alternately touched and irked by his concern. "Not all protests involve burning cop cars."

Evan puts his elbows up on the table and leans his chin against his linked knuckles. "Well, I hope things work out for them, then."

"I do, too."

Then Evan talks about the time his family thought they were going to lose their farm. His parents were in debt to a neighbour. They'd bought his land just before a spell of drought sank them into the red for nearly five years.

"And I know why they call it 'in the red,'" says Evan. "My brother David got a stress rash on his chest," he says, touching to each side of his collarbones, "from here to here. The two of us would get up early, even before my dad, and try to start the chores. We were dead set on saving us all from having to move to the city." Evan waves his hand towards the traffic speeding by outside. "That was our worst fear. We thought everyone in the city was homeless. Or that if we went, we would be. We thought we'd be begging in the street. It isn't intuitive, what you do if you lose a farm."

"Your family would have figured something out. Your parents would have."

"I know that now. But we were just terrified. Then David got cuts all up and down his arm trying to hook up the combine by himself. We'd gotten ourselves up at four in the morning thinking we could help out our dad by starting even before he did."

Hearing him talk, I wonder how much of me is in love with this part of him that he's trying to leave behind. The farm boy just as modest as he is hard-working. The part of him that knows his virtues, the ego or pride that might measure itself against other men and rank itself higher, is buried so deep I've rarely seen its traces. Only one night, out on my porch, he picked me up and threw me over his shoulder and whispered, "I bet I'm the strongest man you've ever known, aren't I?"

I feel flushed just sitting across from him. Then I notice the restaurant is so warm that condensation from the metal ice bucket is dripping to form a wet spot seeping steadily towards our plates. Before we finish eating, one whole side of the clean white tablecloth has leached into a soggy grey.

"I have to tell you something," I say. "I saw Quinn's father."

While I explain about Quebec First and the connection to the Essaids and Ravi's meetings with Sadhana, Evan leans back. When I tell him about Bombay Palace and how I threatened Ravi, he starts to push back his chair.

"You've been hiding this."

"I'm sorry. But I'm telling you now."

"I'm a police officer, Beena, and you're telling me about extortion." With his right hand, he tugs at his hair by the roots. "You know the kind of background check they put me through?" He grabs the arms of his chair, and his wide eyes are frustrated and a gorgeous blue. "I'm not supposed to be in a relationship with someone who breaks the law."

"It's not extortion," I say, swallowing. I can feel the encroaching water reach my wrist on the table, but I keep still. "It has nothing to do with money."

"It doesn't have to," says Evan. "It's about coercion. Jesus, Bee."

"Well, I'm sorry. I didn't realize it was illegal." The truth is I hadn't bothered to think about it. But I feel horrible. "I wish I hadn't put you in this position."

Even seems mollified by my apology, if skeptical. He crosses his arms. "So are you going to call him to straighten things out?"

"No," I say, too fast. Evan looks unimpressed. I add, "I want to see how he reacts. I mean, the damage is already done now, isn't it?"

Evan heaves a sigh, as though defending the rule of law is his responsibility to bear alone. "Fuck," he says. "I guess so. Let's just go."

On our walk to the Metro, Evan is surprised by the housing in the neighbourhood, the blocks and blocks of triplexes. Families packed three-deep in rows of walk-ups.

"A lot more room where I'm from," he says, forging a truce by breaking the silence. "There's a whole field between the road and the houses. Fields in every direction."

"And I bet you knew more of your neighbours."

"Every one."

"Maybe too much closeness keeps people apart."

"Like in New York City."

"Self-preservation."

"I wonder."

~∽∾~

An hour later, at the coffee shop where I warned my son I was going to meet him, I stand outside looking in the window. Quinn and Caro are sitting in the corner, and Quinn is telling a story, it looks like, with his feet planted, hands wide and waving, his whole bright face matching his body in animation. Caro is laughing, arms hugging her chest. Her straight brown hair is pulled back in a ponytail, revealing red earrings shaped like telephone receivers hanging from her earlobes.

I rap on the window and wait for the moment when Quinn sees me and his face falls. There. After a moment, he and Caro come out to meet me.

"Good time?" I ask.

"Not bad," says Caro. This is a kind of teasing for my son, I can tell. She dons a bicycle helmet and bids us goodnight as she unlocks her bike from a pole. "See you tomorrow, Quinn."

"Bye," says Quinn. We watch her pedal off in the direction of her grandmother's house. I notice it is not the direction in which I saw Quinn taking the bus the other day.

Quinn is more forthcoming than he was in the morning, when he heard Evan was coming to town. "Caro speaks three languages, you know. English, French, and Spanish."

"That's amazing."

"She's working on a zillion projects at once, too. The thing with her grandmother. And another thing, about political refugees."

"Oh?" I am not sure whether there is a hidden prompt here to ask about the Essaid family, if that is indeed the story Caro is following. If Quinn is trying to get me to say something, to see if I know anything about his father, he is hiding it well.

"Yeah."

"Well, that's terrific," I say. "She seems very engaged with what she wants to do."

The air is so warm that even our slow stroll is making me perspire. The aromas of different menus cling to all the restaurants we pass.

"So where's your boyfriend tonight?"

I hope he still is my boyfriend. We parted at the Metro without further conversation, Evan turning away from my kiss. "Don't ask unless you really want to know," I tell Quinn.

"I'm not opposed to knowing."

"At a hotel."

"Good."

As we walk home under a sky too overcast for stars, our secrets start to weigh on me while we wind our way along the path through the park. I slow down when we get to the picnic table near the trees, where the other night men called out to me in the dark.

"Are we stopping?"

"I have to talk to you."

He waits, expectant, not looking at me. With his sneaker he traces a soft, grinding circle into the sand and gravel of the path.

"Did Sadhana tell you she was looking for your father? After that time she came to visit?"

"No." There is anguish there. "We didn't talk after she left. I meant to call her. I don't know why I didn't."

So there is to be no late-breaking forgiveness for me, after all. Only the same guilt I've been carrying all along, but for the two of us, and nothing to offer him instead.

"It's not your fault," I say. "You know that, right? It was just a fight. We'd had them before."

Not his fault, but mine. He would probably describe that as something he already knows. He walks a few paces away and lifts up one end of the picnic table, experimentally, before dropping it again to the ground.

"So she went looking for him anyway?" His face betrays nothing about whether he has been doing the same. I suppose I can only assume that he has.

"She found him," I say. "And met with him. And I met with him, too. I wanted to talk about Sadhana."

The anger I'm expecting doesn't rise up to greet me. Maybe it will come later. It is possible I only think I am a part of this thing between them, or that I am a conduit but not a gear in the machine. A couple with a dog passes close by, high on conversation but falling silent as they come near. We stand facing the mountain. Around the tall neon cross at its summit is an emanating glow, a halo caused by the heat of the light.

Quinn shifts his weight, hands in his pockets. "Did he ask about me?"

The lie is out of my mouth before I catch myself. Quinn's relationship with his father, I am almost prepared to concede, is his own business. I might want to stand out of the way, but I am under no obligation to clear the path.

"No, he didn't, Quinn. Not once."

⟞ CLEANING HOUSE ⟝

As planned, Libby comes to meet me at Sadhana's apartment for the final cleaning. At the top of the stairs she cries out. Her hand feels for my arm and she hides her face in the crinkled cotton of my sleeve.

"This is hard, isn't it," she says. And then, "I want it to be hard."

"Are you okay?"

She answers by stepping past me in sure strides to the kitchen. "Let's get down to it."

Libby moves through the apartment with a natural efficiency. She takes charge of half of the supplies and more than two-thirds of the territory, bending and reaching to pockets of dirt beyond my imagining, wielding herself against baseboards and light fixtures. She fills a bucket with suds and starts splashing around the string mop after I have used the broom to not much more effect than a prop in a dreamy Cinderella impression. After forty-five minutes, Libby's hands are already a bright, scrubbed red. I clean the bathroom, as penance, with a large pair of rubber gloves.

"I feel like I've taken advantage of you," I say. "You're a miracle worker in here." I feel unworthy of all the help pressed on me the past few days.

"Nonsense."

When Libby progresses to the feather duster, her intensity abates and I sense the possibility for conversation. My failure to locate Sadhana's diary leaves Libby as my last chance. My only hope of finding out what was going on with my sister. At any rate, I have nothing left to lose.

"Did Sadhana ever talk to you about me and Quinn?"

"Of course. Not your business, but the fact of you. I know how close you were. And she was so proud of Quinn."

"She was, yeah."

"You'll be leaving soon, won't you, now that this is done?" Libby straightens up, and in the full sunlight through the window, now stripped of its curtains, I can see faint lines around her eyes when she smiles. She wears no makeup and no jewellery. "I'm going to be sorry to see you go."

"I'm leaving the day after the demonstration."

We work in silence for a while. By way of the sun and the lemon scent of the cleaning spray, everything seems fresh and golden. When I close my eyes, all I see is yellow. When I open them, I see the light gleaming along the length of the refinished pine floors of which my sister had been so proud.

"Those last few weeks," I say. "I don't know if you know, but we weren't talking."

Libby puts down the duster and looks at me.

"I guess I just want to know if she was happy. Or if she was sick."

Libby stands where the kitchen table used to be and looks as if she is about to say something. Then she steps to the window sill and peers out, placing both hands, palms down, on the lacquered wooden surface.

"I think," she says, ducking her head back in, "we should make sure to sweep the front stairs as well as the balcony." She exits to the balcony, as though literally sidestepping my queries.

"Libby," I call out, loud enough for her to hear. "Please."

She comes back in, looking chastened, and empties the dustpan into the garbage. Tracing her gaze to the floor, I realize that it is her reluctance to talk about herself that strikes me as familiar. Her deflections. She is maybe a little bit like me. Or at least like the way Sadhana said I was.

"I'm trying," says Libby, leaning the broom against the counter. She pulls one of the leftover chairs away from the wall and places it some distance away, nearer the door. As she bends to sit, I see her for one moment without the verve that seemed to be at the root of getting in touch with me. Her hair swings back over her shoulders like straw, and she looks as white and dry and worn as a piece of shell on a beach. Seated, she finally turns to me again. "Okay," she says. "You know we loved each other."

"Yes, you told me."

"You still don't believe me."

"Why not? We had a lot of secrets from each other."

"Well, she had secrets from me, too." Libby brings up her legs and clutches her knees with her hands. "I couldn't stand it." She closes her eyes, head just barely shaking back and forth. "You know, I had an extra key to her apartment ever since she locked herself out one weekend."

"All right," I say. I don't want to risk interrupting her with questions. I lean back against the fridge as unobtrusively as I can.

She says, as if this explains things: "I saw Sadie having dinner with Ravi Patel one night." There is a bitter edge to her voice that I recognize. Jealousy.

"I saw them having dinner," she says again, swallowing. "And I asked her about it and she lied. Then I saw another date with him written down in her planner. Everything between us was so confusing. And I worried that she was sick, too, maybe. She was so thin." She shakes her head. "I had no idea, really."

I say nothing. The refrigerator is warm against my back. It feels so hot in the apartment that I look to the windows, but they have all already been flung open.

"She didn't like it when I got insecure," says Libby, looking miserable, "so I didn't want to bring it up. I even tried to call you once or twice, last fall, to ask—well, I don't know what exactly. To see what you knew about him. Before all this. I don't know what I was thinking. But her diary was going to tell me what was going on." She draws a shaky breath. "I've been trying to find a way to tell you. This whole time."

"What?" My knees quake as though they've already taken on the burden of what's to come. "Wait," I say. I pull a second chair out from the wall and sit down opposite her.

Sadhana, Libby says, had tickets to a play downtown. "She invited me first, to this thing called *Juniper Berries,* and I said no. I already had a plan to let myself into her apartment to take a peek at her diary. She told me she was going to ask her friend Rachelle."

I picture the scene as she describes it. Libby in a panic, mistaking Ravi for a rival. Libby in her black exercise clothes. And Mouse could be left alone at home for the length of an average jog. "I never go for that long," says Libby, as though this is the failure requiring expiation. "And she knows what to do in case of trouble."

Libby coming up the front stairs, silent in her running shoes. Unlocking the second door and leaving it standing open. On the kitchen table, a loaf of bread, and beside it, a bottle of perfume and a notebook. The diary.

"Hold on," I say.

"It was too dark to really read anything," says Libby. "The lights were mostly off, I think."

Bending her head over the notebook, Libby opened it to the last few pages. Then, picking up the perfume, she sniffed it and dabbed some on. Her shirt was sticking to her lower back as she peered at the diary in the semi-darkness, and a trickle of sweat soaked into the waistband of her underwear. It was too warm inside the apartment for all her thermal winter sportswear. It was too warm and humid altogether, Libby realized. Something was wrong. Sadhana always turned the heat down before she left the apartment to save money.

"She was still home," says Libby. "In the shower."

The pair of tickets, Libby found out later, had been given away to some friends of Sadhana's, a married couple. "She told them she was too tired to go," says Libby. "Can you believe that?"

"No," I say. "I don't understand any of this."

Behind her, Libby says, there was a gasp and a thump.

"And that was all."

Her face starting to twist and blotch, Libby tilts her head to one side. I watch her and feel cold. The coldness gives me a strong, lonely feeling.

"What do you mean?" I say.

"She was here, in the apartment, Beena. I scared her to death."

Why I suddenly think of Sadhana flying across the stage in a red leotard, arms stretched aloft in fifth position, I can't say. When she did a grand jeté, it was as though she inhabited every plane at once. The world, as it so often did, seemed to bend to the sheer will made manifest in her body.

"Why didn't you help her?"

Libby's lips tremble. "Why didn't she know it was me? It was dark, but still . . . she should have known." Her voice, for once, is tiny. "It was only me."

"But why didn't you call an ambulance?" I can feel my own tears coming. "Why didn't you tell someone?"

"She was dead, Beena," says Libby. "Her eyes were open. She dropped dead. It isn't just an expression." With a terrible, choking sob, she rises from her chair and approaches mine, crumpling at my feet. Her fingers clutch at my sleeve as she weeps apologies I can barely comprehend. She looks terrified.

I close my eyes and think of CPR or the paddles that can zap a person back to life, as if dying might be a kind of running out of batteries, something that can be reversed if the current is just turned back on quickly enough. Then I feel the coldness again, and once I grab hold of it, it seems like the one strong thing floating in the dark sea of Libby's confession.

I push her hands off me. "Do you know how long she was left here?" My sister, disintegrating on her own floor.

"I know it took a couple of days," says Libby, pressing her eyes closed.

"A week. It was a week." In a week, a body begins to bloat. And smell. It was the downstairs neighbour who called the landlord in the end. I loathe the pettiness of knowing how Sadhana would have hated that.

Libby moans and rubs her nose with the heel of her hand, then wipes her palm on her jeans. "I thought someone would find her." Her voice is hiccupy. "I knew it was too late, so I grabbed everything I'd touched and ran. I would have to explain, and there was just no way to do it." Threads of gold light up in her hair as she moves her head. The sun-soaked kitchen feels like a different place entirely from the scene of fear and death she's describing. "But someone would find her. She had so many friends." Libby's voice is pleading, and she gulps air like it might be running out. "She had you, Beena."

"The diary," I say, ignoring this. "What happened to it?"

"It's gone." Her knee twitches and squeaks as it rubs against the linoleum. "I threw it out."

It may be that she is bent as a supplicant in the very spot where Sadhana fell. I wish she would get up.

Finding my voice, I vacate my seat with shaky legs.

"Get up," I say. "And get out."

~⌒~

There is no redress to Libby's story. There is not even a way to prove she was there. But why it should be proven or who should be told or what should happen now is not something I can make sense of anyway. I am relieved that she obeyed me and left without another word. If she'd kept talking, I'd have to move on to the next thought, the next moment.

On my way home, I cross paths with Quinn in the park. The weather has changed. It is raining again, a warm drizzle.

"Small world, stranger," I call out to him, and he looks up, startled. I take a step closer and flash a smile that must be ghastly.

Quinn is carrying an unopened umbrella. "Hi. Wow. Do you have a tracking chip on me or something?" He swings around the umbrella by a string attached to its handle. "Heading back to Uncle's?"

"Yes. Walk with me?"

He nods. We skirt the opposite side of the park from where we walked the night before, past the playground and a wading pool.

"I used to bring you here when you were little," I say.

"I know."

Of Libby's story, I am determined to say nothing to Quinn. Just now I am less angry with her than I would have guessed, though I feel as sad and sorry as if I were the one in her place. Between our mutual failures, it seems we were unwitting collaborators in Sadhana's death.

"So do you remember the thing we saw on the news?" I say instead. "About the family in the church? The tribunal is going to make a decision tomorrow, and there's going to be a demonstration." I slow our pace so that I can look at him while we talk. "Do you want to come?"

"I'm going already," says Quinn. "Caro wants me to help her film it. Maybe hold a microphone or something. She knows some of the people who are organizing everything." He looks anxious and, if I'm not mistaken, guilty. I wonder if he is feeling some shame of privilege, the luck he owes to where he happened to be born.

"Great," I say. "I hope it will make a difference." The meeting with the Essaid family has stayed with me, as well as the love I have read into their faces. I wonder if there is any chance that Ravi will yield to my threats and throw his support behind them.

"I hope so, too."

As we near the swing set, Quinn cuts off the path and collapses into one of the swings. "So I called him up," he says next. He makes an upside-down V with his sneakers. "My father."

"You did."

"We got together this morning. Caro came, too, though he didn't like that." Quinn looks over at me, and there is a question in his eyes. "Actually, he thought you sent me."

"I see."

There is a small grey cloud hanging over the park, clear sky darkening beyond it in the distance. The rain is holding to a drizzle, but my shirt is wet through across the shoulders. There is no telling what Ravi might have said to Quinn about me. At this point, I'm not sure which worries me more: lies or the truth. More likely, some tricky combination. Politician-speak. I say nothing.

"He seemed concerned you were going to tell his wife or something."

"The newspapers, actually."

Quinn looks bewildered, and I'm about to break into an explanation of the point of the whole thing, the deal I thought I'd struck to help the Essaids, but he heads me off.

"You can't," he says.

"Why not?"

"I promised we wouldn't say anything for now. He wants a relationship, when the time is right."

"Oh, Quinn."

"No." He gets up and steps through the mud of the swing set pit back to the path. "You're out of this now."

⚬⚬⚭

The day of the demonstration breaks overcast, the kitchen curtains pulling back to reveal a sky the colour of murky dishwater. I make coffee and Quinn and I sit quietly drinking it, eyes down into our cups.

"I'm kind of excited," he says. Quinn is trying to make amends by being talkative and by making certain we don't discuss Ravi. "I've never been to something like this before."

"Be careful," I say. "There might be some unpredictable people in attendance." But it is the kind of concern that ebbs with disclosure. Quinn rolls his eyes as though I am being crazy.

"I'm serious." As the words leave my mouth, I remember scoffing at the same caution when it was counselled by Evan.

"I know."

"If you see a police officer," I say, "you run the other way."

"Except your boyfriend."

The word makes me flinch. "Right."

This morning he is drinking his coffee black, his lips recoiling after every sip.

"Are you going with Caro?"

"Meeting her. She's probably already heading over with her video camera and three extra memory cards."

"Great," I say. "I'll see you there." Before the demonstration, Quinn is working a short shift down at the shop, where Uncle is waiting to train him on the cash register. As for Quinn working as a bagel boy, I've shelved my objections for

now. I'll need to save them for dealing with Ravi, if some relationship develops there. Quinn watches me as I let myself out.

"Don't get arrested," I say.

"I'll try." And then, seeing my face: "I won't."

The government building housing the Department of
Immigration is faced by a small park the size of a single city
block. With eight small maples, six flowerboxes, and a large
Victorian iron fountain, it is more of an idea of a park than an
actual green space. There are benches and picnic tables nailed
down at intervals across the concrete square that surrounds
one weedy stretch of grass. It is a place where the employees
can take their lunch and feel some relief.

When I finally arrive, I see that a sizeable crowd has
already gathered. There is a clown wearing flippers handing
out balloons. She doesn't speak but pulls faces and putters a
squat little circle dance around the children and parents who
approach, her arms pumping like a runner. A young man in
fatigues is helping Cherise dish out free samosas and spicy
rice and beans to a long lineup. And all around me, among
the people eating and carrying signs, are people distributing
leaflets to passersby and employees from the adjoining office
towers.

I spot Caro standing on the end of one of the benches,
wielding her video camera. Quinn is at her side, holding a
microphone attached to what looks like a boom rigged out
of an extendable curtain rod. I catch his eye across the grass.
The air is full of energy and chatter, the city smell of exhaust,
and the bite of cooked green chilies. I wave and he waves
back. Whatever happened between him and Ravi, Quinn

seems intact. I wonder if they hugged. What on earth they might have said.

The demonstration is scheduled to start at three o'clock. I don't yet see any sign of Libby. My stomach is unsettled enough to keep me away from the food table, but all around me the mood is light. The word being passed around is that the police are unlikely to get involved, and Evan agrees. He has turned up looking ill at ease in jeans and a black T-shirt, shaking his head to stave off any questions about why he has decided to come.

"The police will hold off unless it gets violent," he says. "No matter what, they'll wait until most of the public has gone home. After all, part of justice is the appearance of justice." He peers around. "Do they have coffee here?"

"That's cynical."

"Not really. Not if you believe that appearances can be deceiving."

"This is all some kind of end-justifies-the-means thing, then."

He points to a table with a large stainless steel urn where a small queue is forming, and he starts moving towards it. "Sometimes it does." He looks at me. "You know it does."

That Evan's morality would have complexity is something that hasn't crossed my mind. I wonder for the hundredth time what Sadhana would have made of him. She had a way of summing people up that I never could manage. Uncle was a stodgy vassal, Ravi a shirking coward, or sometimes a fetal pig. Quinn as a little kid was, more often than not, a jam-fisted monkey. Whether she could see these realities or created them, the effect was the same: she knew the world better than I did.

Evan returns, not with one coffee but two, a gesture that might be nothing but politeness but to me feels more like a valentine. I brush his fingers as I take the cup and he gives me a tight smile.

"I'm sorry," I say, and it comes out in a whisper. The crowd is starting to fall silent in response to some setup activity on the front steps of the building.

"I know," he says at a normal volume. "But I need to absorb all this."

I don't know if he means my flailing attempt at extortion or Ravi's being back in the picture, but it's a fair plea either way. Evan may be the most reasonable person ever to be angry with me.

"Absorb all what?" I ask anyway. I understand the problem of integrating new facets into a picture of a whole personality. If I knew what to make of Libby's confession, I could share it with Evan, but I'm afraid of how he'll react. I can hardly imagine what he might think of her negligence. What I'll start to think.

"I need time," says Evan, "to absorb how secretive you are." His voice is matter-of-fact, but his face is glum. "How untrusting."

The demonstration formally begins with a series of speeches in both English and French, but for me, all the tense energy of the event seems to locate itself in the three inches separating me from Evan. I tug on his sleeve. "Don't be mad."

Evan sighs. He takes one hand from his cup as if to touch my shoulder, but ends up dropping it into his pocket. "Let's just be patient with each other, shall we?"

There are vans from both the English and French media parked around the square, and two men shouldering television cameras aimed at the makeshift podium. A member of the Algerian community talks about Bassam Essaid's struggle to leave that country and his efforts to assist other refugees and new immigrants. A representative from Amnesty International condemns the deportation order. Then Anne-Marie gets up on behalf of No Borders to talk about the exclusionary principles of the immigration system and the lack of basic rights faced by migrant workers. When she finishes speaking, a young man mounts the steps of the immigration building and leads the crowd in a chant culminating in claps and cheers, whistling and the waving of signs. Through a squealing megaphone, he encourages everyone present to stick around until the tribunal hearing is over, to show solidarity with the Essaid family. I check my watch and see that the hearing is not scheduled to begin for another fifteen minutes.

As the demonstration prepares to enter a holding pattern, the silence stretched out for the speeches starts to perforate as individual conversations begin to materialize here and there throughout the crowd. Then Evan says, "Do you hear that?"

Somewhere beyond the square, there is the sound of a march, another megaphone call-and-response being carried out by a group approaching in the distance. "Latecomers?" I say, just as they round the corner to the square.

It is a rally on the move, smaller and older, on the whole, than the group already occupying the square. A chorus of boos goes up, but hemmed in near the centre, I am not close enough to see what is happening.

"People opposed," guesses Evan.

Our attention is distracted from the new arrivals when a black Mercedes zooms up the street between the park and the government block, causing a commotion along the edge of the throng where people had started drifting off the sidewalk. The driver gets out to hold open the door, and the man who emerges from the car is Ravi, dressed in a suit and tie, dark hair shiny and slicked just so. A young woman climbs out from the other side and establishes a portable microphone and PA system on the steps before disappearing through the doors of the immigration building, trailing a coil of extension cord.

"Who's that now?" says Evan.

"That's him," I say, exaltation coming to me in a rush. "That's Quinn's father."

Ravi must truly be scared of exposure, I realize, to reverse his position on Bassam Essaid. He mounts the steps and adjusts the microphone stand. I can't spot Quinn, and I grab Evan's arm for leverage to get up on my tiptoes and scan the crowd.

"That's him?" says Evan, shaking me off as he raises his elbow to cup his eyes against the sun. He sounds bewildered. I make a motion for him to be quiet, and from the corner of my eye I see his back stiffen. Every question I let fall by the wayside is like a little bit of love, let go.

As soon as Ravi starts to speak I realize he has not come to support the Essaids. He introduces himself, mentioning that he is a political candidate. Speaking first in French, he hits a rhetorical rhythm I recognize from televised debates, a predictable cadence as penetrating as a light rain, before repeating himself in English. No matter what the language, I find it hard to focus.

"I am here at the request of my voters, who want to ensure that Quebec is a safe place for the newcomers we welcome."

"Did you know he would be here?" Evan is looking back and forth between me and Ravi, as if he is not sure which of us is the real source of his concern.

"No." I want to kiss Evan, to soothe away his unease, but his whole face forbids me. There is some kind of insecurity there, or maybe even jealousy. "Maybe I could have guessed if I'd thought about it."

Spotting Quinn across the square, I can tell that his father's appearance is unexpected for him, too. He is staring at Ravi with a fixed, hard look. Caro, at his side in a polka-dot dress, is filming.

"At Quebec First, we are pro-immigration. My own parents came to this country before I was born, and together they made a life here. Quebec was a place where they could flourish. What we want is to pace immigration at a rate that will allow new immigrants to acclimatize to our culture and values. So that they, too, can have a chance to flourish."

A woman shouts, "So why do you want to spend three percent of our GDP to increase the birth rate?" Someone on the other side of Evan asks, not loud enough, "Why is your motto 'Reconquer Quebec'?"

"Raising the birth rate is a simple question of economics, madam." I miss Ravi's elaboration on this concept, jostled as I am by a stream of people exiting the square. When Ravi returns to his subject, emphatic now that the bulk of the crowd is against him, he says, "Bassam Essaid is a self-proclaimed atheist, who is preying on our religious conventions in order to flout the laws of this country."

"Who wrote this for him?" I say. "Flout?" I am jeering instead of breaking calm, trying to figure out how to make good on my threats, and if they matter. Quinn is the one who matters now, not my vendetta and maybe not even the truth. Given Libby's confession, I now believe Ravi when he said he never spoke to my sister again. Yet he seems so cowardly up there, appealing to the very worst in people's natures.

But Evan is no longer beside me to answer.

Ravi has one hand admonishing the air. "Bassam Essaid is exploiting our goodwill, our naiveté. If we allow this to stand as a precedent, there is no telling the kinds of criminals, the kinds of terrorists, who will be using these methods to come and stay in our country. Take it from me, now is the time for us to start cleaning house."

Booing starts in earnest as an accompaniment to the existing heckling. Ravi has grown up to be what I suppose he always was. Short-sighted, conservative, and conceited. Sadhana despised him from the beginning, based only on the most cursory acquaintance. She saw, too, in a way I didn't, how willing I was to throw everything over, to toss away my whole life for the promise of one boy's affection.

Back behind the dwindling section of people still standing at attention, I wander into a diffuse group, still lingering at the food table or spread out on the squashed lawn, waiting for news of the tribunal. Evan is nowhere in sight, but I spot Libby sitting on the grass with her daughter. I think I draw nearer because I am curious, or still waiting for the arrival of some deferred reaction. Something like a purposeful rage.

Libby has Mouse between her legs, tucking dandelions into the elastics around her pigtails. She looks up at me with a wan face as I approach, but she seems calm and somehow ready for anything I might say. Her hair has been brushed until it is shining.

"You're here," she says.

"For what it's worth." With Ravi present, it is hard to keep track of the aim of the demonstration, let alone gauge its effectiveness.

Mouse grabs both of us and lays out her dandelion crown for Libby's approval.

"Beautiful, baby," says Libby. I concur. Then Mouse dons her crown and holds out her cupped palm.

"Lucky penny, Mummy," she says, and Libby digs out a coin from her pocket and gives it to her.

"For the fountain," Libby says to me, as Mouse runs off towards the square's ornamental centrepiece. "For wishing."

The penny is a bright speck against the grey sky as Mouse tosses it into the water. Then our attention is drawn away as the chanting starts up again, seemingly in relation to the smaller group of people who arrived just before Ravi and who are the only ones giving him bursts of enthusiastic applause. A line of protestors from the main demonstration is forming to prevent them from entering the square, and there is shouting from both sides that I can't make out. Ravi has stopped talking, although the association between him and the bulk of the dissenting group is not altogether clear. Some of them are carrying signs that read IMMIGRANTS LÉGAUX SEULEMENT and QUÉBEC POUR LES QUÉBÉCOIS. I see him approaching the standoff between the two lines, encouraging people to disperse.

"Boys," says Libby, with a dismissive air. She holds out her wrist to me. Her palm is the colour of the papery husk of a ground cherry. Gooseberry lanterns, that's what Mama called them. It is also deeply lined. "Smell," she says.

I oblige. I detect lemon, a trace of sandalwood and sweet musk. My nose brushes her skin.

"This is the perfume she was wearing," she says, "those last few weeks. Sadie." She pulls her arm back into her sleeve. "I bought it for her."

Mouse has returned. Libby hugs her, holding her tight and teasing her corkscrew curls until the girl starts to squirm. Then Libby lets go, and her daughter flees towards the clown, who is now twisting balloon animals in spite of the light drizzle that has begun to fall.

Libby is waiting for me to say something, to accuse or absolve her. Or tell her what I'm going to do with her confession.

I'm sure my voice is going to come out shaky, but it sounds normal. "What do you think is going to happen with the tribunal?" I ask. Looking past her, I see Evan at last, moving away from the front, stopping to pet dogs and chatting with some of the protesters. There is a bloom of colour all around us as people begin donning rain jackets and opening umbrellas.

"I don't know."

There is a tussle going on at the edge of the square now. A couple of the younger people on either side of the standoff are grappling each other's forearms as they each try to push back the opposite side, a grim game of Red Rover. Libby shifts away slightly, angling herself to face a line of police mustering at the other end of the street.

"We should get out of here," I say.

But Libby doesn't seem to be listening. "Beena," she says, "I didn't throw out the diary. I read it." She looks more ashamed than I ever felt about reading Sadhana's diary when we were teenagers. "Sadie wasn't angry with you. And she wasn't sick. She was trying to do what she thought was the right thing."

"Really." It comes out as scoffing, but I register a jolt of hope.

"Yes, really," says Libby. Turning back to me, she reaches for my arm but falls short, as though only managing the ghost of the gesture she wishes to make. "She just didn't want anyone to know until she had it all figured out." Libby slips her hand into her bag and pulls out a slim green notebook. "Here." She presses it into my hands.

"What do you mean?" I rub my thumb along the diary's soft paper cover with its pattern of cherry blossoms. Then, when a raindrop darkens the green with a wet splotch, I clutch it to my chest.

"She wanted to take care of it all for you," says Libby. "Everything to do with your son and Ravi—she wanted to protect you from that. Look after you in the one way she could." Her voice, for once, is soft. "You know, the way you looked after her."

I know what she says must be borne out by the note-book, or she wouldn't have given it to me. Libby's words and Sadhana's plan coalesce into a kind of dizziness of relief.

The diary is such a small thing, now that I'm holding it.

I thrust it back at her.

But Libby steps back, shaking her head. "Living with what happened, even without that around . . ." She slips her hands into her back pockets, as though to keep them at bay. "No, I don't want it."

"But you were together." And when I hear myself say it, I really understand it for the first time. "There must be things in there, maybe, that matter."

Libby nods. "Lovely things." Her lips tremble. "But those parts I know by heart."

Twenty yards down the street, riot police beat on their shields with nightsticks. After this drumming menace, they begin to march in our direction. People all around us are scrambling to their feet to get away. Libby looks around and leaves me with an apology as she hurries over to Mouse, who is being herded away by the clown to the opposite side of the trees.

I get up and walk away towards the fountain, past the peripheral blur of a black dog, unleashed and bounding after the children. The diary is in my hands and yet I don't think I want it. Relieved as I am, I'm still afraid of what else it might say about me. Sadhana's other diaries have been sealed up, unread, in a box, and maybe that is where this one belongs, too.

It's raining harder, the square emptying of people. The fountain, surrounded just a few minutes ago, is already deserted, and as raindrops strike the water, they generate a rippling mass of circles that radiate and overlap. Spouting iron fish froth the pool from the centre, and drawing near enough to hear the soft bubbling of the water, I remember the moment of lightness I'd felt, releasing Sadhana's ashes to the river.

I shift my weight from one foot to the other. There is a comfortable kind of loneliness is a place that belongs to everybody. Looking to the dark bottom of the granite basin, I see its precious coating of coins bright and dull, the tokens of hundreds of wishes. I feel in my pocket for change and find nothing except some Kleenex. But the diary is in my hand, a light, flat rectangle with so much of my hope riding on it.

I toss it in the fountain with a flick of the wrist, and it only takes a moment to sink to the bottom.

Before I can register what I've done, I hear the charged bark of a megaphone and Evan emerges from somewhere to grab me by the elbow. He helps me scramble out of the way as the police move in, faster than I would have guessed, from the adjoining side. He uses one arm to steer us back through the remaining crowd and the other to keep a tight lock on me.

"They're reading the riot act," says Evan. We are making slow progress to the edge of the park that hasn't already been hemmed in. "We've got to disperse."

Behind us, I can hear the outraged cries of people being arrested. Locating Quinn and Caro beyond the northwest corner of the square, Evan ensures that we are all together and accounted for.

"Mom, you okay?"

Standing next to my son, I can almost feel the bleakness coming off him. "Are you?" He nods.

"I saw someone get wrestled into handcuffs," says Evan. "Looks like he took a couple of bad punches."

"From who?" says Quinn.

Evan ignores the question, which means it was the cops. To me, he says, "You don't look so good either."

I hardly know how I feel. But there is too much to explain. "I'm fine," I say.

Evan reacts to the lie by taking his leave. "Call me later if you want to talk." He seems both rueful and amused. I hope there is enough time left to us to exercise the patience we talked about. "Bye, Quinn."

"Bye." My son watches him walk away before pulling me into step with him and Caro.

"I sort of know the people at this place where we're

going," Caro says now. She doesn't seem dismayed by the arrival of the police, and I wonder if that has anything to do with the footage in the camera she's clutching. "It'll be fun."

ANSWERS

The three of us get caught up in the remains of the group of protesters as it straggles north to a house run by a sympathetic collective. We are a jumbled and roving assemblage, clusters now dawdling, now shooting ahead like sprung elastics. We're in the rear of the procession, where the general attitude is one of defeat. Not that anyone is yet aware of the tribunal's decision, but it looks bad, the peaceful protest marred by a brawl, or the start of one.

Two people walking just behind us are discussing whether they'll still have the heart to continue organizing in support of refugees if they have to keep contending with counter-protests. But as we quicken our pace, we move into the ranks of those who are spinning the day's events into a patchy heroism.

"We gave the fascists what they came for," says a guy with a line of blood on his cheek. His listener slaps him on the back.

"I think more of them got arrested, too." The same guy high-fives Quinn. Just for turning up, we are allowed to belong.

Were it not for Quinn and Caro, I'd walk straight past the party, straight down to the train tracks, and follow them all the way to Ottawa. Yet I'd rather not be alone.

"That was interesting," I say with effort. Quinn nods. His long strides have a bounce at the knees. "Fascinating speeches, especially the last one." Quinn cracks a half-smile but it turns dour.

Caro is more upbeat. "I think the whole thing is so inspiring, people banding together for a cause." She checks her camera bag. "Do you think everyone is going to be okay? I might have caught something that can help anyone who was arrested if it goes to trial."

From our first steps over the threshold, I can sense the gathering has a frenzied edge, fuelled by outrage and exhilaration. It is still early on a Monday evening, but both the kitchen counter and the freezer top are being used to mix drinks and hold opened bottles of wine. At the front of the house, in the living room, a DJ named Spangler is spinning real records on a row of silver turntables. I blink at the records as we go in. Spangler does not look old enough to have even had to contend with cassette tapes. Much of the group is already dancing. Quinn, Caro, and I move past the most boisterous of these festivities and tuck ourselves into the breakfast nook by the back door, well out of the bar and fridge traffic, where we can be ignored.

"This reminds me of that party," says Quinn. "Remember? When I had to sleep in that broom closet?"

"What on earth," says Caro, laughing.

"Pantry," I correct him. I say to Caro, "It was at my sister's place."

Quinn has to raise his voice as the music flares. "It would be hard to fall asleep at this one."

"Not for you," I say, making the usual family joke. He smiles.

Then Caro broaches the subject of Ravi with no hesitation, and I remember that Quinn asked her along to their meeting. "You could still get to know him," she says. "Lots of people have dads who are jerks."

Quinn tenses as though he's afraid of my reaction, but I sit back, well out of it.

"I don't think so," he says. "And I don't care what I promised him." He looks at me. "About not telling, I mean."

"Neither do I," I say, getting up to use the bathroom. There is no need to sort out our separate deals and agreements. Revenge seems like it will take too much energy, too much care. But when I return to the kitchen, I hear Quinn and Caro scheming. They have their backs to me where I hover near an open cooler of beer.

"I can get into the website, no problem," says Quinn. "How much footage did you get when we met?"

"The hidden-camera stuff? Enough," she says. "No need to credit me."

"Don't worry," says Quinn. "Maybe I'll tip off the papers, too."

My fingers tighten around a beer. Sometimes Quinn hacks into websites, pulling pranks. In January, he pulled a stunt with his school's home page that nearly got him suspended. Whatever they are planning now would be a crime, and an obvious one, and Evan's horror at what I tried to do to Ravi is still fresh in my mind. I tell myself that I am going to intervene and repeat it until I am convinced enough to let it go for now.

"Calm down, everyone," I say, coming back to the table. The two of them at least look nervous.

"What's going to happen to the Essaid family?" says Caro. "Have you heard?"

"They're staying." The news is rippling through the house on a wave of elation, and I can make out shouting and toasting from the hall before the music is turned up.

"That's wonderful," says Caro. "A happy ending." She might mean for them or for the movie she's planning, or both. She hops to her feet. "I'm going to go get some interviews."

In the kitchen, as in life, Quinn and I are stuck with one another. I'm not in a mood to make conversation with strangers, and though Quinn has a restlessness in his twitching legs, he's staying put. There is something of a kettle hum about him, the way his mouth keeps moving as if he is about to let loose a speech.

It isn't easy to figure out what to say. All I can comprehend is relief at what Libby claims to have read in the diary — Sadhana's happiness in those last weeks. Her forgiveness. There is still time to decide whether to tell Quinn what I've done with the diary. But steering clear of that dilemma, all that's left for us to talk about are other topics we'd rather avoid.

"Are you sorry you met him?" I say.

"There isn't any point to being sorry," he says. He's having trouble looking at me, but I wait. He's holding a beer in a grip fierce enough to imply his skepticism about my permission. So far he's only had the one sip.

"What?" I say. "It's okay."

"You really don't mind?" he says, looking now, tapping the bottle.

"It's legal, or almost. You're nearly eighteen."

"Not the question."

"It's fine. Really." In emphasis, I take a drink from my own beer, and Quinn looks dubious.

"It's too weird."

"Why? Auntie S always gave you sips of her wine."

Her name between us in any form is still a blow, but it doesn't sting or spin the room the way it used to, given everything that has been happening over the past week.

Quinn nods and shrugs. "It's different with you," he says. "You were always the one in charge."

There is something in Quinn's face that makes me realize he thinks he can get to the bottom of everything if we just keep talking—even Sadhana's death. I've no idea where he might have obtained this trait, certainly not through inheritance. Even after hearing Libby's account of what happened, I feel a long way from understanding how or why accident and illness should have intersected the way they did.

"I never felt like I was in charge," I say. "I'm not sure that I was." I always sensed I was only reacting, making way for Sadhana's condition or pushing back against it, as the situation required. "Anyway, it's hard to say much of anything about the way things really were."

"Why?" says Quinn, as if there is no such thing as an unanswerable question. He scrutinizes me through glasses that have slid half an inch down his nose.

"There are some things we won't ever know," I say. All the times I might have behaved differently, and the hundreds of ways I might have changed what happened. "I mean, definitively."

"Like what? There are things people said that about fifty years ago, and look how far science has come. Look at all the genetic research going on. Look at particle physics."

Even when he's being annoying, I love to hear him debate. "I mean historical mysteries," I say. "Where the facts are gone and there's no way of getting them back."

"You can put the facts back."

"What?"

"You can tell the truth."

"I don't get it."

Quinn holds me in a level gaze. "I found the website for Quebec First. It's kids' stuff."

"Don't do it."

"They might actually win the election."

"They could press charges. You could go to jail."

"Okay, I won't." But he has a familiar defiant look on his face. My sister's face. The smart-aleck look of no regrets. And though we have not said her name again, our thoughts are still running along the same lines.

"I wish we had taken better care of her," he says.

"Quinn, all I've done my whole life was try to help her."

"It didn't seem like it, the way you were at therapy. You hated it."

"No, I didn't."

"Yes, you did. You were always so mean. So different from what you're normally like. I could never understand it."

"She was better than those people." I'm just as surprised as Quinn when this comes out.

"Mom."

"Well, she was. And she had real problems. Some of those girls —" I break off, remembering some of the faces from Sadhana's first hospital stay. Tender-hearted Cynthia, who wanted to be Sadhana's friend. Laurel of the infinite sarcasm. Their helpless inability to understand or communicate their own pain. Of the family therapy sessions that came later, with Quinn, I remember very little of the other young women. Only their parents, wondering what they had done wrong. The way they cried in those plastic chairs in front of everyone, the sniffling that made shivers of disgust creep up my spine. I remember thinking that I would never let myself feel so guilty. Though I judged them, too, even more harshly than they judged themselves.

"I'm sorry," I say. "Ignore me."

Quinn leans his head back against the wall and closes his eyes. "Are you going to marry him?"

"Evan?" I am surprised. "That's not even on the table."

"But would you?"

"I don't know." I am not even sure how to repair the day's damage. My carelessness with his feelings and everything I've failed to explain.

But tonight Quinn will not be put off. The alcohol and the excitement have made him tenacious. "Do you think she was still angry with us?"

"No." It gives me some peace to say this. But pain, too, now, knowing it was mostly my anger holding us apart. That, and, if what Libby said is true, Sadhana's wish to mediate things between Quinn and Ravi. To put that inquiry to rest.

"I wish we could know for sure."

"I'm sorry," I whisper.

"Mom?" He leans forward across the table. I shake my head.

"What about the last time you talked?" he presses. "Before the fight, I mean."

I've been dwelling on those final exchanges for so long that the months before them have slipped out of focus. "No," I say, a little harsher than I intended, and he draws back.

"Fine. I'll go first." Quinn tips back his bottle, wipes his mouth with the side of his thumb. "She told me things were going well." He sounds defiant. "We talked about where I was going to go to school, and if I got all my applications in on time." He takes another sip of his beer and starts talking in a rush. "She asked me if I liked anyone. She said she thought she might be at the start of something new, but it was complicated."

"You never told me that."

"Now you know what it feels like."

"She always told you more than she told me," I say, thinking over what Quinn has reported. "We were never as close as you thought. Not in the way you imagine, anyway."

"I don't believe you." Every lacuna he considers a lie.

I wonder whether there will ever be an understanding between us, and how heavy this question is as it comes to me, as heavy almost as the guilt I have been trying to shed, this notion that even between the two of us, close as we are, there may be no simplicity. Nor was there always understanding between me and Sadhana. And with such a gap to bridge even between the people you ought to be nearest to in the world, people who share your whole history and language, or even blood, anything as simple as friendship begins to seem miraculous. Let alone love. Let alone forgiveness. The people gathered around us, the great goodwill directed to the cause of the Essaids, all that might even be easier. Caring about the well-being of strangers. Tending to principles instead of to people with all of their flaws.

"At a certain point, you're going to have to take my word for it, kid."

Quinn makes the slightest of motions, a movement of his shoulder towards his ear, that hints at concession. It is no wonder he is skeptical. He is my son, mine and Sadhana's, and I am glad that he is clever and full of doubt and sees me more clearly for who I am than as simply the woman who is his mother.

He pushes his chair back from the table. "I guess we've never been a normal family," he says, getting up to move to the fridge. He is looking inside for something, and though I wonder at the propriety of this, people are coming in and out of the kitchen for drinks and nobody else gives him a second glance as he roots around.

"I wish you could have known your grandmother," I say. "She was truly an unusual woman. And she would have liked this party."

"Oh yeah?"

"Yes, she had some remarkable friends. And she never missed an opportunity to celebrate." These are things I've said before, but Quinn always listens as if it were the first time. He turns to look at me as he moves through the kitchen. "If she were here," I go on, "she probably would have baked a cake in the shape of a courthouse or filled the whole house with balloons. She was never afraid of throwing herself into things."

Mama's courage was where our inheritance went astray. The trust she had in her own choices, to follow without doubt the call of her heart, wherever it might lead. Instead of doing whatever else might have been expected. Choosing to be free, choosing to always be choosing, never following. Choosing everything instead of being or seeing only one thing or the other.

Quinn comes back to the table with a loaf of bread and some peanut butter. Before he sits down, he hunts around in the drawers and cupboards, but all he can find is a single plate and a spoon.

"I'm not sure people actually live here," he says. There is no blind on the kitchen window, and though the sun is still up, we can see the gibbous waning moon rising in the east.

We tear off pieces of bread with our hands and scoop the peanut butter on top. The first bite reveals to me my own hunger, and the second tells me something else, that I am alive. That I am here in a kitchen with my son, and we are eating together and we are alive. And the work of getting closer, of loving harder, is the work of a whole life.

⌒∽ ACKNOWLEDGEMENTS ∽⌒

I gratefully acknowledge the support of this project by the Conseil des arts et des lettres du Québec. I would also like to thank the Banff Centre, where I started writing this novel, and Yaddo, where I began to revise it, as well as the Quebec Writers' Federation mentorship program. I am infinitely grateful for the friendships and pages that emerged from these opportunities.

Thanks again to *The New Quarterly* for first publishing the story from which this novel evolved and to the Blue Metropolis literary festival where the issue was launched. Thank you to my agent, Martha Magor Webb, for her insightful reading and belief in these characters.

Profound thanks to my brilliant editor, Melanie Little, for her faith, respect, precision and encouragement, and for understanding everything. Much gratitude also to Sarah MacLachlan, Jared Bland, Kate McQuaid, and all the kind and capable souls at House of Anansi Press who lent their time and expertise to this novel in many different capacities. Thank you to Alysia Shewchuk for the remarkable cover design.

Thanks to Alice Zorn above all for her friendship, as well as for her astute reading of this manuscript, and to Ian McGillis for valuable comments on early pages. Ongoing gratitude to those writerly friends who have been kind enough to read, listen, or commiserate: Matthew Anderson, Jonathan Ball, Linda Besner, Erin Bockstael, Lina Gordaneer, Leigh Kotsilidis, Bob Kotyk, Erin Laing, and Kathleen Winter. Thank you to Atika Mirza for sparking Beena's name. Thank you to all the kind, brilliant, beautiful people I am privileged to spend time with—I don't know what I would do without you. Thank you, too, to friends at a distance for warmth in correspondence. For endless friendship and support, thank you to Mylissa Falkner, Kat Kitching, Jessica Lim, Vivienne Macy, and Rajam Raghunathan.

Love and thanks to my mother, my grandmother, and all of my Ainsworth family. Love and thanks to Vivi and the Webster family. Love and all to Derek.

SALEEMA NAWAZ is the author of the short story collection *Mother Superior* and winner of the prestigious Writers' Trust of Canada/McClelland & Stewart Journey Prize. Born and raised in Ottawa, Ontario, she currently lives in Montreal, Quebec.